"A laugh-out-loud funny, pitch-perfect novel that will have readers rooting for this unlikely, relatable, and totally lovable heroine, *The Overdue Life of Amy Byler* is the ultimate escape—and will leave moms everywhere questioning whether it isn't time for a #momspringa of their own."

—New York Journal of Books

"Filled with love, self-discovery, and plot twists."

—*Madison Magazine*

"Kelly Harms tackles modern single motherhood with flair, swoons, and the most perfect date ever written. In *The Overdue Life of Amy Byler*, readers will connect with the titular character's unexpected journey of freedom and self-discovery, all told with Harms's signature humor . . . I'm a fan for life!"

—Amy E. Reichert, author of *The Optimist's Guide to Letting Go* and *The Coincidence of Coconut Cake*

"*The Overdue Life of Amy Byler* is a charming, relatable, and entertaining look at parenthood, divorce, dating, and everything in between. No one cuts right to the heart of life—in all its hilarity and heartbreak—quite like Kelly Harms. This is easily one of my favorite books of the year!"

—Kristy Woodson Harvey, author of *Slightly South of Simple*

"Amy Byler's life isn't easy—what with an absentee husband suddenly showing up and reclaiming some getting-to-know-you time with their two teenage kids. But what follows is pure wonder. Kelly Harms brings the mom-makeover story to a whole new level, with twists and turns and dialogue that is so funny you have to put down the book and simply allow yourself to laugh. It's well written, it's original, and I fell in love with Amy and all her well-meaning friends on her journey to find out who she really is. So much fun!"

—Maddie Dawson, *Washington Post* and Amazon Charts bestselling author of *Matchmaking for Beginners*

"Amy Byler's husband ditched her and their kids three years ago, so when he shows up, full of regret, we can forgive her for being less than welcoming. Still, she could use a break—and a life. What follows is so engaging I had to clear my calendar. Harms dances on the knife edge between snort-your-coffee humor and bull's-eye insights, often in the same sentence. As a card-carrying curmudgeon, I resist such tactics, but here I never felt played. Instead, I was swept up in Amy's everymom dilemma, her quest for a full life without sinking into the swamp of selfishness. Whip smart and honest to the core, *The Overdue Life of Amy Byler* is a thoughtful, nimble charmer. Did I mention the hot librarian?"

—Sonja Yoerg, #1 Amazon bestselling author of *True Places*

The Good Luck Girls of Shipwreck Lane

"A perfect recipe of clever, quirky, poignant, and fun makes this a delightful debut."

—*Kirkus Reviews*

"Set in small-town Maine, this first novel is a story of rebuilding, recovery, and renewal. Harms has created two incredibly likable heroines, allowing the strengths of one woman to bolster the weaknesses of the other. While the central conflict of the story appears to be resolved fairly early, a succession of plot twists keeps the reader intrigued and invested. In the manner of Mary Kay Andrews and Jennifer Weiner, Harms's novel is emotionally tender, touching, and witty. Great for book clubs."

—*Booklist*

"Spunky leading ladies that you can take to the beach."

—*Fitness Magazine*

PRAISE FOR KELLY HARMS

The Bright Side of Going Dark

"Refreshingly, each character is a true-to-life individual with complicated emotions and unique voices. A surprisingly easy read containing a little romance, a lot of personal growth, and an honest look at weighty topics."

—*Kirkus Reviews*

"Witty, lively, and au courant, *The Bright Side of Going Dark* will make readers think twice about refreshing Instagram for the tenth time today. Tackling thornier questions of mental health and the toll of constant comparison, this will appeal to fans of Meg Wolitzer and Elin Hilderbrand, who'll adore the intertwining lives of Mia, her followers, and those they encounter IRL."

—*Booklist* (starred review)

"*The Bright Side of Going Dark* is about so much more than the moral quandary of screen time. It's about grief and loss and anxiety. It's about mothers and daughters—more anxiety—and about second and third chances. *The Bright Side of Going Dark* is as dark as it is bright, [and] full of humanity: mobile devices, warts, and all."

—BookTrib

"Even casual users know how absurd and unrealistic social media can be—yet keep logging on day after day. Kelly Harms takes this dichotomy to new heights in a clever and unputdownable story of two women whose so-called online lives collide IRL. I laughed, I cried, I came away from the experience with a newfound appreciation for

life—which is to say *The Bright Side of Going Dark* is everything I'd hope for in a Kelly Harms novel and more. I loved every page."

—Camille Pagán, bestselling author of *I'm Fine and Neither Are You*

"Kelly Harms has once again knocked it out of the park with this charming, funny, topical novel about an online influencer who undergoes an unexpected transformation. I honestly had to put my whole life on hold while I read it—laughing and sighing through the clever twists and turns of this plot. Who among us hasn't wondered what it takes to be a person who posts photographs fifty times a day? You'll fall in love with @Mia&Mike as well as the whole cast of wonderful characters. A novel that shines with surprise—and will make you want to turn off your phone and go play with your dog."

—Maddie Dawson, *Washington Post* bestselling author of *Matchmaking for Beginners*

The Overdue Life of Amy Byler

"Librarians and booklovers will fall for Amy, and Harms writes a great light read full of tears, laughter, and charming, relatable characters."

—*Library Journal* (starred review)

"In the easygoing, character-driven style of Liane Moriarty and Barbara Davis, this story of an underappreciated single mom with more freedom than she's entirely comfortable with mixes the self-assured highs with the guiltiest lows of modern motherhood. Harms's warm and witty novel will tickle fans of *Where'd You Go, Bernadette* and *Eleanor Oliphant Is Completely Fine*."

—*Booklist*

"The story is funny and heartbreaking throughout."

—Melissa Amster, Chick Lit Central

"Another perfect summer diversion is *The Good Luck Girls of Shipwreck Lane*. Kelly Harms writes with love about a trio of women desperate for a change and smart enough to recognize it may not be exactly what they planned. Delicious."

—Angela Matano, *Campus Circle*

"The friction between the Janines, along with a few romantic foibles and a lot of delicious meals, results in a sweetly funny and unpredictable story that's ultimately about making a home where you find it."

—*Capital Times*

"Kelly Harms's debut is a delicious concoction of reality and fairy tale—the ideal summer book! You'll feel lucky for having read it. And after meeting her, I guarantee you will want a great-aunt Midge of your very own."

—*New York Times* bestselling author Sarah Addison Allen

"Warmhearted and funny, *The Good Luck Girls of Shipwreck Lane* pulls you in with quirky yet relatable characters, intriguing relationships, and the promise of second chances. Harms's debut is as refreshingly delightful as a bowl of her character Janey's chilled pea soup with mint on a hot summer day."

—Meg Donohue, bestselling author of
How to Eat a Cupcake: A Novel

"Funny, original, and delightfully quirky, Kelly Harms's *The Good Luck Girls of Shipwreck Lane* shows us that sometimes, all we need to make it through one of life's rough patches is a change of scenery and a home-cooked meal."

—Molly Shapiro, author of *Point, Click, Love: A Novel*

"The characters are so well drawn that they practically leap from the page, charming dysfunction and all! A poignant, hilarious debut that's filled with heart, soul, insight, and laugh-out-loud moments. It'll make you rethink the meaning of what makes a family—and if you're anything like me, it'll make you want to pick up and move to 1516 Shipwreck Lane immediately! I'm such a fan of this utterly charming novel."

—Kristin Harmel, author of *Italian for Beginners* and
The Sweetness of Forgetting

"Clever and memorable and original."

—Samantha Wilde, author of *I'll Take What She Has*

"Janey and Nean each have a common name and uncommon hard luck, and when they suddenly have in common a sweepstakes house, their lives begin to change in ways neither of them could have imagined. Their quirky wit will win you over, even as they fumble through their crazy new life. *The Good Luck Girls of Shipwreck Lane* is alive with warmth and wit; I enjoyed it right through to the satisfying end."

—Kristina Riggle, author of *Real Life & Liars*, *The Life You've Imagined*, *Things We Didn't Say*, and *Keepsake*

"Kelly Harms's *The Good Luck Girls of Shipwreck Lane* is a delightful book bursting with good humor, fast action, and delicious food. Aunt Midge is a pure joy, and I loved Harms's surprising, spirited, and generous slant on what it takes to make a family."

—Nancy Thayer, *New York Times* bestselling author of *Summer Breeze*

The Matchmakers of Minnow Bay

"Kelly Harms writes with such tender insight about change, saying goodbye to her beloved yet troubled city life, and hurtling into the delicious unknown. Her characters sparkle; I loved Lily and wished I could have coffee with her in the enchanted town of Minnow Bay."

—Luanne Rice, *New York Times* bestselling author

"The temperature in Minnow Bay, Wisconsin, may be cold, but its people are anything but. Kelly Harms has created a world so real and so inviting that you absolutely will not want to leave. *The Matchmakers of Minnow Bay* proves that a little small-town meddling never hurt anyone and that, sometimes, it takes a village to fall in love. Kelly Harms has done it again!"

—Kristy Woodson Harvey, author of *Dear Carolina* and *Lies and Other Acts of Love*

"*The Matchmakers of Minnow Bay* is a glorious read, full of heart and humor. Lily is the kind of character you'll root for to the end, and the delightful residents of Minnow Bay will keep you chuckling with each turn of the page. Kelly Harms is a talented author with a knack for writing a story you'll want to read again and again."

—Darien Gee/Mia King

"In *The Matchmakers of Minnow Bay*, Kelly Harms weaves together a small town and big dreams into a delightful and heartfelt tapestry of friendship, love, and getting what you deserve in the way you least expect. I was hooked from page one, then laughed out loud and teared up while reading—exactly what I want from romantic women's fiction. Kelly Harms is the real deal."

—Amy Nathan

"In *The Matchmakers of Minnow Bay*, Lily Stewart is Shopaholic's Becky Bloomwood meets Capote's Holly Golightly. This charming tale is filled to the brim with eccentric characters, uproarious predicaments, and a charming (if chilly!) setting. Kelly Harms has created the most lovable character in Lily, a starving artist with a penchant for disaster and a completely unbreakable spirit. One for the beach chair!"

—Kate Moretti, *New York Times* bestselling author of
The Vanishing Year

"Filled with witty dialogue and an unforgettable cast of characters, *The Matchmakers of Minnow Bay* is a complete charmer. I rooted for Lily from the first page and didn't want to leave the magical town of Minnow Bay. Kelly Harms delivers another heartwarming novel that lifts the spirit."

—Anita Hughes

"*The Matchmakers of Minnow Bay* is the perfect feel-good read. An irresistible premise, a charming—though forgetful—heroine, an emotionally involving love story, lovely writing . . . it all adds up to cozy hours in a fictional place you'll wish you could visit. Don't miss this delightful novel!"

—Susan Wiggs

"Sometimes you read a book that hits all the right notes: funny, charismatic, romantic, and empowering. *The Matchmakers of Minnow Bay* is that book. Kelly Harms's enchanting writing lured me into the quiet yet complicated world of Minnow Bay, and I never wanted to leave. I loved it in every way!"

—Amy E. Reichert

"Delightful, and sure to captivate readers and gain new fans for author Kelly Harms. With sparkling dialogue and a winning heroine who finds her big-girl panties amid the disaster zone her life has become and heads in a new direction, finding love along the way, it had me turning the pages into the night."

—Eileen Goudge

"I loved this book! Fresh and devastatingly funny, *The Matchmakers of Minnow Bay* is romantic comedy at its very best. The talented Kelly Harms is one to watch."

—Colleen Oakley, author of *Before I Go*

"*The Matchmakers of Minnow Bay* thoroughly entertains as it explores friendship, flings, and finally finding yourself. Harms tells the story in a funny, fresh voice ideal for this charming coming-into-her-age novel."
—Christie Ridgway, *USA Today* bestselling author of the *Beach House No. 9* and *Cabin Fever* series

THE
SEVEN
DAY
SWITCH

OTHER BOOKS BY KELLY HARMS

THE SEVEN DAY SWITCH

A NOVEL

KELLY HARMS

LAKE UNION
PUBLISHING

Published by Lake Union Publishing, Seattle

www.apub.com

Amazon, the Amazon logo, and Lake Union Publishing are trademarks of Amazon.com, Inc., or its affiliates.

ISBN-13: 9781542028899 (hardcover)
ISBN-10: 1542028892 (hardcover)

ISBN-13: 9781542027090 (paperback)
ISBN-10: 1542027098 (paperback)

33614082336289

Cover design by Liz Casal

Printed in the United States of America

First edition

To Abbie Foster Chaffee and Kris Adams,
two remarkable mothers

Haven't we all had those moments where the "road diverged" and both roads ahead are equally fascinating and equally cool? But you take one or the other and your life happens after that.

—Susan Baroncini-Moe

PROLOGUE

WENDY

Here is how you have a perfect morning:

Step one: Get up early. Really, really early. If your kids need to be at school at, say, 8:06 a.m., and you want to be at work as soon as humanly possible after that, then get up at five. Five thirty at the latest. This means you should go to bed—lights out, no reading, no TV, no sex—at exactly 9:00 p.m. Note: you will never ever achieve this.

Step two: Read a lot of books about good-habit formation, though not at bedtime. (See above.) Listen to them on your commute, if you must. Practice intentional cuing and habit stacking. Make sure you put your pills next to your toothpaste next to your contact lenses next to your antiaging serum. Otherwise you will forget the pills and the serum, because it is very early and you can barely see without your lenses. Only after you have touched all these things can you go have coffee.

Step three: Go back in time to the evening before, and set your grind-and-brew coffee maker to automatically start at 5:00 a.m. Failing this, stare absently at the kitchen wall for four minutes until coffee is ready.

Step four: Drink coffee and make three lunches, two with no vegetables for your children and one with nothing but vegetables for yourself. Put a tiny pouch of Goldfish crackers in your own lunch bag at the last moment and feel rebellious, then wasteful, because some mothers would buy a large bag of Goldfish from Costco and divide them into reusable snack cups themselves.

Step five: Sit in glorious caffeinating silence with your phone for twenty straight minutes. Then rush through a shower before the kids have to get up.

Steps six through forty-five:

Wake up the kids.

Get out the cereal boxes and milk and bowls in the hope that they will at least pour their own cereal this time, just this once.

Put the cat bowl on the counter next to the kid bowls to remind them to feed the cat that they swore to take care of.

Write a note for the husband, who is sleeping and will still be sleeping when you leave, reminding him of the daughter's softball tryouts tonight and the son's field trip tomorrow.

Go wake up the kids again.

Find a purple skirt in the wash that you forgot to move to the dryer last night.

Be accused of "never doing anything thoughtful" for the child who wants the purple skirt.

Ask same child to eat breakfast.

Wake up other child again.

Put on socks for other child because they are "not stretchy enough."

Check on purple skirt in dryer—adjust it to high heat.

Pour skirtless child's cereal, and deliver it to her in front of TV.

Encourage son to go back to room and put on clean underpants.

Momentarily meditate on the sad state of your own six-year-old underpants.

Notice you need to leave the house in seven minutes and somehow the cat has not been fed.

Beg children to feed cat.

Look at son's wardrobe choices in confusion.

Remember purple skirt, take it out, and stretch it out so the shrinkage isn't so obvious.

Ask daughter to put it on.

Ask again.

Take remote control.

Listen to frenzy of complaining and whining over their show being turned off during the "best part."

Tell everyone to put on shoes.

Find everyone's shoes.

Get in car without your own shoes.

Go back inside for shoes.

Go back inside for lunches.

Go back inside to add laundry update to husband note.

Pull out of driveway.

Realize it is 8:04.

Change radio station from "boring news" to top forty.

Listen to seventeen minutes of commercials for unregulated weight-loss aids and used cars while in the carpool lane.

Drop off children.

Return home for forgotten gym clothes.

Try not to wake husband.

Feed angry cat.

Race to work.

Arrive to office twelve minutes late.

Ignore receptionist's unwanted request to let her blow-dry your hair for you at your desk.

Make note to buy office hair dryer.

CHAPTER 1
BEFORE
WENDY

Though I am a celebrated productivity consultant with a standing segment on the local news, a monthly column in a top-one-hundred blog, and a small line of daily planners, there are some areas of my life that could, possibly, do with some improvement. The stress level in my house is generally a bit higher than I'd like, and I do drag around some mom guilt with me everywhere I go. My husband, Seth, is better looking than me, and it's getting more pronounced as we age. As I sag, he weathers. And my kids, Bridget and Linus, are a smidge lazy. Just a smidge. And maybe not actually lazy so much as just living in a different time than the one in which I grew up. My "lazy" is another mother's "unhurried and uninhibited." Their sloth is another woman's "carefree childhood."

But that freaking purple skirt may kill me.

I had to go to an actual mall to buy that skirt. I had to go into a store that had a Wall of Sound approach to identity branding and try to also listen to my eleven-year-old girl try out being a sixteen-year-old. But not an actual sixteen-year-old, with period cramps and zits and low self-esteem. No, a sixteen-year-old from a Netflix series who lives on a cruise ship with her single father, the captain, and her best friend, the rock star. That is who my daughter thinks she is in her purple skirt.

I thought I would avoid this by not naming her Mercedes or Kennedy, but it turns out girls named Sarah or Catherine or even Delores will also be tweens someday. And my tween has figured out that the purple skirt is cool but not that it is uncool to wear the same skirt three times a week. And so I have gone from doing laundry four times a week to doing it every. Single. Night.

And I know exactly who to blame for this.

As I pull into my neighborhood every night, after working my demanding job and running to my kids' activities, I see her. She likes to sit outside. In her front yard. She sits there after dinner—her dinner, which is at six on the nose, of course, and has at least two fresh veggies on the side—and drinks a glass of red wine in plain sight of the neighbors, normal people who are rushing to their homes with cars full of pizza or rotisserie chickens and children who spend approximately ten hours a day under the supervision of other people. Normal people do not appreciate the sight of Celeste Mason, ass in real teak adirondack chair, feet on matching stool, having a nice glass of pinot while her three perfect children romp in her perfect front yard after their perfectly nutritious home-cooked meal.

I am one of those people, in case it is not abundantly clear. I do not appreciate that Celeste, for reasons incomprehensible to me, bought a series of Vogue Teen sewing patterns for her own eleven-year-old tween daughter and let her pick out fabrics and then made her a custom wardrobe of styles that could only be matched in "coolness" by overpriced low-quality knockoffs at the mall store that *does not do free shipping*. I do not appreciate that her daughter noticed aloud the one time my daughter wore the Purple Skirt to school with a two-day-old grass stain on it. I do not appreciate that suddenly my daughter is friends with the kind of child who has grass-stain-removal tips at top of mind, or that she even has something against grass stains, which, until these two girls began to "hang" together, were nothing but a badge of honor at our house. Until Celeste's family moved into the house backing onto mine, a skirt of any kind would have been nothing but pure inconvenience in Bridget's mind. Something you had to layer over shorts anyway to make any kind of meaningful play possible.

Now, if that's not bad enough, Celeste Mason has encouraged her daughter to join my daughter at tonight's softball tryouts. Presumably in a bespoke skort.

Vengeful, I pull into the diamond's parking lot. I hope the tryouts go long and Celeste has to miss her front yard wine tonight. In fact, I hope Zoey, her daughter, makes the team and Celeste has to forgo her wine for the entire season. I hope she has to drag her two other kids to the hot, sticky ballpark every weeknight and stop at the sandwich shop on the way and feed her toddler Sun Chips for dinner all summer long.

I spot Bridget as I find a good parking spot facing the field. She is sitting with Zoey Mason on a large, water-resistant picnic blanket spread with plates of orange slices, ants on a log, sweet grape tomatoes, and . . . good god, is that homemade *kombucha* in jelly jars? And there, in the center of it all, is Celeste.

That had better be almond butter at this peanut-free playground, I think, while hiding the bag of McDonald's under my passenger seat. Peanuts are the number one cause of food-allergy deaths in America. If that's Jif Creamy lurking under those ants on a log, she's officially a monster.

I park. Linus has unbuckled and climbed into the front seat, clutching his Happy Meal, before the car has even released the child safety locks. Linus, my sweet, simple boy, who is still happy to wear Costco joggers and plain tees everywhere. I could leave Bridget's meal in the car, try to signal to her that it's here if she wants chicken nuggets and a fruit smoothie, her annual season kickoff meal. Maybe that way Celeste wouldn't see the fast food. But the jig is up anyway. Linus is halfway to the blanket, excited to tell his sister about the trading cards that came in the box with his hamburger. I grab Bridge's food off the seat and slink to the blanket behind him.

"Celeste," I say, trying to sound, if not happy to see her, at least not audibly mom shamed over some chicken nuggets. "Hello." Then I turn to my daughter. "Bridge! Y'all know you don't have to beg for food!"

"Of course she doesn't," Celeste says, her grating northern accent all consonants and edges. "But I did bring too much, because Samuel is too busy playing soccer over there to even slow down for a bite." She gestures with her head to a passel of boys the same general age as my own son, but each at least twenty pounds bigger.

I smile hopefully at Linus. "Do you want to play soccer with Sam?" I ask him, and he shakes his head. The charm of soccer, like all outdoor pursuits, evades Linus. He likes things you can do inside, like building with K'Nex and playing Minecraft and forgetting to flush the toilet after he poops.

Our son's homebody self drives my husband nuts, but I was an indoorsy kid myself, and I have found the other side of that coin—the side that allows me to spend hours focused on a problem or find rainy-day bliss by a bay window with a book—to be perfectly satisfactory recompense.

Seth, though, is a sculptor. He likes to work outside with big, heavy power tools and sparks flying. He likes weighty work and endurance sports and protein smoothies. I like those things, too, from a distance. I like men wearing welding masks but not actually wearing my own welding mask. When Seth and I met, he was already getting commissions for office parks and city-owned courtyards, and I was in what felt like year thirty of my PhD in industrial organizational psychology. I would bring my laptop to his workshop and stare at data sets while he tossed about great hunks of enameled metal like a Scotsman at a caber-tossing competition, and then, when it was safe to approach, I would bring him beer with the cap already off and gaze upon his sinewy forearms and think, *Well, this is pretty much perfect.*

I think it would still be pretty much perfect if it weren't for the two kids we made, as well as the fact that I finished my PhD and then got a job and then started my own business and now am too busy to bring anyone beers and kind of wish the sinewy forearms I once enjoyed so much spent more time loading and unloading the dishwasher.

If Seth were here, I'd make Linus go do something specific that meant he couldn't play soccer even if he wanted to. I'd give him some homework or have him do my business expenses. I'm my son's sportiness beard.

Happily, Seth's not here, so when Linus says no to soccer, I hand him the book bag I have in the car at all times. He can choose between a new Jeff Smith graphic novel that is probably way too adult for him and *The Hobbit*, which he has already read thrice. He flops, boneless, on the farthest edge of Celeste's blanket and vanishes into Middle-earth. Bridge looks up at me, all eyes and heart. "Don't make me read, Mom," she says. "I'm too nervous."

Celeste hears this and laughs quietly. "Zoey too," she says. "At least they're eating."

So they are. Zoey, with her almost-red hair and too-long limbs, is sitting elbow to elbow next to Bridge, my almost painfully lovely girl, whose beauty is tempered only by an omnipresent sheen of sweat in her brown hair and dirt on her skinned knees. The two of them feast on Celeste's healthful snacks. My McDonald's offering sits greasy and unnoticed while my daughter eats foods with antioxidants and fiber simply because, what . . . they are there? Zoey is doing it? Celeste is using Jedi mind tricks? I don't know.

"Thank you," I remember to say, at last. "For bringing her over here. I appreciate it, I surely do. Is that almond butter?"

"SunButter," she says smoothly. "Last thing I want to do at my daughter's first tryouts is to poison the team captain."

"Oh, is Sofia allergic to peanuts?" I ask. Sofia is the pitcher, and she's got a windup that makes me think their family should be saving up now for a good orthopedist. But Bridge—probably the best hitter on the team—can't pitch to save her life, so we have to bow to Sofia's authority.

"Extremely. Daria sews an EpiPen pocket into all her clothes."

"Smart," I say. "I'm allergic, too, but Daria hasn't offered to sew me anything." I deliver this with a smile. This is me trying to be funny.

Celeste gives me a polite sound that some might call a laugh. That is her trying to be nice. Then she raises an eyebrow. "Daria's probably too busy with her new trainer."

And . . . attempt at bonding instantly over, at least as far as I'm concerned. This is the kind of neighborhood gossip that makes me so, so glad I work full time. It passes from house to house via dog walks and playground chatter, and those of us with real jobs miss out in all the best ways. As for me, I can just lie low and pretend my name never crosses their lips. I mean, what exactly can the Mom Squad say about me? My husband is hot? My son is pasty? I can live with that.

"What are the girls talking about so secretively?" I ask Celeste, to change the subject.

"No idea," she tells me, unconcerned. "It's been going on since pickup. They sit in the way back when I drive them, you know. Even when I don't have the baby and there's room in the middle."

I smile and pretend I already noticed the absence of her third child, who I had momentarily forgotten existed. "Where is Anna Joy?" I ask, the second name poison in my mouth. *Anna Joy,* for heaven's sake. She's not even southern. Where does she get off taking two nice names when there are so few good ones left to choose from in the neighborhood? Because of her greed, some poor newborn is probably going around with the name Bertha-Sue.

"She's getting special playtime with Daddy. I wanted to be able to focus on Zoey today. It's her first time going out for a sport, you know."

I smile gently and try to look reassuring. "It's great that she's giving it a shot." The truth is, our Little League softball team is crazy competitive. Bridge has been playing softball since she was six, and even she's not a sure thing today. Zoey is probably a lamb to slaughter.

"Do you know what's always fun in the fall?" I tell her. "Soccer. There are three leagues right in Birchboro Hills, all with varying levels of competitiveness. It's such a nice thing for the kids. I like the idea of having some team sports that are just for fun."

Celeste looks at me. "The girls are eleven. What else could sports be for, if not for fun?"

"Well, right. Of course," I say. It is a great tribute to my self-control that I do not roll my eyes. If she tells me children should stay children as long as possible, as though I am sending Bridget to work at the Nike factory every day, I may not be able to hold back any longer. "And competition can be really fun," I add, because I can't not. "Girls don't always get the chance to learn that, and some parents seem to think it's something that should be avoided at all costs."

Celeste smiles at me tightly. There's nothing she can say back to that, after all. What exactly can she tell her daughter about healthy competition? That she who makes the best homemade Halloween costume wins? That'll take her really far in life. Exactly as far as it's taken Celeste.

"The girls should go up now," I say. I see the coaches, who feel like old friends, dragging out the ball cages. I nudge Bridge and point to the helmets in net bags that need to be taken to the first base side of the backstop. She hops to it with a team enthusiasm that fills me with pride. Sure, at home she can leave a half-drunk glass of milk on her desk until it's science-lab material, but out here, she's all in.

I lean back on my hands. It'll be warm-ups first, then batting practice, and then the clipboards will come out, and the girls will move through positions. Just like every year, I will pretend I'm happy with any outcome but will watch like a hawk as my daughter plays third base. Her arm has gotten better and better with each passing day, and her father and I agree it's time for her to move to the infield. Her father has to stand at the far corner of our yard now, just forward of a thorny shrub I can't seem to kill, and hit her crazy grounders to give her a real workout. If she stays calm and bouncy on her toes, doesn't sit back on her heels at every down moment, this could finally be her year.

I'm snapped out of my reverie by a series of stimuli, one after another. Celeste, packing up the food, reminding me I'm starving. Zoey and Bridge and the rest of the hopefuls running up to the coaches. Linus sighing and turning over to flop in the other direction. My phone buzzing in my purse—Seth asking if we'll be home for dinner. Presumably he did not see the note, did not finish the laundry, did not renew Linus's bus pass for tomorrow's field trip.

By now, five other moms have arrived with their own blankets and camp chairs. Their daughters, already on the field, run to their breathless moms, grab their water bottles, and then jog back to the field. We all settle in. The other moms tell me about the traffic between town and school—twenty minutes at the best of times, an hour at the worst. We all talk about how we were panicked we wouldn't make it here from work on time. How Sara, who works from home two days a week, offered to run a carload of girls over here from school to save time.

How lucky I am, we all agree, that Celeste lives so close to us and is free all day long to ferry my child around. Never mind that it comes with a side order of guilt.

We are friends, all of us, a small, highly efficient cluster of overworked, overtired women who will do anything for their children. Where we live isn't cheap, but it's one of those magical villages with a wonderful combination of diversity, great schools, and proximity to downtown, where we all work. Two incomes are all but required to afford Birchboro Hills, and the working-mom hustle combined with the team-crazy kids gives us a lot to bond over, normally. But tonight there's a bit less camaraderie. A bit more tension. We are only hoping that it will not be us with the crying child in the back seat on the way home.

It will have to be someone in this group. There are more of our daughters than spaces on the team. Just as there are more tasks to do than minutes in the day, more chores than helpers, more cars than roads, more bills than dollars to pay them. Our lives, as mothers, are made up of these small scarcities—eleven spots for starters but seventeen players good enough to start.

Silence falls, and we watch the girls start to bat. Things start out predictably. Davi is a slugger. Sofia hits like a pitcher. Isla and Jordyn are solid. Bridge settles into a rhythm, hitting one, two, three tight right hoppers.

"No coach could say no to that," says Davi's mom, a lawyer downtown.

"You're golden," says Jordyn's professor mom.

"Who's that?" asks Daria, Sofia's mom, looking at the next batter, who seems able to get her stick on anything in the strike zone. "Is that Zoey Mason?"

I nod. We fall silent for a moment, all eyes sliding over to Celeste, who is barely watching—she seems to be taking photos of her kombucha jars.

"Damn," says Daria.

"Where did she come from?" asks Davi's mom.

"Apparently the minors?" I say.

Isla's and Jordyn's mothers say nothing.

The coach keeps pitching to her. He pitches until he runs out of balls. Not one is coming back to him via the catcher. They are scattered all over the field. Left, right, center. Finally he claps his hands together. "Well, ladies, looks like we have a new secret weapon. Gloves on!"

The girls stand there, dumbfounded. Even Zoey. It's clear she isn't quite sure what just happened.

After a couple of seconds, Coach has to blow his whistle to snap everyone to attention. "Gloves!" he shouts again. "Wake up, ladies!" Our daughters burst back to life, grab gloves, and move into lines for drills. Clipboards come out. I cut another glance to Celeste. Her phone is down, and she seems to be looking back at me and the other team moms. Quickly her eyes slide from our cluster of chairs to some far-off spot in the grass . . . to her son, Samuel. He seems to be chasing his compatriots with a stick the size of a bludgeon. I pat Linus on the back, a silent thanks that he is not that sort of kid. He squirms away. When I look back at Celeste, she's looking at Zoey on the softball field again, trying to keep her expression blank.

But there's no mistaking that smile. It's a 6:30 p.m., adirondack-chair-sitting, wineglass-hoisting smile. She turns it on me and says sweetly, "I'm starting to think you and I will be spending lots of time in this park together in the near future. How fun."

Fun indeed. Tryouts are one thing. There is no universe where I can attend softball practices four afternoons a week at 3:30 p.m., smack in the middle of my workday, and I'm pretty sure Celeste is aware of that. She will be sitting on her pretty blanket with her nutritious peanut-free snacks all alone. Well, not all alone. Now that Zoey Mason is a sure thing for the team, I have no doubt that my own daughter will be mooching food, rides, and extra hand-sewn scrunchies from Celeste on a regular basis.

Guilt, annoyance, and that awful sensation of a never-repayable debt rise up in me. Celeste is a special kind of stay-at-home mom. A woman who plays her leisure against the rest of us at every turn, and all we can do is thank her for it. And here she is now, winning another battle without even trying.

And never missing a chance to let the rest of us feel like losers.

—

CELESTE

In a shocking turn of events, I find I am a softball-mom pariah by the day after tryouts.

The shocking part is sarcasm. Almost a year into our move, I am not a key in the lock of the Birchboro Hills social scene. In this suburb, our homes are expensive, but not "old money" expensive like the estates around the garden or the river. Still, most of my neighbors need two good paychecks to live here. A doctor and a teacher. An attorney and a therapist. Not like Hugh and me. A vice president and a . . . well, a stay-at-home mom, though being at home is only a small part of my job. But there's no good single term for what I do. I do everything. And pretty damned well too.

In Birchboro Hills, using the term *full-time mom* would be slightly ridiculous. Working for pay or not, it is all work. Those few parents who don't have a full-time job have charitable projects and intense artistic pursuits. Whereas I am "just" a mom. I don't run a foundation or do monologue festivals. I just do mom stuff, and ever since we moved here, I've wondered if I should apologize for it. In my childhood, when the shoe was on the other foot and our family couldn't always count on having both a full fridge and the electricity to run it at the same time, my mom would always say, so proudly, "Celeste, honey, you can cope with anything with a smile on your face."

Thinking of her—missing her—I keep trying to plaster on that smile and thaw the ice in our new neighborhood. I started with doing as the Romans do, going against every private bone in my midwestern-girl body. I put our outdoor seating out front—actually, Hugh did it, sweet man; those damned chairs are so heavy. He set them up right smack in the middle of the grass, and now he has to turn them on their sides when he mows and then turn them back again to get the entire lawn. And Mom was right, as usual—I enjoy sitting out front at night while the kids play. I like seeing our neighbors biking with the kids, taking the dog for a walk, or just going out to the grassy play park opposite us to burn off that last bit of energy before bed. My littlest—Joy, we call her—loves taking note of the comings and goings of every dog around as she crisscrosses from one edge of our yard to the other. And Samuel, my middle kiddo, will recruit anyone with a pulse to stop what they're doing and play with him in the thinning light. Zoey will sometimes make me scooch my butt as far over as I can and wedge herself into the same lawn chair as me and tell me important things, like a play-by-play of what's happening in her latest book or who she sat by at lunch today or whether or not she should start wearing lip gloss.

It was on one of these evenings earlier this spring that Zoey told me that she'd seen our neighbor's kid, a girl Zoey's own age, playing baseball in their backyard. "Out the backa the house," as even Zoey calls it now. Bridget Charles, she told me, was the girl's name.

"She was super good, Mom," Zoey said. "She told me the tryouts are coming up for a super fun team." I asked her if she wanted to play baseball, too, and Zoey shrugged. "Is it hard?" she asked. I told her I had no idea and to ask her father, sitting right next to us in his own chair, his ample bottom unscoochable. Hugh explained that down here, the boys' team plays baseball and the girls' team plays softball. And then he made a dad joke, saying that therefore the sport wasn't hard; it was soft. And our humorless daughter said, "Ok, great! I'll ask Bridge when tryouts are, and then, Mom, can you drive us?"

It turns out that as with most things, Zoey is naturally pretty good at softball. Her father came home from work the next night with some gear from the local sports store—lucky Zoey, I would have bought everything used—and pitched her some balls underhand. She hit them all fine. We already knew she'd have no trouble fielding, as her favorite sport is to edge her little brother out of a guy-bonding game of catch with their dad.

Hugh said he'd emailed the coach and put her on the list and used my email on the sign-up sheet, since tryouts were during his weekly daddy-daughter date with baby Joy. And he laughed smugly and said, "Doubt Zoey'll need any help from me anyway, that girl." Could there be any doubt that Zoey has retained her place as her father's favorite through all three kids? And Joy, of course, as my baby, has my heart locked down. Poor Samuel. Though I have a feeling he'll gain favor when Zoey's period arrives.

So tryouts have come and gone, and Zoey has not disappointed Hugh, not that she would ever be able to even if she tried. She made the team as something called a utility player, which apparently is everyone who doesn't know how to pitch or play in the catcher's position. The coach cc'd all the other parents whose kids made it, and I immediately sent an email to all of them saying that I'd love to get a carpool going for practices and have two extra rear seats in my van on practice days to run the kids from the middle school to the field. I got six takers within an hour and had to divvy them up in turns. Daria, who is a big-time real estate lawyer and just cannot be there under any circumstances after school, even told me her daughter was "just hefty enough" to sit in the front seat. I was thinking, *What if Sofia loses a couple of pounds when the season starts? Will she have to ride her bike from school to practice until she can bulk back up? I'd better be sure to bring some high-calorie snacks for the car.*

Zoey was pleased when I told her about the ride sharing. A carload of players meant built-in buddies from the drop. And softball meant new friends at school—an area she could use some help with since we moved down south.

But Bridget's mother, Wendy Charles, is not pleased. Not in the least. She responded too late to get Bridget a spot in my car and now has come over in her uptight work clothes to give me a piece of her mind. It seems to upset her further when she finds me trying to act southern on my front lawn.

"I just saw y'all's email," she says to me. Not *Good evening.* Not *Might I sit down?* Hugh's chair is empty tonight; he's inside fixing a running toilet. She could have had a seat, had a glass of wine, acted like a person.

Instead: "Oh, Celeste, I know you mean well. But I was at work all day; you gotta know that. Doing work," she clarifies. "When y'all are figuring out your carpools, ah'm in a meeting, and now I don't mind telling you I feel hung out to dry."

I look at her, confused, then embarrassed. I guess I did forget all about Bridget and that when Wendy thanked me for giving her a ride yesterday, I responded with a relaxed, "Anytime."

"Oh crap," I say. "I should've saved a spot for Bridget. I just was so excited about the new team I forgot your daughter would need a ride every day."

Wendy seems to soften a bit at my quick regret. "Well, I wish I didn't have to come hat in hand. Wouldn't I like to be sitting here having a glass of wine in the front garden rather than rushing around trying to figure out how to get my daughter from school to her absolute favorite activity in the world? But I wanna stay focused on the positive. She did get in and is looking like a starter, even with all the competition this year. You know, we gotta take the good with the bad."

I try to parse her round-shaped words into something I know how to respond to. "I should make room for her in the car, Wendy. Gosh, I wish I'd gotten that eight seater from GMC." I sigh. "The gas mileage, though."

Wendy waves her hands in the air. "Now, don't be kicking out someone else because of us. Aaliyah's mom, Gemma, is going to take Bridge. She works from home and says she can just slip away for the twenty minutes to and fro."

I smile. "I suppose she wouldn't regret the chance to peek at Coach in his short shorts." Gemma feels like someone I wish I could get to know better. She's funny as can be, with her borderline-inappropriate jokes about the neighbor dads. How the new father the next block over gets his mail in a bathrobe with no belt, or how one of the substitute mailmen makes socks and Birkenstocks look sexy. (He does not.)

Wendy frowns at me. "Ok. That's fihne. But Celeste, and here's the thing, Gemma has a standing meeting on Wednesdays. Don't suppose you could strap Bridge to the bumper on Wednesdays, couldja?" She tries to smile, but it looks like it pains her. "I asked around as soon as I got home, but all the other cars seem to be full already."

"Who drove her last year?" I ask and then immediately regret it.

"Kara's dad," she says plainly. "But then, he'll not be driving this year, will he?"

I grimace. Kara Diforio was a utility player who, by all accounts, got some decent play time last year. She was not on the list for this year. I suppose that might be in some part due to Zoey. "Shoot. I had hoped she was just in the thirteen-and-ups now."

"She'll do the rec team for a year. Regroup. Jane Diforio's mentioned she's got a lead on an amazing private coach. I think the gal they used last year just wasn't up to snuff."

Private sports coaching for eleven-year-olds! I try not to make a face at that. "Well, I'll figure out Wednesdays. Maybe Hugh can come home early on Wednesdays, or . . . I know! We could have Zoey and Bridget bike together, and I could carry their gear? It's only a couple of miles, and I bet they'd enjoy it."

"Bless your heart," says Wendy. I can never tell down here when this is a nice thing to say and when it is meant to be cruel, so I wince whenever I hear it. "I so appreciate that," she adds. I'm about to ask her to have a seat and share some wine, but she is already walking back to the sidewalk, like this whole visit has been nothing but a business transaction.

Or a mugging.

"No problem," I say to her back, because if I was just attacked, it's likely I invited it. I suppose there was a softball-carpooling pecking order, and I have upset it. Or more likely, there was some sort of understanding that softball was Not for Those Yankee Masons from Minnesota, and then I signed my daughter up anyway, and Zoey had the nerve to go and be good at it.

And what's worse, I tried to be just a bit helpful to the very people for whom my lifestyle is a personal affront.

Hugh is right: It's likely that I cannot win, no matter what I do, because to Wendy and her own personal League of Women Judgers, I am everything that is wrong with parenting. I am a woman with no career and three pampered kids who haven't spent so much as a minute in day care. And yes, I admit it, I have a Pinterest board full of fun kids' lunches sorted into a monthly rotation. I am a feminism fail; I am completely dependent on my husband for every penny we have, and I'm perfectly fine with that.

But I seem to be the only one. As the lawyer mom helpfully reminded me a few days ago, we are not living in a community property state, so it's best to "keep up with your waxing and keep things interesting."

Hugh comes out now and asks me, in a faux-fearful whisper, "Is she gone yet?"

I roll my eyes at him, but at the same time I sink back into his arms, hoping he washed his hands between the toilet and me. Linked together, we watch Wendy make her way down our sidewalk to the next block, where her front door stares out in the opposite direction to mine, passing our shared fence.

"Were you hiding the whole time?" I ask him.

"Well, I just figured I wouldn't be much help," he admits. "I never understand all the complicated subtext going on between you moms around here."

"Honestly, Hugh, neither do I. What have I done that's so awful, I want to know?"

"Aw, love," he says. "Jealousy is a three-headed snake—no way to avoid it. Look at her." He gestures, now that she's well out of hearing. "Buttoned up to her chin, shaped like a railroad tie, working herself half to death to prove something to god knows who. And you: beautiful, voluptuous, sexy as hell . . ." He starts to rub the increasingly smaller nook between my wide hips and my wide bust, something that used to make me feel feminine and now makes me wonder where my waistline went.

I wiggle out of his embrace. "You're adorable, sweetheart," I tell him. "But I'm pretty sure she's not jealous. More like irritated at my very existence. And Zoey's, for that matter."

"Well, lucky for her, there's no avoiding Zoey," he says, gesturing to the spot around the side of the house, where Bridget and Zoey are playing catch. That the two girls get on like a house on fire gives me just that slightest bit of guilty satisfaction. I watch as the softball flies from the back of Wendy Charles's yard to the back of mine, crossing over the top of the split rail fence that divides them. "Now come inside; come see what your genius husband has done with the plumbing in the hall bath," he says. "A good flush will perk your spirits right up," he adds to his own amusement, leading me to think of how very, very far we've come from the honeymoon phase.

I follow him inside and applaud his handiwork. But as he explains U-bends to me, my brain wanders back outside, to that ball sailing back and forth over the fence line. A line that exists for reasons I cannot understand. A line across which Wendy's life refuses to acknowledge the meaning of mine.

CHAPTER 2

WENDY

My desk is empty; my email inbox is full. I am ready to do my real work. My productive work. It's the perfect moment in my day, when I can turn the world down and my brain up and be what I am meant to be, if only for a few short hours.

Before me on one large monitor is the synthesis of six different new productivity studies. On the smaller screen of my laptop is a blank page, where I will unfold trends and make sweeping recommendations to present at the championships of life coaching, the annual Upland South Women's Expo, where I have scored a juicy keynote spot just eight short days from now.

Quickly I start to lose myself in the work, falling deeper and deeper into my thoughts and ideas on one simple subject: how much time we have as humans and how to make the most of it. As I work, time ignores me, moves on without me, until my phone goes off and two hours have magically passed. My smart reminders begin to crawl up the calendar pane of my display, my Wi-Fi reconnects automatically, my phone comes off Do Not Disturb, and a banner alert says, *I'm reminding you: ASP tomorrow.*

The reminder merits a sigh. Tomorrow might be Bridge's favorite day of the season. It's definitely Linus's least favorite. I think I'm probably with Linus.

It's called the All-Sports Potluck, an event to kick off kids' summer league sports in our local leagues, and it always happens right after try-outs for baseball, softball, swimming, and tennis. Technically the golfers are invited, too, but there are so few of them, and they've already been playing for six weeks by now, with intense focus and more intense polo shirts. Worse, the golfers are terrible at potlucks. No matter what course assignment you give them, they bring crazy things. Trays of daikon sushi, bruschetta with truffle oil, artisanal pickles: foods that none of the kids will eat and the organizers end up feeling terrible about throwing out at the end of the night. What the kids want is cut-up fruit, ranch pasta salad, cold fried chicken, and little meatballs cooked in grape jelly. The adults want sangria—specifically the Charles Family Recipe—and they want a lot of it. It's hardly rocket science.

I've been bringing sangria to this same banquet for four years, but now, at the ripe old age of eight, Linus has informed us that he wants to stay home this year and send Bridget with the Masons. I dismissed the thought out of hand, but Seth is considering the request, and it has me crawling my mental walls. Uncomfortable though I know it can be, the poor kid needs to get out there, to try to socialize, for his own good.

"They're just not his people," Seth tells me when I call him about this over my lunch hour. "I get it. They're not mine either."

I don't want to start the game called *blame Wendy because we live in the suburbs* right now, so I say only, "Somewhere out there, if he doesn't hide at home every time there's a chance at social interaction, someone will come along to be his people. Everyone's got people when they're patient and they keep looking." I wonder if this also applies to me. I have a few trusted confidants—a guy friend here at work and my sister especially—but all my other relationships are nurtured thanks to a detailed spreadsheet I created with Google Calendar teasers whenever I need to mail a birthday card, send a check-in text, or set up a phone date. I like the other moms from the team, but after the season is over, we always lose touch. After all, who has the time?

"Sure. Ok. But I doubt he's going to find his people at All-Sports," says Seth.

I can't help but laugh at that. If we make Linus go, my money says he'll bring a book. "You've got a point there," I concede. "I bet he'll bring his own people with him, and by 'people' I mean dwarves and elves."

But Seth isn't laughing. "I'm telling you, Wendy. That's the whole problem with this kid. All the sci-fi and fantasy stuff, the depressing stories, the make-believe."

"You're complaining because he's so imaginative?" Seth requires hours and hours to nurture his work and feed his creative muse. Time, I'll admit, I sometimes would appreciate having for our family.

"It's not that he's imaginative. It's that he's a huge bummer. He's not interested in doing *anything* in real life."

"All the more reason to make him go to All-Sports," I say, wishing Seth would just for once stop bagging on my kid. Our kid.

"Tagging along to his sister's event is not the same as doing something. Doing things is how you meet your people."

"He does lots of things," I say.

"Scratch programming? Reading about Scratch programming? Talking our ears off about Scratch programming?"

"Well, what *if* his thing is programming?" I say slowly. It doesn't sound socially great, I'll admit, but the kid's gonna do what he's gonna do. "It's better than cooking meth."

"Programming is not his thing," says Seth. "He's a kid. His thing is kid things."

I'm not sure what to say to this, because it's obviously not true.

"What we need to be doing is giving up on dragging him to his sister's endless shit—"

I wince a little when Seth talks this way about Bridge's devotion to softball—though yeah, it will feel endless by the time August rolls around, and Seth makes sure to make every single game of the season. Credit where credit is due.

"—and start dragging him to his own. What about golf? I know you say the club membership isn't worth it, but look at those kids, with their weird food and their tucked-in paisley tech shirts. Maybe that's Linus just waiting to happen."

I clench my fists. Because he's trying so hard to relate to his son, Seth has tried tennis, baseball, basketball, soccer, and rock climbing with Linus. Each sport with an expensive new set of gear, shoes, teachers, lessons. Linus is indifferent to them all. He doesn't understand the rules; he doesn't try hard; he doesn't always even stay awake between innings. Must we go around this carousel again but with a $1,500 country club membership added to the bill?

I exhale. "The club will set us back financially. The money situation in our house is already too much pressure on me." I am the primary wage earner, to be sure, but I'm also the CFO of the household. Seth's art is expensive to create. Sometimes I have to hide the money to be sure Seth and I have a shot at retirement. The rest of the time I have to hide it to make sure we have next month's mortgage. "How about we consider him visiting your workshop again?"

Seth's offense is practically audible. "Honestly, Wendy," he says. "You know I can't juggle my work and the kids at the same time. It feels so unfair whenever you ask. Would I ask you to take the kids to your meetings?"

I find my eyes studying the far-left corner of my office. There's such lovely molding in here. And the shutter-adorned windows overlook the chicest street in the moderately chic town. "I'm sorry, babe, but I'm running outa time," I tell Seth, because I don't want to delve into the differences in our careers or how his, of late, has started to feel more like a hobby. Besides—it doesn't need to be said. I've seen how much his recent dip in commissions and sales has affected him. I'd do anything to boost him up right now rather than drag him down. "Let's just bring

Linus for one more banquet. He's growing up fast, and my hours are so long. I hardly see him as it is."

"What's to see? He's a lump," Seth says.

I sigh. "Enough with that, Seth," I tell him firmly. "He's really a good kid."

"You're right," he says quickly. "He is. I love him; you know that. That's why I'm not willing to give up on him."

"And I thank you for it," I tell him, finding that once again Seth and I are better off polite than honest. "I'll see you tonight."

"You won't," he says. "Sorry. Gallery night in town."

"Oh, of course," I say. Our local monthly gallery night is huge for him, and for our other friends in the scene as well. They all hit everyone else's shows, sip that crappy free red wine, schmooze among the buyers and owners, and then go to the noodle shop with industry hours and drink soju until the sun comes up.

Once upon a time, Seth and I did that together.

"Well, in that case, I'll see you Saturday morning."

"Ahhhh, actually Saturday night," he says. "Late. Remember? We decided to turn the weekend into Corbin's bachelor party?"

I do not remember this, and I don't have any reminders set. "But that means you won't even be at All-Sports anyway."

"You don't need me—you're a pro. Make the sangria, throw away the golf food, buy the kids too much dessert. Same as every year."

Exactly the same, in that just like the years before, Seth has done nothing to help. Mentally, I underline *work on marriage* on my interminable to-do list. "Tell Corbin congratulations for me, then," I say, because this isn't a fight I want to have right now. The truth is, there hasn't been a fight worth having between Seth and me in years. Nobody wins anymore. It's solvable, I'm sure, but that damned to-do list is just so long. "Have a great time."

Time. In the time I've been on the phone, I have gotten seventy-eight new emails. I'm going to need to hang up now if I want to get any of these triaged before my real calls start. And I'll need to run the calls like a drill sergeant if I want to get Linus from after-school by five. Even then I'll need luck and maybe a miracle to get it all done. I open up the first email. Realize I never took anything out of the freezer this morning for dinner tonight. So now I need luck, a miracle, and the drive-through. Oh, and with no Seth, I'm doing the shopping for tomorrow night on my own. So now it's luck, a miracle, the drive-through, and a ten-minute stopover at the ABC liquors for a case of red wine on the drive home.

In the back of my mind, as I volley back email after email, I ponder it all. Linus, programming, loneliness, how much red sangria thirty moms can drink, if we had rotisserie chicken last night, does Bridge eat broccoli now? Far from leaving me behind, Time is sucking me in now, a black hole of errands and notifications and—oh yeah, I am supposed to be eating lunch. And did I pack the kids any lunch? They would have said something, right? They would have noticed?

I order a salad—the same salad I have every Friday, an automated order on my delivery app. Then remember that I was hoping to go to reformer Pilates over lunch. Realize that I could still make it; dismiss the idea. Consider that I might want to just lie on my office floor for the next twenty minutes until the salad arrives. Answer five more emails. Try to remember if any of Bridge's ride-or-die girls didn't make the team. She told me last night that someone besides Kara got cut . . . she cried over it. But it was someone she didn't particularly like, just felt bad for. That's my compassionate Bridget. Who was that girl?

Brandy. I can't forget the brandy for the sangria. What brand did I buy last year? It wasn't as good as usual. I should have put it in my phone so I don't get it again. Did I? What did I sort it under in my notes app? Do I need to go to the library for Linus's books on hold? Would it be easier to just give the kid a book budget? I'm easily paying twenty dollars in fines each month. It would be a good lesson in limited resources . . . or he'd just use the money and then put more books on hold at the library. It's a good thing to have such a reader, isn't it? Why doesn't Seth see that? Wouldn't other dads be proud of such a studious son?

And on and on clicks my mind, going on while the salad comes, while I eat it without tasting it, while my inbox is cleared. It yammers on when it's time to move myself to the conference room, through a meeting and PowerPoint, and to when the day is over. It goes on until I wake up the next day and find myself in the kitchen cutting up oranges and apples for the sangria on one cutting board and onions for the minimeatballs on another, without quite knowing exactly how I got there and what all I missed on the way.

—

CELESTE

The good news is, my kids are socially successful. When we arrive at Founder's Park for the big sporty potluck thing, Zoey finds Bridget, Sofia, and Aaliyah from the team in an instant, and Samuel can make friends anywhere he can find a ball, a racket, or a stick. Joy and I stick together, and I sometimes wonder if she does this out of pity for me, because she always checks with me when someone wants her to play.

Happily, no one has asked yet—she's one of the littler siblings at All-Sports, and so I use her as a pint-size excuse to spend copious amounts of time setting up a large glass dispenser I found at a garage sale, painted a lemon-yellow chalkboard oval on, and neatly labeled with a fuchsia chalk pen: *pink sangria*. Then I start assembling the recipe. It's easy as pie: two bottles of eight-dollar rosé, the zest of an entire lime, a pint of muddled organic raspberries, and the tiniest splash of this very special artisanal birch-sap vodka I heard about on a mommy podcast where they really seem to know their hooch, if how slurred their words are by the end of each episode is any indication. I had to order it from this place online I'd never heard of, and it cost a fair bit more than vodka should, but it just felt like the sort of special touch that would go far here in Birchboro Hills.

Maybe this will be the thing that helps me make my first real friend in town, I think wistfully. It sure hasn't been the PTA, the boosters, the tutoring, or the carpooling. Not even sitting in the front yard has paid off. Not yet.

When I can fiddle with the drink no longer, I hoist Joy up on a hip, head back to the trunk, grab some more food, and move to the main potluck table. I unpack a tray of deviled eggs with smoked salmon that looks very yummy, if I do say so myself, and encourage Joy to help herself to one. She climbs onto the bench of the picnic table as though all of the potluck—cold homemade chicken, macaroni salads in varieties beyond your imagination (including one with salami?), and, bizarrely, an enormous aluminum platter of pickled radishes, asparagus, and green beans—is laid out for her and only her. Faithfully, she chooses one of my eggs with the biggest garnish of dill and mashes it in and around her face with relish. I take another egg from the other side to make the dish look popular and eat it in two bites, then decide that alone will probably hold down a small glass of my pretty-looking sangria.

When I return to the drinks table, Wendy Charles is there. Her arms are laden with stuff, there's a purse on her shoulder, and she looks beleaguered. But rather than setting anything down, she is staring at my drinks dispenser. "Pink sangria," I hear her read, with a question in her voice.

I smile. Always smile. "You can make sangria with strawberries and prosecco, or white wine and peaches, or really any combo of fruit and wine. But mine is rosé, organic raspberries, and lime zest. And a splash of artisanal single-batch birch-sap vodka," I add behind my hand, like it is top secret. Wendy looks at me blankly. "I know—it sounds crazy. But try it. It's so refreshing." Indeed, I note, the glass dispenser is already a few inches lower than when I set it out minutes ago. No one can resist raspberries in a drink.

"We've never had pink sangria at All-Sports before," says Wendy. Her voice is less singsong than usual. Immediately I know I've screwed something up.

"Oh," I say. Then I channel my dear late mother and add, "I'm sorry."

I know. I know. Why on earth am I apologizing for bringing a refreshing and quite boozy drink to a team potluck on a hot day? Because my mom always said people can't hate you if you apologize for their problems. It sounds a bit codependent, but my mom worked for some real jerks in her life to keep us kids in shoes and socks, and she knew a thing or two about going along to get along. She often told me a quick surrender will take all the wind out of an angry person's sails and make them notice how rude they are being.

That doesn't happen here.

"Pink sangria," she says again. "Not red. Not white. Is that a northerner thing?" she asks. I don't answer because she doesn't wait for me to. "I'm sure it's so . . . yummy," says Wendy, as she pushes the whole dispenser back five inches on the table and pulls her own a bit farther up, as though there's some imaginary potluck spotlight I'm stealing. "But don't take it personally if no one drinks it. It's not about you; it's about tradition. The parents ask me to bring my recipe every year, and I can't say no, though I'm as busy as ever this time of year."

My smile falters just a tiny bit. "Isn't sangria just opening bottles and tipping them in?" I ask. "I mean, unless you use hard-to-find ingredients. But that didn't even take that long—a month to special order is all."

She shrugs casually. "Maybe my sangria is so popular because it's light enough to drink a glass or two before you tip over. I mean, this *is* a family event. Vodka in sangria!" she now says to herself. "Now that's a party right there." She says more quietly: "A party you regret the next day."

Hmph. I hardly think my sangria is going to land someone in the ER. But before my very eyes, Wendy fishes around in her purse, pulls out a black Sharpie, and adds *with vodka* on the label of my sangria. The stenciled label I painted on myself. I guess this dispenser is a one-trick pony now.

"That was chalkboard paint," I tell her, not exactly sure why. She can't un-Sharpie it, can she?

She looks at me. "So cute," she says. "I've seen those labels in the dollar section at Target every summer. I just never have the time to be so crafty."

I give her a look that roughly translates to *!!*

She ignores the look entirely. "Oh, Celeste, chalkboard paint, infused vodka—you're so full of ideas. I wish I could be more like you."

How on earth can she say those words and still make it sound like an insult? I smile tightly. "Maybe I should put this away," I say. "The sangria. We could just hold it under the table for when we run out of yours." Not that anyone in their right mind would care if there were two kinds of sangria at a potluck. No one but Wendy Charles.

"No, no, that's silly. It's already here. It's just . . ." Her voice fades.

"What?" I demand.

"Well, I think you were assigned the vegetarian appetizer course."

"Assigned?" I ask. Is that a thing now—assigned potluck dishes? I grew up clutching a four-dollar Little Caesars pizza on the way to every church potluck, just like half the other kids I knew. We somehow got by.

"On the Google Doc?" Wendy goes on. "Don't tell me you're not in our softball-parents Google group yet, Celeste!"

I know nothing about a Google group. I know about All-Sports because one of the other moms told me about it in passing. "I thought people just brought whatever they wanted to most potlucks."

Wendy looks at me like I'm a complete moron. "Well, then we'd be eating nothing but cantaloupe and deviled eggs if that were the case. Think about it. Everyone would only bring the cheap foods."

I frown and wish I hadn't labeled the eggs with my telltale swirly handwriting. It's true: I did gravitate toward the eggs for cheap protein. You can't take the Little Caesars out of the girl, no matter how much birch-sap-infused vodka I try to pull off.

"Never mind it," Wendy says. "We'll get you signed up, and y'all's family will be up to speed in no time. It helps loads, the docs. I mean, game snacks alone. We'd be duplicating efforts."

Game snacks? I wonder, hoisting Joy into my arms and absently playing patty-cake with her. Samuel's school soccer team gave me a twenty-dollar bill at the beginning of the season, and I brought cut-up orange slices to every game. On the last day, I brought cupcakes decorated like soccer balls. I sort of figured this would be the same thing, only with less black frosting. Why does everything related to Wendy Charles have to be so *complicated*?

There's a quiet coming over the pavilion, and aside from a few people milling by some bacon-wrapped dates, I see that most of the parents are gathering toward the front of the tables. "What's this?" I ask Wendy, because she's standing closest to me. Because both of us are refilling our sangria glasses with our own respective sangrias, I notice reluctantly.

"Oh, this is the fundraiser," she says. "Maybe the whole point, to be honest." I look around at our kids, all romping joyfully in the large park, playing soccer, digging in the sandbox, or playing on the climbing frame and swings. *That* seems like the whole point to me. But I don't say that.

"Before everyone eats," Wendy explains, "you can go bid on a chance to visit the dessert table." She gestures to the far side of the food options, where brownies, cookies, cakes, and doughnuts are piled high. "The top fifty bidders win an all-you-can-stack dessert plate. So we all go hog wild to win our kiddos a plate, and the teams make a mint."

"Whoa, really? There must be way more than fifty kids here, though."

Wendy nods. "Course, the kids are crushed if you don't bid high enough, with all those sweets out on full display while you try to get them to eat a piece of broccoli covered in ranch."

"The kids would be crushed?" I ask incredulously. "I'll be crushed. I love lemon squares."

Wendy gives me a good-natured—for her—smile. "Lucky you. I don't mind telling you, Hugh seems every bit as sweet as marshmallow fluff. Whereas Seth lets me know when I gain so much as an ounce. I can't even look at a lemon square."

I smile. "Hugh is so sweet," I say, though I don't quite understand what that has to do with my love of desserts. Oh! Wait! I get it: He's sweet to love me even though I'm curvy, I suppose. I guess only the nicest sort of fellow could bear to look at this body unclothed. Stung, I add, "But I'm sure Seth indulges you in his own way." Meaning at least Hugh doesn't have to live with a sangria-obsessed b-word-that-rhymes-with-witch.

"I'll give you a tip," says Wendy, missing my sorry attempt at a sick burn. "Just bid twenty dollars per kid. You can't see what others have bid, which the committee always hopes will make people go crazy and overbid. And for a few people it does. But most of the crowd just bid five to ten bucks, because that's all they can see a plate of cookies being worth. So you come down right in the middle."

"Can't they just let everyone have a cookie each and take donations?"

Wendy shakes her head. "Doesn't work. Same as the cantaloupe and deviled eggs. *This* is what works. This is how we raise enough so that every kid will get a uniform, a helmet, whatever they need, no matter their means."

I reach right over Wendy, pull my sangria container back to the front of the table, and pour myself a too-big glass. "Even though the same kids who need uniforms probably won't be able to afford cookies."

Wendy just shrugs sadly. "Those kids probably aren't even here."

Right, because who would invite their parents to the Google group? "What happens to the leftover desserts?" I ask.

More shrugging. I want to shake her by those apathetic shoulders.

All at once, though I was doing fine before, I feel the sangria start to hit home. In a surge of tipsy insecurity, I wish Hugh were here rather than in the company box of the Braves game schmoozing important clients. Hugh is brilliantly personable, a people person if ever there was one. But he doesn't truck with this sort of snobbish nonsense, not at all. He'd tell our kids we were going out for ice cream later and refuse to bid on dessert. He'd personally buy ten uniforms for kids in need rather than play along with this dumb stunt. He'd tell this Wendy with her perfectly colored hair and small, flat little body what he thought of her red sangria and then eat every bite of cantaloupe and deviled eggs in the place personally.

Is it any wonder I married the man?

But without Hugh, I can only just simmer. I simmer and pour myself yet another pink sangria (*with vodka*). Then, fortified, I stomp over to the bidding table and write down not four but six dessert-plate bids, at twenty dollars each. Three are for my kids, though they are not going to be eating more than a couple of sweets each, because in my family we can respect healthy limits. One is for me and means that yes, I will eat twenty dollars' worth of lemon squares or die trying. And as for the last two bids, well, I put them in for Bridget and Linus, the long-suffering children of Wendy the Sangria Shrew, so that they can know that at least one person in their neighborhood knows what it's like to be generous.

Or maybe I do it just so I can watch Wendy's face when her kids each get *two* plates piled high with sweets thirty minutes after their regular bedtime. Maybe—*sorry, Mom*—preemptive apologizing isn't nearly as satisfying as the sweet flavor of artisanal vodka infused with passive-aggressive revenge.

CHAPTER 3
SURREAL SUNDAY

WENDY

I wake the next morning with a splitting headache and the sense that something is very, very wrong. Immediately I suspect that damned pink sangria. That damned sangria in that gorgeous, perfect Williams Sonoma five-quart sangria dispenser from the popular "I'm Better Than You" collection. I shouldn't have had any, but I had to know whose was better. And then I had to double-check my results.

And yep, after Linus ate so many brownies he had to throw up in the Port-O-Johnny and Bridget cried from little-brother embarrassment and I packed up all the leftovers like cantaloupe—no one even *likes* cantaloupe—and threw away all the artisanal pickles, not a drop of my famous red sangria was left in the entire park, while three solid inches of raspberry mush remained of Celeste's recipe. And yes, technically that means I won the potluck.

But I'll be honest right now. I do not feel like a winner. I feel like something that died over the winter and was found by a stray cat, carried into this bedroom that I swear I have never seen before in my life, and deposited on this bizarrely comfortable bed, where it has been chewed on idly ever since. And in that case, the best thing to do is to let myself go back to sleep, or back to being a rotting corpse, whichever the case may be.

—

CELESTE

My head is pounding when I get up the next morning. My head is pounding, and my husband is snoring. That's weird. He rarely snores. But then, he did show up to the potluck late last night after I, slightly drunk, SOS'd him around nine. He was quickly surrounded by three miserable children in sugar comas who had no hope of making it home without a ride, even if I somehow carried all three on my swaying body the mile home.

And he and I did fight after we put the kids to bed—fought over the stupid moms Hugh was convinced I was overreacting to, about whether I should have spent $120 on team donations made in spite, and about whether we should have ever moved here for his job when we could have stayed up north in our one-bathroom Queen Anne with the bats living in the roof. Even if the secondary schools were closing from low enrollment and furlough was a very real possibility. Even if five people in one bathroom was indeed a bit much.

And—I remember now—I did blame him for my loneliness and, somehow, for my overconsumption of pink sangria (with vodka). I told him that I missed talking to him for more than three minutes a day, that he seemed more focused on the kids than he did on me, that I worried I bored him just as much as I seemed to bore everyone else in this village. And he retorted that if I didn't see how much he cared about me when all he wanted in the whole world was for our family to be happy, maybe I was the one with the problem.

So yeah, with a night like that, I suppose it stands to reason he should be snoring a little. Because he's right, of course. He shows me how he cares in a thousand little ways. The problem is, I can never seem to believe he really means it. And he probably went to sleep mad, probably tossed and turned worrying about me, and probably will wake up feeling crappy, all because I couldn't manage a skirmish over a potluck dinner. It makes sense.

What doesn't make sense is that he should somehow now be . . . smaller?

—

WENDY

When I wake up again—I don't know how much later—I am still, to my shock, feeling a bit drunk. Seth is still sleeping; of course he is. My eyes are bleary to the point of near blindness—nothing in the bedroom looks quite right. I need to get my contacts in. I think I cried last night on the walk home, which is humiliating enough, but it would be worse if Celeste saw me and thought I was crying over sangria. I am a confident, intelligent woman. I wasn't crying over a mixed drink. I was crying over a million little stresses of my life. And also over a mixed drink.

Oh no, did Bridge see me crying? I need to know she didn't. She can't be thinking I'm crying all the time if I'm supposed to be inspiring her as a successful working mother so that someday she can be a successful-er working mother. Linus probably wouldn't notice a few sniffles, but Bridge is a sharp kid and empathetic.

Should I go try to wake her up early so she and I can talk about this? Or wait—it's Sunday. Sunday is the one day each week when Seth is supposed to get up with the kids, except it's the first Sunday, which means he had gallery night on Friday and the bachelor thing with his art buddies last night, which means . . . I lean very, very close to his sleeping body to smell him. If he came home sideways on good bourbon, I'll be able to tell by my nose.

I smell nothing alcoholic whatsoever, except some kind of acidic citrus flavor on my own breath. To my surprise, my husband smells . . . kind of good, actually?

But wait. Where did his hair go? Did he shave his head?

What the hell is happening?

—

C ELESTE

Wendy's husband is in my bed. I press my eyes shut, open them again. And stifle a scream.

Pardon me while I have a heart attack.

Wait. Stay calm, Celeste. There has to be a reasonable explanation for this. Breathe.

This isn't my bed.

This isn't my room.

It's similar. Same size, same general layout. But there's a hole in the drywall above the TV. Also, there's a TV.

Where the *heck* am I?

CHAPTER 4

WENDY

Very, very quietly, I throw my feet over the side of the bed.

The first thing I notice is that the floor is closer than it used to be. This is a freaking awful hangover. How much sangria did I drink?

And while I'm asking unanswerable questions, why did Seth shave his head?

Why is our bathroom on the wrong side of the room?

Why are my breasts on the wrong side of my navel?

With a start I realize I'm going to be sick. I am going to go to the wrong-side bathroom and barf in the wrong-side toilet—if I can get there in time. I'm not going to make it.

Ok, at least I made it to the toilet.

What a nice toilet it is, I think to myself, drunk as I am. So clean. And what a nice tile floor. Is this floor heated? I've never thrown up anywhere so pleasant before. And what a strange thing to think, and how strange that these towels have sea stars embroidered on them, just like the sea stars we picked out of the waves when Bridge was a toddler and Linus was in my arms and we went to Tybee and were all together as a family. How long ago was it, now? Was that the happiest moment of my marriage? Am I delirious? And if I'm delirious, should I tell someone?

No. I should go back to bed and close my eyes tight until the room stops spinning and my brain starts working and I'm back in my own bed.

Yes. That's what I'll do. I'll go back to that other bed and lie down again and assume this is all a weird, confusing dream. Next to the bald, quiet Seth, who, strangest of all, for the first time in his entire life is not snoring. This is an excellent plan. When I wake up, none of this will have happened.

—

CELESTE

Well, I know where I am. And it's very, very bad.

I am in Wendy's bedroom. I know because I am surrounded by Seth's art and pictures of Bridget and Linus, which I can only just make out, because everything more than ten feet away is very blurry.

I have no idea how I got here, but I know I need to leave immediately.

Heart racing, stomach churning, I stand up and pad as quietly as I possibly can into the big unfinished bathroom with grout that needs resealing, close the door behind me, and contemplate slipping out the window. It is a first-floor bedroom, but at the moment I am so confused and horrified I think I would be willing to chance multiple stories just to get out of here. But I have to pee first, and it's one of those bathrooms where the toilet faces a bathroom door with a mirror hung on the back, so when I close it and pull down my pants and sit down, I'm staring at the body of Wendy Charles, and it is everything I can do not to scream at the top of my lungs.

No, I tell my brain firmly. *Stop being crazy.* I am the one on the toilet; I am the one peeing. I feel my pelvic floor doing the work of peeing, I feel the cold seat on the back of my legs, and I hear the tinkle with my ears. But the woman looking back at me in the mirror is Wendy.

Wendy Charles. Wendy Charles's blonde hair with no gray and Wendy Charles's pointy nose with no humor.

My heart begins to race. I look at Wendy in the mirror, shut my eyes tight, and then open them again. Her mouth opens in horror just like mine. I hold up my hand, and she holds up hers in perfect symmetry. I grab some TP and wipe; Wendy reflects it back. At last, I stand up, undies still around my ankles, and move right up to the mirror, but the image of Wendy moves, too, closer and closer, until I knock my forehead against the mirror and watch Wendy raise her hand to her head in pain. A tiny, stifled gasp of horror escapes my throat, but it's not my voice.

I look down at my chest. I'm in a thin, hole-filled T-shirt I've never seen in my life, so I lift it up and over my head and stare down.

And those are definitely not mine. Those little B-cup handfuls that point upward are not my breasts; they aren't a tenth of my breasts. They are as neat and tidy as mine are pendulous and unpredictable. Those breasts could only belong to someone as anal as Wendy.

Similarly, that trim stomach can only be Wendy's trim stomach. That C-section scar must belong to Wendy. The navel that is taut, not deep like a cavern? That must also be Wendy's.

I look at my crotch. My god. Does Wendy have a brazilian?

Am I Wendy?

Do I have a brazilian?

—

WENDY

Refusing to let myself think, I lie back in the bed, this time on my side. I smoosh the bald Seth. He grunts and says, "HEY!" and then sits up, looks at me, and says, "Honey, what are you doing?"

AND HE IS NOT SETH!

He is Hugh Mason. Celeste's husband. The squishy, middle-aged sales VP with the fancy grill setup Seth lusts after.

I jump out of bed and start to scream.

"What are you doing here?!" I screech.

"What? Celeste, what's wrong with you?" Hugh pops up in bed and throws off the covers. He is naked. He is totally naked. I scream some more.

"Are you having a dream?"

"Did you just call me Celeste?" I ask him hysterically as I cover my eyes.

Hugh is out of bed already, before I can tell him to cover up, and heading over to my side of the bed. In a horrified panic I flee toward the bathroom, shouting, "Cover yourself!" Confused but always obliging, he turns to grab a robe from his closet, and I stare at his bottom, at the thatch of light back hair toward the top of each shoulder blade, the muscle and heft of his biceps, the strong, thick legs and slight dad paunch. What the hell is happening here? What is happening to me? Did I go to bed with Celeste Mason's husband? And if so, my god, why?

"Celeste, honey. Are you sick?" he asks the minute he comes close to the wrong-side bathroom. "Oh man. Is it still the sangria?"

I try to find someplace to put my eyes, to quiet my screaming brain. It's like I've been hit by a hammer in the area of my cortex where reason used to live. But my eyes . . . they're not blurry anymore. They're clear. Clear, as in clear enough to see details on things on the other side of the room, though I am 99.9 percent sure my contacts weren't in a second ago. I can see the details of a half-open wall closet with frumpy women's clothes in it. The folds of pretty, feminine curtains on the windows. The curves of bold accent wallpaper in the wrong-side bathroom and the pretty tile that is sending comforting little heat waves up into my panicked toes.

"I'm sorry," I say. "I don't know what's happening to me. I have no idea what I'm doing here." I lurch out of the bathroom, try to stay upright and evade Hugh-in-just-his-bathrobe to flee for my life.

Hugh takes me by the shoulders—bathrobe still wide open, nakedness perfectly in focus—and says, "You don't need to apologize. If you're this hungover, you need to be in bed, not running around making yourself upset. Lie down with a cool washcloth, and I'll take care of everything. Oh, sweetie. I'm sorry we fought last night. I didn't realize how far gone you were. How much of that stuff did you drink?"

I have no idea what this man is thinking, but I'm not going back to bed in someone else's house with someone else's husband no matter how hungover I might be. I push past him to the open closet, start looking through the clothes for something I can wear outside.

But my reflection, perfectly clear, in the large wall mirror across the room catches my eye.

That and some pendulous breasts that seem to be attached to my chest.

Pendulous breasts that are somehow at once hard and saggy. I freeze in front of the mirror, tilt my head, watch the head looking back at me tilt too. My mouth, as well as the reflection's, slowly drops open. I see curly shoulder-length hair, reach up and touch curly shoulder-length hair. I see the overgrown grays dominating the first inch of her part. A little button nose, nice white teeth, large clear black eyes. I straighten my head. The face in the mirror straightens. My brain cracks.

I seem to be seeing Celeste in the mirror. The mirror is some kind of hallucination, or trick, or weird fitness device, maybe? But that doesn't really make any sense. My panic rises, and I worry I'll be sick again.

"Baby, what are you doing?" Hugh asks. "Are you ok?"

I think of all the things I could say to him right now. I could say, *I'm not your wife. I'm not your baby. I'm your neighbor. And I have no idea how this could be remotely possible, but it seems I'm trapped in your wife's body.* I could say, *Excuse me, good sir, but would you put on some pants and make some coffee? I have to get sober and then go straight to the ER, because I've lost my mind.*

I could ask, *Did I get hit in the head last night, and no one told me?*

But none of that makes any sense, does it? No. I'm Wendy Charles. I'm not Celeste Mason. I don't look like her; I don't have her generous boobs and round butt and understyled hair. I don't have her hairy-backed husband. I never went to bed in this house. These are not my beautiful things.

I run to the bathroom and look in that mirror. Celeste Mason is there too. She is me. I am her. My brain is my brain, but my body is someone else's. So . . . then . . . I've gone insane.

Great.

I turn from the second mirror, take Hugh by the hand, and look him directly in the eyes so he will know just how serious this situation is, and I say, "Hugh. I don't know what you're seeing right now, but this is Wendy talking. Can you please call an ambulance? I think I've had a terrible stroke."

CHAPTER 5

WENDY

Hugh won't stop laughing. I mean, he just will not stop. I am not finding a single thing about this situation funny, and he's having a big chortle.

"Ok, ok. You've made your point. Wendy's got a stick up her ass, sure. But then, sweetie, people might say that about you from time to time. You're the one who told me: Sometimes what looks powerful on a man looks rigid on a woman at first glance. The trick is to look harder. And that has served me well for years."

I stare at him, mystified.

"Do you know what I think?" Hugh asks me in his newscaster accent. "You've been telling me for months now that a break would do you good. And now here you are showing me exactly why I need to listen carefully when you tell me things are getting rough. Why don't you crawl into bed and take the day off, see if that doesn't fix you right up?"

I look over at that gorgeous bed. It looks so much better than the mental breakdown I'm currently having. I try to talk myself into doing the right thing. "I've got to get up. The kids . . ."

"You need to rest, Celeste. For real. I know people have been treating you like your life's a cakewalk around here, but they don't see what I see. Let me take the kids."

For a second I think he's talking about my kids too. About Bridget and Linus.

"All of them?"

He laughs again, a warm sound full of assurance. "Lie down, and when you're feeling ready, I'll send in the monsters for a movie and cuddle if you like."

It's the thought of the cuddle that snaps me back. I have two children at my house all alone with my husband and his own likely hangover. Shouldn't I rush over there and take care of things? And where the hell is Celeste?

"Where the hell *is* Celeste?" I ask.

Hugh looks at me funny. "Is this about that identity crisis book you wanted me to read?"

I look back at him, his broad smile and the wrinkles by his eyes. It's all so warm and welcoming. I just want to get in that nice big bed and go back to sleep. What is wrong with me that I'm seriously considering it? The sheets look so clean. "What book?" I ask drowsily.

"The one about Bernadette."

"*Where'd You Go, Bernadette*?" I ask. We read that in book club a year ago.

"Yes, that's it. I know you said you wanted us to read it together. I'm sorry. I just . . . it's so hard to get into fiction right now." He claps his hands. "I'll get the audio right away, listen to it on my commute. Ok?"

I nod, confused.

"Are you having a where'd-you-go moment, Celeste? Please don't even think of packing up and leaving us. I know we've been a little weak in the romance department lately, but you're what I live for; you know that." He cups my face in his hand. "So you got drunk at a barbecue. So you smell like . . . I don't want to say. Not great. Your life is not slipping away before your eyes. You're not going to suffocate to death in the oppression of a nice neighborhood with good schools. You just have to find your people."

"My people?" I ask. I'm back in that conversation with Seth. My people, Linus's people, Celeste's people. So many people.

Hugh gives me a pat. "Go brush your teeth, take a long, hot bath, and then get all tucked into bed and just take the day off. When you wake up, you'll feel a million times better, and the kitchen will be clean, and the kids will be clean and fed and exercised."

"My kids?" I ask, already moving toward the bathroom sink to brush my teeth, realizing in just one more disgusting cherry on this insanity sundae that I'll have to use Celeste's toothbrush.

More chortling from Hugh. "Who else's?" he asks. "I'm going to give Samuel the WetJet and let him go crazy with it."

"Well . . ." It's just a quick bath. And Hugh seems so reasonable. Maybe there's some kind of explanation for all this. Maybe Celeste is over at my house, happily feeding the kids homemade flaxseed granola and waiting for me to come over and swap back with her. Maybe this sort of thing happens to her all the time. Maybe she's magical, and that's why her kids always have on clean clothes no matter what time of day it is.

I look in the mirror at Celeste's face. I've lost my mind. Or maybe . . . she has, and she thinks she's me? In which case real me is over at my house with my snoring husband, not knowing anything is wrong? Or maybe I'm even drunker than I realize, and this is all some weird brandy-induced dream? In which case I might as well go back to sleep and wait it out, right? And not just sleep, but . . . I look into the mirror and see the deep soaker tub filled with jets. When was the last time I took a bath?

I want a bath.

I am going to take a bath and lie in the jets and relax, until either I wake up from this dream and am myself again, or I start convulsing and Hugh takes me to the hospital. I turn on the water, make it hot, as hot as I can possibly stand. I take off Celeste's camisole—*Is this an old nursing tank?* I wonder when it unwinds in the front—and her unreasonably soft pajama pants. I look over the soft, round evenness of her belly and the thick curves of her thighs. Then I look into my eyes. Her eyes. I look as deeply as I can until I think I can see my own eyes in her sockets. I swear I can see flecks of my own hazel in her brown-black eyes. That must be me in there somewhere, right?

Feeling colder every second, I slide into the bathtub. It is the most singularly comforting place I've been since . . . well, since my honeymoon, when I was in a similar bathtub, my back resting on Seth in relaxed bliss after he'd washed off a great deal of accumulated sand from honeymoon-type behaviors. We were so in love then, and now things are so cold between us that I'm having a nervous breakdown in my neighbor's bathroom. I think I'm someone else, and I'm taking a bath in that someone's bathtub.

And just when things can't get any more insane, my own body, in a ratty old fleece jacket and stretch pants I had forgotten I even owned, comes bursting into the bathroom shouting in my pretty southern drawl, "What in the name of high heaven are you doing taking a *bath*?"

—

CELESTE

I mean.

Can someone try to explain to me what kind of person, after experiencing an otherworldly body swap, takes a bubble bath?

A crazy person, that's who.

Only if she's crazy, so am I. Because I see her there, and she's me. She's my face, my body, my voice, and she's naked, so I am one hundred thousand percent sure who I'm looking at here. I look at her in my too-soft body and too-fat knees and feel, on top of fear and confusion, that hot flush of shame that I always feel when forced to reveal my body to a stranger.

"Celeste?" Wendy asks me, the water sloshing as she moves to sit up. "Are you . . . in there?"

I nod sadly.

"How can this possibly be? How can I be you and you be me?"

"We swapped bodies," I say needlessly.

"Like *Freaky Friday*?"

"I guess? I mean, I went to sleep me. I woke up you."

"No. That can't have happened. *Freaky Friday* is not a documentary," she tells me. "It's a Disney movie, like *Frozen* or *Up*! You can't fly houses with balloons, and you can't swap bodies from drinking sangria! This can't really be happening."

"Yet here we are."

She stares at me, looking just as dumbfounded as I feel. For a long moment we just gape, openmouthed, my archnemesis and I, trapped in one another's bodies for no apparent reason.

"May I inquire as to why you're taking a bath in my bathtub?" I ask at last.

"Oh, is there a correct post-body-swap etiquette?" she asks me sharply. Her voice is my Yank accent, but the words are pure Wendy. Except now I'm too upset to play the role of So-Sweet Celeste. Now Wendy gets to see how I really feel.

"I mean, forgive me if I didn't start a Google Doc," I snipe back. "But taking off all my clothes and having a spa day might not be the most natural first step after stealing someone's actual *body*." I notice for the first time that I seem to have Wendy's soft drawl. I try to stifle it. "Would you just get out of the bath?"

Wendy puts an arm up. "Pardon me, did I violate your privacy, madam?" she asks. "My apologies. Next time I lose possession of my corpus, I'll be sure to bundle up. Though you might want to give a similar chiding to your husband."

I gasp. A terrifying thought hits me.

"You didn't . . . Hugh wasn't . . ." He often wakes up, if not exactly in the mood, well, then two blinks away from it. If this woman had sex with my husband . . . I try to think how to ask this delicate question, knowing that the answer could lead to some light homicide. "You were dressed in bed, right?" I demand. "I went to sleep in my pajamas. I'm sure I did."

"Oh my gross—I know what you are asking, and no. No, no, no. Y'all know he has back hair, right?"

With my accent and my voice, Wendy's *y'all* sounds so affected. There's a hiccup between the *ya* and the *all*, like the *a* is repeated twice. Is that how I sound when I try to fit in? I hereby vow never to try to say *y'all* again so long as I'm in the South. And wait, what did she just say about my husband?

"He doesn't have back hair!" I say, a moment too late. Although I suppose maybe he does. I never paid it any attention. After fifteen mostly great years, he's really just my Hugh, hairy back and all.

Wendy shrugs. In my body the gesture looks childlike, and I wonder, *When was the last time I changed my hairstyle? It can't have been college, can it?*

"Look," I say. "It's very awkward to be standing here staring at my own naked body while trying to talk to you. Can you get out of the bathtub and put on a robe or something?"

Wendy looks upset. "You have no idea how good this bath feels. I'm having a nervous breakdown, and this is literally the only thing that makes any kind of sense. Just give me five more minutes," she says. "Then, if you want, you can take one next. This tub is amazing."

"I am well aware of the qualities of the tub, since it is mine, as you might recall."

She ignores me. "You know what? I think we are having a mutual hallucination. I had to read something about those back in Psych 101, but I've retained nothing, and I have no idea what we should be doing about it."

"Going to the hospital?" I suggest. "Or the psychiatric ward?"

Wendy sloshes. "Ok, so imagine we go into the ER and tell them we've swapped bodies. We're modern mothers, both under a lot of pressure. They're going to sedate us and say we're having concurrent nervous breakdowns. Frankly, I don't disagree. I think I've been staving one off for about four years."

"I'm not having a nervous breakdown!" I insist. "I'm not under a lot of pressure!"

Wendy's head rolls back. "Well, I suppose that's true, with nothing to do all day. But I am. I've got a company, three employees, a huge mortgage, a tortured-artist husband, and two very different kids. I'm never more than one bad night's sleep from a minor meltdown. This is probably it, right here."

I want to scream at her. "I can't understand how you can be so blasé! You do understand what's happening right now, right? You're me. I'm you. This is not desirable."

"Look," says Wendy. "What do they do in *Freaky Friday*? They try to run directly into each other until they practically concuss themselves. They scream and shout and cry. Then, eventually, after a lot of carrying on, they get dressed as the other person and try to go about life as normal until their bodies switch back. Shouldn't we just skip to that part?"

I blink at her in absolute shock. I feel like I have a lot more screaming and shouting and crying in my future. "Is that what's happening? Are you trying to go on as normal? Do you always take a bath on Sunday mornings?"

"Are you kidding? I never do. You've seen my house. The tub from our bathroom became a sculpture, and the one in the kids' bathroom leaks down to the subfloor. Oh—good reminder. Whatever you do, don't take any baths while you're me."

I frown. Wendy's house is in a bit of a state. "How long do you think that will be, exactly?"

Wendy shakes her head. "A day?" she says, but we both know it's a wild guess.

I sigh and sit down on the closed toilet lid. "What happened to your bedroom wall, by the way?"

"What do you mean?"

"The hole in the wall, by the TV? Surely you've noticed it."

"Oh yeah. I've just completely forgotten about it. It's been there for years. Seth had a copper installation there, and he got angry and ripped it down one day after a bad review during the triennial. It's no big deal."

That does, actually, seem like rather a big deal. "Does he have a bad temper? He's not hitting you, is he?"

Wendy laughs. "Oh sheesh, no. Don't worry; you're safe. The kids, on the other hand . . ."

"He hits the kids?" I ask.

"No! Lord, what do you think of us?" she asks. "No, he's never once laid an angry hand on any of us. All I mean is, the kids are home alone with him, and he had a big bachelor weekend that went for two straight days. Savion Glover is probably giving a live concert in his skull right now while the kids run amok. You've got to go back there, or I do." She pauses to have a think. "Which would make more sense? Can it be you? I am really into Hugh giving me—or you—the day off. And if the neighbor lady came over to care for them, they'd just be confused."

I shake my head. "Your kids are fine. I wouldn't leave kids alone and untended in the house. I got Seth up, pretended everything was normal, and sent him downstairs to make the kids breakfast."

Wendy sits up from the bath and cranes her head to look at me. She looks nothing short of astonished. "And did he?"

I frown. "No. I mean, he went downstairs and then came back up and said he couldn't find the toast and tried to get back into bed."

Wendy just laughs sadly. "Sounds about right. The kids won't eat his toast anyway. They say his toasting makes the bread too crunchy."

I just have to laugh too. "What does that even mean? Where do they come up with this stuff?"

"Well, either way, thanks for feeding my kids," says Wendy.

"Oh, I didn't," I tell her. "I put a cold, wet towel on Seth's face and told him I had no idea where the bread was and he should probably ask the kids for help, because I was coming over here to have a cup of coffee with you."

Wendy's eyes get large. "Was he surprised at that, at least?"

"He said he had no idea anyone had moved into this house."

Wendy sighs. "Oh my god, Celeste. I just went insane, my neighbor stole my body, my kids cannot get themselves a piece of bread without help, and my husband is completely freaking oblivious to his surroundings."

"I have to agree with you there. We've been here for ten months now. And how does he not know where you keep the bread?"

"It's not great. But at least he doesn't have back hair," she says.

"Hugh doesn't have back hair!" I exclaim.

"When was the last time you saw him with his shirt off?" she asks me.

I cross my arms. "Two nights ago, not that it's any of your business."

"Ok, when was the last time you saw him from behind with his shirt off?"

She has me there. I shake my head.

"Boring sex life, eh?" she asks, as she steps my body out of the bath and wraps up in my Egyptian cotton bath sheet.

"Don't pretend this"—I waggle my hands between us—"this psychological glitch or whatever it is opens me up to discussing intimate matters. It does not. We are not"—I stop myself before I say the word *friends*. It would seem mean, somehow, to proclaim that we're not, though she has to realize. Sangria contests and carpool standoffs aren't exactly the stuff of soul connection—"that close. Besides," I add, recovering, "I can think of absolutely no conjugal position in which I would be facing my husband's back."

"Course you can't," she says. "You know what they say about Yanks in bed."

I sniff. "You realize you're the Yankee now, right? How does that feel?"

She pads toward me in her bare wet feet. "It feels smug and superior, actually." She puts on an exaggerated accent straight from *Forrest Gump*. "Y'all know whut? Maykes me sound rell smarht." She drops the accent. "When I go to work tomorrow, I'm going to call up Boston College and see if I can't get them interested in our new productivity study. Maybe they'll say yes to this voice."

"You're not going to work, though, are you? Not if things don't get better."

"What do you mean?" she asks. I just look at her until she says, "Oh. Right. Shit! You can't be going to work for me!"

I exhale. Finally the gravity of this situation is setting in. "We could just talk to our families. Try to explain things. Swap for a bit, until this"—I look heavenward—"mutual hallucination is over."

She looks at me for a long time and then just shakes her head.

"They'd lock us away in the loony bin," I agree. "I'm about to lock myself in the loony bin."

Wendy inhales deeply. "Let's just give it one day. One day, and then we can go to the doctor," she tells me.

"Wendy, tell me the truth. Are you just saying this because you want a whole day off from your husband and kids?"

"Course not!" she exclaims. "Not at all. I love my family. Now, it's true I've never been told to stay in bed on a Sunday morning before. It's not the worst thing that's ever happened to me."

I put my head in my hands. This *is* the worst thing that's ever happened to me. I don't want to be Wendy Charles. I don't want to walk around like I invented being busy and everyone else should be grateful for whatever it is I do. And I really don't want to sleep in her husband's bed!

Another penny drops. I really, really don't want thin, lithe, sexual-position-expert Wendy Charles sleeping in the same bed as my husband.

Except.

I mean, for this one little second, I *am* thin, lithe, sexual-position-expert Wendy Charles. I sneak a peek of my current body. I'm ridiculously fit. I have abdominal muscles. My small breasts are pointing upward, and I didn't even put on a bra. Now, I love Hugh, and I don't mean to forget it, but right now I look freaking great, and my back doesn't hurt. Tomorrow, if this keeps up, I'll put on pretty work clothes and go into the city and talk to adults all day. For lunch I'll get a nice fresh green salad and a chunk of grilled salmon on top from the public market and eat it in total peace. And both of Wendy's kids—she only has two, blessed be—are past the age of pull-ups and independent and spend the entire day in someone else's care. Just this once, I could see how the other half—ok, the other 75 percent—lives.

"Ok," I say. "You're right. No need to panic. Let's give it a couple days."

Wendy arches her eyebrow. "One day's enough."

"One day, then," I say, but now I'm thinking I'm getting the better end of this deal. I wonder what Wendy will say when Joy makes her lunchtime appearance today or crawls into her bed at two in the morning and takes up an impossible amount of mattress. What about when Zoey asks if she's got her schedule sorted out for the week? Or Samuel falls asleep on the floor of his bedroom and she has to figure out how to get his sixty-five-pound body into bed using only my weary, sleep-deprived body?

What about when Hugh tries to smother her to death when, after sixteen seconds of spooning, he rolls over and falls asleep on her?

"A day or two," I try to sneak in. "Now, to be clear, there should be no touching the husbands." Wendy's husband may be a hot artist, but there is no way I want Wendy's hands, in any form, on my sweet, unsuspecting Hugh.

Wendy looks at me like I'm crazy. "Oh, that will *not* be an issue for me. You're the one who needs to keep your—well, my, I guess—panties on. I mean, no offense, but look at Hugh. And now look at Seth."

I grimace. How on earth could one not take offense at that? But I decide to willfully misunderstand. "Exactly. Your husband is safe in my hands; I can promise you that."

"And the kids?"

"What on earth do you think I'm going to do to your kids?" I ask, offended even further now.

She rolls her eyes. "Tell them anything. I just don't want you to tell them. They do not need to know what's going on."

"Oh," I say, embarrassed. "Right, ok. No telling the kids."

"And if you do go to work as me," she says, "you have to be cool. You have to not be . . ." She wiggles her hands in place of finishing the sentence. "Just try to act like me."

"Uptight and unreasonable?" I ask.

"Like an adult, professional woman. Don't bring in any healthy recipes or Pinterest projects, ok?"

"Is that what you think of me?" I ask her.

She gestures to the homemade gallery wall on the east side of my bedroom, where all the frames are made with shells from different beaches we've visited as a family.

"Fine," I say. "No crafting at work. I will try to act exactly like you. And you can try to act exactly like me. It will be good for you."

"Yeah. Restful."

I growl.

"Shall we shake on it?" she says.

Of course I shake. "Text me later with your schedule so I know where I'm supposed to be tomorrow, ok? If we don't . . . I mean . . . if we're still hallucinating?"

"Fine," she says. "We won't be, but fine. Good luck with everything today." She looks, even in my body, a little maniacal. "If you need me, I'll be sitting on the front lawn with a glass of red wine in my hands."

"That's mighty thoughtful of you," I say, laying Wendy's natural drawl on thick. "But I'm sure I can handle your life just fine."

CHAPTER 6

WENDY

When Celeste leaves her bathroom, I crumple. The booze has worn off, but the awful hasn't. I'm so tired, and my body hurts, and it's not even *my* body. I know I've been doing too much; I've been told by my sister, my colleagues, even my often-nasty mother-in-law, who feels my time is better spent driving to her house, where she is better able to criticize me. In fact, I've been told I do too much by everyone except the people for whom I'm doing too much—my needy clients, my distracted husband, my demanding kids. They all believe I'm not doing enough. And now, instead of pulling up my big-girl panties and putting all my productivity expertise into action, I've gone and lost it. I think I'm someone I'm not, and someone else thinks she's me, and I'm living in a 1970s children's book that's been remade by Disney at least forty-seven times.

And the worst part? I can't even do this right. Almost every single day, I lecture one of my clients about the futility of multitasking. That said, because doctors never take their own medicine, I am an inveterate multitasker. Even when I am having this mental breakdown, I think, *Well, I'd better make it count!* I can use this time to catch up on admin work, polish my speech for next Saturday, and fix Celeste's hair situation while I'm at it.

Immediately I grab for my phone, planning to call my salon and do my emails at the same time. While the phone rings, I start to scroll and wonder what the hell happened to my email inbox for a moment. Then it hits me. This isn't my phone. It's Celeste's—we own the exact same model. It opened to Celeste's facial recognition. And this is Celeste's email.

It is the most blissful inbox I've ever seen.

I hang up on the salon and take in the wonder. There are zero work emails. Nothing, not a single thing, flagged "priority." In fact, the inbox is completely empty—not read, not tagged, but *empty*—except for seven emails that came in this morning. All of them are on pleasant subjects—sales on steak at the organic butcher, new styles at the kids' fair-trade clothing shop, a 10-percent-off coupon for sports equipment online. There's a newsletter about an online parenting club—socializing! for leisure!—and a forward from a Dottie Mason to a large distribution list that's just a funny meme from social media. There are only two emails that are even really meant for Celeste specifically: a request for a driver to a school field trip on Thursday—I immediately volunteer Celeste without a second's consideration—and an email forwarded from Hugh about a charity gala his company is sponsoring this Wednesday evening with the forward note, *No one I'd rather eat rubber chicken with. Let's get a babysitter!*

Damn, Celeste! The event is black tie. Sure, Hugh's got a dad bod and some deferred manscaping, but his heart is certainly in the right place. Seth doesn't even invite me to gallery night anymore, much less take me to swanky fundraising galas.

Which, if I spend too much time considering it, is kind of sad. Of all the reasons I fell in love with Seth, sharing in his talent had to be one of the best bits. His works have always filled me with pride and inspiration—exactly the qualities his best reviews say they inspire in everyone—and talking about what it means to make something from nothing always united us. But that was when the work was going well.

Now, whenever I want to talk about art, he thinks I'm pressuring him. When I ask about seeing our old friends' shows, I'm rubbing in the lack of his own. If I splashed out and bought us two tickets to a charity event, he'd ask me what I thought we had to prove. When the only thing to prove is that we still love each other enough to try a little.

I look back at Hugh's email, and my heart tugs for that kind of affection. Would it really be that bad if I had to be in Celeste's body for a few extra days and put on a beautiful gown and be wined and dined for a change?

I shake my head. Of course it would. *Besides,* I think, as I put down Celeste's phone, *I'd miss my family too much.*

Not that I won't see them constantly, between the backyard and softball and school stuff. With a sharp stab of mom guilt, I realize that I'll actually see my kids more than I normally do, going to softball practice every day after school and hanging out in the backyard with both sets of kids while I'd typically be inside on my laptop.

Still.

Usually, when Linus wakes up on a school day, he is so slow to come awake fully that he is, ever so briefly, my little baby again. I sit on the edge of his bed and gently tousle him awake. He lifts his arms to me, and I have to peel him up to sitting, and he flops over into my arms and tells me about his dreams, and if he didn't have dreams, he tells me what he wishes he'd dreamed about. Tomorrow, if things aren't better, he'll be telling Celeste about his dreams.

When Bridge goes up to the plate during games, she touches her batting glove to the knob of the bat three times, tap tap tap, if she feels nervous about something. It's just a little tic, but I know to ask about it if I catch her doing it, and she will tell me everything on her mind.

Will Celeste notice it too?

I pick the phone back up, google *Body Swap,* and get a huge list of reported events. The first several sound like cranks, pranks, and/or delusions. Then there's a massive list of body swaps in fiction. *Freaky*

Friday's on the list—all the different versions and the book. *Prelude to a Kiss*—that was a weird movie I saw in a Meg Ryan support binge when my sister was going through a breakup. A bro romp with the guy from *Arrested Development* and one of the Hot Ryans. And a lot of others.

Hundreds.

Wow. Fiction loves body swaps.

I start scrolling through synopses.

It seems like the conventions of the genre indicate that the swap will last until another major head injury or magic spell is cast. But I do not remember either a head injury or a magic spell. I just remember the dry, sugary drink of last night and the terrible headache of this morning.

Hmmmm.

The drinking. Not just my own sangria but the glass I sneaked of Celeste's when she wasn't looking.

What was that stuff she was bragging about adding? Artisanal sap infusion from some tree or other? Didn't she say she had to special order it?

Did she order . . . magic vodka?

That's ridiculous. Right?

Still, this feels like a lead. Maybe we should make another batch of pink sangria tonight and have one or three glasses of the stuff, just to rule it out.

That doesn't seem like such a bad way to spend a Sunday.

I scroll through Celeste's contacts and find my own name. Of course she has me all programmed into her phone—first name, last name, proper spelling of both Bridget and Linus under *Notes*. She'll see my phone at some point today and wonder what crazy person never puts a single contact in by their real name. She will probably come up in my phone as *Zoey's mom*. But come on. Must we know the full names of every mother of every child our children have ever talked to? I scroll Celeste's contacts some more. Apparently, we must.

I send her a voice memo: "Listen, I think we need to get drunk on your sangria. We were basically the only ones drinking it." I pause and try to make an apology come. "I could have been a bit nicer about your fancy ingredients. You were obviously trying really hard." I hit stop on the memo, thinking I should rerecord it, but push the wrong thing. It sends automatically. Oh well, in for a penny. I try another. "I have no good explanation for this switch, except that we drank that weird stuff before this started, so that's what we should try to make it stop. Right?"

I hit send. Recognize neither message was any kind of apology, find the prayer-hands emoji, and send that too.

Then I climb back into Celeste's bed. It's so much more comfortable than mine. Why is that? The clean sheets I didn't have to wash? The deluxe mattress I didn't have to pay for? That warm, milky smell that comes off Celeste's very skin?

I add it to the list of unknowable mysteries of the day. When I get back to my home, I'm going to get a new mattress. I'm going to get this exact same mattress Celeste has and find out where she buys her sheets. And get some of the bath milk I saw by the tub too. And a bathtub to put it in.

Till then, I'm going to make the best of this. I'm a full-time working mom with a very full slate of parenting responsibilities and a never-ending list of to-dos, and I'm suddenly allowed to impersonate a housewife, just for a day or two. Or maybe three.

As my eyes grow heavy, my phone buzzes. It's Celeste texting back from my phone. The "weird stuff" was birch sap infused vodka from the Alaskan interior. But presumably if that was the cause, we would both have had to drink it.

Just before I drop off into slumber, I write back. If you must know, I may have had a sip when you weren't looking. I just wanted to know what the big deal was.

What I don't add: that the weird stuff was goddamned delicious.

What she writes back: Ordering more weird stuff asap.

—

CELESTE

Wendy's house is my worst nightmare.

If, during this strange shared hallucination or whatever it is, I kill Wendy and end up in the eternal fires of damnation, this house will be a close approximation of what I can expect. It is two messy stories of projects, dirt, and palpable guilt. Every closet I open is full of clutter. Every crevice has ten years of dirt pushed into it. And it contains three of the laziest human beings I have ever laid eyes on. Every time I see one of them, they are draped somewhere as though there are no muscles in the middle of their bodies. They are human throw blankets.

For the first time in my life, I feel sorry for Wendy Charles. Have I been, since moving to Birchboro Hills, very compassionate to the Wendy Charleses of the world?

Have I, once or twice, resented her for being too busy for the rest of us?

Have I put myself in a different category than her—have I thought of myself as an ever-so-slightly better mother?

I look down at the mess I'm standing in. It is hard to be compassionate to a woman who seems to put herself ahead of me. Who believes her paying job is more important than my full-time dedication to my family's well-being.

But honestly, Celeste. Taking sides in the Mommy Wars? Isn't that so 2010? I can do better than that. I can see past insecurities and guilt to the truth. Are working moms and stay-at-home moms really so different?

Well, in the case of Wendy Charles, we are very different. She is an uptight jerk, and I am not. But in the case of working outside the home or inside it, we are the same. We are two roads that diverged in the wood. I'm not sure which of us is the road less traveled by—I flatter myself that it's me, sacrificing personal glory for familial bliss—but both of us work hard, live tired, and struggle with the culture of unreasonable expectations for women. Judging by the amount of home repairs needed, Wendy is living close to her means, forgoing financial cushions so her partner can pursue his goals unencumbered. Just as I do everything I can to make one income possible on our end, from sewing Zoey's clothes to avoiding restaurant food for all but the most special occasions.

I shake my head. My mom would have seen it right away: I need to open up my darned heart immediately to this neighbor, try to be of service, and see if it doesn't come right back to me.

Having been forced, by me, to survive on bread (with almond butter and bananas) and water for breakfast, the children have turned down a trip to the park on this absolutely gorgeous Sunday morning. Instead, they are melted like candle wax all over the family room. Their heads are slightly swiveled toward an enormous television playing reruns on Disney Plus, and their fingers are twitching—in Bridget's case, over a phone screen, and in Linus's, up his nose.

Wendy's husband was last spotted back, for the third time, in bed. He slunk off, hair of the dog in hand, in the hope that no one would notice.

I noticed.

So that leaves me, in this supercharged, energetic body, to do as I please while I wait for my body back.

I please to fix this dump up.

The closet I'm standing in front of is ostensibly the cleaning cupboard. There is a broom and dustpan, a bucket, and sprays and such. There are also enough plastic bags of all shapes and sizes to smother a whole elementary school full of children, as well as an opened family-size package of Milky Ways stuffed way, way back behind a book on home repairs covered in dust.

So this closet does get *some* use.

Except, Celeste, you aren't judging Wendy anymore. You're better than that.

Remember?

Amid the chaos is a bag of cleaning cloths—the kind you have because you tried multilevel marketing in an attempt to make friends and extra cash and have nothing but a box of a hundred cleaning cloths to show for it. (Or, in my case, single-purpose kitchen gadgets.) I grab the unopened package and wrest the cloths free. Then I locate a multisurface cleaner. I apply latter to former and clean the closet's light switch, its doorknob, and the handle of a bucket I fill with useful supplies. I am away.

There is nothing, truly, more stress relieving than deep cleaning. As I learned from my own mother, the act can be a meditation, a devotional, when done in one's own time. When there is no shame attached (*I should have taken care of this weeks ago*), no regret (*I wish I'd never bought this many gewgaws to dust*), and no anger (*How does one even get raspberry jam on the top of a picture frame?*), and there is nothing to do but just clean the room you're in from the ceiling down, one thing at a time, it's actually quite restful. If a child isn't "helping" you, if you have all day, if you've been well rested and fed, cleaning is no different from a peaceful walk or a nice yoga class. You know what to do, you do it well, you breathe deeply and move gently, and when you are done, you can see everything you've accomplished.

The dining room, the nookiest and cranniest room in this house, will soon be gleaming. I will, before the children so much as solidify into human form again, have this one shining example of a clean, hygienic house. It is here I will meet with the youth of tomorrow and explain how they, too, can enjoy rooms as clean as this. They will breathe in the fresh air and take in the newly conditioned dining table and vow to the woman they think is their mother to help her keep the house in this lovely, restful state to the end of their days. I Windex the glass of the picture frames. I use a toothbrush—one of the kids' that looks like it should have been tossed months ago—to clean the grooves in the sideboard's legs. I lightly moisten the dustcloths with water and get to the baseboards, seeing, as I do, that a touch-up on their white paint would not go amiss. I wonder where the honey-do list is in this house. A chalkboard? A notepad? No matter. I will start a new one and give it to Seth when he gets up. I spend the next hour and a half in this deep state of happy achievement, and when I am finished, I alert the children that they are needed around the table.

But nothing happens.

Are they dead?

I crouch over the boy, Linus, and feel for a pulse.

"What are you doing?" he asks. He doesn't sound upset or mean, just curious.

"Oh, good," I respond. "I thought maybe you'd died."

His eyes drift from the TV to my face. He's seeing Wendy, I remind myself. Wendy's get-up-or-else face might be less effective than mine. His eyes glide back to the screen.

I do what I would do with Samuel the odd times he's not bouncing on the couch cushions or climbing around on the top of the sofa, unable to pay attention to the screen. I grab his shins and flip him over on his stomach. "C'mon," I say. "I'll wheelbarrow you to the family meeting."

"What's a family meeting?" he asks absently, scooching around on his stomach to watch TV in this new position, his shins still in my hands.

"It's how we sort out who is doing what around the house," I say, wondering what process Wendy normally uses to delegate, or if this meeting is, in fact, going to come as a terrible shock to these kids.

"I pass," says Bridget, who has, in that unnerving tween way, been following events on her phone, on the TV screen, and in the room without moving an eye muscle.

I am taken aback. Momentarily. I move, as casually as I can, toward Bridget's side. The remote is on her armrest, the phone cupped in both hands. My hand darts out like a cobra striking. Hit one, the phone.

Hit two, the remote. Phone in pocket, TV off, remote in other pocket. *Take that!*

"MOM!" the children shout in unison. They look really surprised. And angry. Wendy must be a far nicer mom than I am. No wonder the house is a pit and the kids seem to think they don't have to take care of their things.

"Screens are for helpful children," I say. I skip off to the dining room. It's so rare I get to torture my own children this way anymore. I feel a lovely blast of nostalgia.

Bridget sits tight, but in a matter of seconds Linus is there, surprising me by walking straight between my legs where I'm sitting admiring my handiwork. He puts his head on my shoulder, and his voice whines, "I'm helpful, Mommy. You always say I'm helpful." I feel tears on my neck. Oh dear.

"Of course you're helpful, Linus," I say. Is he? I have no idea. He certainly didn't seem it just now. I think quickly. "And now you're ready to level up to the kind of helpful that helps people even when it's not convenient for you."

He looks up at me. "I don't think I want to level up."

"Oh, but leveling up is the only way to get to the good stuff," I tell him.

"Prizes?" he asks. His tears have vanished. No, they're on my shirt collar, with some snot. But they've stopped coming.

"Maybe," I say, kicking the can down the road. "Or the satisfaction of knowing you are doing the right thing."

He frowns. "I want prizes."

Of course he does. "This meeting is the place to start. But we need your sister. Can you go annoy her into coming in here?"

His face brightens. "Is that helpful?" he asks.

"Extremely."

"Be right back."

In a matter of moments he's back with an angry tween. I study her face. So different from my own baby girl. Sharper. Prettier, maybe? I don't know. I suspect they'll both be gorgeous in a few years. But Bridget is edges and lines and a tight ponytail. She moves with command and conviction. It's intimidating, and it's a perfect facsimile of her mother. A woman (to be) who has it all. And doesn't even see what she has.

"Phone, Mom," she instructs. She says it with such authority that for a moment I lose my way and consider giving it back to her. But then I remind myself I'm not parenting someone else's children—not from their point of view. I can treat them as I would my own. Not that my own would ever talk to me that way.

"Sure," I tell her, calmly. "Once I'm done, it's yours."

She crosses her arms. "Go, then."

"I want you listening," I tell her. "Not just thinking of what you're going to text your friends in two minutes."

Her eyes bug out. "I'm not texting, Mom. I swear!"

Oh, is she not allowed to text? This is interesting. Even Zoey has texting privileges. Perhaps I should rethink that.

I clear my throat. "Do you two notice anything different about this room?"

Their eyes roam the dining room. They shake their heads but say nothing.

"Nothing?" I prod.

"Did you paint?" asks Linus. "It looks shiny."

"I cleaned, Linus," I tell him.

Bridget sums it up when she asks, "Why?"

I squelch the urge to cry, *Because you're living in squalor, that's why!* "The house is dirty. So I cleaned part of it. But I need help to keep it clean. And it's Sunday, you have no school today, and you obviously have nothing to do, so you're the perfect people to help."

Much moaning and complaining ensues.

"Plus," I remind them, "you live here. You get to use all this nice stuff. You have to keep it nice."

"Dad lives here, and he doesn't clean," says Bridget.

Doesn't he? I wonder. That's a bit sad for Wendy. "But he earns money," I say.

"He does?" asks Bridget, incredulous. *Oh dear.*

I don't answer, because I have no idea. I know Seth is meant to be a successful urban artist. Don't successful artists in thriving art scenes like the one downtown make loads of money?

I have this powerful urge to text Wendy to ask about these questions. But coming from me, it's not like she'd open up. "Let's focus on what you can do," I say. "You can clean. You'll actually like it, too, once you realize how good it feels to have a clean home. You, Bridget, can do loads of laundry on Sundays. While you, Linus, can run the Roomba."

"We have a Roomba?" he asks, mystified.

I grimace. "Um . . . we're getting one. Today you'll just vacuum and dust."

"We have a vacuum?" he asks again.

"Don't we?" I ask.

"You gave it to Dad when it broke, remember?" Bridget says.

I don't remember, because I wasn't there. Not the point. "Well, he'll have repaired it by now, then," I say.

"Mom?" Bridget says. "I'm, like, ninety-nine percent sure Dad used the vacuum in his artwork. You told him he could. You said the Merry Maids have backpack vacuums, so why did you need one here anyway?"

"I did?" I ask.

Both kids look at me funny.

"Well, right, I did." I'm chewing on all this. They have a housekeeping service, yet the house is filthy. The husband, Seth, took a vacuum to his studio and never brought it back. This is the same husband the kids just told me doesn't clean or make money. This is all a very curious situation. "Let's get you guys started. We need laundry baskets and, um . . . dusting wipes . . . and music."

Before long I've got the two kids working. They're not bad kids and seem totally game to help out their mom once the path is made clear.

They are listening to Top Forty played very loudly on the TV speakers and picking up all kinds of things, things I wouldn't have necessarily had down as toys rather than trash, like Linus's collection of acorns and a stack of box score sheets that Bridget assembles and files in an elaborate system in her bedroom desk. In an hour and a half the children are back in front of their screens, only now Bridget is getting up every fifteen minutes to address the laundry, and Linus to dust one more room. Meanwhile I take up residence in the kitchen, taking pantry items that are minutes from expiration and cooking, cooking, cooking up a storm. In four hours everything in this house is honestly livably clean, there are six freezer meals ready to roll, and a mound of clean clothes is being folded at the speed of snails as Disney Plus resumes and the kids feast on turkey sandwiches and apples cut into eighths.

I want to run across the backyard and get Wendy and show her what I've accomplished in her house in half a day of walking in her shoes. I want to walk through the house taking "after" photos. I cannot wait for Seth to return from wherever it is he's gone and see what a nice home he has so I can get him started on some of the long list of overdue repairs it needs to be its absolute best. I'm not exactly clear on how to replace porch screens or fill in drywall, but Seth is a sculpture artist. He'll know his way around a staple gun and plaster repair. And I certainly know how to paint the dining room, which, now that I look at it, could really use a warmer color, one that isn't quite so hunter green. I could try to strip the white paint off the baseboards and return them to the pretty dark walnut they used to be too. Without meaning to, I slip into the slightest little fantasy of me and Seth—who is, let's face it, the hottest husband on the block—in painting clothes, rolling a rich, creamy light brown on the dining room walls side by side, and him embracing his lovely wife in a tender moment, and his wife being me . . .

And then my eyes fly open in horror. I have been in Wendy Charles's body for less than a day, and already I'm fantasizing about stealing her family, her home, and her husband.

CHAPTER 7

WENDY

When I come to again, it's midafternoon on a Sunday, and I've done nothing today but rest. No kids have come in to shout at me about the Wi-Fi being down or to demand a ride, a bagel, or a ride to buy bagels. It is just me, the wonderful bed, and my dreams. The only way in the world I could get this kind of break is by stealing someone else's body, and the truth is, I resent that.

I was there, sure, when Seth and I decided together that he would pursue his passion and I would pursue our health insurance. But I don't remember when we agreed that he wouldn't bring in any money anymore, after years of selling his works. Or when we agreed all the costs of his art would fall to me, and the success of my business any given month would determine whether we could afford special family trips, date nights, or other perks, like, you know, the dentist.

I would like to reconvene that meeting ASAP, and I would like to renegotiate my terms. As soon as I get my body back tomorrow, that's exactly what I'm going to do.

There is a planner next to Celeste's bed, and reading it would be wrong, but tearing a page out to write on seems borderline ok, so I do exactly that. At the top, in my prettiest writing, which is not pretty at all, since I have been writing in all caps since I was seven, I scrawl,

THINGS TO CHANGE SO I STOP HAVING HALLUCINATIONS
Under that I write:
Let me sleep in on Sundays.
Get Seth to sell a piece but not spend the money right away.
I pause and look around Celeste's bedroom.
Install those room-darkening curtains I bought three years ago, I add.

I think about what else would make my life better. Ideas leap to mind, but when I pull those threads, a thousand things our family needs to operate come unwound. If someone else does the laundry, the towels might all come out pink. If someone else picks up the clutter, Linus's beloved trading cards could end up mangled. When it's Seth's night to cook, we get expensive takeout 100 percent of the time, so that's not something I can increase the occurrence of without going broke. And if I run away to Rome, I will definitely miss everyone. Most days.

But what other tasks can I delegate? Financial management, maybe? Managing our household finances is the most stressful part of my life, because the people in my house don't quite get how money works. But for that very reason, sharing the money duty would end in bankruptcy.

I draw lines through *laundry, cleaning, cooking, money* on my list. Not much is left.

Still, I'd really like to sleep in on Sundays.

I underline that item twice and then fold the paper in half and then fourths, knowing it would confuse the hell out of Hugh if he saw it lying around. Just as I'm doing that, there is a tiny low knock at the door. "Mommy?"

The sweet baby-girl voice is unmistakably Anna Joy.

"Mommy, you've been in there all day. Now can I have milk?" she asks.

"Course you can, sweetie," I tell her, not needing to channel Celeste to feel a warm affection for the little one. "You need help?"

"I'm coming in," she says. The door opens, and the small girl tumbles into Celeste's pretty sanctum. I pat the bed beside me, and she comes to the edge and flings her tiny body up onto it. With a deep, contented breath, I take her in. She is pocket size, wispy haired, and dressed in cotton brights that look like that email ad I saw in Celeste's inbox earlier. I can't remember if she's three or four, but she's pretty as a picture and still has those giant baby eyes that are impossible to say no to. My heart tugs. Three children sounds like a recipe for disaster, but this little girl makes my ovaries cry out for more. *Hush, ovaries.*

"Did you get a good nap?" she asks, and before I can answer, she tells me that she and her daddy went outside and planted flowers from the nursery and Zoey can hit a ball into outer space and Samuel is mean.

I put my arm around the small girl. I want to tell her I had a pesky older sibling, too, but the truth is, Samuel probably isn't all that mean, and if Celeste has siblings, I don't know anything about them. "What happened?" I ask instead.

"He says I'm a booger."

I can't help it; I laugh.

Her face crumples up. "I am not a booger! He's the one who tried to pick his nose and wipe it on me!"

I cringe. Kids are repulsive. "Oh, hon. You're nothing like a booger. Unless"—I pause for effect—"did he mean to say you are a unicorn booger? Those are very magical and beautiful. That's probably what he meant."

She tilts her head, giving this some thought. "That's what he meant," she agrees, with a giggle. Then, out of absolutely nowhere, she lifts up my shirt and dives in toward my breast.

"Hey!" I shout, startled. "What are you doing?"

"You said I could have milk," says the muffled voice, and then, bam, in horror I feel the sensation of someone else's toddler latching on to my nipple. My brain shorts out. *WHAT IS HAPPENING?* shouts every neuron in my body. I wrench back, only to feel a sharp yank of pain, a hot sting, and then, dear god, milk letting down.

I haven't had this sensation in seven years, and I remember every tingle, every swell, as if it were yesterday.

And I *hate* it.

Without thinking it through, I put my palm on the child's face over my shirt. "Off!" I cry. "Stop!" I sound like I'm shouting at a strange dog. "Child!"

She comes to and stops. I feel breast milk—Celeste's milk—run out under my breast and down my stomach. Ugh. "What are you doing?" I ask her again.

She wrenches free of my shirt and looks up with big innocent eyes. "I ate all my lunch," she tells me. "I ate the peas." As if I am worried about vegetables right now.

"Honey," I say, softening. I want to ask her, Does she do this every day? How many times a day? How fast can I get her to stop? But instead I flounder, flail around, and decide, Ok, this isn't my place. I'm not the preschool nursing police. If Celeste doesn't want to wean her last child . . . that's her business. Right?

I'm selling no one on this open-minded business. I am judging. Hard.

Still, I'm not going to scar this child for life over a hallucination / magic spell / injury-related delusion. Instead I say, "Oh, sorry, sweetheart. I should have told you Mommy is feeling funny today, and my milk . . . is feeling funny too." I try to relax my previously bugged-out eyes as I say this.

"What kind of funny?" she asks.

"Just a little cold. But . . . the virus hurt my head, and I can't remember how old you are?"

Anna Joy's eyes brim with tears. "Mommy! I'm three! Are you sick with Old Timers' like Great-Grandma? Are you going to die?"

My heart plummets. "No, no, honey. I'm ok. It's just a headache, and I'm still drowsy from my nap. I'm totally fine, and I'll be able to do . . . what we normally do . . . in a day or two. Do not worry." I say again, "I'm fine."

"But I can't have milk," she checks.

"Yes. I'm fine, but no milk today—that's right. If you're thirsty, I'll get you something from the fridge." And get myself a strong belt of whiskey while I'm up. My eyes narrow at the sterling-framed wedding photo of Celeste and Hugh on the dresser. Did she say anything about this when she was here earlier? She did not. A heads-up that a full breastal assault was coming would have been nice.

"Can I have cookies, then?" she asks. "Cow's milk and cookies? Since I ate my peas?"

I look at her sideways, the innocent young girl who just violated my swimsuit area. What other attachment parenting delights are awaiting me in this house? Family bed? Cloth diapers? Guatemalan wraps?!

When this is over, I am going to have a strong word with the woman who stole my body.

But that will wait until after I find out what kind of cookies they keep around this joint.

—

Celeste

After I've fed Seth and the kids a pretty little stir-fry in homemade orange sauce that makes even red peppers fly down the children's hatches, after I've washed up the dishes and started planning a week of packed lunches and cleaned out and rearranged Wendy's cutlery drawer, I go to find my phone to send out carpool schedules for the week ahead.

But, of course, it's Wendy's phone on the charger, and on it are three texts from my phone number—so Wendy—asking me if I seriously expect her to nurse Anna Joy (yes), if I want to try getting drunk again to swap our bodies back (yes and no), and if Bridget did her

World History assignment yet (what does she take me for?). I ignore them for a beat, then tell her what she needs to know, and I add the bad news. I went back to the website where I ordered that birch-sap vodka . . . and found nothing but an ad for web hosting.

She responds instantly: What's that now?

I hover over the phone screen. I'm not sure exactly how to tell her that after an hour of frantic googling, I've found a liquor store in Seattle that, with expedited shipping I gladly paid through the nose for, can get it to us no sooner than Friday. At the earliest.

As in, almost an entire week from now.

Do I say, *Hey, girl! Just so you know, I have to live in your hot mess of a life for a week, so I'm gonna try to Mary Poppins this dumpster fire you call your existence into something safe for humans before I give it back to you?* No. Even a nice, reasonable person would take affront to that. A reasonable person is not who I am dealing with. Considering I gave Wendy an out-of-body experience by bringing a better sangria to a party than she did, it's best if I soft sell this turn of events in person.

But before I can even sidestep, she texts back. Never mind. I'll find it myself. God, how do you make everything so COMPLICATED?

Be my guest, Wendy, I think. Nothing could make me happier than to be rid of her and her life ASAP. I tell her good luck with that and ask her when her kids go to bed. I assume it's much later than it should be.

She writes back immediately. Linus: 8:30. Bridge, 9. She doesn't ask about my kids. I guess they'll go to bed when Hugh puts them to bed. He usually excels at bedtime, an area where he is especially motivated.

How are my kids? I text back. Three dots, then nothing.

Five minutes pass, me fretting the whole time, before she finally writes back: Sam has been outside playing with some neighbor kids since after lunch. He only has been back for food. He eats a lot. Zoey is still doing her homework. She needs batting practice—do you guys have a punch card to the cages? Oh, and Anna Joy is fine.

Just fine? I wonder. I wait for her to say more or ask about her own kids, but she does neither.

This mode of communication, or lack thereof, is killing me. I text: **Meet me in the backyard at 9:30.** It's late for me, but then, with Seth in bed most of the day, maybe he'll do the morning routine with the kids tomorrow to even things out.

Maybe? Why do I sort of doubt it? So far today he's done nothing helpful except for an hour of softball training with Bridget. If he's acknowledged Linus's existence today, I certainly haven't seen it.

It's a good thing he's hot.

Poor Hugh, I think. He's a gem of a man, so why am I having all these roving thoughts about someone else? Sure, Hugh's not Adonis, per se. Or any other god, for that matter, not since he stopped replacing his worn-out boxer shorts about five years ago. But he doesn't deserve me ogling the neighbor man.

Wendy finally writes back: **You don't, by any chance, have any left-over fancy vodka from the potluck that you're holding out on me?**

No, I write back. There's a long pause. I imagine Hugh climbing into bed with her and running his hands around her back, spooning up close, and my stomach lurches. If God wants me in Wendy's body for me to be of service, fine. So be it. But I am willing to lay down good money that he does not think Wendy should sleep with my husband as part of the bargain.

Then I'm not coming. Hugh defrosted a lasagna and opened a bottle of merlot. If I have to be you, I might as well enjoy it.

I groan. I would really like to be in *my* adirondack chair with *my* merlot right now, not organizing chore wheels for someone else's lazy kids. **It's important,** I text her. Important that we make some plans for the week ahead, before she screws up my kids and damages my marriage.

Finally she writes back. 8:35. Bridge reads in bed when Linus goes down, and I'll have you back in time to tuck her in and turn out the lights at nine. Meet at that thorny shrub you can't see from the house.

I sigh. What will Bridget think if she gets up for a glass of water and finds her mother missing? What will Hugh think when "I" just walk out the door right before we usually sit down to watch an episode of *The Great British Baking Show*? Why can't Wendy just at least put in the tiniest bit of effort to hold up her end of my life while I'm over here Cinderella-ing the heck out of her house, life, and family?

Why couldn't I have body swapped with someone who has just a tiny bit more of a clue? What did I do to deserve Wendy Charles?

But then, I think I know exactly what I did. I got very, very lucky, and now it's time to even the score.

When I was ten weeks into my maternity leave with Zoey, I got a formal letter from my college's HR department. I worked, back then, full time as a math teacher at a local community college—not at all like the flagship university system that is the backbone of Minnesota but a little satellite two-year program for people from all walks of life. My 200-level classes were mandatory for secondary-ed majors, future actuaries, and nighttime MBAs, while my surveys were requisite for most everyone else. I remember my pregnancy with Zoey as nothing but grading, grading, grading, and the endless string of petitions for unearned good grades that I euphemistically called my office hours.

Zoey, when she arrived, needed no grading. She was one of those babies, the angel kind, who eat, sleep, and poop in an endless, predictable cycle. And Hugh made things even better. Each morning before work as he kissed us both goodbye, he told me in no uncertain terms: "If I hear about you cleaning or cooking while that baby sleeps, you're in big trouble." He made me feel like the very act of growing, birthing, and nursing Zoey made me a goddess suitable for worship, or at the very least unrequested foot rubs.

Even on the weekends the rules were the rules: if Zoey was asleep, I was to be resting too. Mostly I slept, but sometimes I wasn't exhausted, and Hugh propped me up in my bed with a happy baby in my arms and set up an unending stream of *The Office, Parks and Rec,* and *House Hunters* for my entertainment. Or he took the baby from me, wrapped her up in a woven sling he'd insisted on mastering, and handed me a romantic novel and a strawberry smoothie on his way out the door.

Her waking hours were almost as blissful. Mostly she and I walked around the neighborhood in slow motion, but sometimes we'd do chores, wash and fold her tiny clothes, and take photos for her baby book. Though my daily planner was always close at hand, I refused to turn to the next month's pages and fill them out in advance as I usually did, because I knew the day I had to go back to work was approaching fast. The closer it came, the sourer my mood, and Hugh noticed. He revved up the preparations, knowing I was going to be worried about every little thing once Zoey wasn't in my sight all day. We called in my mom to come be with Zoey for at least the first couple of weeks. Found a dreamy day care with a one-to-two care ratio and the kind of attention to safety and snuggles only another mother could replicate. Ordered some milk-bottling supplies to keep at work, got one of those Velcro pump bras that make you feel like a dairy cow in an industrial feedlot, met with a lactation specialist to prepare for the change in nursing schedules. And every night I cried myself to sleep.

The letter that came the week before I was to return, however, changed everything. Everyone knew the school budget was being hacked to pieces, salaries were frozen, and class sizes were going up. Even in my baby bubble I'd been keeping up with all the news. What I hadn't heard was that they were buying people out of their contracts. If I wanted to be one of those people, I could get paid through the rest of my two-year contract at a 20 percent rate and never set foot on that campus again.

I didn't tell Hugh about the letter right away. First I ran numbers. What would we have without my salary? What would we have to give up? How would it affect our retirement, our dreams, our plans? I made charts, ran scenarios, even did a cost-benefit analysis. I tried to make it make sense—show that we'd save money on my lunches and work clothes and day care—but the numbers just didn't add up. There was no doubt: he'd be working longer, we'd be living smaller, vacations would be campouts instead of beaches, and the next house wouldn't have any more bathrooms than the one we were already in.

I decided there was no point in even bringing it up.

I threw the letter away and ordered some more stretchy work pants and nursing shirts. My mom arrived. I told her how I was feeling about going back to work, and she, having been through it all herself, only with two jobs, four kids, and no supportive partner, let me cry as much as I wanted.

Then, the Friday before I was to go back, Hugh came home from work waving a piece of paper like he'd won the golden ticket.

He forked it over, and I recognized it very well. It was a cost-benefit spreadsheet, just like the one I'd made, showing what my going to work would cost us and what it would earn us. Mine had come out miserably. He, however, was grinning like an idiot and pointing at it erratically. "Look here! We just need three kids!" he said excitedly.

"What?"

"We want three kids, right? I mean, if that's what we're given, that's what we're going for. We always agreed on that. You still feeling the same?"

I smiled sadly. "I think so. I mean, it all depends on how things go when I'm back to work. But yes, I hope for three. Why?"

"Well, that's the crossover point, baby. Look at this graph! Three kids—well, two and an eighth, but it's hard to have that many, from what I hear—that's when we save more from you being at home than we make from you working. That's the tipping point that lets you be home with the kids!"

My jaw dropped. I had not even considered taking the math out through two kids, much less three.

"But that won't be for years," I said. "It's a moot point as far as Zoey is concerned."

"But remember you won't be driving to work," he went on. "We just need to be creative. One job only needs one car. Like your Corolla, which is cheap to own and as reliable as the tides. If we sell my truck now and don't buy another car until the third baby comes, we can really make this work!"

I remember how I felt, even now, when I got that news. Ever since I had taken care of my little siblings as a teenager, I had known I wanted to be a mother more than anything else in the world. Now, thanks to Hugh and a quirk of educational funding, all my dreams were about to come true. That wonderful day I didn't worry about getting back into the workforce someday or being a good feminist or defining myself as someone other than who I wanted to be in that very moment. Who I wanted to be, with every bone in my body, was solely and exclusively my daughter's mother.

CHAPTER 8

CELESTE

Wendy is late. I have found the "thorny bush," also known as an English tea rose. It should have been cut back last October, but it's on her side of the property line, and how she's supposed to garden when she's so busy with Sangria Policing I'm not sure. Fresh wood with cream-colored buds winds its way through old growth of years and years past.

I know where the hedge trimmers are. It's not dark yet, and Wendy'll probably still be struggling to get Joy to sleep with no milk. Or maybe she's nursing my baby—who knows. My stomach feels funny. I mean, it's my milk, my boobs. Wet nurses have been a thing for millennia. But still. Wendy might be nursing my kid right now. This, this whatever it is, just gets weirder every single time I consider it.

Stop considering it, I order myself.

Instead, I go into the garage via the side door and find the hedge trimmers.

Only I also find Hugh.

"Wendy?" he asks.

My eyes bulge with the realization: I went to my own garage. Now Hugh thinks he's seeing the neighbor woman stroll into his woodshop like she owns the place.

"Oh my goodness, Hugh!" I say. Only Wendy isn't religious, is she? She'd just say *oh my god*. Or *holy shit*. She's got no qualms with taking his name in vain. Frankly, I have fewer qualms than I probably should, but I don't mind following the rules when it has the handy side effect of keeping curses out of my children's mouths. I try again with my Wendy impersonation, forcing my mouth to form the right words, the right drawl. "God, you scared me, Hugh," I say. I pretend to catch my breath. Or maybe not pretend. This whole mess has me gasping and wheezing.

"I'm sorry," says Hugh, like he has anything to apologize for. He spreads his hands wide, and I see how familiar they are compared to Seth's. "Are you looking for me?" he asks. "Or Celeste?"

Every day, without fail, Hugh finds a moment to throw an arm around me and pull me in tight. To me that's the moment when, after a long day, we both come home. If only I could hug him close now. "Celeste told me to come on over and help myself to her hedge trimmers." That sounds like something I would tell Wendy exactly never, not that she'd ask. "She's so neighborly," I add. I kind of like how soft and slowly words unfold from Wendy's lips. It makes my accent seem choppy and terse. I look into Hugh's eyes to see if he likes the lilt as well. Or maybe whether he can feel that I'm in here? But his face just looks tired—something I've never noticed before. Has he had a bad day? Or is he overworked all the time lately, and I haven't paid attention?

"I've got some roses out back, about fixin' to devour any little children who come too close."

"Ah well," he says. He doesn't even make eye contact. Notices nothing about me whatsoever. "Help yourself. But I know that plant; Celeste has pointed it out to me—"

HUGH! I mentally scold. *Don't go selling me out!*

"And if you don't mind hearing it, I think you'll need chain mail up to your neck to cut that sucker back," he goes on, no idea how he's sinned. "You can just leave it to me, if you like. I can get it with the power trimmer when I do the boxwoods next weekend."

"Oh," I say. Well, that sure sounds a lot better than getting thorn scratches on every inch of my arms. It's certainly what I'd do if I were Celeste. But what would Wendy do now?

She'd say no, of course. She doesn't want our help with anything. And Hugh knows it. Otherwise I bet he would have done this months ago without so much as asking.

"Nah," I say. "That's nice, really, but I've got it. Won't take a minute."

"You sure?" he asks.

"You bet. I'll just grab these"—I move too easily to the shears and take them down off Hugh's orderly wall—"and get out of your hair."

His head tilts. I bet he's thinking Wendy is in here more than he realizes. I bet he's thinking she's using our garden tools all willy-nilly. I wonder if he'll report me to, well, the person he thinks is me.

Or maybe he'll reason that if Wendy were in here all the time, her yard wouldn't look the way it does. I call my thanks behind me and make for the bushes, wondering if I'm about to become a blood donor. I'll just come at them from underneath, I decide. Surely I can spare myself the worst of it. I get down on my knees and start thinning, the work satisfying, if spiky.

"What the damn hell?" I hear suddenly. I start to stand up, get a face full of brambles, and retreat out the bottom, practically belly crawling to get out of the roses alive. When I get to standing, I dust myself off and take in my counterpart, my body dressed in a camisole, a loose cardigan I didn't realize I even owned, and some terribly unflattering joggers. They're comfy, and I normally wear them all the time. But never again.

"Ah, there you are." *Don't look at your watch, Celeste. Don't do it.*

"What are you doing with those?" Wendy asks.

"I'm trimming the dead wood," I tell her. "To pass the time." Shoot, there it is, the verbal equivalent of a deliberate watch check.

"Well, stop it. That's not your dead wood to trim."

The words feel loaded. Are we talking in metaphors right now? I put my hands up. "Suit yourself," I say. I'll just cut it tomorrow while she's, what, in the bath instead of doing the hundred things I have on my plate every Monday?

I set down the trimmers and ask, "So how did today go?" My voice has gotten hushed. I don't want anyone besides us to hear anything from here on out.

"It was fine. I lay low. Spent the day hoping we'd be swapping back tonight."

I frown. It's clear she had even less luck chasing vodka than I did. "Wendy, about the vodka . . ." I break the news of the expedited shipment's specific timing. She screams an obscenity.

"Hush!" I whisper back. "Do you want to wake the dead?"

"FRIDAY?" she scream-whispers.

"You looked; I know you did. And you didn't do any better."

"But I cannot have you being me until Friday! I have a huge work event Saturday that I cannot miss. My entire fiscal year depends on it."

"I have a lot going on too—" I say, but she just rolls her eyes. "And I miss my family already. This isn't what I want either. But if it comes by Friday, we'll survive. You'll have yourself back for your big crucial work event. I'll have myself back before my house starts looking like . . ." I stop myself before I get to the word *yours*.

Her shoulders slump. "I just want my life back," she says. "And not a week from now. Today."

"Me too, believe me," I tell her. "But, Wendy . . . ," I start slowly. "Do you think maybe it's about more than my sangria? Like maybe . . ." I am not sure how to proceed. "Like this is some kind of, um, divine intervention to help you out with things?"

She looks at me, shocked. "Help ME out?" she asks.

"Well, yeah," I say. "You're always so rushed and stressed out. Your life seems so hectic, and your house . . ."

"What about my house?" she asks defensively.

"It's . . . well, there's a hole in the bedroom," I try.

"Seth's fixing it," she says. "You can't rush an artist."

I want to ask about all the other things that need fixing or the family of dust bunnies I found multiplying under every piece of furniture in the house like . . . well, like actual bunnies. Instead I say, "I guess not," meekly. She's taking even more offense to this line of discussion than I predicted. "But look, maybe we can put a good spin on this, since it's happening."

"By fixing my terrible life," she says.

"I will say today has been the most stressful day of my life in several ways," I tell her.

She laughs, a dry, joyless laugh. "No surprise there. Compared to my life, yours is a cakewalk. And not because I have a hole in my bedroom wall. Because I have a huge, time-consuming job that supports my entire family and am raising two very different children at the same time. You don't know anything about the kind of stress I'm living with."

I rear back. "Oh, don't I? I know I only have the small, meaningless-by-comparison job of taking care of three children who will make the world a better place, supporting the local schools, and, oh yeah, driving YOUR kids from place to place, but believe it or not, my days can be stressful too."

"Hardly," she replies.

I roll my eyes. "If your life is so darn hard, maybe you should change something about it."

"That's probably the most naive thing you've said to me yet. This is what it is to be a working woman. Take it from me—you can have it all, as long as you don't ever want time to *enjoy* having it all."

I say nothing to that. It's just too tremendously sad to respond to. But she must see the bleakness on my face.

"Look," she says. "I know you'd like to spend all night out here criticizing my homelife and cutting down my shrubbery, but we simply don't have time. You've got to say good night to Bridget in ten minutes, and I've got to go . . . what? Pack color-coordinated bento lunch boxes and iron T-shirts?"

I set my face tight, as if I weren't just slapped. "Just pack Sam and Zoey turkey and provolone on whole wheat. Add some sprouts from the window box by the kitchen sink, and throw in a few carrots—but be sure to wash them first. The whole thing will take three minutes. I do laundry on Mondays, so they're fine for clothes for one more day. Which my children can iron by themselves, I assure you, if the need arises."

Her face gives away nothing. "Fine. And as for you, try to get the kids to school with their after-school gear and money for lunch, because there's no coming back for anything once you head toward the city for work. And you have to dress nice." She gestures to the only clothes suitable for cleaning I could find in her entire wardrobe, old gray leggings and a yellowed T-shirt. "Like really nice. Like a real person with a job."

I didn't think I could narrow my lips angrily more than I already have, but fortunately Wendy has very pointy lips.

"And shower," she goes on, "and get to my office by eight thirty. I'll text you the address. After that I can send you more instructions and answer the important emails remotely if we trade phones. Oh, and do you have some kind of system so I can figure out where I'm supposed to be all day?"

I nod and send up a silent prayer that she'll follow through on my obligations just as rigorously as she expects me to do for her. "I have a planner in the top drawer of the nightstand on my side of the bed. Everything in my life is in there. Zoey is yellow, Samuel is blue, and Joy is lilac. Hugh is red."

"What color are you?" she asks.

"Huh?" I respond, shaking my head at the question. "I don't have my own color. I'm all of the colors, obviously."

She snorts.

"Just follow it to the letter, ok? There's PTA work and Kindermusik and tutoring and—"

"I'm sure I can handle it," she says, so smugly I find myself wishing her three kids with flu and head lice at the same time. Then I remember: those are my kids. Goodness. And this experience is supposed to be bringing out the best in me.

Grounding myself in that reminder, I tell her, "Let's review the rules. Quickly. Before Bridget comes looking for you. Me. Us."

"Fine. The rules. Easy. One: don't fuck up my life."

"Or mine," I say. "Which includes keeping your language PG, please."

She rolls her eyes. "Two: don't let the kids find out."

"Ok. Right," I agree.

"Three—and this is the most important one. Don't. Touch. My husband."

"Obviously," I tell her. "I'm a happily married woman!"

"To a man with more hair on his back than his head," she says. I want to smack her. What is her obsession with my husband's hair situation? I would certainly rather have some roaming follicles than a head full of hair covering a brain full of indifference.

"What are you going to say to Hugh?" I ask.

"What do you mean?" she asks.

"When he comes on to you or goes for a kiss or whatever. I thought I'd tell Seth I had a yeast infection. Or maybe it's my time of the month? Or . . . I'm coming down with something? What do you think?"

Wendy's gaze seems to search mine. "You don't need to say anything. If you don't bug him, he won't bug you." She says no more, but then, she doesn't have to. That one little sentence speaks volumes. Unhappy volumes. Again I am grateful for Hugh's touch, even if he doesn't always have the best timing.

And I don't want Wendy anywhere near him.

"Tell Hugh you're ovulating," I tell her. "He'll treat you like you have the plague."

"Oh my god," says Wendy. "Of *course* you use the rhythm method."

"What is that supposed to mean?" I ask her.

"Mom?" comes a small voice from Wendy's house, before she can answer. It must be Bridget. Oh, I hope it isn't Linus. That poor kid. Everything seems to make him worry. Getting him to lie down in his bed tonight and go to sleep was like wrestling an octopus with an attachment disorder.

"You've gotta go," says Wendy. "Here—take your phone, and give me mine. And be nice to Bridge. Tomorrow's the first real practice of the year. And she's riding her bike to the field by herself for the first time ever."

"I thought you said Gemma was driving her."

"I lied," says Wendy. "She'll be fine. She's eleven. She's just a bit nervous. But straight up, if one single girl is late to the carpool line tomorrow, I'm taking Bridget instead."

I nod. It's totally unfair, and I would do the exact same thing for my daughter.

"Remember the rules," I tell her.

"Oh, I'll remember them. It's you I worry about."

I can't begin to respond to that, so I walk away, to Wendy's house, to tuck Wendy's daughter into bed. And "be nice" to her. As if I would do anything less. *I'm a nice person!* I want to shout. *I cleaned your entire house. I taught your kids to do laundry!*

But then, she didn't ask me about any of that, did she? She asked me what I planned to wear tomorrow. And if all she cares about is what I wear to her office tomorrow, how much more effed up can her life really get?

———

WENDY

That night, after the shrubbery confab, I come back into Celeste's house to find three sleeping children and a sleeping husband. Samuel is tucked into a slumbering ball on top of his bed, no covers, fully dressed, as though he passed out after a frat rager. I put a throw blanket over him. Zoey is in her twin in her own room, also asleep, even though it's only 9:20 p.m. The children in this house know how to *sleep*.

On the giant squishy leather sectional in front of the cooking channel, I find Hugh and Anna Joy, snuggled up together, both out cold. It is the sweetest thing. It reminds me, with a pang, of my maternity leave with Linus, six short weeks when I gave myself over entirely to that strange cocktail of joy, hormones, and fatigue of infant motherhood. Linus's sleep was disorganized and he stayed up late, so I'd put him in a baby swing in the corner of the room while I tucked in his big sister, sang her to sleep, and, if Linus would have it, spent twenty or thirty quiet minutes doing nothing but watching her sleep and him swing, blissed out on the motion and the mobile above his happy head. Then he'd fuss for his turn, I'd scoop him out of the swing, and we'd collapse in my bed together, Seth happy to be relegated to the guest room for the time being.

When I went back to work, Bridget went back to preschool, but there were two weeks to cover before Linus was old enough to go to the well-rated day care I'd signed him up for before he'd so much as shown up on an ultrasound. Seth was prepping for an installation for the museum's big triennial, so my younger sister, Ruthie, moved in with us and watched Linus in the interim. I was always home for Bridget's bedtime, and I remember thinking that life was just about perfect. Sure, I was making good use of a preemptive dose of Zoloft to avoid PPD, that scourge so many women know can cut you out of the good parts of early parenting, and yep, I was tired. But I was needed at work *and* at home, just enough to feel like I was doing right by both. My sister was so loving to Linus that I never felt guilty leaving him in her hands—I didn't cry in the car when I left him each morning, like I had after Bridget had started day care. I was over the early expectations I'd had with Bridget about perfect parenting, and six weeks away from the office had done me a world of good. I really thought I'd feel as happy as I did those short two weeks forever.

Reality crept up slowly, like the sneaky bitch she is. Ruthie returned home, Seth reclaimed his spot in our bed, and Linus got on an earlier schedule thanks to the experts at his day care. Our bedtime routine became a rush from the moment I walked in the front door, work demands grew, and over time Seth and Linus's bonding failed to take off as it had with Bridget. Linus clung to me when I was home, and guilt clung to me when I was at work. Things just . . . got real.

Melancholy, I sit near Hugh and the toddler as their bodies rise and fall with each relaxed breath. In the quiet, I clear out a few weekend emails on my phone, grateful to have it back, and then wonder what my next steps should be. Do I wake up Hugh so he can sleep in bed and try to relocate a sleeping Anna Joy? Do I put her in that little toddler bed in her brother's bedroom and hope she stays asleep through the transfer? It certainly doesn't seem right that I should be allowed to sleep in a grown-up room by myself in perfect solitude after doing zilch for the family who thinks I belong to them. And yet I don't feel right about sharing the bed with someone else's husband. No, if anyone should be spending the night on the sofa, it should be me.

But that means waking up two happy sleepers I barely know.

Feeling utterly unnecessary and lonely for my own home, where I might still be chatting at Bridget's bedside or working on my laptop in front of the TV, I go back into Samuel's room. There's no sign that the white toddler bed has been used for anything besides storage. It's made up tight as a drum and covered in stuffed animals and folded boys' underpants. That's right—folded size-eight underpants; my suspicion that Celeste mostly makes extra work for herself all day and night is confirmed. Perhaps she's one of those people who expands the task to fit the time she has to work on it. Perhaps I'd become that, too, if I were knocking around this big house alone all day like I am now.

Tomorrow, she told me, is laundry day—a whole day just for laundry! I imagine her home alone while her kids are at school, hanging their clothes out on the line instead of throwing them all in the dryer with a fragrance ball, and then later folding each pair of Spider-Man boxer briefs lovingly, while listening to a critically lauded audiobook, maybe, and contemplating a slowly braised dinner. Sounds luxurious, if I'm being honest. Meditative. No rushing, no stress, no psychotic breakdowns over potluck beverages.

But then, how many times have I read a think piece about rejecting the cult of busyness and wanted to shout at the well-meaning writer, *It's not like I have an option!*

I do not.

Except, for now, I do.

As Celeste, I can reject the hell out of that cult of busyness. I can go sleep in that big bed by myself tonight, figure out that color-coded planner tomorrow, and go through the motions of Celeste's idyllic little domestic fantasy until all this is over. A week, I think, as I pad to the master bedroom, alone, without anything whatsoever to do. I can stand to do nothing for a week. It might even do me some good.

CHAPTER 9
MANIC MONDAY

WENDY

The next morning I wake up slowly to the sun, thinking I'm myself, and when I slowly remember the swap, I'm not as surprised as you'd think. After all, the bed I'm in is not my bed, the pretty pink pajamas could never be mine, the ache in my hips is not my ache, and the icy toes on my back belong to someone else's slumbering toddler. In the bathroom I look at the mirror reluctantly, but of course I still see Celeste. My fingers rise to the underside of her eyes, trace the spot where my real face would be puffy and sallow on any given Monday morning. Instead I see smooth olive skin and full, glowing cheeks. I tilt my head in surprise as I take the time to give this other woman a real look. Celeste is one of those women with great raw materials and absolutely nothing done with them. It's 7:00 a.m., and I am probably needed in the kitchen, but maybe later it would be nice to give her a little glow-up. Maybe Celeste was half-right, and this strange experience is meant to improve her life, not mine. Seems like the least I could do in exchange for the vacation.

In the pretty white kitchen with hanging copper pots, things are grooving along nicely. Hugh is eating a boiled egg. The kids are eating . . . what? I look closer. Breakfast burritos? So the Earth Mother lets her kids eat frozen burritos for breakfast, eh? Well, they look damned great, and my stomach rumbles. Don't mind if I do.

But in the freezer I find a horrifying sight. Shelf upon shelf of plastic Ziploc bags, meticulously labeled, jammed with endless homemade foods for reheating. Two gallon-size bags full of "breakfast wraps—bacon" and "breakfast wraps—spinach" respectively. I pull them out to get a look at what's behind them and find five—FIVE!—homemade pizzas, mummified in loads of plastic wrap, each labeled, on cards, with baking instructions. Then two lasagnas. One broccoli and sausage, one traditional. A moussaka. A shepherd's pie and a cottage pie. I don't even know what the difference between those two pies is, but apparently Celeste does and has labeled them accordingly. Then there are packages of prepped raw ingredients frozen flat and shelved upright like books. *Crock pot fajitas. 6 hrs, medium. Instant pot salmon pilaf. Add asparagus after quick release.* It goes on. I see premade veggie soups. Precooked quinoa. Bags and bags of rich tan chicken stock.

Jesus on the cross. Is this woman expecting an apocalypse? One with working small kitchen appliances?

"Mom," says the boy child. "I ate the last sausage wrap."

"Ok," I say, because he is telling me this as if it is actionable. As if I am going to go and make a dozen more sausage wraps, individually package and label each one, and stack them in the freezer for these children to eat when—HELLO—they SELL these things at the store. Not to mention Eggos. Not to mention has anyone in this house heard of cereal for breakfast?

"We're fixed for eggs, though, thanks, babe," says Hugh. He comes at me looking kissy, and I duck the whole ordeal like I'm a boxer. Hustle and flow. Or is that float and sting? I don't know; I just know I'm doing some kind of sporting cliché to avoid touching Celeste's husband. And ugh, hard-boiled-egg breath first thing in the morning? Hard pass.

Zoey looks toward but through me, exactly like Bridget does. Must be a tween skill. "Mom, did you figure out what I'm supposed to wear today?"

I look at her blankly. "What do you mean?" I reply.

"To softball!" she says. "Mom!"

"Oh, right," I say, and I'm reminded of rule one. The way Zoey just spoke to me definitely feels like I'm on the edge of fucking up something important. I should really go get that planner and have a good look. "I haven't had my coffee yet," I tell her.

Hugh looks up. "I thought we were quitting coffee? For the frogs in the rain forest? You've gone without for three months!"

I have no idea what he's talking about, so I just nod and say, "Yeah, that's how long it's been since I had my coffee!" with a forced laugh. "And it'll be three more. Don't worry." Like hell it will. I will have a double espresso in my hands the minute that man turns his back. What is Celeste trying to do to me? "It's just an expression, you know. Anyway, practice gear. You just wear a T-shirt and shorts. Stuff you can move in."

"Are you sure?" she asks. "Did you talk to Bridget's mom like you said you would?"

I raise an eyebrow. "I absolutely did," I tell her. I'm talking to her right now, as a matter of fact.

"Then I'm screwed," she says.

Samuel says, "She said 'screwed'!"

Hugh looks at both of them, very daddish. They both look down for a minute; then Zoey hands Hugh a quarter from her backpack.

"How are you scr—stuck?" I ask.

"I don't have any shorts, remember? You told me my tennis skort would be fine. I'm going to look so stupid, Mom."

I put my hand to my chin. "No shorts?" I ask. "Not one pair?"

"I had those old ones from last year, but they made me look stubby," she said. "Remember? I looked like a tree stump. You agreed."

Hugh and Samuel are watching this conversation like tennis spectators. They look highly interested, the way you'd look if you were about to, say, witness a street brawl. So I shake my head. "If that's true, it was the shorts' fault. You'll look great in any decent shorts. You'll look like an athlete. I'll get you a few pairs today while you're at school. And remember, the point of softball practice is to get better at softball, not to win a fashion show."

Zoey scrunches up her face. "Can you win a fashion show?" she asks snarkily.

I want to roll my eyes, but then I think of Zoey's beautiful hand-tailored clothes and realize this whole fashion thing is a big part of this girl's identity. "If anyone can," I say, "you would win for sure."

She looks at me, surprised. "Thanks, Mom," she says. "That's really nice."

"No problem," I say. "You'll rock it tonight." She beams. And because I can't resist, I add, "Just do what Bridget does. She's a great friend to have on a day like today." Silently I give a prayer of thanks that Bridget is able to be herself on the field and not fret about what she looks like in her sweaty, dirty, never-stops-smelling softball gear. She's really a pretty down-to-earth kid, purple skirt aside. And for god's sake, she owns a few pairs of shorts like a normal human.

"Samuel," I test out. "Do you need shorts too?"

He looks at me like I'm crazy. "I'm good, Mom."

Hugh laughs. "If not for basketball shorts the kid would be pants-less three hundred and sixty-two days a year, Celeste! Besides, you buy him two new pairs every time you go to Costco. I think he's set."

Oh, I see how it is. Hand-sewn Vogue Teen clothes for the dress-up-doll daughter. Costco athleisure for everyone else. Even Celeste herself is resigned to yoga pants that come in three-packs. Something I definitely should work on while I'm here . . .

"Actually, Hugh," I venture, since he seems fed and happy at the moment, "I might like to get myself a few things while I'm shopping anyway. You don't mind, do you?"

"Mind?" he asks. "I've been telling you to do this for months! And you need something for the work thing on Wednesday too. Do you want me to call that sitter Gary recommended?"

I don't know who Gary is, but I assume he's not a serial killer if he's friends with these squares. "Yes, that would be great." And it is *so* great! This guy is sending me shopping to buy a dress to wear to an event for which I don't even have to hire the sitter myself. I may have to get Hugh to pass along some pro tips to Seth.

"Get something sexy," says Hugh. Zoey makes a retching noise. I try not to join her. "She's a beautiful woman, kids," he tells them. "Even if she is your mother."

At that, the baby stumbles into the kitchen, bleary eyed. I'm not sure where she slept last night. Or where Hugh slept, for that matter. I hope it wasn't that toddler bed. "Mommy!" she cries. "Are you well enough to do milk today?"

Hugh shoots me a look. I arch an eyebrow back at him—just one. I've never been able to do that before; it seems to be Celeste's special talent. "I wonder if maybe it's time," I say quietly to Hugh. "She's almost four."

His eyes widen. "Amen!" He claps his hands together. "And praise be! Ok, kids, finish it up and show some hustle! I'm taking you to school today. Mom's got a project on her hands here. Lunches?"

I think he's telling the kids to make their lunches, but for some reason, he looks at me. I remember the sandwiches I didn't make last night. Whoops. "School lunch today!" I say chirpily.

The kids look at me like I just grew a second head. "Seriously?" asks Zoey.

"Oh, for Pete's sake. Seriously. It's Chili Monday. Just buy a bag of Fritos from the vending machine, dip 'em in the chili, and boom, you've got nachos." My kids love Chili Monday. Three dollars and fifty cents each for lunch, the chips, and a can of Coke. A bargain at any price.

"Fritos?" says Samuel. "What are they?"

I try not to do a spit take. "You'll love them," I say.

Hugh looks at me in true awe. "Can I have Fritos too?"

"I don't know how to answer that," I say honestly. "I have no input on what a grown man eats for his lunch at work." And Celeste probably shouldn't either, I add mentally.

Hugh coughs in surprise. "Well, if you're sure . . ."

"Fritos for everyone!" I tell them. "Put it on my tab!"

A tiny voice wafts up from around my kneecaps. "Can I have a Fritos, Mommy?"

"If you go a whole day without nursing," I tell her, "you can have *unlimited* Fritos."

She's so excited she starts running through the house crying, "Fritos! Fritos! Fritos!"

Hugh winces at this. Perhaps I've violated the family all-natural-food ethic with just a touch too much gusto. But even so, he wrangles the school kids, hands out cash for lunch, shovels them all into a car, and drives away after failing on two more marital-kiss attempts.

"Good luck to you, babe," he says when one foot's out the door. "Have fun shopping for yourself for a change. But careful. Don't forget the corn poops," he adds with a sad laugh.

I pretend to laugh back, as if I'm in on the joke. But immediately after they leave, I text Celeste.

What, exactly, are corn poops?

—

CELESTE

I will tell you right now about a suspicion that we stay-at-home moms have about working moms. We would never, ever say it to their face—as mentioned, we are way above the Mommy Wars. But still.

We think they have it easier.

Every day while we are living our lives of servitude, they go to a place, in real clothes, where they are paid to sit comfortably among adults and think entire, complete, punctuated thoughts. Often this place has free coffee round the clock and cake on their birthdays.

Yes, work is work, and no, not every day is a joyfest. But here is what I did not realize when I handed in my resignation at the community college and became a professional mom: if you work outside the home, for eight or so back-to-back hours every weekday, you wipe zero butts that do not belong to you.

And to be clear, butt wiping is pretty much the *easiest* part of stay-at-home-mom work. I would gladly wipe ten more butts per day if it did away with even just the raisin-related tantrums. If it meant I didn't have to stand outside in every kind of weather saying, "I see! I'm watching!" while one of a succession of toddlers does absolutely nothing of interest for the tenth time in a row.

If you have a full-time job outside the home, that means that for eight solid hours every day, no one asks you to go down a wet slide or starts crying because you're not pushing them "right" on an impossibly low swing while you stand there hunched over, staring into space, begging yourself not to look at your watch yet because zero time has passed in the last seventeen hours; it is the same exact time it was when you arrived at that park, before your butt was wet with something smelly and before you put your hand on a fireman's pole covered with bird poop, and before someone else's child sneezed directly into your face. Time stands still when you are a stay-at-home mom, and working moms are always saying, *Oof! Where did the day go?* and I am always thinking, *It did not go. It will never end. I will never get to the part where I sink into a comfy chair with a glass of wine, because this is the longest day of my life.* Until tomorrow.

So yes, I'm very glad to be sitting in Wendy's pretty reclaimed-warehouse office with gorgeous architectural details and story-and-a-half paned windows looking out over one of the cutest, busiest hot spots in the city.

Wendy has a fancy ergonomic chair and a sit-to-stand desk. Here at her workplace, people care if her body is properly aligned and healthily engaged. They care if she is comfortable. Sometimes Anna Joy comes into our bedroom in the middle of the night, snuggles sweetly with her dad, and puts her cold baby feet directly on top of the soft, smooshy pouch she and her siblings left behind on my stomach, where all my internal organs are just lying in a misshapen postpartum blob. Then she presses those feet onto me as hard as she can. She somehow continues to do this even after she's fallen asleep. I will wake up bent exactly in half with my rear end frozen outside the covers and my head not so far from my knees in an attempt to escape her sleep stompings—and no, that sort of rest is not terribly refreshing. When I get up, my body makes sounds no living thing should have to make.

I would like an ergonomic chair.

Wendy has sent what feels like a hundred texts to get me set up in her office, where she is, unsurprisingly, a productivity consultant. In a string of messages, she's sent log-ons and passwords and a who's who and a very fast tutorial on the intraoffice Slack policies. I am ready to get after it, workwise, but soon after skimming over several of her emails, I decide that not only is her job not a good use of her mind, body, and intellect, it is also entirely nonurgent. If she-slash-me slacks off for a day or two while I try to set her homelife to rights and give her some small chance to stop being such a word-that-rhymes-with-witch, it's no big deal. Wendy is not an ER nurse or an insurance adjuster. She tells people how to cram more work into their waking hours. Everything, literally *everything*, about her job can wait.

I close Wendy's email tab and open a browser window. This is the perfect day to browse for fun activities to keep the kids learning during the upcoming summer break. But to my surprise, Pinterest autocompletes in her address field before I've even typed the *N*. Huh. Wendy did not strike me as a Pinner. I click around her home boards to see what's caught her eye.

It's an education. Besides a few pantsuits, short haircuts, and "the only macronutrient counter you'll ever need," all her pins are articles. A very specific kind of article:

"Working mom's minute-by-minute schedule after 5 p.m."

"13 game-changers for busy moms to make up for quantity time with quality time."

"Six ways to be present with your children during working hours."

"Secrets for extra energy from real working moms."

"What you can learn about your kids from a stay-at-home mom."

I click on that one instantly.

It takes me to a blog called *Only Real Moms Know*. Immediately I wonder what the hell a fake mom is. A mannequin of a mom at the Children's Place? An alien trying to impersonate a human mother in a bid to infiltrate the species?

And then I keep reading and realize, *Oh.*

It's me.

I'm the fake mom.

Real moms, according to the *About Us* section of the website, know how important it is to be role models to their daughters and sons. Real moms work hard and play hard. Real moms know how to walk side by side at home, but at work they walk out in front. Real moms can afford to nurture their children's gifts because they're not scrimping and saving every penny to make up for living in a one-income household. Real moms *love* working and love that they're not dependent on their partners to pay the bills.

Oh, and did I know that Science Proves that working moms' daughters:

- earn higher salaries over the course of their lives?
- get better educations?
- are less likely to be caught giving handies behind the bleachers in the ninth grade?

Ok, maybe I invented that last one. I scroll backward on the touch screen to get back to Pinterest, to get out of this weird bullcrap dichotomy. No one really believes this nonsense, do they?

Sure enough, on the next click I end up on an essay called "10 Reasons I Regret Staying at Home with My Kids." I wonder if maybe I should avoid it for my own mental health, but Wendy's pinned it, and I want to know what malarkey is filling her brain. And then I get a burst of hope, because at the top of the post there's a chart showing that 60 percent of moms think stay-at-home parenting is better than working parenting. I mean, I shouldn't care about "better" or "worse," but after that last site, I'm smarting a bit. I scroll on.

And cringe. The number one reason the writer bemoans her stay-at-home years is because she was a disappointment to those who came before her.

I sigh heavily. *As if Gloria Steinem gives two S-H-I-Ts whether I work or not,* I think defensively.

But truth be told, the sigh isn't exasperation. Not really. It's recognition. How could first- and second-wave feminists *not* care what my generation does with the freedoms they fought for? What debt do I owe Margaret Sanger, bell hooks, Sojourner Truth? What about all the women born before me who would have been so, so much happier if they'd had the choice to work, to have their own money, to be free? I do constantly wonder if I owe them anything. I constantly tell myself they fought for me to have choices . . . and then hope and pray they might have seen my own choice as a legitimate one. Another long, hefty sigh. I should stop reading this list right now, but I can't.

The next entry makes my stomach churn: *I had too much time on my hands.*

Was I busy? asks the author. *Sure. Busy worrying too much, helicoptering my kids, and making up standards of perfection that only served to make other mothers feel bad. I remember running around like crazy, being the default parent to anyone's kids, taking on every drop of volunteering work I could find, signing my kids up for too many activities and special events because I needed to feel like I was putting myself to use. But in the end, if you ask my son what I did while he was young, he'll say, "You didn't do anything, Mom. You didn't go back to work until I was in high school."*

I push back from the desk, stand up. This is claptrap and garbage, and I'm not buying into it.

Except it's what runs through my head almost every day, in almost the same exact words. Am I busy with purpose or just busy? Am I smothering my kids? Sure, I love sewing Zoey's clothes, and the two of us have more fun at the fabric store than just about anywhere else, but what happens when she gets older and wants real store-bought clothes? What happens when Samuel is old enough to bike himself to his activities and friends' houses? Those days aren't so far away. Will he, in a jam, tell his friends, with their lawyer and doctor moms, *My mom can take us to the movies. Don't worry; she doesn't do anything?*

WENDY

Corn poops are a thing, I learn by the end of the day, and they are no joke. I mean, they should absolutely be a joke, and after I catch up on the last four seasons of *The Marvelous Mrs. Maisel*, I'll probably find they already are. But after finding no coffee in the entire Mason kitchen of the Mason family, and knowing I'm going to need Fritos stat or I'm going to get accosted in my bosoms again, I grab the toddler, bundle her into ladybug boots and a raincoat, and head for the biggest grocery store on this side of town. It's a giant fluorescent nightmare that sells everything for at least a third less than it would cost elsewhere—except the wine, which is always half-off and as such has become part of my weekly routine since having kids. Here, produce is loose in huge cardboard bins that lean and bend precariously. The deli meat is all presliced and wrapped in plastic increments of a half pound, something that could have happened this morning or six weeks ago. Most shocking: in the back left corner by the corn dog selection, they have a chest freezer with bulk chicken nuggets you take out with a big plastic scoop. But the deals!

Anna Joy is completely unfamiliar with the place, and the minute I set her on her feet in the store, she runs for it, a fat little bowling ball in a raincoat rolling down the huge aisles toward the endcap of Cheez-Its, aiming for a strike. She careens between carts, and I get a couple of glowers until I realize—oh yeah—this is my kid, for all intents and purposes. I'm the mother of a toddler again. It's up to me to go chase her down. One of the glarers is a mother with two kids under three sitting in the front of the cart, something I completely forgot about doing now that my littlest is eight. I scoop up Anna Joy and put her in the cart seat and clasp the buckles. She bursts into tears. "I want to be FREE!" she says dolefully.

I laugh at her. "Girl, I thought I was free until I realized you'd be home all day."

She stops crying out of confusion.

"Anyway, there's some good news for you, sweet dear," I tell her. "I'm going to do something I wish I'd done with my kids. I mean, your siblings. I'm going to bribe you to be good and make my life easier, and I'll feel no guilt about it whatsoever."

She looks at me, still mystified.

"How do you feel about cheap plastic toys, Anna Joy?"

She eyes me carefully. Suspiciously.

I lean to the left. As usual, next to the junk food displays there are toy risers running up the shelving like parenting IEDs. Closest to us are small stuffies with freakishly large rainbow-colored eyes. I grab a kitten.

"KITTEN!" she shouts.

"This kitty's name is"—I look at the tag—"Meowsie. Meowsie, meet Anna Joy." Anna Joy tentatively takes the cat. "Meowsie is yours if you're good. You can hold him the whole time we are in the store, and if you are so nice and make shopping fun for us both, then you can keep him when we leave. And if you are naughty, I will put the kitty back."

She clutches Meowsie close to her chest. "I'm very good," she tells me.

"I believe it. I've met your siblings. Now, where in this store can we find espresso beans and one-hundred-calorie packs of Starburst?"

Together, we wander through the massive store, emptier on a Monday than it is on the weekends, when I usually end up here, but still well populated. Anna Joy doped up on bug-eyed Meowsie is so good and angelic that people stop me to tell me loudly how sweet and beautiful she is. I think of Linus and Bridget, both of them clingy and loud at this age. People never stopped me at the store to say, *Wow, that pair of barnacles howling and scratching your face while you try to shop sure are sweet and beautiful.*

That said, no one would have been able to catch a word with me anyway back then, even if they'd tried. I've never had more than an hour free to get through a grocery shop start to finish, and I normally zip like lightning from item to item on a list sorted by aisle, like a cast member of *Supermarket Sweep*.

By contrast, on this trip I walk down aisles I've never visited just because I can. Pets—who knew they sold actual betta fish here? Sports drinks. Miles of them. And look! This is where they hide those sugary Frappuccinos in glass bottles I thought you could only get at the gas station. I put a four-pack in my cart, then open the first and slug down a quarter of it before we even pull into the next row.

When we finally leave the store, I have bought seventy dollars' worth of easy-prep groceries, plus a few more weaning bribes for while I am in Celeste's body. I put it all on Celeste's credit card because I have no idea if she has any cash on the debit card. In fact, since she doesn't work, the Masons may be downright poor. Or maybe, since she doesn't work, they have to be downright rich? I have no idea what her real financial situation is, come to think of it. Meowsie costs a mere $3.99, worth every penny for my sanity, but since I'm not sure where Celeste stands, I buy the bribe separately with cash, holding on to the receipt for the rest to pay her back later as needed.

The money considerations get me thinking. I have always sort of assumed that despite race, religion, or creed, everyone in Birchboro Hills is generally like us financially: a huge mortgage, one good salary, one crap salary, and very expensive kids. The math on that kind of lifestyle means we look rich—a big house, two cars, fancily clad kids in any activities they desire, and takeout five days a week. Yet we feel poor—no money left over to travel, no time to sleep, no energy for sex, books, hobbies, home cooking, the stuff that makes you stop and enjoy being alive from time to time.

But then, maybe not everyone lives like this. Celeste can clearly afford to fix up her house—something out of reach for us. She doesn't have to work, which means whenever she's tired, she can rest. She can cook at home at her leisure—the freezer is proof that she enjoys it—and the stack of books on her nightstand says a lot about her intellectual growth as well.

And then there's the upcoming gala.

What did Hugh say about me buying myself some clothes? He's been trying to get me to spend some money for months? Maybe the Masons are loaded.

I pay the store to load my bags into the car for me. Then I buckle in the little cooing creature and her rainbow-eyed cat and say, "Anna Joy, sweetheart, Mommy wants to go shopping for a new look."

She looks up. "But shorts for Zoey," she says. "And I want shorts too."

I smile at her. "Macy's, then. Shorts for everyone and a couple outfits for Mommy and, if you're very sweet, maybe some cute new something for you too."

Her eyes grow huge. "Can I keep the kitty?"

"The kitty is yours, sweetheart," I tell her. "You earned it."

And apparently I earned *this*. I don't know how. But as I pass through Macy's with Anna Joy happily staying within my sight, I wonder what, exactly, I did to be so lucky that instead of spending a day in my own stress-filled life, I am shopping with someone else's money on someone else's time, and there is plenty of both for the first time in many years.

CHAPTER 10

WENDY

Anna Joy gets hungry just as I am checking out in the women's section. Once I got her dress size right, I found five great separates that make Celeste's waist look shapely, two bras that move her breasts back into the correct position, and a pair of shoes that say both *I'm a great person with something meaningful to say* and *If you're lucky, I'll leave these on during sex*, at the same time. *Lucky Hugh!* I think to myself, only to remember that Celeste can't have sex with Hugh right now, or I would also be having sex with Hugh, and there are rules for a reason. Still, I might leave Celeste with some notes on how to use tools like these shoes and bras and the pair of lacy undies I doubt she will be pleased to find in her drawer when she gets her body back. Once everything is paid for and bagged up, I take Anna Joy to the excellent dumpling restaurant a block away. Just as she has never seen a Frito before, she's also never seen a soup dumpling. She looks from it to my boobs suspiciously.

"I want milk," she says.

"You can have cow's milk," I tell her firmly.

"I want mommy milk!" she clarifies at the top of her lungs. "FROM YOUR BOOBIES!"

I am calm. This is Celeste, not me, whose kid just shouted *boobies* in a dim sum joint.

I take out a bag of Starburst.

"These are very chewy," I tell her. "Come sit in Mommy's lap like you were going to have milk, but instead try chewing on one of these while I stroke your hair."

She looks at me dubiously. I unwrap a strawberry Starburst, eat half exaggeratedly, and say, "Yummmmm, so chewy!"

She comes to sit on my lap, and to my surprise my breasts start to tingle and let down. Not caring what anyone thinks about Celeste in this place, I stuff three napkins inside each bra cup and push one arm against my nips, using the other to hold up the sweet baby girl who is probably missing her real mommy so much, even if she can't quite figure out why. Pangs of emotion and the pure desire to just give in and nurse her bang around my head and squeeze my heart. The hormonal surge that accompanies the milk letdown brings on happy memories of my own babies. Bridget at three was chubby like this one, and she was speedy and zoomy, too, but she didn't fall for new things so easily. If I had told her to eat something specific—no matter how sweet—at three years old, she would have refused on principle. If I had said to sit on my lap, she would have lasted two minutes before trying to stand on my shoulders and leap over the top of me. But oh, how she made us laugh.

By contrast, Anna Joy cuddles in deep, takes a candy, and puts it in her mouth, then grabs a fistful of Celeste's deep-brown hair and twirls, twirls, twirls.

To my own surprise, I'm sympathetic to Anna Joy's plight. Linus probably would have nursed till fourteen if I hadn't had to go back to work, where my breasts laughed in the face of my breast pump and closed up shop within three weeks. He loved, and still loves, cuddling with me as tightly as possible. When he was this age, he would bring books up to me at every hour of the day, sometimes even when I was sleeping, and get as close to me as he could without fusing atoms. Then he would open the book onto my face. If I was too tired to start reading, he would tell me the title and then recite the story from memory, turning the pages completely at random. It made Seth crazy. "I'm trying to sleep here!" he'd tell us from the opposite side of the bed.

"You're not the one with a book on her face!" I'd call.

"It's three a.m.!" he'd say.

"Go to the guest room!" I'd tell him back. "At least you can breathe! Linus, honey, let Mommy have her windpipe back, ok?" And Linus would adjust his hug to pinch my kidneys instead and resume his narration.

Anna Joy sighs, not a contented sigh but a longing one, and I do the same. It is a strange irony of motherhood that you start yearning for another baby before your first one can say her own name, before you've had a good night's sleep in ages, before your body could possibly handle another pregnancy. The baby itch that you think will be finally soothed with a beautiful, healthy child in your arms after nine months of waiting comes back so fast, and stronger than even before the first kid. I thought for sure it would be gone after Linus, he of the six months of morning sickness and the forty-eight-hour labor, but no. Around nine months later I started to think that if I must have sex in this baggy, stretched-out, tired body, maybe I should have it unprotected so we could try for a third.

Even now that Linus is eight and Seth has been snipped by mutual agreement, I find myself watching mothers of three jealously, as though I don't already have an embarrassment of blessings. My perspective vanishes, and it's suddenly all about what I don't have after all. Look at those multiparous women, with their one last baby, their last midnight snuggles, their last stroller walks. Their last maternity leaves and their last diaper changes and their last slow lukewarm baths and the chance to say a proper goodbye to every stage, knowing for sure they have done it right this time, that they have learned what there is to learn, that this child, certainly, will be the one to give them three perfect grandbabies and let them snuggle them as if they were their own when the happy time comes.

At two kids, you think, *I'm so tired. Two has to be enough. Two healthy children; I'm as lucky as they come.* And your husband, or at least mine, is ready to walk as it is.

But still, you break down some mornings around your ovulation. You dream of another baby, and when you wake and find she is not real, you cry. You cry when you sell your stroller to a neighbor, and you cry when you take your baby bottles to Goodwill. Each laundry day you sort out what is too small for your youngest and cry a little then too. You wonder, Would three really be so bad? The other two would be in school all day, and it would be just you and the baby. And now here I am, in Celeste's body with her baby on my lap, pressing my arms to leaky nipples and thinking, *If only I'd had one more.* This would be my life. This toddler in my arms gazing up at me lovingly, and nowhere to be except here with my favorite soup dumplings within easy reach.

This is Celeste's life.

A sorrow as keen as knives opens inside me.

"Mommy," says Anna Joy. "Why are *you* crying?" She makes it clear that she is the one who should be crying here, and she indeed seems very close to tears, though she is trying this new thing with her whole heart.

I think about what to say that won't freak out this kid for life. "I am so glad you're here, that's all. You are a little precious gift, and your mommy is so lucky to have you."

She smiles. "Can I have milk, then?"

"No," I say. "My heart is made of stone. Sorry, darling."

"Maybe tomorrow," she says and takes another Starburst. Lemon.

"You never know," I say in return, both to her and to myself.

—

CELESTE

There is a knock on the office door. Wendy told me in no uncertain terms not to shut her door—apparently her PhD thesis was on the power of "architectural/subliminal information in the compassionate workplace." But I ignored her because she doesn't get what it's like to never, ever, *ever* be alone. She gets to sit in this office all day and read these articles to make herself feel smug about her choices. She uses an office bathroom with a lock on it. In her office desk she has a stash of what looks like leftover Easter candy that her children will never, ever find.

I call for whomever it is to come in.

"Wendy?" says a man with a full foot of height on me—well, on Wendy, who is just short enough that in her body the whole world looks slightly bigger. The man has the nicest sort of shoulders that he has to angle to squeeze through the half-open doorway. My, or Wendy's, body kind of wakes up when he's in the room. My very first thought: *Is Wendy sleeping with this guy?*

Looking carefully at him, I'm not sure I could blame her.

"Everything ok in here?" he asks. His accent is a rich, creamy British, and he looks genuinely concerned.

Do I look funny? I wonder. *Is my Celeste showing through?* "Why do you ask?"

"The door," he tells me. "You never close that door."

Oh, right. My lack of architectural compassion.

"I wanted to try some new workplace stretches," I tell him, the lie tumbling out surprisingly easily. "And I was afraid I'd look a bit goofy my first go-round."

He smiles. "As if looking goofy has ever stopped you," he says warmly. I tilt my head. *Wendy* and *goofy* don't belong in the same sentence, unless you're talking about two costumed characters at Disney World. Being goofy would require a sense of humor, and Wendy Charles hasn't got one. But the man, the strapping, tall man, gestures with his head toward a five-by-seven picture taped up on Wendy's back wall, one I've never noticed before, and sure enough, in it Wendy's dressed up as Cheri Oteri's character from those great old *SNL*s when she and Will Ferrell are cheerleaders with way too much school spirit. The Strapping Man before me makes an excellent, hot Will Ferrell in his trim white pants and red tank top. And pom-poms.

My mouth drops open, and I try to close it up. "Well," I say. A beat passes while I try to be clever. "If I'd had my cheerleader costume on, it might have been different."

Strapping Man's eyebrows lift, and in a hot rush I realize both of us are imagining me in a cheerleader costume, stretching. In my version he is definitely in the room with me. And the door is definitely closed.

Wow, Celeste.

Wow, I mentally add. *Wendy, you dog.* One look at this guy's face, and I know with complete certainty that if she hasn't slept with this man, he'd certainly like to change that soon. Holy cats.

At this precise moment, Wendy—real Wendy—calls me. I sneak a glance at my phone and see a string of text messages from her that I've missed. Oh dear. Somehow it's gotten to be afternoon, and that means it's pickup time, and that means I should put *it* back in my pants, as Hugh's crass brother likes to say, and make sure the right assortment of children is in my minivan right now before Wendy drives off and strands half the softball team. I exhale.

"I'm sorry—I have to take this call. My kid's school," I lie to Strapping Man.

"Not a problem. Actually, I was just checking on you because of the closed door. Wanted to see if you were taking a nap day."

Oooh, is that a thing? I think it might have to be tomorrow if I stay up late cooking and cleaning again. "Wide awake . . . and wondering who forgot their soccer cleats," I say, because I've learned that whenever a mom mentions soccer, all nonmoms, men or women, are guaranteed to flee any room. (Pro tip: in the event of a zombie apocalypse, clear any overcrowded bunker by talking at length about kids' league sports.)

Obligingly, Strapping Man says, "I'll let you handle that, and we can catch up later," and books it outa there. On the way out he leaves the door wide open, and I wonder if it was out of habit or a commentary but leave it be. I remember the promise I made to Wendy last night like a solemn oath: *Don't ef anything up.* Maybe I closed her office door and spaced out for half the workday, but I haven't had sex with Strapping Man, divorced her husband, or sent her kids to school in circus costumery. I'm doing fine.

And as for my counterpart . . . I answer the phone too late. When I call back, no one picks up. I scroll back to catch up with her texts.

WHY ARE THERE TEN KIDS TRYING TO GET IN YOUR MINIVAN RN? reads the first text.

Oh ok, reads the second one, which came in two minutes later.

Then: I'm looking in the rearview mirror at three girls, two boys, and a toddler. Does that sound right? I frown. It does not sound right.

A new one pops up now. Wait, do I take this rando boy? Hugo? He says his mom says it's ok.

I text back quickly. Hugo is supposed to walk to his grandma's and he knows it. It's two blocks. Tell Samuel no friends except on Fridays. And make sure he has his backpack. Hugo, not Samuel.

Then I keep texting: Did he get a check-plus today? Samuel, not Hugo.

And more: What is Zoey wearing? Did you see in the planner that you were supposed to get her some softball clothes? Can you tell if Merine has lipstick on? Her mom wants me to watch for rogue makeup.

No answer. I keep texting. Oh and before you drive away, can you send Zoey into the school kitchen to pick up a Nesco cooker for the soup sale?

That's the only message she responds to: The turkey fryer things?

Roasters, yes. But just one. LMK, I type, and Let me know, please autocompletes on my phone before I hit send. This little moment of technological zen took fifteen minutes of watching YouTube instructionals and searching my iPhone settings, but it's so worth it. When I die, someone will say, *RIP, Celeste Mason. Her text messages were always complete sentences, and polite too.*

I wait for her to answer all my other questions, but the screen goes dark. Um . . .

For ten minutes I wonder who is in that minivan. I try texting Wendy two more times. I make a written list of which girls I am supposed to take each day and worry about whether any kids are stranded at school. What would they do if they were? Wouldn't Zoey tell Wendy if someone was missing? Would Wendy even listen?

I stew in the silence. If Wendy didn't get that cooker, she'll have to go back to school and get it after practice. But the school is locked by that time. Crap. Maybe Dr. Randall will still be there? But maybe not, because this is the Monday of the school board meeting. If I don't have it, then what? No gazpacho in Dixie cups to sell to kids at the monthly Go-to-School Night tomorrow night. No extra fifty dollars to supplement the state-funded snack with fresh-cut vegetables for the following school year. *Come on, Wendy. Just tell me you got the Nesco.*

Ok, no response, so time for plan B. I can probably make enough gazpacho for the fundraiser if I use a couple of lobster pots. I assume Wendy has a lobster pot. A Nesco is eighteen quarts, so two ten-quart pots will work, except I like to cook the white onions first because they're too sharp for the kids otherwise, so I'll cook the onions in one pot, then transfer them to two and add the tomatoes and seasonings before I puree with my stick blender, and if I use enough plastic wrap, I can probably get the pots sealed up enough to get to school tomorrow without incident. But the Nesco has a locking lid . . . so much easier . . . and tomatoes inside my light-tan minivan . . .

I startle. To my great shock, there are three people standing over my desk, blinking at me. How they got there I have no idea. They are all strangers to me, but I pretend to know who I'm looking at and say,

"Whoopsie! Lost in my thoughts." And then, because I guess I'm more off kilter than I realize, I say, "What can I do you for?" like a doofy character from an office sitcom.

The three of them stare at me more.

Finally one rouses and says, "Did you get my email?"

"Or mine?"

"Or ours?" they all seem to ask in unison.

Email. Didn't I just read somewhere that it was a scourge on productivity? My emails never scourge me that much—but I click over to Wendy's Outlook window and am startled all over again. There are So. Many. Emails. What is it that Wendy even does, again? How does she ever get anything done when this many people are pestering her? My goodness.

"I'm sorry, guys," I say. "I'll have to get back to you on these later. I've got to run. There's a school emergency."

One of them visibly gasps. She's the one who greeted me this morning in surprise by saying, "Wow, Wendy! Your hair is dry!"

"Are your kids ok?" she asks now.

"Fine. I just think that . . . uh . . . Bridget got left at school today by the mom who is supposed to drive her to softball. And I'm not sure about Linus."

"Doesn't Linus just go straight to after-school every day?" says the smaller of the three women in my office.

Oh, right. He does wraparound childcare. That's what Wendy told me yesterday. I pick him up from after-school at five thirty.

I'm not exactly sure what after-school involves, I now realize. Do they feed him? If not, won't he be starving by then?

I think of that huge mess of emails and the top one on the list. The subject ominously reads, *Confirming today's 4pm intake meeting*, and I don't know what that could even begin to mean.

I really should go make sure Linus has something to eat.

I grab keys and wallet and the light wool jacket I threw over my blouse this morning to make me feel like a boss. "Gotta scoot."

The crowd in my office looks at me like I'm a freak. "What?"

"But what about that intake with the referral client?" asks one.

"Did you look at my reformatting for the presentation?" asks another.

"The planner proofs have to get back to the printer by Friday," says the third.

"Ah . . . ok. Rebook the client—but for next week, at the earliest," I tell the first. "And the reformatting is awesome—nailed it," I say to the second. "And the proofs . . . I have to get back to you on the proofs," I say to the third, as I run for the door. *Book it, Celeste,* I think. *Before someone asks you for the nuclear codes.*

I'm two steps down the hall before someone says, "Don't forget to lock your door!" and I double back, look at all the keys on Wendy's ring, and then just decide to use the push button on the other side. There. Crap. All these colleagues, plus now hot Strapping Man, are flat-out staring at me. Clearly whatever it is Wendy does requires three staffers and can have its stressful moments. Roger that.

Luckily I did nothing all day, so I have probably not effed anything up too badly. *That was clever of me,* I think as I race out of the office hallway, away from the staring eyes. It's three o'clock, which is not exactly five but not noon, either, and I just spent an entire peaceful workday impersonating an employed person, and I think I got away with it! *Ta-da!* I think victoriously. *Take that, Ms. "Good luck being me, my big, important life is so hard and complicated you'll never do it right."*

Except the victory fades pretty fast when I get out to Wendy's car. Though I have never seen one in real life, I know exactly what is locked onto her rear wheel, and I'm pretty sure it means despite all my best attempts, I've failed at rule number one of Body-Swap Club. Yep. That big yellow metal thing that promises Wendy's body and I aren't going anywhere right now is most definitely a boot.

CHAPTER 11

CELESTE

I am a good girl. I was born a good girl, raised a good girl. I didn't do anything even remotely irresponsible until I was in college, and then I felt extremely guilty about it. So no, I've never parked illegally in my life. I've never breathed illegally in my life. My most borderline-unethical act heretofore was when I returned an open bag of seaweed snacks to Costco because they tasted like . . . well, seaweed.

That was years ago. Now here I am with a head full of gazpacho logistics and an impounded car. There's a phone number on the boot contraption, and I call it.

"Please listen carefully, as the menu options have changed," it tells me, and I wonder, *Who, exactly, calls about a boot on their car enough times to master the impound line menu?* But I listen carefully. More proof that I cannot rebel.

I get to an option about wheel-restraining devices and impounding in place.

It sends me to a website.

I say, "AGENT!" into the phone. This works a treat whenever I have to rebook Hugh's flights for travel.

Nothing happens. Automatic Menu Lady keeps giving me options. I navigate to the website while staying on the phone and holding for further assistance. It turns out I need to pay a fine by credit card, so I autofill with my own card. Lord knows this isn't Wendy's fault, and I'm getting the inkling that she couldn't afford it if it were. I put in Wendy's plate numbers and hit "Complete Payment." Phew. Now I can get to school, pick up any stray children, check on my own kids and Wendy's, and know that there will be soup made in time for tomorrow's fundraiser. Thank goodness.

The next screen tells me a reversal agent will be by in the next two to twenty-four hours to unboot my car.

I feel like screaming.

What if I did scream right now? I don't scream when I'm frustrated; that's not who I am. But then I, as far as anyone else knows, am in my minivan with an uncertain assortment of children on the way to the softball field in Birchboro Hills. Wendy is the one who parked so very illegally that she can't go anywhere for the next two to twenty-four hours.

So Wendy can definitely scream.

I open my mouth and let out something utterly bloodcurdling. It feels amazing. People all around me on the sidewalk turn and stare. I sustain the scream until my lungs are totally empty, then raise a hand, wave, and say, "I'm fine. Everything's fine," to the observing population.

And actually, I really, really am.

In the end, I get a ride from the unlikeliest of people. At least unlikely for Celeste. After my scream, I think of calling Hugh for help but remember the hedge-trimmers incident and decide that would be extremely confusing for him. I don't have Seth's phone number. I try to think of who Wendy's close girlfriends might be—the kind of friends who would offer her a ride to get her kids in such a situation—but I don't see any one person in my mind's eye with any kind of clarity. That means it's time to call a ride share.

But then I see him. Strapping Man. My goodness. He has his jacket off now in the May heat, and he looks like . . . everything good in the world. *Sorry, Hugh,* I send up mentally. *Not my body. Not my hormones.*

"You have a boot!" he observes.

"I . . . ," I gracefully reply. "Have a boot . . . ," I manage.

"Why, Wendy," he asks. "Did you park in the tow-away zone? And if so, why?"

It's a fair question. Real Wendy would presumably know the parking regulations near her office. Fake Wendy didn't see the sign. Fake Wendy was a bit out of it this morning.

"To be honest," I say, though honesty is sort of beside the point today, "I have no idea. Do you ever just feel like . . . you're not living your own life?"

He laughs. It's a nice laugh. Not as rumbly as I might have suspected, him being so tall and broad and his chest so . . .

Goodness, Celeste.

"I know just what you mean. A couple of days ago, I pulled into my garage"—I try not to visibly swoon at the pronunciation of *garridge*—"with no memory of how I got there," he says. "I was so wrapped up in thoughts of work that I just . . . I guess I went on autopilot. It was not a great feeling."

"Yes!" I say. "That's it exactly. I was just not . . . present in my own body, and someone else was running the show."

"Thank goodness for muscle memory," he remarks. "It's funny you say 'present.' After that garage incident, I decided I need to work on being much more present for the day-to-day moments in my life. I don't want to move through my days just through muscle memory. Matter of fact, you're the one who inspired that decision."

"I did?"

"You did. When you were telling me about how you had to really focus after work to be in the moment so you got quality time with your kids. Remember that conversation a couple weeks ago at lunch? I had the strangest sensation while you were talking. Here, get in my car; I'll tell you all about it. Where do you need to go?"

For a second I am tongue-tied. Where do I need to go, again? Wendy, if I remember my text instructions right, goes to the store after work to buy a frozen family dinner or pizza and bagged salad, then puts it in a cool bag and goes to softball to pick up Bridget. Then she gets Linus from after-school camp at five thirty, rushes home and puts the food in the oven to reheat, and does twenty minutes of stationary cycling in the basement while the kids do homework. She then feeds everyone, and they watch TV together until Seth gets home.

Uh, no, that's not happening. I can make a pretty vegetable frittata tonight. Broccoli, cheddar, and caramelized onions, fresh and fragrant and warm on the table in twenty minutes with stuff everyone keeps in their house already. I can serve it at the now-pristine dining room table and wrap up leftovers for tomorrow's lunches. And I can certainly skip the spin bike. As for right now . . . well, I can get Linus before I go to softball, let him play soccer with the other boys in the fresh air, catch the second half of practice, get my eyes on my own kids, and let Bridget know her mother thinks her activities are really important, like look-up-from-her-emails important.

"Can we make two quick stops?" I ask Strapping Man. "They're very close to each other."

He smiles. "Of course. Does this end with us lying on a blanket in a park?" he asks.

Oh, how my head fills with that image. But wait, he's not supposed to be joking with Wendy about rolling around on a blanket in the woods! *Celeste! Get a grip! What would Wendy do?*

She'd be in a huff. "Pardon me?" I ask, trying to imitate Wendy's trademark outrage.

Strapping Man's cheeks wash pink. "I mean to say, watching softball practice." He coughs, stammers a bit. "You know. Last time I ran into you in the park, you were on that big plaid blanket. That's what

I was referring to. The blanket. For sitting on. While you watch girls' softball. But not in a weird way."

I crack up. I can't help it. This poor guy. Six feet plus, built like a brick wall, stammering and awkward. He tries to laugh, too, but he's still dark purple and tongue-tied.

"I get it now," I tell him as reassuringly as I can. "I thought for a minute . . . but, of course, no."

"Of course," he echoes. "No. You're married!" he adds. I realize that if this is the reason he cites to clear things up, it probably means he would be all too happy to roll around on a blanket with Wendy if it weren't for her wedding ring. Very interesting.

I follow him to his car, still smiling to myself, and say, "Tell me about being present."

As we buckle in, he tells me about how he and I—well, Wendy—were discussing how she uses a special series of reminders to get her into mom mode after a long day at work. I listen, impressed. She's very systematic about everything she does, but it's clear that it's important that her kids know she's all in when she's with them. I think about this in my own life all the time. When you are home with your kids constantly, you forget to be *all* there sometimes. There's no urgency about the quality of the time you spend together, because there's so much quantity. But sometimes, when you can get grounded and present with them, they pick up on it right away, and they respond differently. Despite all our differences, it's clear that Wendy has figured this out too. I think of Bridget's and Linus's eyes when they stop to look at their mom. They're lazy little stinkers, but they love her. There's trust that goes down to their bone marrow.

"So when you told me about how you always turn off the radio and drive in silence on the way to pick them up and just focus on breathing and letting your workday slide away, I was inspired. I know it's not the same without kids, but I don't want to just . . . I guess, daydream"—his voice rises, checking the word—"right, daydream away my own life.

When I was a kid, daydreaming was the best sort of pastime. But now, instead of thinking about how I would design my own footie cleats or animate cartoons, I think about emails I didn't send or when I need to change my furnace filter or what will happen three months from now if I forget to renew my plates and I get pulled over. It doesn't result in any useful actions. It just pulls me away from the life I really am having."

"If you ever get pulled over . . . ," I say slowly. Our city cops are constantly in the news for being certified in this or that implicit-bias training, but they still have guns and adrenaline and lifetimes of faulty programming like in any other city. I don't even know Strapping Man's name, and I feel afraid for him.

"I know, I know. You've told me a hundred times. I've heard it from my mother, my aunts, my cousins . . ."

"I'm going to renew your plates right now," I say. "For the next ten years, if I can."

"As if following the law makes it safer to be brown behind a wheel."

Without thinking, I move my hand on top of his. He startles, and I do too. But I don't—can't seem to—move my hand.

"I assume we're going to the softball field," he says after a moment.

"Actually, to Birchboro Hills Elementary first," I say, pulling my hand away. "I want to get Linus early."

"Oh. Ok, ok. This is brilliant. I've always wanted to meet the fellow."

Uh-oh. He's never met her kids. I imagine telling Wendy I introduced her son to her extramarital crush. Assuming she has a crush and it's not just one way. Which is a pretty big assumption, but then . . . look at him. If she doesn't have a crush, she's dead inside.

On the other hand. Wendy's husband is . . . let's just say in the twenty-four hours I've been his wife, I haven't been dazzled. Maybe he could use the feeling of a little competition to get him to try a little harder.

"Great! You'll love Linus. He's very . . . sweet."

"I know I'll like him. I just hope he likes me," he says, a comment so telling that my heart tugs a little.

"It's hot," I say, knowing exactly how to start a successful new friendship for any young boy of eight years old. "If you're not in a hurry, should we grab some ice cream and four spoons?"

—

WENDY

The weird thing about pretending to be someone else's mother, even for two days, is that you quickly find you don't have to pretend that hard.

When I get to watch practice, I am usually laser focused on my own kid. She works harder than her peers, and she gives more of herself to her team. I never have to pressure her or lean on her to get her head in the game. I know she has visions of landing an athletic scholarship someday, and that would be wonderful, but I don't care if she plays 4A or some coed keg league at community college, as long as she's able to get through school without the mountain of debt I faced down. Each month I set aside cash for each kid in a college savings plan, and there are months that feel like that's money we don't have. It's money that would pay for a bathroom remodel, a drywaller, or maybe a dry basement year round. But I believe a college education for a kid who works hard goes much, much further.

Today I enjoy the chance to watch Bridget practice, but my eyes are drawn to Zoey too. The girls are lined up, doing the very first lessons of pitching: the toe rockers, the low snaps, the work that is, for most of the utility players, largely about team unity. But Zoey doesn't know up from down, and she studies Bridge's heels, her arms, looking lost and uncertain, always a beat behind.

She needs Seth, I think. He played baseball as a boy, and when Bridge was starting out, he taught her everything he knew—which meant she was always pitching and batting just a little bit wrong for softball. Then, when she was around seven, he went to a couple of her games, saw how hard she worked, and let her start to teach him. Now he knows the mechanics of a good slow pitch and can teach Zoey too. Or he could, if he were home.

My heart sags a bit. Seth has been not home for two years now. I don't mean to say that he moved out or anything. He's present. But he's just not *there*.

He does bedtime once a week so I can catch up on nonurgent emails during the off-hours, when no one can possibly write me back. I do love a good Inbox Zero.

And he gets Linus from after-school and then does dinner on Wednesday nights, so I can catch up with my sister and have happy hour.

He always does movie nights with the kids on a weekend night. Some Saturdays he takes Bridge to the batting cages or takes Linus to laser tag.

But that I can list the things he does for our family on one hand worries me so much that sometimes I find myself imagining a life without him. Just imagining—I am not really going anywhere—but I think he knows this. Is that why he's at his workshop so much? Or is his art really on the cusp of a huge breakthrough? I really can't tell. I used to obsess about it, ask to go to the studio, hoping, I suppose, that something big was coming and that something would allow us all some breathing room. But the last time I was there, I saw scrap metal and unfinished works, vape pens and a new couch long enough to nap on. I didn't see a breakthrough. And when I asked him about *that*, he told me his work was one step forward, two steps back, and no, he wasn't really smoking again, but also, "Wendy, you've always loved me for being an artist, and artists have bad habits. You know that." Do they? Is that true?

When I spoke to my sister about him, she always seemed to imply that he was hurting me on purpose. This is a fundamental misunderstanding that a lot of people seem to have about Seth. If I mention resenting him, that he doesn't earn money for the family or pull his weight around the house, it is because I need to vent. Just vent. This is who I married; this is what I signed up for. If I want to complain about Seth, what I really am saying is, *Marrying a tortured artist is a bad gig. He loves me and his kids, but his work is everything to him.* Work isn't something he does. It's something he *is*.

My baby sister married a lawyer. His biggest client is a major civil rights organization. He works long hours and some weekends and travels as an expert witness. They're working on conceiving now, and I try to tell her what's coming, parenting with a passionate careerist, and she tells me she'll stay home if she has to. She can, I guess. She's an ESL teacher, and I know she loves the kids she teaches, but she seems confident that she can drop in and out of her workforce as her family requires. She's probably right.

And yes, today was fun. Anna Joy is good company, and she napped easily at the exact time Celeste said she would, and for almost two hours. Besides shopping and lunch out, we did basically nothing all day. At 3:00 p.m. I loaded up the van with an assortment of children and drove them here, and that also required zero brain cells. The kids all were pleasant and said thank you and behaved themselves. I gave them all Fritos. Now I'm sitting in the warm sunshine, one of three parents who stayed for practice, daydreaming while Samuel entertains himself with the monkey bars and Anna Joy watches PBS Kids on my phone.

Celeste's life is good.

If it weren't for missing my own kids, I'm not sure I would want my old life back just yet. But I do miss them. More than I could have predicted.

But then, as though I conjured him, Linus comes running down from the parking lot out of absolute nowhere. I rise to my feet and call his name, delighted to see him, wanting some snuggles and quite sure he's wanting some too.

He looks over at me, a confused expression on his face, and then waves awkwardly. "Hi, Samuel's mom," he says.

Right. For all intents and purposes, I'm Samuel's mom. Which means Linus's mom is . . . *where?*

Celeste, in my body, emerges from a car I don't recognize, carrying a reusable shopping bag, and behind her, coming from the driver's side . . .

Is that Davis?

Did she bring my work husband to softball practice?

What. The goddamn. Hell.

"Mommy! Swears!" says Anna Joy. Apparently I said that out loud. "Mommmmmmmmy!" she says, delighted. "Goddamn hell!" she adds.

When Celeste hears this, her face—my face—scrunches up, and she shoots me a look that would wilt a lesser woman. Unwilted, I shoot her the same look back. Why did she bring Davis Pereira to softball practice? Why did she pick up Linus early and drag him here when he would much rather be building with LEGO with his friends at afterschool? Why isn't she at my office, for that matter?

And what did she do with my car?

"Mind if we pull up a blanket?" Celeste asks me, as though I would let her out of my sight right now. She spreads out my large lawn blanket and starts taking bowls and spoons out of a reusable cool bag.

I say nothing.

Davis leans over me. I look at him, confused, wondering what he's doing. But he's only introducing himself. "Hi, I'm Davis Pereira," he tells me. "I work with Wendy."

I swallow. Davis, a sports-psychology coach from the UK who's been a partner at Wendy Charles Consulting since a few years in, has become a good friend, but his friendship has been heretofore relegated to the office. Outside of the professional setting it's much, much easier to notice how masculine his presence is. With his suit jacket off and his shirtsleeves rolled to the elbow, he's the kind of good looking that embarrasses me to look at too carefully. "I'm Celeste Mason. Nice to meet you," I say. I try to think of what else a normal person would say. "That's my daughter over there doing the snap drills."

"Looks like she's picking it up. First day of practice, Wendy tells me."

I nod. Wait until he sees Bridget, I think. Now there's a snap drill with some panache.

He turns away from me but says, "Wow, Wendy."

"Huh?" I ask, but then cough and pretend I have a tickle in my throat. I find this body-swap thing so confusing.

"Your daughter looks exactly like you."

Celeste smiles. "Doesn't she?"

I study Bridge, then Celeste-as-me. It's really rare to get a chance to just observe your own physical self from the outside. Am I as pretty as my daughter is? *Nah.* I mean, I'm old, and I have crow's-feet, and my C-section scar poofs out over the top of every pair of underwear I own.

Still . . . I look at Celeste again. My face, with her brain behind it, seems carefree, less dour and wrinkly than I always imagine it. My torso seems less boxy and more muscular. The creamy silk blouse she's wearing hangs well off the sharp lines of my shoulders. I haven't worn that blouse in years. I should add it back into the rotation.

I look pretty good, even if I am still doing battle with the same ten pounds since I had Linus.

"Ice cream!" says Celeste.

Oh, come on. I just notice I'm looking ok, and *she* tries to ruin it with ice cream. I sneak a look at the container. Full-fat ice cream? The nerve. Those calories will go on my body, and I won't even get to taste them!

"So, *Wendy*," I say. "Before you eat, let me ask you. Aren't you usually at your office at this time?"

"Took an early day," she says lightly. "It's the first day of practice, you know. And the carpooling situation made me a bit nervous."

"You needn't have worried," I say a bit too sharply. "As you can see, Bridget is here."

"She sure is. Looks like an eleven-year-old biking six blocks wasn't such a huge deal after all," she tells me with a little shrug.

"Well, now you know, so you can get back to the office," I urge.

"To be honest, my own daughter's convenience wasn't my only concern," she says pointedly. "In fact, I was a bit worried because earlier I was talking to one of the moms who drives the carpool for other kids, and I asked her some questions to make sure everything was ok, but she never responded."

I narrow my eyes. "She was probably busy driving and running errands. Picking up turkey roasters. Dropping off strange boys at their grandmothers' houses. That sort of thing."

Davis watches the conversation ping-pong with wide eyes.

"Didn't strange boys walk to their grandmothers' like they were supposed to?"

"Strange boys don't take that much room in a van for a two-block drive," I tell her.

"So . . . they shared a seat belt, then?" she asks, her voice rising to a pitch most audible to dogs.

"And everything turned out just fine," I say. "Four softball players, Samuel and Anna Joy, and me, all at the diamond, all alive."

She pauses for a moment as if satisfied, if grudgingly so. Then, with a tilt of her head, she asks, "What's that Anna Joy is doing on this gorgeous sunny day?"

"Watching PBS Kids," I say blithely. "She loves *Martha Speaks*."

"Does she? And here I thought you guys were a no-screens-on-school-days kind of family," says Celeste pointedly.

"Oh, well, a little TV on a Monday isn't a big deal. She's three. It's not like she needs to be doing algebra homework or studying music theory."

Celeste scowls. "And I had heard three was such a great neurological age for absorbing new educational experiences."

"She's absorbing the heck out of that show right now," I reply, just to see if smoke will come out of her ears.

"Is she . . . is she also eating corn chips fried in vegetable oil?"

"Yep. She just loves Fritos," I tell Celeste with an absolutely shit-eating grin on my face.

Celeste exhales loudly. For a second I think she's beaten. "You know what I love?" she tells me, a wicked smile creeping over her. "Huge servings of Oatmeal Cookie Ben and Jerry's."

I frown. I *cannot* underestimate this woman. "That sounds very caloric," I say.

"Oh, sure, but I'm having one of those lucky days where I can eat what I want and never gain a pound," Celeste replies smoothly. "I might eat this entire thing."

Davis laughs nervously, clearly mystified by our undercurrent. "I hope you save me a bite."

"Oh, of course I will. For you, anything," Celeste says, her body angled toward Davis but her eyes looking straight at me. "You really came to my rescue today!"

What is happening? Is she flirting with Davis? She should NOT be flirting with one of my coworkers. Especially not the guy who pays me a little too much attention as it is. And not in front of our kids!

While he looks at her, I make that cut-it gesture, a quick slice across my throat with a flat hand. She just turns to Davis and gives him this killer smile I didn't even know I had in me.

He seems to sit an inch taller, and the way he looks at her . . . I have to wonder if I've been kidding myself about him.

"So, Linus," he says, forcing the boy to look up from his own single-serve container of strawberry swirl for the first time since he arrived. "What do you like to do for fun?"

"I like to play LEGO," he tells Davis sharply. "That's what I *usually* do at after-school with my friends."

Give 'em hell, Linus, I silently cheer.

Davis presses on. "Your mum told me you were a brilliant reader. That is so cool. When I was eight, I was so into one series of books that I read it three times. But it's fantasy, so you may not dig it."

"What's it called?" Linus asks, properly taking the bait.

"Redwall," he says. My ears perk up.

"I loved that series when I was a kid," I say. "Brian Jacques, right?"

"Mm-hmm," says Davis, as though I barely spoke, and turns back to Celeste-in-my-body. "Wendy, did you ever read it?"

I want to wave my arms and say, *I'm over here!* but that wouldn't make any sense to Davis. So I catch Celeste's eye and waggle my brows while nodding.

She looks at me and then says, slowly, "Yes . . . ? But! It was a long time ago? And I can't remember anything about it?"

I shrug. Good enough. Davis and I can have a good chin-wag about Cluny the Scourge and the other classic characters in the series another time.

"Maybe Linus can give you a refresher," says Davis, tapping a few buttons on his phone and then handing it over to my son. "I have it right here on my book app. Linus, do you like scrolling action or page turns?"

"Page turns for sure," says Linus excitedly. "But I know how to use this app either way. What is a novice?" he asks, already scanning the book's description.

"A monk-to-be," Davis says at the exact moment I say, "A future monk."

"Exactly," he adds to me with this cute tilt of his head. I've never seen him do that before. Or maybe I've never noticed? It's probably the latter—I'm not supposed to be noticing cute head tilts or anything else cute about Davis. He's the guy who tells me if I have lettuce in my teeth after lunch or warns me when our assistant is sobbing over a breakup at her desk. I'm the woman who listens to him describe a bad date or his niece's trip to the ER over jasmine tea in the lounge.

"What does *scourge* mean?" Linus asks.

I want to tell him it means someone who causes pain and suffering, like a meddling neighbor who steals your body. But Celeste says, "Let's make a note and look it up later. That way you can do your best to try to figure it out in the context and then compare your guess to reality when we get home."

"Look it up how?" asks Linus. "Are you saying you don't know?"

Celeste just smiles. "We can use the dictionary together. You know, the big book with all the words?"

I am 99 percent sure I don't own a dictionary. Linus looks at Celeste like she's gone mad, but then he looks at the e-book and says, "I think it means someone who is bad or, like, causing trouble. Making things hard on people."

Davis gives him a pat on the back. "Nailed it, kiddo."

I look away, sheepish. Why don't I ever handle his questions that way instead of blurting out the answers and getting on with things?

I am further chastened a few minutes later when Linus tells Celeste he's thirsty, and instead of buying him a Costco juice box from the team cooler for fifty cents like I would do, she says, "I believe you took a water bottle with you to school this morning. You're welcome to refill it at the fountain."

Linus pales. "I left it at school. I think."

And Celeste just smiles at him and says, "That's ok. The water fountain isn't that far away," and resumes talking to Davis.

I am speechless when Linus just gets himself up without a word of complaint and gets a slurp of free water. Or I would be speechless if anyone were talking to me. And I realize, aside from a few words to strangers in the stores and Celeste just now, I haven't spoken to an adult today or typed a sentence or read a paragraph. I turn to the other side of my blanket, where Davi's mom sits, scrolling on her phone. "Hi, Sumeta!" I say. I'm not exactly sure what to say next.

She looks at me and gives me a weak smile. "Hello, Celeste. How are you?"

"Great. Had such a relaxing day."

"That's nice," she says coldly. Then her phone buzzes five times in a row. "Sorry. It's work. I tried to take a half day to see the first practice, but my team comes to me for every little thing anyway—what's the point?"

"Oh yeah, I so know," I say. "And you think, *Why can't they make these decisions for themselves? Did I train them to become this dependent?* But I think maybe this latest generation of grads is actually just striving to be communicative. I truly believe the overreporting behavior that is a trademark of younger staff is fixable with patience."

Sumeta looks at me with increased interest. "I didn't know you worked, Celeste. I thought you were just at home during the day."

I bite my lip, exposed. "I mean . . . that's what Hugh tells me, my husband. He has a lot of . . . summer interns."

She nods. "Oh. Yes, of course, I see. And by the way—I shouldn't have said 'just at home.' I apologize. Staying at home with three kids is probably a ton of work."

I shrug. "I don't know about that. The older kids are in school all day, and this one is so easy. Just give her a phone or a tablet, and you're good. It's really been a bit boring. No one needed me all day today."

This time Sumeta's fake smile doesn't even reach to the corners of her lips. "Well, in that case, I should get you to come to my house sometime. You won't be bored; I promise you that." With that, she turns back to her phone.

I turn back to the field, feeling somehow shamed. I thought Sumeta would be glad to hear the truth. But, of course, now I realize I just sounded smug. She can't possibly know that my days are usually exactly the same as hers. She doesn't know that a boring day was a reprieve. All she sees in Celeste is a Pinterest mom with all the time in the world and none of the cares. Someone who makes the rest of us look incompetent, with her perfect sack lunches, perfect birthday parties, perfect educational craft projects and screen time limits and healthy snacks on compostable dining ware. In other words, she sees Celeste exactly as I do: a personal indictment of my best attempts at motherhood.

I turn back to Bridget and Zoey and Davi all playing together, hustling around the field in safe-slide drills. They're getting filthy and laughing and are liberal with the high fives. In twenty years, will they be sitting here on three separate blankets like their moms, trying just as hard as we are to justify the different choices they've made for their families?

I really hope not.

It's just that I have no idea how to prevent it.

—

CELESTE

My mom was a very patient woman, but there was one thing she did while we were growing up that made everyone in my family run for cover.

So I notice right away when I get home to Wendy's house, unload groceries, start laundry, think up dinner, load up the dishwasher, and somehow manage to do it all at a hundred decibels. "How exactly does one loudly fold laundry?" we always teased my mom after the danger had passed. The trick, I now see, is lots of huffing.

I huff as I look at the morning's cereal bowls near and in the sink. I huff as I take in the kitchen floor, which I mopped yesterday and which now has three gooey spots on it. I huff again as I see that Bridget has taken her softball clothes and thrown them toward but not into the laundry room, then left her gear bag in the middle of the hall and reconnected her butt to the sofa seat she was in all day yesterday.

I huff because Linus left his muddy shoes on when he came inside and is now looking around the kitchen for something to eat even though I am clearly chopping tomatoes for dinner.

I huff because it is almost six, and Wendy's husband is nowhere to be seen.

I huff because after Davis left for his weekly poker game, Bridget, Linus, and I had to get a ride back to the car with Wendy and my kids. The boot was off when we got there, and I thought maybe I would get away with the whole thing without Wendy ever knowing, but there was a new parking ticket on the car windshield. As though I could have moved the car if I'd wanted to. And the whole affair was me trying to tell Wendy to stop feeding my kids ultraprocessed foods and wrecking their frontal lobes with screens and her replying that only an idiot would park in a loading zone and could I maybe keep her homelife separate from what is obviously, at least to me, an office affair just waiting to happen.

And in the back of my van, the kids all shouting at each other, and Linus and Samuel having a slap fight over the top of Anna Joy's car seat, and Bridget telling Zoey she needs new, expensive athletic shoes, and Wendy saying absolutely nothing to the kids about any of this.

So yeah, now I know how my mom learned to take her feelings out on kitchen appliances. In fact, I wonder how many times I can slam this microwave door before somebody asks me if everything is ok.

But on slam number four, I start to chill. I'm being ridiculous, and there's no earthly way two kids under twelve are supposed to pick up on this passive-aggressive tantrum I'm having with myself in here. I've got to use my words on these kids and save the grumping for adults. Like Seth, if he ever shows his face. I bend over, hang loose at the waist, and take some deep breaths.

Then, like a ninja, I stealth into the living room and say very quietly, almost in a whisper, "Bridget, I have a proposition."

You have to be patient when you try to ninja your kids. Nothing happens at first. I'm expecting this, so I just pick up a gossip magazine—why does Wendy's coffee table look like the waiting area in a cheap nail salon?—and read about what's happening with the royals.

After a page of *Stars Are Just Like Us*, Bridget looks up from her phone.

"What?" she says.

I reply in a voice so quiet she can't possibly hear me.

"Why are you whispering?" she asks.

"Come over here," I say. "So you can hear me."

She looks weirded out but comes to sit by me.

"I wonder how you're enjoying school lunch," I ask her when she gets closer.

"Ugh, it's gross; you know that."

"If you could bring anything to school every day, what would it be?" I ask her.

She doesn't hesitate a second. "Sushi. California rolls."

"Hm," I say, then get up and go looking for Linus.

"Wait . . . Mom?" she calls after me. I ignore her. I'm building a long-term conversion campaign, so I can't go explaining everything to my customers. I have to create mystery.

"Gotta go make dinner, babe," I call back to her. I find Linus standing in front of the open freezer, staring.

"We're out of bagels," he tells me.

I want to ask him why he's looking in the freezer for bagels, but then I realize. He's taken out an empty box of something called pizza bagels and is shaking it upside down, ignoring flakes of diced imitation pepperoni that fall to the floor as he does.

Why is an empty box in the freezer? Why isn't he taking any care to keep the floor clean? Why is he trying to feed himself junk at exactly dinnertime? These are all reasonable questions, but I say instead, "Come wash your hands; I need your help in here."

Linus looks at me like I'm insane.

"Go on," I say and pretend to poke him with the end of a wooden spoon. He laughs but moves, washes up, meets me at the kitchen island.

"Eggs," I say. "Remind me—can you crack them with one hand?" He shakes his head.

"Can you crack them?" I follow up.

"I guess?"

"Oh, this is going to be good," I say. I get out a mug—the best container for young ones cracking eggs. "Egg cracking is one of the great human feats. I've read that so far no artificial intelligence has come along that can teach robots the right way to crack an egg for cooking. It's all about using the right amount of pressure and then stopping before you go too far." I demonstrate how to put an egg in the center of my palm, move my thumb to the top, crack on the edge of the mug, and pull my fingers open wide to split the eggshell one handed. The egg comes out, yolk whole, and I move the whole thing to a second bowl. "Now you go."

He bangs the egg too hard and ends up with a handful of shell. "I can't do it," he tells me.

"Yes, you can. We have eight practice eggs. Keep trying until they're gone, and then we can get serious."

"I'm supposed to waste eight eggs?" he asks.

"You're supposed to crack one egg at a time until you've got the hang of it," I say.

"Then what?"

"Then you'll cook the eggs, silly."

"On the stove?"

"It's not quite hot enough to use the sidewalk yet," I reply. "We need music." I put my phone onto my favorite salsa channel. It makes me cook faster. "Here we go. Get crackin'! Get it?"

"Ugh. You're being so dorky, Mom," Linus says happily.

I start salsa-ing around with the tomatoes. Linus starts cracking more eggs. He's making major improvements. Egg four is just right. I throw up my hands in celebration.

"Go show your sister this perfect egg," I tell him, thrusting the mug into his hands. It's covered with egg white and totally gross, but whatever: the floor is a lost cause by now, and no one's eating off it anyway.

Linus runs into the living room and makes Bridget look at his egg.

Like magic, she comes into the kitchen and asks what we're doing. I give myself a mental high five.

I tell her we are making music videos. Then, with a pan in one hand and a fistful of parsley in the other, I repeat a complicated hand-and-arm jive that Zoey taught me last week. Only she would never say the word *jive* out loud.

"Are you TikToking? How do you do that arm part?"

"What's that?" asks Linus.

"Take a video," I tell her. "Just be sure you put an emoji over my face if you want to put it up, or your friends will know it's your mom."

I repeat the dance for Bridget's camera.

"Mom. That's OP."

I can't remember what *OP* stands for, but I know it's good. I turn away from her. "Linus, you are on fire." There are six good eggs in my egg bowl.

Beaming, Linus cracks an egg for his sister with a flourish.

"How do you do that?" she asks him.

Soon she is working over a mug. I only need eight eggs for this recipe, but Bridge is starting on the second dozen. I stifle a laugh and get Linus started on beating the eggs while I take the broken bucatini off the stove and drain it—pasta in a frittata is surprisingly delicious. All three of us are wedged into this tiny work triangle between the stove and the sink and the island, and while we jostle around, I shake my hips to the music, bumping the kids around like pinballs.

Working this way, a fifteen-minute frittata takes forty-five minutes, and no one cares. It turns out Linus has never worked at the stove before, and Bridget has never been allowed to touch the oven. Both of them get a proper lesson on egg doneness and fight over the pepper grinder. When we're done, they look at the frittata topped with green salad like it's an extralarge pizza bagel with double cheese.

"I'm sooooo hungry," Linus says.

"It smells soooooo good," Bridget says.

"I'm eating standing up," I tell them. I'm hungry enough to eat a horse for some reason. Probably the stupid grilled-chicken salad—no cheese, no dressing, no bread—that Wendy's office manager ordered her at lunch. I slice the dish into fourths and slide three onto plates.

We are eating and laughing at the enormous pile of eggshells when Seth finally walks in through the garage door.

"Dad!" Linus announces as his father lingers in the mudroom. "I made dinner!"

"What?" he asks. "That's great, kid." He shoots a glum look at me. "Frozen pizza?" he asks as he comes around the corner.

"What's this called again, Mom?"

"Bucatini frittata," I say. "The kids made it together."

Seth looks at us, surprised. I'm expecting whoops of celebration, or at the very least a request for details. All he says is, "That's great. How's my slugger?"

"Are you going to eat some, Dad?" she asks.

"Ate at the studio, Bridger. More for you. Any guess about field position yet?"

She shrugs. "It's day one. I won't know for a while."

"Third base or nothing, right, kiddo?" he asks.

Bridget looks down at her dinner. Her face is blank.

Something just happened here, something complicated, between Wendy's daughter and her husband. But I'm not sure what it is. It doesn't feel good. So far, very little surrounding Seth has.

Well, looking at him feels good. He is hot—there's no denying it. But that's starting to run really thin, really fast.

I'm going to ask Wendy tonight exactly how this marriage is supposed to work. I add it to the mental list that feels about forty miles long and then text her a quick note.

Same time, same place tonight? I type, and as I do, I feel daunted. I want my body back; I want this to be over. But there's so much to do in this home, so much to fix. And from the way Seth keeps slipping in and out of this house, I'm guessing it's pretty much on me to do it all myself.

CHAPTER 12

CELESTE

At 8:15 p.m. that night, I am drop-dead exhausted. Even though I did next to nothing all day behind Wendy's computer at work, every single second afterward has been jam-packed. I clean up from dinner, mop the floors again, get the kids going on homework, and dash out for a quick grocery run. When I'm home again, I do another load of laundry and fold the cleans, watch three sushi instructionals online, and then make and package up two california rolls for Bridget's lunch. For Linus, I make deli sushi—a.k.a. turkey, spinach, and cheese wrapped in a flour tortilla.

Then I prep a Crock-Pot meal for tomorrow. I pick up the living room, trying not to huff even though three people are sitting there watching TV while I do so. I draw up a chore chart that will be slowly, slowly revealed to these lazy people over the next day or two. I download some software that will automatically change the Wi-Fi password every morning and send the new password only to me so I can get some motivated assistance. I clean out the microwave, which is vile, using my hot-wet-sponge technique. I want to bake the kids homemade pita chips to dip in fresh veggie hummus for an after-school snack, but I run out of time before I've got to tuck them into bed and get out to talk to Wendy.

But when I get out to the trimmed-shrub meeting spot, Wendy is nowhere to be seen.

I text her again. I compose a message saying why we need to meet and how much I will appreciate catching up with her about how things went today. I hit send.

Ten minutes go by.

I send a text that says, **Are you ok?**

Another five minutes.

Then she bursts out of the back door and stomps to the bush. "I cannot believe you canceled my four o'clock!" is what she says to me. Though I thought I was ready to discuss screen time and childhood nutrition calmly, my blood instantly roils. I have swallowed a thousand huffs, and now they are all going to come spilling out, and Wendy Charles, a.k.a. Birchboro Hills' Mother of the Year, had better watch out.

"I cannot believe you fed my kids garbage and gave them TV all day," I reply sharply. "I asked you to do a few easy things. Did you get the Nesco?"

"I got your precious Nesco," she replies. "Did you pay the parking ticket?"

"Don't worry about it," I tell her.

"I can worry about what I want to worry about," she snaps back. "I checked my email tonight. You didn't even answer the easy ones, you didn't take a meeting, and you sure didn't bring my attention to any issues. What exactly DID you do all day?"

"What did *I* do? What did *you* do?"

"I weaned your daughter," she says smugly.

My jaw drops. "Excuse me?"

Wendy gestures to the bags under her—my—eyes. "Look at these dark circles, Celeste. Hugh has a matching pair. You have a preschooler, not an infant! It's time for her to sleep through the night."

"You can't go weaning MY child!" I shout. "She's not ready."

"Says who?" Wendy asks.

"Says HER MOTHER. Who else's vote matters?"

"Well, your husband's, for one. You should have seen the look of relief on his face when I told him I was shutting down the milkshake machine. It's not just about the milk, you know. It's about getting good sleep, having the bed back to yourself, and not having this terrible back pain." She gestures toward the entire left side of her body, which, I've forgotten already, usually hurts whenever I sit, stand, or rotate. "Think how glad Hugh will be when your boobs go back to recreational items after eleven years."

I cross my arms. I know Hugh is ready for us to be done, but he's not the one with the hormones and the extra calorie burn. "Nursing has nothing to do with him," I say. "He doesn't get a say."

"It's his daughter you're talking about, and he does a lot for that girl—and for you. Sheesh, you have any idea how much he does for your family?"

"Do you have any idea how LITTLE your husband does for *your* family?" I ask her.

Her face falls. "Yes. I do, as a matter of fact."

My eyes bug out. "Well, what the heck, Wendy? Why are you putting up with it?"

"Putting up with it? As opposed to what? Lysistrata? That only works when the guy wants to sleep with you in the first place."

Oof. It's hard not to feel a twinge of sympathy when she tells me that. But she doesn't need my sympathy. She needs my skill set. "As opposed to this," I say and present her with the chore chart. It's two circles on top of each other, held together by an office brad. The top one is divided into pie slices by name, the bottom one by chore—dishes, laundry, mopping, and tidying.

"You've got to be kidding me."

"It works! This is how Hugh and I got into the swing of things when we first married!"

"Adults do not give other adults chore charts," she tells me.

"Why not, if he's not doing his fair share around the house?"

"Well, for one thing, he's not my child, and he won't appreciate being treated like one. And for another, a load of laundry is not worth it," she says. "Seth isn't some working stiff who knocks off at five and then mows the lawn. He's a gifted sculptor, and his work takes a lot out of him. If I wanted laundry help, I should have married someone else."

"On this we are agreed," I say. I wave the chore chart. "But this is cheaper than divorce."

The expression on Wendy's face goes dark. "Fine. You just go right on ahead and infantilize my husband. It's not like I needed a happy marriage anyway," she says sarcastically.

"Ok, and you go ahead and wean my baby. I didn't need a happy child anyway," I echo.

"What does weaning have to do with happy?" Wendy asks. "Weaning is about you getting to sleep through the night and get your health back."

"What's wrong with my health?" I ask. "My health is fine."

"Is this fine?" asks Wendy. She rolls up her short sleeve and holds out her arm, then flaps the bottom, the flabby wing under my arm bone, like she's trying to take off from the ground.

"Everybody has those," I say.

"I don't," says Wendy.

Curiously, I lift up my own arm, look underneath. It's just muscle. What a B. "Well, congratulations! You're thinner than me. How's that working out for you?"

"It's nothing to do with thin. I have muscle tone because I get to do healthy exercise. I get to do healthy exercise because I don't have to take a nap every afternoon to get through the day. I don't have to take a nap every day because my kids sleep through the night. Which is because they don't wake me up in the middle of the night knowing they'll get a delicious, fresh decaf latte if they do."

"Breast milk is insanely healthy," I say.

"Anna Joy is insanely healthy already," she replies. "Kids can be healthy without nursing until they go to college." She pauses. "I barely nursed Linus, and he's fine."

"He's fine? It's May, and he's still roughly the color of fresh-fallen snow. Does he ever go outdoors? Or move his body voluntarily?"

"Do you?" she replies bitterly.

"Are you calling me fat?" My voice is shrill and getting louder.

"Absolutely not! I'm calling you tired. And I am living in your tired body right now, and I can tell you confidently, weaning is a good idea."

"Not if I don't want to!" I feel petulant. Attacked.

Wendy softens a bit. "But will you ever want to? Anna Joy is growing up. She's healthy and happy and a wonderful kid."

"She won't eat anything but bananas and toast."

"So she eats bananas and toast. Child Protective Services is not exactly on the doorstep if you get the rest you need and help her move into her next stage of life. Besides, Hugh said something this morning about how you've wanted to do this for the last year."

I start to get choked up. "She's my last baby," I say, anger and nostalgia making for a strange feelings soup.

Her voice loses its edge. "I get it. It's hard. And the hormones are no joke. I was crying in a Chinese restaurant today."

I wrinkle my face at her. "What were you doing in a Chinese restaurant?" I ask. "There's nothing healthy to eat there."

"You're very controlling," Wendy says. "You know that, right?"

"What did you feed my daughter?" I ask her.

"Besides crack cocaine?" she replies.

I snarl at her.

"Tofu veggie dumplings," she replies.

"Soy has been linked to early puberty."

"Anal retentiveness has been linked to early murder," she shoots back.

My anger hits the roof. "There is no one in this world I'd less like to swap bodies with than you," I tell her meanly.

"How do you think I feel? You didn't respond to even the most straightforward emails today, and you missed three meetings. You brought a man from the office to meet my kids and made me the subject of gossip for every softball mom on the team. You got my car ticketed, ate four thousand calories, and ignored my kids in favor of flirting with a guy who is not my husband."

"Oh, really. That's what you think of how I spent the day?" I reply. "Pretty telling about where your values are. If you look at it like any decent mother would, you could also say I gave your kids some healthy food for a change and taught them how to feed themselves, put some energy toward being nice to your business partner, and filled your fridge with easy-to-complete Crock-Pot kits. Oh, and I cleaned the revolting place you call a kitchen. I mean, what even was that on the microwave keypad? I think it was breathing."

"Why are you so obsessed with cleaning?" she asks me.

"Why are your kids so lazy?" I shoot back. "And your husband! Sunday in your house was the most surreal day of my life. It was like there was a gas leak!"

Wendy looks consternated. "Our family likes to relax on Sundays. Bridget works hard in softball and gets straight As in school. When things get too messy, that's when we call a housekeeper."

"Well, our family likes to clean on Sunday. And Zoey works hard at everything she does. Including helping around the house."

Wendy's expression gets as tight as her . . . well, forgive me, but you know what I was about to say. "Believe it or not, Celeste," she says, "I'm not actually raising Bridget to be the perfect housewife someday."

I reel back like I've been slapped. How dare she?

"A little housework won't hurt your kids one bit," I tell her, wanting to sting back. "Nor will a little sunshine, in Linus's case. Look at him. His skin is the same color as . . . well, I don't want to say a Jordan almond. But there's a minty cast."

"Come on," Wendy says. "Linus didn't do anything to you."

I flush—I've gone way too far. "You're right. I can get a little defensive about my kids . . ."

"I've noticed," says Wendy.

"But I'm just trying to say there's a lot worse things that could happen to your kids than becoming stay-at-home parents if that's what they want to be. For example, they could get married to someone who doesn't respect them. They could miss their kids' entire childhoods while they answer emails on their phones."

"You don't know everything about my family," Wendy replies.

"I know you're living in a house full of holes, in more than one sense, and using TV and takeout to try to patch them."

I take a big breath, knowing I have gone Suzanne Sugarbaker on this woman but also knowing I am right. "You look at a few chores like it's some great offense to your entire being—like your entire family is too good to cook or clean or take care of your home. Whereas that's the whole ball game, Wendy! It's a good meal and a loving family that will make for your kids' happiness down the line, no matter what they choose to do for a living. Even if they don't want to be entrepreneurs telling other people how to run themselves into the ground."

She sighs, and I realize not only have I driven this point home, I've driven it into the core of the earth.

Wendy puts her head in her hands, and for a second I wonder if I've made her cry. "Seth is going to hear about Davis."

"Maybe that's not such a bad thing, Wendy. And Davis is a great guy who cares about you for some reason. What is going on with that, anyway?"

"Nothing is going on with that," she replies. "Davis is nice. He's friendly, and he's always got a listening ear for me. He's a great coworker. But that's all it is."

"Well," I say, not believing her at all, "it's not the end of the world if Seth gets the idea that he has some competition for your affection."

"This isn't high school, Celeste. This is my marriage and my workplace."

I shrug. "Fine. I just see why you work such long hours now."

"I work normal hours!"

"I've seen your email inbox, don't forget. I know you normally answer messages practically twenty-four hours a day. And I've seen your house. If you weren't a workaholic, there's no way it would look like that."

"SOME OF US HAVE TO WORK!" she cries, surprising us both.

There's a silence. I feel like a jerk. We are both red in the face, angry, and exhausted. We are both such terrible wrecks. I look at her in my body, my tired, saggy, overextended body that hasn't gotten so much as a five-minute chair massage in years. I look at the weird clothes Wendy has dressed me in—far too formal for the real me. I think of what I changed into the minute I could. Pajama pants.

I start to laugh.

"What?" she asks.

"It's just . . . we are so bad at this thing," I tell her. "You'd think if we were having a mass hysteria or whatever, we'd be better at it."

She shakes her head at me, mystified.

"We're both highly competent people, right?" I say. "I mean, I taught math. You have a PhD. We have five happy kids between us. Safe homes and long marriages and attached garages with two cars each. How is it that we're having such a hard time at this? We are successful women!"

"I'm not having a hard time," she replies. "Your life is easy, Celeste."

"That's because you're doing it totally wrong," I reply simply. "In my real life I cook everything from scratch so that we save money and eat organic. I never let my kids use screens during the week when they could be playing or doing homework. I don't go to Macy's ever, because I might spend money there. I make gazpacho for Go-to-School Night and tutor during second period and drive four hundred children around town on behalf of their own working moms. Don't get me wrong: I love what you've done with my eyebrows there"—I gesture to the pretty shape they've been tweezed into today while I wasn't in my own body—"but I don't usually have time or energy for the troublesome beauty stuff, and no one looks at my face anyway."

"Maybe because they couldn't see it underneath all the eyebrow hair," Wendy says. And it's not mean, the way she says it. It's just funny. Funny like this whole situation is funny—or would be funny if it didn't stink quite so hard.

"Maybe so," I say, with a hint of a smile. "And you're right—I'm being extra cautious about the kids. They're the only ones I have!" I think of Davis. Seth. Bridget. Linus. "I know we said we weren't going to screw up each other's lives—"

"We said fuck up—" Wendy interrupts.

"Whatever. We said that. But we are totally screwing things up."

Wendy smiles weakly. "Yeah, agreed."

We both sigh.

Wendy reaches out awkwardly. She puts her hand on my arm and sort of pats it. "Let's just do things in the way that feels right in the moment, ok? This can't last too much longer."

"Can't it?" I ask.

"It absolutely cannot. The vodka is coming, right?"

I open my phone and show her the confirmation email. Scheduled to arrive Friday by 3:00 p.m.

"Oh, thank god," she gasps.

"You sure do have a lot of faith in this vodka."

She shakes her head. "It has to be the vodka. It has to. I have to have my life back by Saturday morning."

"The huge work event."

"Huge. A keynote address for the Upland South Women's Expo. Hundreds of ticketed guests. Live web broadcast. My business needs this. Badly."

I inwardly gulp. "Hundreds of guests?" I repeat. "Maybe I should prepare a little, just in case."

"There's no 'in case,'" she insists. "We're switching back Friday."

Her lips to God's ears. "Even if you're right, we still have to get through the rest of this week. We have to keep the wheels on, be separated from our families, and fool everyone we come in contact with." I try to keep the panic at bay.

For just a second, Wendy looks panicked too. But then she squares her shoulders and takes a deep breath. "Listen to me, Celeste. We can survive this. We just have to lower our standards a bit. If I get a little backlogged at work and your kids get a little TV time, it's not the end of the world, as long as when this is over everyone is still in one piece."

I mimic her deep breath gratefully and nod. "You're right. That sounds like a good philosophy."

"We'll just stick to the other two rules."

"No sex with anyone," I confirm.

"And no telling the kids," she answers back.

We shake on it.

"I'm sorry about Davis," I say. "I see now why that wasn't cool."

"I'm sorry about the weaning," she replies. "I should have talked it over with you. I just panicked."

"It's ok," I admit. "I do actually think it's time. I'm ready to be done. You're right about that."

"And you're right about Seth," she says. "Maybe competition will bring out the best in him." She doesn't sound convinced.

"I hope so. The kids will be ok?" I ask her, not sure why I want reassurance from her but wanting it all the same.

"What they don't know can't hurt them. They'll be totally—" Her voice stops suddenly when we both startle to a loud thud.

"What was that?" She looks at me, eyes wide. I am looking at her right back.

Just like that, rule number two shatters into pieces.

CHAPTER 13

WENDY

The sound isn't a whisper or the crackle of a twig. It's a thud. The thud of the other shoe dropping. The thud of this surreal situation Wendy and I are in going from a two-woman hallucination to a full-on family psychiatric event.

Or the thud of a small boy falling out of a tree.

"Samuel!" Celeste hollers. We both run to him, lying under a cherry tree, his body a dark puddle over the top of the pretty fallen blossoms. He is still for a moment, and my heart stops beating; a strange time-stopping sensation falls over me—not panic, not fear, just primal readiness as I race to his side.

Before either of us can get all the way over there, he's up, popped to his feet, and pointing at us with a wicked grin on his face. "WHAT?!" he demands. "What can't we know that won't hurt us?"

"Samuel Mason, you scared the ever-loving Pete out of me!" Celeste exclaims. I elbow her hard and cross over to Samuel.

"Young man," I say. "What were you doing up in that tree? Were you spying?"

Samuel shakes off like a wet dog. "Don't you want to know if I'm ok?"

I eye him. "I can see perfectly well you're fine. Now come over here."

"I have to get Linus down first," he says.

Linus? Is in a tree? I shoot Celeste a concerned look, but she ignores it, still stealing glances at her own son to see if all his limbs are attached.

"Linus?" I call.

"Hi, Mrs. Mason," he says. "It wasn't my idea."

"Sellout!" says Samuel.

"It's all right; it's ok," says Celeste. "No one's in trouble if they tell us what they're doing out of bed right now and . . . what they think they overheard." She reaches up a steadying arm, and I watch nervously as Linus slowly slides down the tree to safety.

"We couldn't hear anything because you were whispering, and Mom, you are NOT supposed to keep secrets, remember?" Samuel whines.

I look at Celeste. What the hell kind of crazy rule is that? The entire job of parents is to keep secrets from their kids. Tooth fairies? Wizarding worlds? The accursed elf on the freaking shelf? "Sorry, dear, but I also don't think you're supposed to be spying on adults. Or be out of bed at this hour. Now off you go."

Samuel hangs his head and starts to march back to the house. Linus, being my child and far less obedient, wheels on Celeste. His eyes narrow. "Are you guys talking about me?" he asks.

Celeste makes a face. "No, silly. We're just having a chat."

"What kind of chat?" he asks.

"The kind of chat friends have," Celeste says to him.

Linus looks at her skeptically. "But you guys aren't friends. You said Mrs. Mason makes you as mad as a wet cat."

Celeste's brows rise slightly, and I brace for that temper of hers, but to my relief she shrugs slightly and says, "Oh, she does. But sometimes you find yourself annoyed by the people who are most like you."

"And sometimes," I interject, "you're highly annoyed by people who are very different from you too."

"Either way, you're annoyed, and yet you can still be friends, right, Mrs. Mason?"

I inhale. "Right, Mrs. Charles."

"Ok, now," I say to Linus. "You run along to bed, or you'll be dog tired for tomorrow's coding class after school."

He looks at me. "How did you know about that?" he asks.

"I told her," Celeste quickly says. "Off you go; I'll be inside to tuck you in again in five minutes. I just need to say good night to . . . my *friend* Celeste here."

Linus tucks tail and heads inside, slowly, quietly, in case we say something good, but still, he's doing as he's told. When he finally disappears inside my back door, both Celeste and I let out exhales of epic proportions.

"Oh my lord," she says. "That was close."

"Too close. We've got to be careful, or we're going to have bigger problems than gazpacho and emails."

Celeste nods. "You're right. From now on we've got to try to play nice. No more constant sniping at each other, or the kids really will figure us out."

"And then they'll tell the guys," I continue.

"And then it's straight to the padded cell for us," she finishes.

I nod. "What does it say about me that right now the padded cell isn't sounding so bad?" I ask.

"After a day running around in your shoes," Celeste says, "I hear you one hundred percent."

CHAPTER 14

TRAUMATIC TUESDAY

CELESTE

Everything Wendy owns is just slightly too small. Which is bizarre, because her actual size is pretty much the social ideal. She doesn't have extra weight on her body, and none of her clothes have any stretch. That means that twenty-one days a month, assuming the normal postperiod loss of water weight, this woman is walking around being uncomfortable for no good reason.

It's ridiculous.

Further, when we were texting this morning, she wrote: Please go to Pilates today. Pleeeeeeeease. You have no idea how fast I can gain weight. Or how long it will take me to lose it.

I don't understand this dynamic one bit. Too-tight clothes, punishing workouts, skipping meals—on purpose. If I were Wendy, I'd take a garbage bag and fill it with all the clothes that don't quite fit and take them straight to Goodwill. Actually, if I were her, I would never have bought them in the first place. Think of all the money she could have saved. Money she wouldn't need to work so hard to earn. If time is money, Wendy's closet full of name-brand clothes, overpriced convenience foods, expensive gym, and utterly useless housekeeper are all hours of her life she could have back.

Unable to stop myself, I start sorting through her closet. On the floor is a pile of clothes clearly needing cleaning, alterations, or new buttons. There's a pair of pants with the tags still on that, when I hold them to Wendy's waist, are easily four inches too long. If I were her, I'd have these pants altered in twenty minutes.

I *am* her, come to think of it. I could sew buttons, remove stains, and fix zippers without breaking a sweat. I could pull everything that's too tight, too itchy, or too uncomfortable out of the mess and donate it to women in need of professional clothing, where it could make a real difference. I could give Wendy a proper make-under she could badly use without spending a single penny.

That said, sending her clothes out for resale seems a bit antagonistic. Instead, I spend an early half hour taking the too-small stuff and moving it into the guest room closet. I pack up a big tote of mending and one of those hotel sewing kits from the hall closet to take to work for the times when I have no idea what to do with myself. What's left— stretchier skirts, kindly cut jackets, and light cotton cardigans—suits me just fine and looks a heck of a lot less uptight than what she was wearing before. As I close the closet and take my Wendy-ness in with some pride, I consider: maybe the reason she's such a pain in my rear is because she's slowly suffocating to death in her normal clothes.

Next up, I take in her row of pointy black high heels hanging from shoe compartments on the bathroom door. I could box those all up, too, but when I put them on, I feel my alignment change and my shoulders straighten. I put my hands on my hips like Wonder Woman and remember how I would wear heels on dates with Hugh, back before children. How glamorous they made me feel. How they made Hugh's world—miles away from the hand-to-mouth way I'd grown up—feel less daunting, thanks to the three-inch shift in height.

Ok, fine. While I am Wendy, I will wear heels and put on pretty red lipstick. I will even go to that workout class she wants me to do. It will probably be fun.

I clip-clop over to Seth in bed. Yes, in bed. He has snored through an entire early-morning closet reorg and a high-heel fashion show. On hardwood. "Seth," I say as I shake his shoulder gently. "I'm going in to work early."

"Mmrfph," he replies.

It occurs to me that perhaps he is not going to remember this conversation unless I take drastic measures. "Seth," I repeat as I turn on the bedside lamp. "I'm going to work early. You *will* take the kids to school, right?"

His eyes open fully; he groans and clamps them shut tight again and says, "School?" like an idiot.

"That's right. You need to take your children to school," I say. I have a firm look that's very similar to how I look at my kids, designed to take the place of the words *AND I MEAN IT*. I give him this look.

"Fine. Fine," he says, turning away from the light. "Can you send me a pin on Google Maps?"

"A pin to what?" I ask him.

He sighs, beleaguered. "A pin to where you're supposed to drop the kids. I let them off in the wrong place last time, remember, and you got that passive-aggressive email from the Twerp?"

I wonder which twerp this is, exactly. Probably Ms. Kranz, the school secretary, who enjoys policing the carpool line more than anyone really should. Personally I adore her, because before she took it on as her personal mission in life, the school parking lot was mayhem. But it makes sense that Wendy, who is too busy for rules, thinks she's a twerp.

"I'll send a pin," I promise, though I'm very tempted to not follow through and let him develop competency on his own. After all, if Hugh asked me where to drop the kids for school, I'd take him in for a brain scan. I bet all Wendy's problems would be solved a lot faster if she'd only just raise her expectations and demand some help. *But then,* I grumble uncharitably, *if she asked for help, she couldn't pretend she invented busyness.*

Seth rolls over and settles back into bed. He's definitely going back to sleep. I wonder—briefly—if the kids will get to school today on time, and for a moment I think perhaps I should rethink my plans for today. In the end, I decide it's ok if they're ten minutes late. You see, I really want to get to the office early today.

After all, Wendy has a breakfast meeting with Davis.

—

WENDY

On Tuesday morning, I am still in Celeste's body. I'm not as shocked about this as I was the last two days, but it's safe to say that it's still not the best way to wake up. Furthering my annoyance, my phone is full of text notifications from Celeste about what the day should hold, what lunches should be packed, where I should be when, and with which kids in the car. This doesn't stop me from giving the kids money for school lunch—Taco Tuesday, of course—and spending the beginning of my day playing with Joy. Somehow I have forgotten in just a few years how busy a toddler can be. She's alternating between potty accidents (I forgot you have to remind them if they start dancing) and finding dangerous things despite truly over-the-top childproofing (did she crack the drawer locks?) and just generally taking things you set down for a millisecond and immediately losing them. Through all this she is staying weaned, technically, but still requires a lot of bribes. Thank goodness Celeste gave this her blessing yesterday, or I would feel awful today. In retrospect, perhaps telling another woman what to do with her boobs—even though I may be temporarily attached to them right now—may have been a poor choice.

Similarly, I may be forced to admit that there might be a smidge more to her life than gourmet lunch boxes and afternoon minivan rides. Every time I take a peek in her planner—which, by the way, I desperately want to replace with one of mine; she would love it—I see I've let another ball drop. As I try to field messages from my job that, I have to admit, aren't *all* of the highest import, she's forwarding me emails about envelopes she promised to stuff for a gun-safety town hall and the upcoming school play. I try to tell myself it's all busywork that can wait or just not happen, but then, did I realize she was going into the third-grade classrooms to provide talented-and-gifted challenges every week? At last year's referendum we had to choose between funding third-grade music or third-grade TAG, so without her there'd be absolutely nothing going. That will be Linus's classroom next year. And to help the summer all-sports budget, she's in charge of stitching the entire swim team's initials on their new warm-ups—saving fifteen bucks' personalization fee per order. Zoey isn't even *on* the swim team. Ugh. Celeste. She's just so . . . freaking . . . *helpful*.

And then there's the fact that she's the quintessential housewife, and without her the place is going to pieces. There's an ominous pile of wet towels on the floor of the once-pristine laundry room, and the groceries—Samuel eats more than Linus and Bridget combined—are running down fast. And this morning, as I dodged kisses and a booty pat—the guy is so crazy in love with his wife—Hugh told me sweetly that he couldn't wait for some more of my home cooking soon. He said, "It's better than anything you can buy in a store."

He should just wait and see about that.

Meanwhile, I saw a truly shocking sight this morning—Seth in the carpool lane with my two kids in the back seat. When they got out, they were each carrying lunch bags. Somehow Celeste is beating me at my own life.

But with the things Celeste said to me last night still ringing in my ears, stuffing envelopes becomes something of a contact sport. *Is she really right?* I ask myself as I mangle brochures and envelopes that seem designed not to fit together. Are my kids unhealthy and spoiled? Do they need to learn some new skills if they are going to be able to cope as adults? The idea has taken root. I think back on times I've seen Seth around his mother and shudder at the idea that I might be sending Linus in a similar direction. But at the same time, I'm not sure I know any other way to parent. I'm gone all day every day, sometimes weekends too. I cannot be home with them enough, and when I am home with them, I hate it to be a struggle. I want it to be nothing but happy times. I *want* to give them what they want. I owe it to them.

Right?

Maybe tomorrow, I tell myself, if I'm not myself yet, I will try on a little Celeste impression at her house and see what I think of it. I can be Celeste Lite. *Yes,* I resolve. Tomorrow I'll make almond butter and jelly for the lunch boxes and bake that casserole on the side of the noodle box for dinner if I have time after my Expo prep session. I can even do some laundry. Laundry can be very relaxing, when there's not an eleven-year-old shouting at you about it and a staff meeting in an hour. Or at least, that's how I remember it in my twenties.

But turnabout is fair play. If I'm going to pay any mind to what Celeste said to me, I should also be able to bring a little Wendy to Celeste. For instance, in two nights, she gets to go to a black-tie event with her husband, be shown off to all his colleagues, and enjoy fine dining, live music, and socializing with interesting people who are neither clients *nor* children. It sounds positively fabulous. I am going to go in full Wendy mode. Chic clothes, sparkling conversation, and all the free chardonnay a girl cares to drink. Hugh will get to see what his wife looks like after a shower and a little makeup. For just one night, Celeste can turn all that loving, boundless energy onto the person who's given her—what did she call it?—the whole ball game.

Since I have a window coming up today while Joy is supervised at a children's music class, I call my fitness studio, tell them I'm sending a friend in to use one of my virtual guest passes, and then take myself to the place where all the most invigorating torture happens. I cannot wait to give Celeste's body a little workout, get some blood flowing, and realign her slumping muscles. It's not that Celeste doesn't have energy—in fact, despite the shape she's in, I feel more vital in her body than I do in mine, probably because she feels so much less constant stress—but there is a sag to her that speaks to me of insecurity or inattention. It's a lack of self-care, I decide. She doesn't give herself any time to go out with friends or treat herself to the spa, even though she totally could. Certainly she could do a couple of barre classes a week. If she wants to feel better, she has the materials.

Or so I think, until after one excruciating boot camp session. Celeste is out of shape, and everything I'm used to doing in my body is an experiment in pain tolerance in hers. Her legs shake halfway through squats, her arms can't handle the lightest weights, and her shoulders, while strong from picking up so many kids, seem to float up higher around her ears with each rep. Rebounding, my absolute favorite stress reliever, is off the table—Celeste seems to be more than slightly incontinent.

The worst comes when I hit the floor for core work. On my back, knees bent, I try to engage my abs and lift my head and shoulders off the floor, but nothing happens. I look down at the void that is Celeste's midsection and see it tensed properly, but there's something seriously wrong when I do at last manage to crunch up one time. There's a big bulge right down the middle of my stomach like a kind of hump. While I writhe around on my tailbone trying to get even one decent set of medicine ball crosses in, the active trainer comes over, gently leads my shoulders back to the floor, and says, "Have you been checked for diastasis recti?"

I lie down, panting, and try to think what she's talking about.

"It just looks like maybe your abs aren't coming together correctly when flexed," she adds, and I remember being warned about this while

I was carrying Linus. It's some kind of normal but gruesome tearing of your abdominal muscles during gestation—common, but it doesn't always self-heal. Dear god, I think. Poor Celeste. Her body is totally broken.

"What should I do if I have it?" I ask the trainer, who probably has the same amount of medical training as my mechanic, but still.

"Talk to your doctor and get physical therapy," she says. "And absolutely no core work until you know what's up. I mean, real credit to you wanting to come in here and work, but you just had a baby. This may be a better time to rest and get centered," she says invitingly. I flop on the floor and shake my head in wonderment, knowing there's no use in telling her the baby is three years old. Well, then. Celeste even gets to nap during abs.

CHAPTER 15

CELESTE

Can you develop a crush on someone else's work colleague while you're operating inside that person's body? This is a question that has likely never come up before in the history of the world, and yet here I am pondering it. Davis is so handsome, so tall, so not Seth, but equally—and I feel very guilty saying it—not Hugh.

When Hugh came into my life, that's the day that everything changed for me. We were both taking econ at the U, and there was something about him I loved from the start. I remember my very first thought was that his chest looked so *solid*. His background (dead center of middle class), his dreams, a job with a good paycheck and benefits, his appetites (vast quantities of hearty food and long make-out sessions on his futon with old movies playing in the background): all of it felt at once grounded and exhilarating.

Now I almost laugh to think I could use that word to describe him. Hugh is my everything, my night and day, my love, and yet after twelve years of marriage I've heard most of his jokes and seen most of his moves. He's shared my goals and dreams, brought me solidly into the middle class, stood by me when we lost my mom, been an amazing father to our children, and listened while I've tried to explain the quagmire that is stay-at-home motherhood in Birchboro Hills. And somehow I still have moments when I feel lonely, misunderstood, and overlooked.

This, my mom would have said, is what it means to commit yourself. It doesn't mean you're never lonely or distracted. It means you're lonely or distracted and you give your whole heart anyway. It's great advice, I know. I just am not sure how to follow it.

In every fundamental love relationship, we ask our partners to be both solid as a rock and thrillingly fun at the same time, and it's utterly unreasonable when we get annoyed that they can't do both. That my partner has revealed himself to be dependable and a bit boring is, by my measure, a huge win. The fun ones are useless. My mom always said how much fun my father was.

Take Seth, Wendy's husband. He makes no money, shows no interest, and can't even find the damned carpool lane at the kids' school. His nice looks seem to be fairly moot: when he comes to bed, it's before or after me by a fair bit, and with zero designs, even though Wendy is very attractive by every measure. What good is hotness if it comes with celibacy?

Hugh, the other side of the coin, has never faltered in his attention and has, occasionally, had to be swatted away with a cookbook I'm trying to read. When I'm not in the mood, I'll come to bed in ancient Hanes and a sleep shirt with pit stains, but even then he'll say, "Wow, babe, you can make anything look sexy."

Without question, I have the better deal.

These thoughts leave me wondering: Which sort of man is Davis? He is nice to look at, and his accent is irresistible. He shows interest in the kids and in Wendy as a person. He has a job with a paycheck. He has already successfully navigated the carpool lane.

And he is definitely into Wendy.

"Did you buy out Dunkin' Donuts?" I ask him when I see the spread on our conference-room table this morning.

Wendy's office has a style unlike any workplace I've ever imagined. This is the sort of office one has if one wants to be featured in a glossy magazine, and in fact, there are framed photos of the office taken from local magazines scattered among bright prints and local photography when you first enter the suite. Past the reception desk and the luxe velveteen chaise, there's Davis's office, Wendy's office, a kitchenette, three cubes, and this airy room lined with paned windows and papered in a delicate sage William Morris reproduction. The glass door that leads to it is etched with **THE EXCELLERATOR**, which would make me groan if the room weren't so gosh-darned excell-ent. Based on the long, labeled drawer units by the far wall, this is where the "visioneering" happens, as well as the "initial consult materials" and the "moonshooting" and the "staff meetings." I laugh at the mix of jargon and practicalities and marvel at how damned organized it all is. This is the same woman who basically sprints through her life in a haze of email and to-do lists. Here in the office I see a different Wendy, someone who takes care with detail and presentation. Who strives for perfection and, it certainly seems from the testimonials on the website, hits it frequently.

I want to ask Davis what moonshooting is, exactly, but since I'm supposed to be Wendy, instead I praise the spread of pastries.

"They're from the Italian Labor Society," he tells me. I've seen that place downtown, but as it has no off-street parking, I have never gone and may never go. The bakery is in a converted Workman's Club that now sells fresh European baked goods during the day and red-sauce Italian at night. "The best part about living downtown is being able to walk there before work," he tells me.

"Did I know you live downtown?" I ask, hedging for Wendy.

"Probably not," he admits. "I mean, why would you?"

Why indeed, I think. Certainly not because I was wondering if Wendy had already paid him an intimate visit. "Because I take an interest in my coworkers," I say with a soft smile.

Davis takes a beat. Then he says, "Do you?"

I can't tell if he's flirting or challenging my assertion about Wendy. Flirting seems better, but knowing Wendy, I'd guess she's never asked anyone she works with the slightest thing about their personal life. She probably has a policy about that that is as forced as her policy about open doors. After breakfast I should take a look around her office for a file marked *Policies*. Or perhaps a file titled *Things to say to your coworkers to make them think you care about anything besides work.*

"I had fun meeting your son," says Davis, "speaking of interest in coworkers. He's kind of a paler version of me at that age."

I look at Davis, who is quite fit. Muscular, even. "Really?"

"Yeah. I was a bookworm and nowhere near as wild as my sisters, who couldn't hold still for love nor money. My mom put me in football, and it was . . . well, comical. You should see the match tapes. But I had fun, and it helped me make friends." He tilts his head adorably. "It did not spark a lifelong love for team sports. I'll take a weight room over a pickup game any day of the week."

Well, that explains the biceps, triceps, and all the other -ceps. "I cannot imagine Linus in a weight room," I tell him. "Not that he isn't a great kid." I fish around for a way to describe a kid who is the opposite of every other little boy I've ever met—my son and my little brothers especially. "He's just small and . . . sort of delicate."

"That's because he's eight and he's living in his own imagination," Davis says lightly. "When he starts getting moody and aggro as a teen, you can let me know, and I'll show him how to use a weight bench to get the feels out."

I imagine Davis shirtless on a weight bench and think that perhaps that's something Wendy would enjoy seeing much sooner than Linus's adolescence. "Linus shows zero signs of ever being an adolescent," I tell him. Compared to beefy, rough-and-tumble Samuel, he is still a baby. "Zoey, on the other hand . . ."

Davis looks confused. "Wait, who's Zoey?"

Oh crap. Wrong kid. "Um, Bridget's friend. She's, um, er . . ."

"Girls grow up fast, if my niece is any indication," Davis says into my conspicuous stammering. "Bridget is so awesome, though. She reminds me of my student-athlete clients, even though she's ten years younger. I can't believe what those kids can do on the field."

I frown at the thought of Zoey and Bridget turning into little adults so soon. That's not what I want for these kids. "I'm a bit concerned about how competitive the team is, to be honest."

Davis is taken aback. "Really? I thought . . . you told me that you thought that was the whole point of doing softball. You were worried that kids weren't competitive enough, didn't work hard enough for what they wanted."

"Did I say that?" I ask. *Sheesh, Wendy,* I think. "I guess I'm not worried anymore. Maybe I was being silly, worrying about the competitive drive in a tween."

"Not silly. You should know the value of competition. You didn't get this far in business by lying around."

I think a minute. Though I've been treating Wendy's work almost like a hobby, this is, in fact, a real business. I've never really thought about what must have gone into starting it or why a woman who has everything—at least by comparison—cares so much about coaching other women from the ground up.

"And then there's the fact that your competitive drive opened so many doors for you at her age. I'm thirty-eight years old, and I still have ten thousand dollars in student loans. You paid yours off in, what . . . two years?"

"I did?" I say. "I mean, yes. Well, that's true," I say. But I'm shocked. If it weren't for Hugh's great job, I'd still be paying off the high-interest credit cards I used to buy books and ramen in undergrad. How on earth did she pay off college in two years?

Also, inserts my libido, *Davis is thirty-eight?* Is that too young for me? I mean, *for Wendy?*

"So maybe Bridget just inherited her mom's love of competition," Davis continues.

"Maybe. But maybe she's not . . . you know, balanced enough. She doesn't have to be focused on one thing all the time."

"Sometimes what bothers us most in our own lives is what we project onto other people," Davis says.

I nod. "That makes sense. But . . . my life is fine. I think so, at least," I say. Wendy acts like she invented Doing It All, and she certainly seems proud of herself for it.

Davis frowns. "You've told me yourself you're stressed all the time. You've talked about the constant mom guilt and how everyone else seems to be doing so much more than you for their kids."

I try to compose my shocked expression, but I can think of nothing to say that wouldn't give me away. We sit for a moment in silence.

"You know what I think?" he asks me.

"What?"

"I think these are the strawberry mojitos." He points to a filled doughnut with white frosting.

"Is that a kind of doughnut?" I ask, grateful for the topic change.

"Coconut-rum frosting, strawberry-and-mint crème."

"My goodness."

"I got the cocktail mix," he tells me. "Because I wasn't sure what you'd want. I've never seen you eat a baked good before, to be honest."

I laugh. "I think I can be too hard on myself. I'm working on that," I tell him, picking up one of the two mojitos. "Starting right now. You want the other?"

"Nah, this one over here is a mudslide. That's where I'm putting my energy."

"What are we going to do with all these doughnuts?" I ask him.

He looks at me wickedly. "Eat them all?"

"Maybe not," I say, though would that really be so bad?

"Just kidding," he says. "You know I try to limit sugar." Aha! So this paragon does have a fault. A fault Wendy would be super into. "But the doughnuts will find homes. We've got a full house today. The book-keeper will be in, and you've got that intro session with what's-her-face, and the women's expo is just a few days off, so maybe a little pick-me-up later won't go amiss."

I pretend the thought of speaking to a crowded hall about produc-tivity doesn't make me want to lose my breakfast. "Ah . . . the women's expo." I take a beat, say a little prayer for the vodka's timely arrival. "You'll be there too, right?"

He looks at me funny. "Of course I will. Forty percent of my annual earnings come out of that expo. And your keynote is already sold out in person, down to webinar availability only."

"Sold out?" I ask, growing suddenly quite concerned. What if I actually do have to give this speech? "How long do you think a keynote should be, exactly?"

"Very funny. Like you haven't written and edited it to perfection already. Twice, maybe. I know how it is. You're in the room with me, but your brain is adding high-impact graphics to your PowerPoint."

"Heh-heh, right. So I give the keynote, which I'm totally ready for," I say slowly. "And you . . ."

"I'm giving your intro and doing the seminar on salary negotia-tions. Small beer. You're the one who has to come up with all the new microinsights and generate media attention."

"Right," I say again. I don't know what any of that could possibly mean. So instead I say, "How exactly did we get our job assignments, remind me?"

"You sure you're feeling ok?" he asks me.

"Fine, fine," I say. "Just a bit nervous about the sold-out keynote."

"Just remember what we tell our clients: passion wins. If I was up there speaking, it would be fine; I'm a good speaker. But when it's you talking about what you really care about, women getting ahead despite the thousands of challenges . . . the room just turns on." Davis shakes his head and puts up a finger to signal I should wait before saying anything further. "I think the doors are open." He pokes his head into reception and says, "Yep, Cat's here."

"How did it get to be nine already?"

"Right? I'd better get to it," he tells me. "See you back here at eleven," he says on his way out.

"Eleven?" I ask.

"The in-house planning session for that charitable thing you're all hyped about? The free seminars for women on parole. That is today, right?" he asks, already halfway through the door. He checks his watch. "Yep, that's today. See you then."

"Wait, what?" I say into the empty room.

I stand there slack jawed. I came here to suss out Davis further, but instead I got a crash course in Wendy that doesn't fit with anything I thought I understood. Suddenly I feel like I'm not just in someone else's body—I've become someone I don't even know.

—

WENDY

When I finally try to get up after my workout, everything hurts. Calves, thighs, groin, butt, shoulders, and especially all those tiny little muscles on the backs of places you didn't know you had. I try not to groan aloud as I franken-walk to the changing room and out of the studio and sink into the blissfully comfortable minivan. I sit there at the wheel, poking and prodding at the middle of Celeste's body, where on my real body there is a modest wall of muscle. But on her it's an open space that goes clear to . . . where? Her abdominal cavity? I shiver a little.

Why hasn't she gone to the doctor about this? I text her exactly that question, with a link to the condition from the university hospital's site, and then put on the sweater I brought along today, even though it is not cool outside, to protect my tender underbelly. Thankful for the soothing effect of this minivan's heated seats, I pick up Joy, Samuel, and the girls, take them all to the softball field, and unpack the bag of Goldfish I picked up on the way to keep them all from the brink of starvation. And then, just as I'm about to settle in and put on some *Martha Speaks*, Samuel clears his throat. "Um, Mom?" he says, quietly.

"Yes?" I answer, because something is wrong; any mom can tell that.

"I need you to sign this note," he says, then hands me a piece of paper.

It's a memo from his school, saying that Samuel is getting an in-school suspension tomorrow unless a parent or guardian—that would be me—shows up today, in person, before the school closes at 5:00 p.m., to discuss his behavior.

"What the HELL is this?" I ask him.

"Swears, Mom!" says Anna Joy.

I put my hand up at her. "Oh, I'm swearing. Your brother has been very bad."

I immediately call the school. They won't tell me anything. I have to come in, they say. I tell them I'm responsible for other kids right now, and my daughter is at softball. They say maybe then my partner can go.

"My partner has a job!" I say. "These are working hours!"

"But it says here that you're unemployed."

"Well, that doesn't mean I sit around all day waiting to rush to school on someone else's terms!" I announce.

There's a long pause.

"We have a policy, Mrs. Mason. Unless Samuel can come in and discuss his actions in person, he is receiving an in-school suspension applicable tomorrow at start of day. And the law is clear that you or another guardian has to be present for such a discussion."

I sigh loudly into the phone. What would Celeste do? She would take her kid's side no matter what. All her kids. "You know what?" I say.

"Do your worst, lady. Samuel is a good kid, and I'm proud of him, and I'm committed to being where I am right now. I'm keeping him home tomorrow, and he and I can discuss this ourselves."

Then, still channeling Celeste, I hang up the phone, give it to Anna Joy, and say in no joking terms, "Samuel Mason, what did you do?"

"I called someone a bad word. He was picking on a small kid and driving me nuts, so I said, 'Do you wanna fight me?' And he said he was gonna tell on me, so I said, 'Then you're a pussy.'"

If my hair could just all spontaneously fall out from surprise, it would, right then. "Ex*cuse* me?" I say, but then, since I don't want him to say that word again, I shift to, "In what universe do you think it's ok to start a fight? Or say that word?"

He looks down guiltily, and I can see I've hit home. "Sorry, Mom."

I shrug. "I'm sorry for you, because now you have to learn where that word comes from, understand why it's so offensive when used as an insult, and write *I am not a misogynist* fifty times in cursive."

He looks at me like I've lost my mind, which, ok, is accurate on a semantic front. "I don't know cursive," he says.

"Well, then it's going to take you a really long time."

"Mom?" he asks. "I don't actually know what it means—that word."

"Misogynist?" I ask.

"Yeah, but also the other one. The one that made you so mad."

I sigh. "I'll explain later. For now, can you promise you will never do that again?"

Samuel frowns. "Ummmm . . ."

"Why are you not promising?" I ask him.

"Because I'm not sure it would be true, and then I'd be in trouble for breaking a promise."

I swallow the urge to laugh at this solid reasoning. "You cannot be going around starting fights and calling names, Samuel," I say to him with my straightest face. "There's no acceptable reason."

"But you told me—you said, 'Treat Linus like a friend you just haven't made yet, and he'll come around in time.'"

"I said that?" I ask.

"And I can't let someone pick on my friend, can I?"

The wind goes out of me with those simple words. I look at Samuel, hard, and see in him for the first time a kid with a heart as big as his appetite. How did I miss this? Does Celeste know how lucky she is?

But of course she does. She's the one who made him this way.

"You're going to have to apologize to that kid," I finally say, recovering. "And do the punishment."

He nods.

But then I wrap my arm around him. "Samuel, kid, you know what?"

"What?"

"Linus is pretty lucky to have you as a friend he hasn't made yet."

CHAPTER 16
WILD WEDNESDAY
WENDY

When Hugh walks into the bedroom a half hour before the gala starts and sees what I'm wearing, I am afraid I'll need to get a Taser.

"You are amazing," he tells me. "That dress—when did you get that?"

I look up from my own reflection in the mirror to his. Celeste does look really good. He's right. I got the makeup done while Joy waited patiently in my lap between nap and pickup today. I picked out dresses from Nordstrom and tried them on over yoga pants while Samuel read books to Joy right outside the fitting room after school. I paid for this dress using Celeste's credit card (with her permission—look at me evolving) and am breaking out the shoes from Monday with the pointy toes.

After I pick her up from softball practice, I tell Zoey to go borrow Bridget, mostly because I miss her, and let the two girls do an amazing wrapped bun that puddles Celeste's curls into a pretty pile on top of her head and makes the silver-gray streaks look like all part of her master plan. Zoey is surprisingly excited about this—apparently she's been wanting to wear her own hair in elaborate styles for some time but has been discouraged because she looks too "grown up." I know where Celeste is coming from, for sure, but I also know that Zoey is all about expressing herself through her style, and anyone who gets in the way of that is eventually going to feel like the enemy, no matter how good her intentions.

"Now you're beautiful, Mom," Zoey tells me proudly. And then pauses and says, "I mean, you're always beautiful. Sorry. But it's, like . . . did you get taller?"

"It's about confidence. About throwing your shoulders back and putting on something that makes you feel great and saying, *This is me, world!*"

The two girls look at each other conspiratorially. I take her hand and Bridget's. "You guys doing ok?"

Bridget tilts her head. "You and my mom have been acting really weird lately. Ever since you guys started hanging out, my mom's been, like, cooking and showing us how to do things. And being kind of mean to my dad."

I try to keep a poker face. "Mean how?" I ask her.

"She's just . . . like, she's not here for it right now. You know how you sent Zoey over for drills with him last night? He said he was too busy, but he didn't seem busy, and my mom saw the whole thing and loudly told everyone she was cleaning the oven so everyone had to get out of the house to avoid the fumes and he might as well go help us out. And she said it pretty, like, bossy. I mean, I didn't even know ovens could be cleaned, so this was an unusual thing. I think she's mad at my dad."

"These things can be more complicated than a kid can understand," I start to say. But it sounds ridiculous in my mouth. I'm not the kind of mom who speaks with authority and makes sweeping statements.

Zoey raises an eyebrow. "But, Mom . . . you're being weird too."

"I am?"

"Look at you," she says, gesturing to the mirror. "It's like you've had a whole makeover. And you're suddenly ok with us eating normal-person lunch and leaving the block on our own as long as we're home by seven. Now you're letting me do a braided topknot, and Samuel told me you refused to go in to school to talk to Dr. Randall because you just didn't want to." She pauses for a breath. "And also, you know, you kind of hated Mrs. Charles until, like, three days ago."

"Oh, no. I didn't hate her. Did I?"

Zoey frowns a bit. "I think so? I mean, she's been kind of not nice to you for a while now. Sorry, Bridget."

My darling daughter just shrugs, the traitor.

I frown and tilt my head. "How has she not been nice?" I ask. Though I quickly regret it.

"Well . . ." Zoey looks down at the sink. "The cookie thing, right?"

"What cookie thing?" asks Bridget.

Zoey shrugs. "We moved in a year ago here, because my dad got this promotion, and we were really nervous about moving so far away from home. But your mom never came over with cookies."

"Came over with cookies?"

"You know. It's a thing. Whenever someone moved into our old neighborhood, we made cookies, gluten-free ones in case of allergies, and then we took them over to the new people to say hi."

"Ok," I say cautiously. "To be clear. That's nice and all, but most people do not actually do that. That's kind of specific to . . . our family."

"They don't?" Zoey asks.

"No. I mean, there's nothing wrong with baking people cookies, but it's not a thing you *have* to do to be nice. Most people are way too busy to drop everything and bake whenever a stranger shows up in a moving van. Besides, not everyone wants cookies."

"Sure, but we got plants. And a cheesecake, and that biryani dish that I learned how to make in the Instant Pot. And mostly people here just visited to say hi."

"Exactly," I say. "No gifts necessary."

"But Mrs. Charles never even said hi."

"Well," I prevaricate, "it's a big neighborhood."

"But in the entire time you've been here, no one new has moved in except you guys," points out Bridget. "And our backyards are touching."

"Bridget!" I scold. "You're supposed to be on my—I mean your mom's side."

"I am. Which is why I'm trying to figure out why you used to hate her."

"I never hated her," I say, praying that's at least sort of true. "Especially not over cookies. I understand that people are busy in Birchboro Hills," I tell them. "Do you know what it means to be productive?"

"It means to cough something up," Zoey says.

"What?" I look at her sideways.

"A productive cough is when you're sick, and then you have to go to the doctor because you start coughing snot out of your lungs." She turns to Bridget. "One time, they gave me an x-ray, and it was pneumonia, and my mom asked the doctor if it was because my dad let me swim in an outdoor pool when it was fifty degrees out. And the doctor said no, that wasn't necessarily it, but my mom told my dad if he did that again it would be his lungs on the line, and he said, 'I'd better sleep with one eye open, kids,' and then Samuel told him no one could do that, and Dad said he could, and Samuel tried to stay up all night to prove that he couldn't. And then Samuel got sick too."

Great story. "To be clear," I say, "the word *productive* means producing something, not just coughing things up. You can produce work or products or happy customers, for example. Bridget, your mom knows a lot about productivity, because she is an expert for her job. And she and I are . . . different kinds of productive."

Zoey looks at me. "So, then, you're saying that you can produce a ton of things like kids and meals and cookies and clothes from patterns, and Bridget's mom can't produce as much, because she's spending all day stuck at her office?"

I try not to make a growling sound.

"Zoey," I try. "Not everything someone does or makes is productive. Only doing or making something *useful* is productive."

"Samuel is not useful," she says. "So I guess he doesn't count toward your productivity."

Bridget has a good laugh at this.

"Ok, sure," I say, not entirely certain my point is coming across. "See, Mrs. Charles works and employs people and supports the economy. And she pays taxes on what she earns, and that money goes to everyone's benefit. What she does at work may not look like she's *making* anything, exactly, but she's actually way more productive at work than if she were staying home."

Bridget nods. "My mom kicks butt," she says, and inside, I give myself a mental high five.

Zoey thinks this through herself and then nods. "Ok. Ok, I get it." She turns to Bridget. "It's not that your mom meant to ignore us when we moved in. It's that her cooking is awful, so her cookies would not be useful, and she's a productivity coach, so she can't do things that are not productive, like bake awful cookies."

The two girls nearly hurt themselves laughing. I decide to let them concentrate on my hair.

—

CELESTE

Between two kids who are running back and forth between houses constantly and Wendy's texts, by Wednesday midday I realize that my counterpart has started holding up her end of our bargain. Even better, the birch-sap vodka has shipped and should be here by tomorrow, a full day early. I text her about meeting for a drinks date over Thursday lunch.

She writes back quickly. You're having lunch with Davis and the staff for Cat's baby shower. Dinner.

Right. Do we have a present?

I keep a stack of gift cards to Target in my upper right desk drawer. Six o'clock Thursday?

I can't be away from your kids at night, I type back. What I leave unsaid: *I have no idea if or when your husband will show up.*

Sure you can. They can come over to my house. Your house. Hugh can watch them all.

Well, that is true. Why have I never offered a bit of childcare respite to Wendy before? I've seen how crazed her days are.

Abashed, I spend the day determined to nail Wendy's life, and that means faking my way through two meetings. She's already sent me PDFs of all her training materials and bullet points on what I need to cover today, and let's face it—she tells people how to do more stuff. I can tell people how to do more stuff! Watch less TV, right? Cook on the weekends. Maybe exercise with your kids so you can kill two birds with one stone. I'm all over this productivity stuff. Right?

Cut to me coming home that night with a layer of flop sweat dried on every inch of my body. It turns out that the people I had meetings with today are not exactly new to the concept of getting things done. The first client showed up with a branded planner—made by Wendy, because who knew?—and every single inch of it was filled with meticulous notation. She had already done away with the low-hanging fruit: TV, sleeping. She was on to trying to cram forty-eight hours into every twenty-four. I spent a lot of time making mouth noises and praising what she'd already accomplished.

And then there was the meeting about prospective pro bono work, a home for woman parolees that wants Wendy to coach their clients as they make the adjustment from prison life. Now, how can Wendy go and do cool, meaningful things like that and still be such a pain in my rear? I didn't get into that at the meeting, but I did definitely delegate my fool head off and have all three of Wendy's staff sit in for the session to cover for me.

Then I looked over what felt like a thousand different ink samples to try to figure out which blend of cost and clarity was the way to go for next year's planners, approved layouts that all looked exactly the same to me, and signed off on payroll in a program called QuickBooks, which has neither quickness nor books involved. Then there was bumbling around her scheduling app trying not to mess things up, a Webex conference I accidentally logged into on two devices, and the ensuing chaos of that feedback loop. Oh, and there was the constant in and out of her most junior staff member, a young woman who simply cannot do the simplest task without telling Wendy about it before, during, and after.

The truth is, I'm starting to understand that the work she does is relentless, and I feel sort of ashamed over how quickly I've lost control of her household. Her grays just started coming in—and here I thought I was the only woman our age going gray—and I keep forgetting to shave her legs, since normally I wear jeans every single day, and Seth's toothpaste spit is once again crusting up the bathroom sink. I'm so exhausted after her long days of meetings and work and kid wrangling that dinner is becoming less gourmet and more boxed with each passing evening. If I didn't have Bridget doing her own wash now and Linus picking up after himself, all would truly be lost.

And then there's this keynote speech, and if the vodka doesn't work and I have to give it, it's going to be an absolute disaster. I've seen the research she did for it on her office computer, and it's chock full of extremely daunting advice, like how you should never go to sleep at night without knowing your next seven days are planned and "goal-mapped." You should always be the first one in the household to wake up, because that is when studies show people do their most effective work. Assuming you can stay awake. Multitasking is bad, but also, when you are driving, you should always have a notes app available that you can dictate ideas into. Best to have a similar setup while in the shower. Stay away from distractions like social media, except when thinking outside the box, at which point consider following new people to change your perspective. Also good for changing your perspective: sitting in a new place in your office or home or working out of a coffee shop. But not a coffee shop with distractions, obviously. And try to never eat while you're working. So a silent coffee shop where you're the only one there, at five in the morning, without your phone, and with nothing to eat.

Awesome.

Just as I'm about to go home and probably—let's face it—get a rotisserie chicken on the way, a text comes in from Wendy reminding me that tonight's the night she has a video call with her sister, Ruthie, back in Alabama.

I have time now before the gala, she adds. Come do it at my house. I'll sit in the background and help you out if you get stuck.

I sigh and point her Jeep toward the village. Parking in front of my own house feels surreal, but not as surreal as having the door answered by myself, only much, much prettier.

"You look amazing," I say to Wendy.

She smiles. "Yes, YOU do," she says smugly, doing a quick spin in a beautiful new outfit I've never seen before. "The girls did this bun, and Samuel and Joy helped me pick out the dress."

I gape. It's so bizarre looking at yourself, only not yourself, in your home, talking about your kids and your clothes and your hair as if they don't belong to you. I am hit with a hot blast of longing—I would give anything to be able to step back into my own body right now, this instant, just to give my kids a hug.

"Hey!" Wendy says. "Are you crying? Don't be crying. The vodka is coming. The end is near."

I press my lips together and nod. "It's just that it was a long day today. Your life . . ."

"I know," she says. "Tiring. And just wait till you meet my sister. I'll log on. You take some deep breaths and pour yourself a glass of wine."

I follow Wendy's instructions, reluctantly impressed at how she can keep managing one thing after another, day after day, even in the most trying of circumstances, without losing it entirely. But once I am sitting in front of a Zoom screen, I realize where the excitable genes in the family ended up.

"Oh my stars, Wendy! You're so on time today!" declares a bright blonde with an even more lilting drawl than Wendy's. Ruthie's voice is chipper, and her hair seems to bob when she moves her head, like it's excited too.

"Thanks!" I say, stupidly. "I mean, light day at the office?"

Her eyes bug out. "Liar. I know you're going straight home after this to commune with your inbox. Matter of fact, where are you?"

I look up at Wendy, who is miming something that looks like a clown juggling beach balls. Ignoring that entirely, I say, "I'm at a . . . a friend's house. I'm, uh"—now I watch Wendy gesture like she's putting out a house fire with a garden hose—"watering her plants."

"Now, isn't that nice of you. You drinkin' her wine too?"

I blush. "She offered," I say. "And things have been busy at home."

"Isn't it always? To be honest, I thought maybe you wouldn't show again."

I frown. "For my sister?"

Ruthie rolls her eyes. "I need a drink too!" she says. "I'll get the first round, har har."

She pops off the kitchen barstool she's perched on with the same relentless energy Wendy has, and while she's gone, I pause the camera. "What do I say to your sister?" I ask Wendy.

"You don't have to say anything," Wendy replies. "She talks constantly. Just lean back and let it wash over you."

"Did you turn off your camera? Who are you talking to?" Ruthie asks, bouncing back faster than it would take me to open the fridge, much less pour a glass of wine.

"Nobody. Well, I was texting my, ah . . . friend. Celeste."

"The bee-yotch with lunch boxes?" she asks. Before I can answer *that*, she raises her glass in the air and says, "A toast! But wait. Before you drink yours, look at mine!" She holds up a highball glass that's clear and fizzy. "Guess what I'm drinkin'!"

I peer at it. "Uh . . . gin and tonic?"

"I'm drinking Sprite!" she says in her pretty drawl. "You know what that means!"

I do not at first, but she fills in the blanks. "I'm pregnant!"

You don't need to be this woman's sister to know that a high-pitched squeal and a hug are the correct response to this news. "Congratulations, Ruthie!" I say. "This is so exciting!" I look up at Wendy, and her eyes are wide in happy surprise, and despite everything, I wish I could go over there and give her the biggest hug at the news.

"SO. Exciting," she repeats. "I'm 'bout dead. Ok, I'm dead. I mean, I was starting to worry! And then we made the appointment, like you said, and kapow. Sperm, meet egg." I steal a glance at Wendy, who is shaking her head in amusement. "Dickie is THRILLED. He was really freaked out about all the samples. I said, 'You get to jerk off into a cup, while I have to have needles stabbing me all day and night,' and he said, 'How am I supposed to explain to the partners that my billable hours are down because I'm spanking it in a clinic bathroom?'"

At this point, Wendy is doubled over in mirth, and I'm trying desperately not to let her start me laughing too. But Ruthie is oblivious. "And I said, 'Richard Pickely Kleinbaum the Third, you get in there, and you do what you need to do so we can start our family.' And then that night, I don't know if he was just too worried about his billables or what, but here we are!"

And then, just as I think it's my turn, she starts to cry.

"Eight years!" she says. "That's how much the cousins will be apart in age. How can this even be? What'll we do?"

I know the answer to this one! Zoey and Joy are eight years apart. "Actually, I think it will be wonderful, Ruthie. Linus is going to fall in love with this baby, and Bridget's almost old enough to babysit. You'll be glad for the help." I glance up to Wendy and catch her smiling at the thought.

"You are so right! To be honest, I'm already kind of nervous about how hard it will be. I know the first three months are going to be just all eat, sleep, poop, but then after that . . . I just do not want to have to quit my job."

"Yes, I remember thinking those things," I say.

"Obviously," she replies. "Even if you had wanted to quit your job, there'd be no way, I know. Dickie and I are right on the edge. We can make it without my salary, but I'm just so afraid I won't be able to hack it at home. And then what happens when the kid is older? What becomes of me?"

Oh man. I lock my eyes on my wineglass so I don't have to see Wendy's reaction to all this. If I could answer that question, I'd sleep a whole lot better at night. This is what I worry about all the time. No matter how happy our choices make us right now, the day is coming when I won't have anything between me and the profession I left eleven years ago, except the fact that I never particularly liked it. Hugh says that will be my "season to shine." But this is my time right now. Mothering may well be the only thing I'm good at.

I take a decent sip of my wine. It's as familiar as this kitchen I'm drinking it in—a favorite from the eight-dollar bin at Kroger, and it's an excellent stall technique. And anyway, Ruthie has just gotten a fresh wind.

"I don't suppose Seth's given any more thought to that adjunct art-teaching gig I told you about? I know it's beneath him and all that, but it's only ten hours a week. It's worth another conversation, right?"

"Mmm . . . ," I say, noticing Wendy is getting more fidgety the deeper this conversation goes.

"And anyway, when was the last time he sold something? Dickie said to me yesterday, 'Maybe we should hire Seth to do the childcare,' and I was like, 'Hardy har har,' but then Dickie heard that Seth didn't even apply for the latest commission for the Downtown Initiatives Fund. Not even apply? Wendy, you have to do something about him."

I frown, and for a moment I wonder if I should take the laptop somewhere Wendy can't hear us. But, of course, this conversation is supposed to be *with* Wendy. These words are meant for her ears, as surprising as they may be to mine. "What do you propose?" I ask her, looking up to catch Wendy's eye.

"Leave him?" she says.

My jaw drops. Wendy's eyes dodge mine, and she turns to my fridge, retrieves the wine bottle.

"Ok, ok, sorry. I didn't mean that. I know you love him. I know how talented he is; I really do. But, like, what is talent if you don't do anything with it? It's like having a big dick but not being able to get it up," she says. "And also refusing to take Cialis. Which Seth ALSO does."

Oh no. Oh, that explains so much. I look up at Wendy again, but now she's studiously pouring herself a glass of wine. A generous glass.

"Ruthie," I begin to say, trying to warn her, though of what, I'm not sure.

"Ok, ok. You always get so prickly if I say anything even slightly critical of Seth. I'm your sister. I say it out of love."

I clear my throat, lock eyes with Wendy. "Just keep in mind, it might hurt to know your sister and her husband are discussing your marriage," I tell them both.

Above the laptop screen, Wendy sets down her glass and looks at me as if she's reassessing me. Ruthie, meanwhile, just smiles sadly. "You're so, so right, sis. I will cut it out, yesterday. Besides, I remember when he used to make you so happy. He should get credit, too, because he supported your decision to start this business, and now look at you. The keynote Saturday! You're going to kill it."

I open my mouth to respond, but she says, "Dickie and I were talking about division of labor, right, for when the baby comes. And I know you told me it's all fun and games until there's a crying baby at four a.m. and you can't even wake your husband up, but Dickie said, 'If you can't wake me up, hit me in the face with a baseball bat if you have to.' Isn't that sweet?"

I take another drink of wine. "I guess?"

"And it just made me think about your deal with Seth, right?"

"My deal?" I repeat dumbly. In the background, Wendy is unscrewing the wine bottle again and filling her glass even fuller, even though she's barely taken a sip of what she already poured. Either she really loves this wine, or she really hates this conversation.

"It's just that I have had those baby-crazy hormones now, and I know how badly I want this and how, like, everywhere you go, all you see is new moms and their buggies and their diaper bags, and I totally get why you promised to do all the work of child-rearing to talk Seth into getting pregnant. But after eleven years, I just don't think you have to keep that deal."

I stare at her in shock, forgetting for a moment that Wendy is even in the room. She promised to do everything kid related by herself for the rest of her days? And Seth let her?

"You talk to me about being a good feminist, right?" continues Ruthie. "But then you do everything in your house. You do the kids, the food, the clothes, the money. It's cray!"

Wendy coughs quietly. Her lips are set in an unreadable line, and her eyes seem stony, but I can still imagine what she's feeling right now, and my heart pulls for her.

"He did play softball with the girls the other night," I stammer in shock. Inside, I am reeling. Is this why Wendy is doing everything by herself? To keep an impossible promise?

Ruthie doesn't seem to notice she's made her way into such murky waters. "I know parenting is so complicated these days and that Seth is an artist and this isn't what he signed up for when you guys got married, but Dickie said, and he's totally right, you know, 'What kind of husband expects his wife to keep a promise like that? What kind of man doesn't parent his own kids or wants to see his wife so overworked?'"

In the background, I watch, concerned, as Wendy walks off, wine forgotten, into the living room, where Joy is playing with a stack of board books. Only half out of view, I can see everything as she scoops up my daughter, pulls her in tight, and drops a sad kiss on the top of her head that speaks volumes of her sorrow, her personal pain. I want to follow her, but what could I say to Ruthie? And what could I possibly say to Wendy that would make her feel any better after all this?

"Ok," Ruthie goes on. "That's the last thing I'll say about Seth, I swear."

She looks at me expectantly. I fish around for the right words and end up with, "Thank you." But inside I'm absolutely roiling. Poor, poor Wendy. This explains so much about their relationship and why her expectations are so incredibly low. It doesn't explain how Seth can hold her to this, but then, I'm not sure anything can.

I wrap up the call as quickly as I can. Another excited congratulations, a virtual toast, a shared desire to give her a big hug soon, vague agreements about finding a good date for the shower. As soon as I close the laptop, I go to find Wendy but find all three kids—my beautiful kids—instead. To my great amazement, they are all hanging out together, playing some kind of online Harry Potter trivia game I've never seen before and probably never would have let them touch in the past. Samuel, in his halting way, is reading the clues to Joy, and they all laugh when she incorrectly answers two questions in a row with "Hermione."

After they notice me, I ask after their mother, stuttering only a little on the words, and Joy looks at me hard for a second before telling me in her goofy syntax, "That mommy went up to rest her eyes before the babysitter comes."

For a second I think about going up there. But then I realize, as I drag myself out of my real house, my real life, to go live someone else's,

I don't have the right. I'm not Wendy's friend; I'm not her family. Yet I now know far more than she ever wanted me to know about the inner workings of her life. I finally understand that she made a deal with the devil for the thing so many of us want most in the world. And now that she's paying the price, she's convinced herself there's no going back.

—

WENDY

I am standing in Celeste's master bathroom staring at myself—at herself—in the mirror, feeling more lost than I've ever felt in my life, when I hear footsteps on the hardwood. Hugh peeks in through the open door and cracks the widest smile, a smile so bright I could do my eyeliner by it. He is gazing at me like I hung the moon. "How did I get so lucky, babe?" he asks me. Before I can fully come to, he gets in a peck on the cheek, and I realize there is absolutely no harm in that. There is no harm in letting a tiny incremental bit of the love that Celeste basks in every day filter down onto me.

And I do feel it. I feel that there is nothing I could do in this situation that would change how Hugh feels about me—about Celeste. This is the reason, I am starting to understand. This is what makes Celeste want to be homemaker extraordinaire. The guy isn't a teen dream or an artistic genius. But he is so present with her. He is so available to her. And the same for the kids. All week, as I've bumbled the juggling act around here, I've never had to ask him to do a thing to cover for me. Hugh just does what needs doing, by default. If the kids need care and feeding, he cares for and feeds them. When Celeste needs a night out, one appears.

And, I think guiltily, I've nabbed that night from her and left her with Seth.

The event is being held in a beautiful historic hotel downtown, with original chandeliers dripping from the ceiling, lush red carpet, intricate plasterwork, and finely napped chaises by the entries. The hall is a-mingle with a good-looking crowd. That magic of black-tie clothing, the way everyone stands up straighter and looks a little more timeless, lets me imagine for a moment that I'm in a period drama. Before that stupid video call with Ruthie, Celeste directed me to an enviable jewelry box where she keeps the gifts Hugh picks out each Valentine's Day, and I was able to adorn my look with dangly gold drops that glisten halfway between ear and shoulder and a tennis bracelet that gives me instant confidence among all these swanky donors.

I will need it. Even if Ruthie's call hadn't shaken me up, this gala would. I do a lot of events for my business, but my clientele are not the sort of people who are usually in a position to write huge checks to worthy charities. At least not *before* I work with them. That's where we're going, if we strive hard enough together.

To be fair, until Linus came along, there used to be scads of art-related schmoozing events to go to with Seth. But those were all about the cultural elite, and by their very nature the cultural elite are broke all the time. This doesn't mean they're not a lot of fun, but it does mean I'm a fish out of water tonight. Celeste, I have to imagine, was born for this. And Hugh is a natural host. He introduces me around everywhere. He seems to know every soul in the room and understand their connection to this charity, a fundraiser for the local domestic-abuse-intervention services. With easily two hundred people here and handbags I can mentally price out from my online-window-shopping habit, it's safe to say the event will raise some serious funds.

Hugh is here at the invitation of his counterpart at another company, where they do something even more dull than whatever it is Hugh does—he tells me that when I ask him to clarify *corporate reinsurance*. We're sitting at their table, and Celeste has apparently met two of the women here before. Both of them give me cheek kisses when I arrive, and one of them, a small brown-skinned woman with a pixie cut, pats the chair next to her. I sink in gratefully. The rounds of greetings took

Hugh more than forty-five minutes, and though I think of myself as reasonably attentive and astute, I can only remember maybe two names, and then only because they were Dandelion and Ziggy. My brain hurts. Plus, pointy shoes.

"Great to see you," I say when I sit down, to be on the safe side in case they are already the best of friends.

"You too. That dress! It must be new." Ah yes, they do know each other! Celeste has a friend! *Quelle surprise.*

"Do you love it?" I ask her. "I couldn't decide between three." In the end, I picked this pleated and embroidered cream dress because it looked like it would be the hardest possible thing to make from scratch, and I thought Celeste would see the value in it.

That, and she looks hot.

"I do love it. I was expecting the black one. You love the black one."

"The black one looks like a Hefty bag," I blurt. My compatriot nearly chokes on her drink. When she's recovered, she tries to say something in response but instead just gapes at the air a bit.

"See?" I laugh at her. "You think so too. I took one look at it in my closet yesterday and realized, *Celeste Mason, you can try harder.* Not to surrender overmuch to the patriarchy, but if Hugh is nice enough to drag me along to these events, the least I can do is excavate my waistline."

The woman—Celeste's friend—laughs gaily. "You and the patriarchy, always in heated negotiations."

Is that so? I wonder.

"Am I?" I ask her.

"Well, of course. No matter how many times I tell you staying at home is a worthy choice, you'll never stop being weird about it. I blame that ticky-tacky suburb of yours."

Gulp. "By the way, you look great yourself," I say, desperate for a topic change.

"Thank you. You know I hate these things, but this is as good a cause as can be, and Ziggy is the mother of one of Arvind's classmates.

I'm going to be coming after her in a few weeks for a table at the president's dinner."

I pretend to know what and who she's talking about. "Oh yes, of course," I fumble.

"Speaking of, you getting tired of that public school yet?" she asks me laughingly. "I know you guys can swing tuition now that Hugh's gotten yet another promotion . . . ," she leads.

"We're good," I say. Wow. Celeste rolls with private school people. And sews her own kids' clothes. Go figure. "It's a wonderful school district, you know," I add. It really is. Ticky tacky though our suburb may be, the kids' school is fairly utopian, between its excellent teachers, diverse population, and community focus. That's how we ended up there. Those great schools are Seth's archenemies.

"I know, I know," the woman responds. "But ours is a wonderful school with a forty-five percent Ivy placement."

I try not to look shocked at this. My goodness, that's high. Should I be sending Bridget to a school like that so she can go to Harvard or Yale someday?

Get real, I remind myself. Schools like that are for kids of women like Celeste. Not for us. I go searching around for a fresh topic.

"How is Arvind?" I ask, grabbing hold of the one proper noun she's shared so far.

"Too clever by half. Zoey?"

"Same, but also, she did my hair tonight, so I'd better give her credit where credit is due."

"It's stunning!"

As though she were my own daughter, I fill up with pride. "Thank you. Zoey's got such an amazing flair for style—watch for her on an upcoming series costarring with Tim Gunn."

I am interrupted by the arrival of a stranger at my table. No, it's not a stranger. It's Ziggy.

"There you are, Jaina!" she exclaims. Off they go, kiss kiss. "And it's Celeste, right? Hugh's wife?" she asks me.

"Very good," I congratulate her, grateful for her steel-trap memory—we met for maybe ten seconds earlier. And also, now I know the name of Celeste's tablemate, which will make the remainder of this evening a lot less awkward. "Ziggy? Do I have that right?"

"It's short for Ghislaine," she explains, without explaining. "Such a mouthful. What I wouldn't give for a nice normal name. And do I even look like a Ghislaine?" she asks me. I have to admit she does not, as she is neither a mermaid nor a bottle of perfume.

"I'm thrilled to see you both here," Ziggy goes on. "This time of year everyone is. So. Busy. I don't take any guests for granted, especially not for a more intimate event like this one."

I keep my eyebrows in place.

"Celeste, I'm not sure if you know this—I'm also the development director for the Downtown Initiatives Fund. Our big night is in January every year. The Snow Ball?"

"Of course," I say. I've never been to the Snow Ball—I don't know if you have to be invited or what—but I've certainly heard of it from the photos that run in the local magazines. "How did it go?"

"Oh, let me tell you. I am such a mess leading up to it, but it was huge this year. Huge. The only downside is that now I have to top myself next year. Speaking of which, I don't suppose you're looking for a tentpole for next year's social season?" she asks me with a twinkle.

I think about Celeste and Hugh. If she has a social season, this is the first I'm hearing of it. I wonder if she'd be thrilled to be invited to the Snow Ball or if she'd groan and get out the Hefty bag again. "It's a bit early, but I should connect you to my friend," I tell her. "She runs a productivity-coaching consultancy that might be interested in partici-pating, and her husband is a celebrated sculptor. Seth Charles?"

"Oh, Seth. Of course. Very gifted. Actually, he used to be actively involved in the DIF. Submitted a proposal last year, which of course we'd love to have used, though you might whisper in his ear that his fees are astronomical for a young organization like us." I groan inwardly. "Not that he's not worth every penny, I'm sure." She snaps her fingers. "Why don't you and Hugh buy a table next year and bring the wife along? I could certainly use a new friend who's an expert in productivity, right?" She titters at herself.

"Couldn't we all?" says Jaina. "Every year I think I can't get any busier, and then I do."

"Too right. You pretty much have to be a productivity expert these days to get even a second to yourself," says Ziggy. "And what is it you do, Celeste?"

Jaina gives me a worried look, and when I realize I have to try to answer this question for Celeste, I start to feel worried myself. "I'm a homemaker," I try. That is what Celeste told me when we first met. That must be her wording of choice. It sure beats *life of servitude*.

"A homemaker? That sounds lovely," Ziggy says, barely listening to herself. "Oh, your husband is so lucky to have you at home doing everything. He can just focus on his job, I suppose. You're the woman behind the man."

I cringe a little. Poor Celeste, if this is what everyone says to her when she drops the bomb. What did I say when she first told me? I try to remember. I'm sure it was something about how relaxing her life sounded.

"I tutor at my children's school," I hear myself say, but Ziggy isn't listening, turned toward Jaina now, talking about work. I'm making this announcement to no one but the swirly pats of butter found on every hotel banquet table in the history of mankind. Feeling sheepish and suddenly quite left out, I stand up and scan for Hugh. He's in line for the glass of white wine I asked for ages ago, and I join him.

"Oh, Dale," he says to a tall, striking woman when I approach him. "Let me introduce my gorgeous wife, Celeste." I am embarrassed for both of us by his overt fawning.

"Hi there," says Dale. "Nice to meet you."

"Dale consults for us sometimes," Hugh explains. "Always gives me loads of trouble," he adds with a laugh. "Especially when the bill arrives."

Dale and I shake hands. "And what is it you do?" she asks.

"I . . ." I decide to try different language. "I'm a stay-at-home mom," I say.

"Oh," says Dale. "That's nice." She says nothing further, and before I can do anything to stop it, a heavy silence folds over us. Hugh pats me on the back, reassuring, and as Dale wanders away muttering about crab-stuffed mushrooms, he tells me not to worry about it. "They just don't know what to say," Hugh tells me, and I can tell it's not for the first time. "Everyone is so used to making conversation about their work at these things. It has nothing to do with you."

But as the evening goes on, the interaction repeats, repeats, repeats. I've always wished people could resist asking each other what they do for a living in first meetings, but I understand the need for a short-cut to connection. Now I learn that for Celeste, the question shuts down any hope of connection, and my answer seems to make most people uncomfortable. People respond by saying, "Lucky you, Hugh," as though I'm not there. They say, "Don't you miss working?" One woman even wonders aloud how much money Hugh has to make to make such a lifestyle affordable.

Only one response strikes me as even remotely sensitive.

"I could never stay home with my kids," says a woman close to me in age. "Your job is probably the hardest job in the world."

I color bright pink. It's not, I want to reassure her. Being stressed about my small business twenty-four seven while feeling like a terrible mom is worse. But then I take a moment. Celeste is right: if I were doing her job *well*, I'd be wrecked by now. And without my business forming my identity, who exactly would I be on a night like tonight? I'd be the person no one knows how to talk to.

I'd be Celeste.

CHAPTER 17
THIRSTY THURSDAY
CELESTE

For reasons I don't totally understand, I get such a huge barrage of text messages from Wendy between Wednesday night and Thursday morning that I think for a second she's finally gone the rest of the way round the bend. But then I realize, no, she is still in the bend, exactly where I left her, but something must have come up at the gala that upset her. Maybe the usual stuff about how awkward those events can be, how no one knows quite what to say to me if I don't make it easy on them by joking about watching soaps and eating bonbons all day and then quickly turning the subject back to them.

Whatever the reason, she's being strangely nice, considering what happened the last time I saw her. She's asking how things are going and if I need anything and telling me what a nice house I have and how helpful Zoey is being. And dammit if I'm not softening toward her too. That bomb her sister dropped yesterday has completely shifted how I see her. Sometimes I'm critical of her parenting, but could there have been a more loving act in the world than the sacrifice she made to bring Bridget and Linus into it?

Maybe, I think, I'll tell her that when we meet up tonight to get blitzed on artisanal sangria (with vodka) and switch bodies again. As I've done a hundred times in the last few days, I pull up the tracking number, wondering what time it will arrive today.

Then I set down the phone and have a dark moment.

When I recover, I text Wendy: Vodka delayed till tomorrow. Still want to meet tonight?

Within moments I get back the swearing-face emoji.

A few minutes later she writes: TACO BARN 6pm. Need margaritas.

I have never been in the Taco Barn, an actual barn-shaped restaurant that sits just outside the village. In a long-past life a place like the Taco Barn would have seemed like the best of indulgences. But in my current life, Hugh and I have two date nights a month, with our brilliant sitter filling in, and we always go someplace worth the trouble of paying someone ten dollars an hour to keep our humans alive.

Plus, Hugh loves to try whatever spot has just been reviewed in our alt weekly—his small nod to hipness. Because the Taco Barn has a sign under the neon sombrero logo that reads MARGARITAS AS BIG AS YOUR HEAD, I feel quite sure that fine dining is not the thrust of this place and that the carnitas will not be from heritage pastured pigs.

In fact, I find as I slide into a vinyl booth right at six, ground beef and "Barn Blend" cheese are your only choices for all the traditional Tex-Mex fare, and then for a two-dollar upcharge you can have shrimp "diablo," and there's a little asterisk that indicates that diablo items may be too spicy for milder palates. Around our table are many, many mild-looking palates, most of whom are under the age of ten or over the age of seventy. The kids are squirmy and the seniors tipsy. This is why I cook all our kids' meals at home.

But Wendy, despite being in my body, looks utterly at home when she slides into a booth here, and she immediately waves over a server and orders a house "marg, rocks, no salt." I get the same, because when in the Barn, do as the animals do.

"You're late," I blurt.

She just shakes her head at me. "I thought you had a stick up your butt before this whole experiment," she says in reply. "Now I think you have Big Ben up your butt, chiming on the hour."

"Are you kidding me?" I ask her. "You're the retentive one. Normally I have the nice, pleasant life you're living right now. Because of you, now I'm the one racing around like a chicken with her head cut off."

"Are *you* kidding *me*?" she echoes. "You showed me your planner, you know. If I were following it, I would have made six nap pads for next year's 4K classroom, sold cold pureed tomatoes and garlic for a dollar per half cup, and baked fifty cupcakes for a classroom event that requires zero freaking cupcakes. Talk about beheaded chickens."

"Oh no. I forgot about the cupcakes!" I say, whipping my hand over my face. "Wait, you didn't do the gazpacho?"

"I didn't do the gazpacho," she says shamelessly. "No one likes gazpacho."

"I earn at least thirty dollars with that fundraiser every week!" I argue.

"I will give you thirty dollars not to make me swallow a Dixie cup of cold soup," she replies.

I inhale sharply. "A lot of parents love that soup."

"Maybe so, but the kids hate it, and that's who they try to feed it to. Until you can learn to make something the whole family enjoys, I'm sparing the citizens. Have you ever considered a can of Campbell's?"

"You are infuriating! My gazpacho is healthy and organic. It's great for the kids."

"Not if they don't eat it."

I level her a glare. "If a kid is hungry enough, they'll eat anything."

"For a buck fifty, a kid can get four chicken nuggets at McDonald's."

"For a buck fifty, a kid can make a mayonnaise sandwich and keep the other dollar forty," I say before I realize how much about me this gives away.

Thankfully, just then our table is charged with drinks, chips, and extra-spicy salsa, which Wendy asks for without consulting me. I am delighted when she takes a bite, finds my taste buds unequal to the challenge, and starts wheezing and guzzling water to put out the fire. Curious if the transverse applies, I take a bite.

Ooooohhhhh, it's heavenly. It's a lovely, fruity blend of tomatillos and chilies, and instead of tasting nothing but painful heat, I get notes of smoke, roastiness, and bright-green flavor, which, yes, is a color, too, but that's really the perfect description. Green and bright and so good. "Wow," I say. "That's amazing! That's what salsa is supposed to taste like?"

"Ugh. God," she replies. "My mouth is on fire. Argh! Why did we even come here if I can't eat the salsa?"

"I was going to ask you the same thing. But that was before I knew about this salsa."

"I come here all the time with the kids. They eat free on Tuesday. On Fridays, they have a special deal where for every ten hours your kid reads, you get a free drink and they get a scoop of ice cream. It's genius, because think about it—who really makes those monthly reading charts happen? The moms, that's who. Don't we deserve a bribe for it too? Plus, they give out game tablets at the tables with kids so you don't even have to deal with the monsters; you can just drink in peace."

I gape at her. I don't even know where to start with that little soliloquy.

"Right, right. Judge me. But that's how I found out about the salsa. It's out of this world; admit it."

I look down and realize I was just about to eat it with a spoon. "Ok, it's amazing. But only with *your* taste buds."

"Yeah," Wendy says, napkin to her eyes. "Did you grow up eating nothing but oatmeal? I feel like I just made out with a ghost pepper."

"Oatmeal would have been an improvement," I say, and seeing her face, I add, "We didn't have a lot when I was growing up."

"I mean, presumably you weren't too poor for Taco Bell," she says. "Is there such a thing as that poor?"

I look at her hard.

She colors even redder than the salsa. "I'm an idiot. Sorry. I . . . it was a stupid thing to say. I had no idea."

I smile weakly. How can I blame anyone around here for not relating to the feeling of being hungry? Their monthly mortgage payments would have bought me and my siblings a year's worth of groceries. "It's ok," I say. "The hot salsa is probably punishment enough."

"The heat was awful," she says. "And then there's the taste of foot in my mouth. I'll be needing my second margarita soon."

"Don't get too trashed," I tell her. "Even when we're sober, it's hard enough to play nice with each other."

"But that's the thing," she says to me, around gulps of her drink. "That's *exactly* what we're doing wrong."

"Dealing with each other?" I ask.

"Well . . . ok, yes. That isn't what I was going to say, but sure," she says, shaking her head at me. "When we switch back, I have no doubt we'll probably never speak again."

For some reason, the comment hurts. I take a glug of my margarita. And another.

"That's right—feel the dark side," she tells me. "Have a stiff drink in the Taco Barn. See how it feels to be a human person."

"Why can't you just make the cupcakes?" I blurt out. "They are so easy compared to last year's cupcakes. Those had to be topped with volcanos that really erupted."

"Zoey says you were supposed to make fifty cupcakes because there are fifty entries to the school science fair, and everyone who loses gets a cupcake. Is that right?"

I nod. "There can only be three real awards. That's a lot of disappointed little scientists."

Wendy snorts. "I cannot think of any less necessary cupcakes in the history of cupcakes. And that includes the time when there were three cupcake trucks parked next to each other downtown fighting for business."

"What about all the kids who don't win?" I ask her.

"They get the joy of doing science."

I shake my head. "They also get cupcakes."

"Not this year," Wendy tells me.

"Wendy, please. I am going to have to make them myself if you don't, and I'm going to be up all night tomorrow baking." I narrow my eyes. "When exactly will we have time to switch bodies if I'm busy frosting fifty little DNA helices until four in the morning?"

She lets her head roll back and stares at the ceiling. This is exactly what my tween does when I'm being "unreasonable," and I hate it.

"Ok, Celeste, imagine this. Imagine a world where instead of you creating an extra thing to do for the science fair, you go home and read an inspiring memoir."

"Oh, that's rich. I've searched your house and found only four books outside the self-improvement realm, and none of the spines are cracked," I respond.

Wendy draws her phone like a Wild West sheriff in a gunfight. "E-books," she says, showing me her digital library. It's enormous. "Read 'em and weep. Literally, because I mostly read historical fiction set during World War Two."

I stifle a smile, refusing to acknowledge that she almost made me laugh. "Well, fine. Let's say I don't make one little batch of fifty cupcakes, and instead I read a few chapters of"—I zoom in on Wendy's most recently read title—"a novel about a French Resistance fighter who saves a brie factory from the Nazis. The end result? I stress eat a wheel of brie, and forty-seven kids leave the science fair without a, ahem, sweet taste in their mouth." I salute my little pun internally. "In that group of children is one little girl who has the potential to cure cancer, but in that moment of losing at the science fair and being sent home with nothing, she decides to major in art history."

"You're telling me the kid who can cure cancer is so easily defeated that she gives up due to the lack of a consolation prize?" she asks me, amused. "I sure hope she gets cancer curing right on the first try! Also, why wouldn't this hypothetical genius have won the Birchboro Hills Elementary School science fair, exactly? What kind of fair are you imagining? Is it full of former Nobel winners?"

I cross my arms. "It's just nice to hand out cupcakes," I say.

"It's nice to have meaning in your life. Baking consolation prizes isn't meaning."

"Is being mean *your* meaning?"

Wendy puts a finger up and then takes a long, long drink of margarita. "Celeste, for real, I have been you for almost a week now, and no matter how much I now appreciate the intricacies of your life, I still do not totally understand your choices. If I comprehend correctly, you somehow dedicate your entire life to the comfort of three people, two of whom do not even have fully formed frontal lobes. Additionally, the moment you get free time, you spend it doing things for complete strangers' kids. Things that largely go unnoticed and unappreciated, like science fair cupcakes and unpaid Ubering. Yesterday night I went to that big event with Hugh, and everyone was dressed up and on their absolute best behavior, and I—well, you—looked straight-up stunning. And still, literally no one wanted to talk to me—you—except Jaina, and I suspect only her because you and Hugh bought a table at her private school fundraiser. You don't even have kids in private school! How can you possibly tolerate that?"

I shrug. "It's not as bad as all that," I say.

Wendy scoffs. "The minute someone asked me what I did for a living, the conversation was dead. No one knows what to say to you. Your life path is the conversational equivalent of asking about a bad rash. Is that how you really want to roll?"

It's like she whipped a BB gun out of my nice big handbag and shot me in the forehead. I'm not dead, but I'm furious. "You," I tell her, putting my margarita glass down hard, "are awful. Just awful. And I was just starting to think you might be human."

"Hey, I was being sympathetic," she says.

"You were being rude. Do you know how much I've done for you since we switched bodies?" I ask her. "For your kids?"

"Let me play devil's advocate: What exactly have you done that a housekeeper couldn't?"

If I were a cartoon, smoke would start coming out of my ears. "You want to know what I've done? Taught your kids to cook, for one thing. Taught them to get off the stinking couch. You have an eleven-year-old who didn't know where the washing machine even was and an eight-year-old who can't make toast. He told me he had literally never used a toaster before."

Wendy looks sheepish but shakes her head. "You can't understand. When I get home from work, I haven't seen my kids in hours," she tells me, as if I haven't been her for a week. "I miss them; I care about them; I think about them all day. If Linus wants toast, I'm happy to make him toast."

"But not dinner," I say sharply. "As far as I can tell, your kids are surviving on pizza bagels alone."

She rubs the back of her neck. "Celeste, does it matter what they eat on any single day, as long as they are fed, safe, and healthy? Honestly. Be real."

I think of this question. The old me would have said no. Fed kids who are loved . . . of course that's good enough.

But the me of this moment isn't so sure. "They need to see you modeling good food choices. They need to eat organic so they don't get Red Number Three disease, and avoid excess carbs so they don't get bullied, and eat the rainbow every day even though there are really only so many blue foods. And they need to eat local. Being the family food gatekeeper is one of the last acts of useful environmental activism," I say.

"I think we read the same mommy blogs," says Wendy. "I've heard all that before. But unless you have nothing to do all day but cook, it just translates to 'You have to be perfect all the time, in every way, and do nothing that doesn't better the childhood of your precious offspring, or you're a parenting failure.'"

I frown. "Is it women staying at home with their kids that you have a problem with," I ask Wendy, "or just ME staying home with my kids?"

"It's how you *do* it, Celeste," she says, and my name comes out with such a weight of compassion that I find myself leaning forward to listen further, or maybe to get ready to slap her, if the need arises. "We both know there's nothing fundamentally wrong with choosing not to work outside the home. If you can't earn enough during the day to afford childcare, then it can be absolutely necessary. Conversely, if you just don't want to work and can afford not to, fine, be my guest, Mrs. Moneybags. But what you do, the designer baked goods and the perfectly planned birthday parties, the vegan organic school snacks and the sanctimonious health tips—that would offend me whether you did it during the day or after working hours. You are basically creating busywork to make the rest of us feel bad. Most women need to work, not just for money and health insurance but because we want to have a life outside of our kids."

"Oh, so now I'm the one making YOU feel bad here."

"Actually," she tells me, "you're the one making both of us feel bad, because all of this is at the cost of your own happiness. If sewing kids' clothes and cooking three-course weeknight dinners and slicing SunButter sandwiches into the shape of 3D endangered species lights you up and fills up your heart, then fine. Tell me that's the case, and I'll lay off. But if you're just competitive mom-ing on Facebook to try to make others feel they're losing at something that's unwinnable . . ."

I say nothing. Do those things light me up? The lunch boxes, the craft projects, the meal planning? I don't know. Maybe, kinda, sorta?

I've wanted my own kids since I was the boys' age. That's when I started taking care of my own siblings while my mom was at work, and that's when I felt most of use. But even before then, I had a dolly with me everywhere. I changed her diaper, cooed to her, burped her after her "bottles" of water that dribbled down her plastic chin.

But those days are coming to an end. And after that . . . I don't know what will become of me.

"I rest my case," she says into my silence.

"Can I ask you a question, Wendy?" I finally say. "What about you? Does your lifestyle light you up? After work, which I now understand is a consultancy that tells other insanely busy people how to take on yet more in their lives, you come home to two sweet but pretty demanding kids. You shove subpar food into them, basically do their homework on their behalf, and then let them watch TV while you clean up their messes, cover for your husband, and torture yourself on a basement spin bike."

Wendy makes sort of a dismissive noise. "You just described the second shift," she says to me. "You're finally understanding how ninety-nine percent of the female population lives."

"Well, let me tell you, the second shift first-degree sucks."

Wendy actually laughs.

"Pardon my French," I add, feeling the margarita acutely. But still I go on. "Your life would be so, so much easier if you taught your clients to stop bugging you after hours, made your kids do some chores, and asked your husband to, you know, participate in the family."

She lets out a joyless laugh. "In the week you've been there, have *you* had any luck with Seth?" she asks.

I shake my head. "But I've had some luck with Davis," I reply too quickly.

Wendy nearly snorts her margarita. "Don't even start with all that. Davis is a work friend," she tells me. "I'm not having an affair."

"I know. Seriously—I can tell. But he's nuts about you. You may be leading him on."

"I'm not leading him on!" she says. "I'm trying so, so hard not to lead him on," she amends. "He's an amazing guy. He deserves the best."

"He seems to think you're the best."

"Well, what does he know?" she jokes.

I shrug. "It seems like he knows you pretty darn well. He knows you're a workaholic with a secret soft spot for the underdog," I say, thinking of that meeting we took with the director of the halfway house. "He knows all about what's important to you and what's important to your kids. Unlike me, I think he even knows what makes you tick."

A blush of recognition crosses her face. "You're right, Celeste. Davis is amazing. He makes me smile, cares—there's no question I could love him if I wasn't married. But I am. And yes, the situation isn't perfect, but if it's what it took for me to get my kids . . ." She shrugs. The sentence doesn't need to be finished, not for the sake of any mother I've ever met.

Maybe that's what makes me soften at last. That realization that no matter how different Wendy and I may be, we are in complete alignment on this most vital thing. There is nothing, literally nothing, we wouldn't do for our kids, and it starts before they are even born. Whether that means the way my mom worked eighteen hours a day so that we could eat, Wendy selling herself out for a baby, or me setting aside everything else to make sure my children get the perfect childhood I always dreamed of. How much we all give up, we mothers. How much we willingly hand over. Our bodies. Sleep. Sometimes safety. Often passion. And, of course, our dreams. We'll give up our very dreams, if that's what it takes to see to theirs.

To my surprise, Wendy reaches over the table and puts a napkin in my outstretched hand. "Don't cry, Celeste. Don't cry for me, at least."

"I'm not crying," I tell her. But I do dab my eyes with the napkin and give her a meek little smile. "It's the margarita. Is that server *ever* coming back to take our order?"

"Oh. No." Wendy gives a little laugh. "I sit in her section whenever I come here, and I never order anything but chips and drinks," she tells me. "We can't eat dinner *and* drink this many calories. Not if I'm going to get into my normal clothes when I get my body back."

"Who cares if you do, Wendy?" I gesture to the bias-cut skirt and flowing blouse I chose this morning. "These clothes are nice, and you can breathe in them. And besides," I say as I wave the server over, not just for some darn tacos on the double but also for another drink, "Davis likes these clothes." My eyebrows arch high to the sky.

She sighs. "Davis is a good man," she says.

"He is. And he would like you wearing anything. Or better still, wearing nothing."

———

WENDY

The thought of Davis follows me home that night, haunts me as I politely tell Hugh I have a raging yeast infection and need space, get ready for bed in the closed bathroom, and then slip under the covers ten minutes later, after he is already fast asleep. I wish I could take time, while I am being Celeste, to talk to Hugh, to understand him better, but I am so afraid if I do, after all Celeste and I have shared these few days, I'll learn that he's not a unicorn, that a helpful partner isn't too much to hope for. And if I start to think that, what hope is there left for my marriage?

I think back on Celeste's words. Could she be right that despite what I promised Seth twelve years ago, when the yearning for a baby had become so strong and so blinding I would have given up a kidney in the negotiations, I deserve better now?

I'm not brave enough to ask. Not again. Asking could be the thing that finally kills our unspoken agreement that we will let each other be, and in exchange we will be able to hold on to what we have and maybe, someday, make it better. I am tough; I can do almost anything I set my mind to, but I don't think I can survive upsetting that delicate balance.

It's because I once tried that awful conversation years ago that Davis and I became friends. Seth was in a tenuous equilibrium with his art, where it earned almost exactly as much as it cost us, and my business was growing faster than I could keep up with it. And then I got pregnant with Linus. Neither Seth nor I had really discussed the terms of a second baby in the way we had with Bridget, but I seem to remember we were both there for it in the actual moment, no cajoling or promising necessary. Seth was besotted with Bridge; he was possessive of her when we went out as a family, loved her rough-and-tumble spirit, and let her into his studio from time to time to play with little whatnots he made expressly for her. Now on to baby number two, Seth responded in all the right ways. But his own joy was pretty muted by six months in, as it became clear that I was getting too tired to run the house and the childcare single-handedly. I was behind on laundry, behind on everything, and one Saturday I fell asleep while I was on the floor right in the middle of a game of pretend with Bridget. When I woke up, it was because she was screaming bloody murder. She had half eaten a Tootsie Roll while I was out cold, lost it in her frizzy baby curls, then gotten it hopelessly stuck in a wad of hair and gone to find Daddy to get it out. I ran toward them, screaming in a panic, and watched as Seth cut the disgusting wad of candy out of her hair with scissors while Bridget sobbed. The look he gave me was chilling. Not angry, not compassionate. Just annoyed. It was the look you'd give an employee who'd screwed up her job royally.

After that, things had their ups and downs until Linus was just about to start 4K, and the wheels came off. At the encouragement of my naive sister, I waited until Seth'd had a good day in the studio, poured him a glass of wine and myself a half glass, and nestled up to him on the couch. He told me he wanted to rent a new studio with an outdoor courtyard so he could add some smelting back into his process. He knew of just the place, an old factory turned makers' space in the city, short walks from the art museum and three important galleries, so the schmoozing would be built right in. Thinking the cost of studio rent was a fair trade for getting a little help at home, I quickly said yes and then introduced my own ask.

"I'm having trouble keeping up with everything right now." My mouth spilled over with reasons. "It's the work," I told him. "I never thought the company would grow so fast or be so popular. I don't want to miss out on the career opportunities, but by the time I pick up Bridget from school and Linus from day care, get them home, feed them, bathe them, and get them tucked into bed, I can barely keep my own eyes open. If you could just take the lead with the kids on the weekends, my life could be a lot more doable."

"Oof, babe," he told me. "You must be wiped."

"I am," I said honestly. "I don't remember being so tired with Bridget at this age. I guess because I only had one kid, and Linus isn't exactly Mr. Independent."

Seth put his hand on my knee. "Wendy, weekends are kind of huge for me," he told me. "When I'm at work, it's not all emails and meetings and, like"—he waved his hands in the air like he was conjuring a magic spell—"PowerPoint presentations to clients. I can't put in an earpiece and just sit there on my computer all day. I need hours and hours of extreme focus." He shook his head. "Focus I can't get in the 'bonus room' anymore," he said. "I want to help, but if I don't get some sculpting in on the weekends, I'll be working on my next show until I'm eighty."

My face fell. "You've been working on this show for so long now anyway," I tried.

"I don't need that rubbed in," he snipped. "Look, I know you're tired. It's a lot, for both of us. I can definitely babysit at least one night during the week, if that will help. You could use that night to stay at the office and work as late as you like."

"Seth," I said, slowly, not sure what to try next, whether to start with the word *babysit* or just try to let that go. "Bridget's only awake for an hour and a half after I get home from work as it is. I don't want to come home after she's asleep. I won't get to see her that day at all."

"You can see her in the morning," he said, and the hormones must have shifted just enough, because that harmless comment was the last straw.

"I know I can see her in the morning," I hissed. "I am the only one who sees her in the morning, because you never, ever get out of bed before we are both gone for the day. One would think you'd want some extra quality time with her on the weekends, that being the case."

Seth looked stung. "Are you saying I'm not a good father?"

"I didn't say that," I replied. But I was thinking, *You're certainly not a good husband.*

"Getting up at six in the morning has nothing to do with being a good parent," he told me firmly. "I'm not a morning person, and Bridget probably wouldn't get up at that hour, either, if she didn't have to so you can leave her at day care all day."

Day care. My Achilles tendon of guilt. "Do you have a problem with us needing childcare?" I asked sharply. "Because you could certainly stay home with her."

"I have no problem with day care. I have a problem with how much you constantly change the rules of our relationship," he replied smoothly. "You know who you married, and yet every time I want to sit down with a glass of wine, I get to hear about how I'm a terrible father and a neglectful husband."

The ground under me shifted. "I never said either of those things."

"Wendy, do you have any idea how *trapped* these conversations make me feel? Every time you start one, I want to drop everything and just run for my life. And you did trap me; you know that, right? You loved me as the artist I was, and then you slowly, slowly started to change me, to take away this freedom or that. You wanted a baby, you got a baby. You wanted good schools, we moved to this suburban hellscape. Then baby number two, your own business, a bathroom remodel, check, check, check. Wendy wants, Wendy gets. Now you want me trying to create meaningful, significant art in a room the Realtor suggested we use for 'teen gatherings.'"

"I didn't argue with the new studio!" I said.

"Your face told me everything I need to know. You think I'm not worth the rent. You think I'll never sell anything again. Do I tell you my doubts about your passions? Do I say anything about how bourgeois and just . . . small . . . the very concept of a productivity consultancy is?" I tried not to let my face show how much he was hurting me, tried to keep my composure. "When we met, you were studying philosophy."

"Psychology," I corrected. When, I started to wonder, had this man I loved started to care so little for me? And what on earth was I supposed to do about it now that we were in so deep together?

"You were pursuing a life of the mind," he said. "Now you're selling branded planners?"

It hurt. It was too much. "You said they were beautiful planners."

"They are beautiful planners, sure. And you've never been sexier than after two C-sections. And I love eating frozen meals every day and cutting chewing gum out of my daughter's hair, and no, this lifestyle doesn't make me want to run away in the night to a place where you can never find me."

My mouth went dry. Not because I was angry—I had been angry a lot. The anger had become a trusted companion. But this was different. Now I was scared. Scared that he would run away in the night. Scared that he would leave us. Scared that he wouldn't, and this would be the rest of my life. This man. This argument.

"Do you really feel all that?" I asked him.

"I'm not going to kill myself, if that's what has you worried," he told me. "Though it would be nice if you cared about it for more than logistical reasons."

"Why would you say that, Seth?" I asked him. "Why are you trying to scare me?"

"I guess I'm trying to let you in on how things are going over here. Somehow you've missed the fact that my art has been sucked out of me by the terrible, endless, soul-sucking *repetition* of daily life, and you're saying you want me to give you more time to answer emails? Maybe you don't recognize the seriousness of this situation to our marriage."

There was nothing to say back to that. I could only blink at him. Blink and then watch him stand up and leave, go out somewhere, I didn't know where. While the wine I'd poured him sat on the table, ignored, right next to the contents of my heart.

A week later Davis came into my office with a bowl of fresh figs trimmed and cut in half.

The move struck me as overtly sexual, and I was cold to him for about three seconds until I realized there was nothing outright rude about figs, except that I was feeling a lot of feels about the state of my marriage and reading into everything as a result. I asked him to have a seat and tried not to get overtaken by my seesawing emotions.

"Do you not like figs?" he asked me. "You are looking at them like they're poison."

"I like figs. I actually love figs. I love how ephemeral they are. Unless you live in a fig-producing area, I guess. Then you probably feel that way about peaches." I blushed then, because if figs were maybe a bit sexual, peaches absolutely were. I was just making things worse. I changed the subject to the least sexy thing I could think of. Productivity.

"So you have probably noticed the pace picking up around my office," I told him.

"Hard to miss. You must be going hell for leather."

"It's all to the good. In your experience as a corporate coach, do things like this happen cyclically? Are they tied to the economy?" Davis had recently moved into my office suite from a larger operation, where he'd been forced to travel constantly to work with newly promoted VPs and underperforming execs. My business, on the other hand, had started from the ground up, and I did a lot of my coaching remotely, working with people whose dreams were bigger than the hours in their days.

He frowned. "Well, you and I serve two different populations," he pointed out. "I coach people who already have what they want and need help dealing with it. You coach people who need strategies to get closer to what they want. So our cycles are different even in times of external growth."

I nodded. "True. But when people have money to invest in themselves, that's when each of us comes into play on our consulting business. So it follows, then, that if people don't have money to invest, things shrink."

"How long have you had your business?" he asked me then. It had been five years. Five years, and it had grown bigger than I had ever dared imagine.

Davis tilted his head. "Whenever you and I talk, you draw lots of conclusions about what's going on in the outside world that affects your day-to-day income and growth. But those things are outside your control. Why not focus on what's going on in your inside world and see how that challenges or supports you?"

I looked down at my desk. I kept it—still keep it—pristine. No one wants to walk into a productivity coach's office and see a mess. I had my monitors and laptop on a sit-to-stand desk, I had beautiful pens in a white porcelain pot, and I had my own planner, with my name engraved on it, sitting on the right-hand corner. Then, on the left side, was a photo of my young family. Seth with Bridget in his arms, making "ta-da" hands next to his recent public park installation, a breathtaking work in reclaimed wood shingles, two matched wings, swooping dramatically in the array of weathered grays that the lake had created over the years. If you came upon a viewer standing in the middle, the wings seemed to sprout from under his arms, left and right, and in your imagination he took flight over the water. In the photo, the space between the wings was empty, and it was there that I always imagined myself. But heavy with my disappointment, there were no wings that could possibly lift me today. I turned from the photo to the bowl of figs, and I started to cry.

Davis's response went from classic male horror—he actually said, "Wait! What's happening?!"—to this kind of yielding compassion I can never quite forget. He reached out his arm across the desk and took my hand and did nothing more and said only, "Right, then. Right."

When I had cried for a long time, I took my hand back, cleaned myself up. Blew my nose.

"I feel," I started to say, not sure where the sentence was going. And then I knew. "I feel so much better," I said. "What is it about a good cry?"

He looked at me hard. I could tell he thought I was faking the relief I felt, but it was real. I felt the same as when I was ten and cried my heart out when my best friend had dumped me loudly at recess for buying the exact same shoes as her. That night my parents had wrapped me up together in their arms and let me sob and sob, let me go on and on. My sorrow for my dilemma with Seth was deeper, but somehow, with the lightest touch of Davis's outstretched fingers, I felt just as safe.

It made no sense, it was inconvenient, and I decided there and then to ignore it. But Davis did not get the memo. "Wendy," he said softly. "You must know how I feel about you by now."

I looked up at him, startled. I had guessed but not really been able to believe it. After all, it made no sense that a young, hot, successful guy with a great accent would be attracted to a married woman who had wrecked her husband's life. The friendship connection made so much more sense to me, and that's what I reassured myself with whenever I let the question come up. Now I could only nod. If I had been able to pretend before, now that pretending had to be over.

"I can't be a monk and wait for you. Too much pressure for us both. And I care enough about you as a person to want you to be happy in the marriage you're in now. I want your family to be exactly as you imagined it."

I shook my head. He was kind, handsome, and caring. I couldn't encourage him, not even a little. "I just want that too," I told him honestly. "I really do want what I have."

"Of course," he said sadly. He mustered a smile. Then he squared his shoulders and seemed to change from my friend to my colleague, right before my eyes. "Well, in that case, keep this in mind: coaching people who want to keep what they already have is my area." He thought for a moment. "You've been bushed lately. Let's go in together on a higher-level assistant. Keep Cat on the front desk and bring in someone to do questionnaires, marketing, admin. This is what I'd recommend if you were my client. Your extra bandwidth can all go into ramping up planner production. If you can make that income stream cover the cost of outsourcing eventually, you can return your focus to client service and generation after the baby comes. It will give you more flexibility. More security."

I looked at him in wonder. "More sleep," I added gratefully. His idea was brilliant, and better still, it was utterly doable. "Davis . . . ," I started to say. I'm not sure if I wanted to apologize for loving my husband, for letting Davis help me so much when I had nothing to give him back, or what, exactly. Finally, I settled on, "Thank you."

He nodded, saying, "Let's never talk about that other stuff again, ok? I'm not cut out to pine. I'm a man of action." He laughed and then wiggled his eyebrows. "And I can be flexible. After I change my mindset a bit, I'm sure I'll be happy enough just to sit back and watch your star rise. No one deserves it more."

But it didn't matter what I did or didn't deserve back then, I realize now, as I lie in Celeste's bed, listening to her husband breathe in and out evenly, as reliable in sleep as he is each day. Come Saturday, if all goes well, my star will rise, my business will flourish, my coaching calendar will be booked out, and my fiscal year will be made. I will improve more lives, build more dreams, and make my little corner of the world just that much better.

And yet all the success in the world won't change who I married and what kind of man he's become.

CHAPTER 18
FREAKY FRICKING
FRIDAY

WENDY

The next morning the text comes in: Lord willing, it's the last day of your life as me. I have a present for you. A sitter is coming for Joy at noon. I'll take all the kids after work and we'll do pizza and a movie night all together, just for a big sendoff.

I check twice to see who sent this. Celeste? Is that you? Have you had a lobotomy?

> It's me, and you should shut up and let me be nice to you. No softball tonight so no carpool, Samuel's going into after-school with Linus, and Sofia's mom is picking up the girls and hanging out with them in the park until I get home from work. The vodka's en route and should be here any minute, and you've got a big speech tomorrow. I'm giving you the day off.

My throat catches, and it's all I can do not to cry. But when my wits return, I shake my head. Not fair. You're the one who deserves a day off, I write back.

Shut up and relax, she writes back. Go into the city and do something fun.

I don't remember how to have fun, I write back.

Museum? Matinee? Pedicure? she texts me.

I think for a moment and laugh. You can get your own toes done tomorrow. I'm going to go sit by the river and have an indulgent lunch completely and utterly alone.

Perfect. Enjoy your day-drinking, she quickly replies.

By the time I've packed the kids a modest lunch to save them from Friday meatloaf, run them to school, cut out a hundred math manipulatives and laminated them, and run an errand to the local awards-and-trophies store, it's almost lunch. I cannot believe I'm even considering taking time out today, much less that someone I was brawling with a week ago is the one who gave me this chance. But I've learned my speech forward and backward, and Celeste's right: this is my last chance before I go back to being Wendy, the Woman Who Has It All—something I am desperate to have happen and yet . . . not entirely sure I'm ready for.

I know exactly where I want to spend this respite: the Water's Edge, one of my favorite prekid date spots. It's a stodgy old bar and grill with a patio where you can sit by the river on a gorgeous day like this one and have a perfectly made sidecar and just stare for hours at the boats and the ducks and the clouds and the people passing by.

Or you could do all those things if you weren't a woman with far too much to do.

Well, guess what. I'm not that woman for a few more hours. I slide into the Water's Edge, find myself the perfect barstool, half-in and half-out of the building, where the sun can only reach me through a vine-covered pergola. I order one of those sidecars I remember from a visit here years ago, with a wedge salad to make it look like lunch. They show up almost at the same time, first the pretty ruby-colored drink served up with sugar on the rim, then the quartered head of iceberg dripping with blue cheese, bacon lardon, and bright-red cherry tomatoes, the most indulgent way to eat vegetables that I know of short of fried zucchini.

I ask the bartender if they also have fried zucchini, and he says, "Not on the menu, but I can arrange it," so I order that too. Then I turn my eyes to the river, eating, drinking, wondering what to make of my life.

If you had asked me before last week if I was happy, I would have told you, quickly, that of course I was—and considered you weird for asking. My daughter is a starter on her softball team, my son is a sweet kid with a voracious appetite for books, my husband is working tirelessly to break through with his art, and my self-made business is earning more with every quarter. But a far, far more accurate answer would be that I had no idea, because who has the time to think about happiness? Happiness is for people with nothing better to do.

But it's one thirty on a Friday. I'm at the bar with breaded, seasoned, fried slices of zucchini and a glorified cognac delivery system right in front of me. I have nothing scheduled but to watch the world go by, and guess what: I have time to think now, and it's very dangerous. Basically, the second I slowed down—by force, hallucination, magic, or some combination of all three—every single hole in my drywall, real and metaphorical, has started to show through. My kids are indeed a bit coddled. My husband is maybe not the artistic genius I thought I married. And the job I love so much is hardly curing cancer or solving climate change. Am I throwing away the most precious moments of my children's lives for my own selfish dreams?

Suffice it to say I order another drink. While the bartender makes it for me, I ask him rhetorically, "Where did it all go wrong?"

Before he can give me an answer, the front door of the bar opens, and Seth walks through it.

My jaw opens. There is an awful lot I'd like to say to Seth right now. I have a head of steam and just enough of a buzz started to think it would be better to give him a dressing-down he dearly deserves than continue to sit here in the sticky cauldron of my own feelings, where no one but me can truly take the blame. I think of all the things I'd like to tell him. Things I have been holding in for a long time. That he hasn't sold a piece in years, that he's doing nothing to help our family, that he's a colossal disappointment to me in almost every way—things that are hurtful and mean and that will be really, really hard to take back.

But just before I can even get started, he says, "Oh, Celeste! What a surprise!"

Right. I can't take my fury out on Seth, because I'm Celeste, and Celeste shouldn't have any fury toward her next-door neighbor's husband. Actually, right up until this moment I didn't even know Seth knew who Celeste was, exactly.

"Hello," I say, forcing a weak smile. "What brings you here?"

"Oh, I'm here every Friday. My studio's a few blocks away, and this bar is the perfect place to get centered when I'm stuck," he tells me. "I'm a sculptor," he adds, as though I asked what he was stuck on. (I didn't.) "Sometimes the studio just gets so oppressive. This is where I come to take the pressure off."

I nod. "I see. I didn't realize sculpting involved so many cocktail breaks."

"The muse works on her own time," he tells me with a charmingly wry grin.

I'm not in a charmable mood. "How is the muse treating you these days?" I ask him, not just because it's what a neighbor might ask but because I genuinely want to know—*What's going on in that studio of yours after all this time? What do you have to show for yourself?*

"Damned poorly," he says. "I must have pissed her off at some point." He flashes me a grimace that's leaden, sorrowful. "To be honest, I haven't liked much of what I've been making for a long while now."

I look at him for a moment. Of all the weirdness that I've experienced since Celeste and I swapped bodies, this is the weirdest. Talking to my husband when he has no idea he's talking to me. Seeing him without the fog of *Who emptied the dishwasher last, and what time will you be home, and did you put a new chain saw on our credit card?* is like seeing him for the first time in years. His handsome face, his backlit blue eyes, a start of a shadow creeping across his jaw as the sun rises up high in the sky. A sadness at the corners of his eyes and lips that speaks of talent frustrated, hopes fading, life disappointing.

There's no way to look at this man and not be overcome by all the things we've shared. The day he proposed, the first gallery show, the parks installation, my opening day of business, and most of all, the children, Bridget and Linus, our greatest acts of cocreation. My heart seems to contract as a wave of memories washes over me. All at once I remember what Celeste said early on—how perhaps there was a greater meaning to this swap—and I can't help it; I wonder . . . could this moment be it? Maybe this is the very, very beginning of how I find my way back to him. Maybe this is what it has all been for.

I swallow hard. "Why don't you order a drink and tell me about it," I ask him. I'm hoping that without the tension of our sorry marriage, I can get a better idea of what's going on with his art. Maybe then I can understand how we've gotten so far apart.

He frowns. "You have time?" he asks me.

"Taking a day off," I tell him. I pause for a moment. "I'm just taking some me time to figure things out."

"So I'm not the only one," he says, with a little tip of the head. "Can I get a beer?" he asks the bartender. "Something local and hoppy?" he adds.

The bartender offers him some goofy-sounding brew and gets to pouring it. When it's in front of Seth, I watch him take half a sip, set it down, and shake his head.

"Before I got married," he tells me, "I had almost bottomless energy for my artwork. Art craft, I should say, because the craft of it was more important than some arbitrary standard about what made something art back then. I could just . . . do me . . . and make it the best I could, really, and sometimes, when all the stars aligned, what I wanted to make was what galleries wanted to see too. And then the reviews came in, and . . . the things they said about me."

"Mmm?" I lean in. I remember all the hours we spent talking these things over, the late nights dreaming of what he might create next, of what art meant to us, of all the beautiful things our future could be.

"I mean, *ARTnews* called me 'the next must-acquire sculptor,'" he tells me now.

It's a review I have etched in my memory, and I pass a framed copy of it every time I walk through our hallway, but how long has it been since I thought about that moment, the champagne and the celebrating and the tears of joy?

"Wow," I say. "They covered you? They don't mess around."

"Exactly," he agrees. "That kind of feedback, it's so exhilarating, you know?" He pauses a moment. "Wait, I'm so sorry. I forgot to ask you what it is you do, Celeste."

I think fast, not wanting this conversation to get shut down by Celeste's standard answer to this question. "I work from home," I try.

He nods. "Go on?"

"Just part time. Ah . . . in fashion," I end up saying, because no one can argue that the things she sews for Zoey aren't perfectly fitted, stylish, and well chosen. If she hired me as her coach, I'd definitely see if she wanted to take that gift any further.

Although one can guess she would never hire me in a million years.

"Fashion!" says Seth, pleased. "So you get it. Where the art meets commerce . . . that's where the magic happens." He pauses. "Or doesn't," he adds sadly.

"Stuff isn't selling?" I ask.

"Not selling. Not even getting press. I can't remember the last good review I had. My work lacks assurance. That's what the last one said. I'm in a crisis of confidence. Ever since . . . well . . ."

"What?" I ask. "Ever since what?"

"It's nothing," he says, shaking his head.

"It's not nothing to me," I tell him, wishing he knew just how true that was for the real me. "I'm interested."

He takes a long swig of beer. "It's just, Celeste, you have to understand my wife. She's an amazing woman," he says.

My heart seems to expand outward with pride. I never dreamed he would say things like this about me, after all this time. But then he keeps talking.

"Too amazing. She seems to think everyone should be able to work at the level she does, which is nonstop. She thinks I should be working nine to five and bringing home a fat paycheck. And if I can't do that, she wants me home all the time, to just drop everything—my art, my passion—and become the perfect family man. No offense, there's absolutely nothing wrong with that in a guy. It's honorable, is what it is, if you can do it without losing your soul. It's just not who I am. I'm an artist."

I furrow my brow. "That's what Wendy said?" I ask, feeling confused, startled even. "That she wants you to drop everything?" *Didn't she pay for your studio downtown so you could work uninterrupted and be inspired by the art scene in town?* I think, trying to keep my face placid.

"Oh, no, no—that's the whole thing, Celeste. She never actually says it. If she did, she'd have to hear me say no and face up to who I really am. Instead she just walks around in a constant state of disappointment. Apparently if she can be the perfect mother and perfect businesswoman and earn big bucks, the man she married should be able to do that too."

I shake my head. He's got it all wrong. I want to take him by the collar and say, *That's not what I want! I really want you to be happy.* "I don't think she'd really think that, would she?" I ask him, panic rising.

He looks at me. "Oh, Celeste. Of course that's not how you'd treat me in her shoes, I know. A fellow creative wouldn't squash my ambitions and leave me drained of all inspiration. That's why it's so hard for you to imagine anyone else doing it."

I grimace, my face warring with the growing unrest in my stomach. This is so far from the truth, these things he's saying. That I squash his ambitions? I have been his biggest cheerleader since before we were even married.

Why would he say such a thing to my next-door neighbor? And why does he think he knows so much about what Celeste would and wouldn't do in the first place? How well does he even know her, when I could have sworn she said Seth didn't know anyone was even living in her house until last week?

He takes another big gulp of his beer. It's half-gone now, and my second sidecar is sitting there untouched. I stare at him, trying to hide all the chaos going on in my head. "You don't know what I'd do, Seth," I say at last. I think of all of Celeste's disparaging comments about him. "If I were in your wife's shoes, I might be even harder on you than she is."

"I can't believe that," he says, and he takes a bit of Celeste's curly brown hair and moves it out of my face in a move so stunningly intimate my throat tightens up. "Look at you. You're the opposite of her. You curve where she's all edges. You give where she takes. You're gentle . . . and beautiful," he tells me. That's what he tells someone who he thinks isn't his wife. "I refuse to believe that you're shrill like her."

I freeze up, ice on my skin, in my veins, coursing into my heart. "Wendy isn't shrill," I say.

"Spoken like someone who doesn't live with her," he replies.

"She's busy," I say, my voice tight, clipped. "She has a lot on her plate." I can't believe I even can talk right now.

"Her so-called plate is more like a trough," he says. "It's never enough. Before she gave her life over to that business, she was happy enough working in a normal job with normal hours. If she still did that, she'd have plenty of time for the kids. Maybe she'd even still have time for me."

Happy enough? I think, growing colder and colder still. I worked with sexist idiots in that old HR job and watched them waste half their days on cat videos while I got paid eighty cents on the dollar and saw my female mentors get stuck in middle management.

I started this business because I dreamed of something bigger for myself. For all of us, the entire family. For him.

"What are you thinking?" he asks me now, because I have been silent for far too long. Seething. Roiling. Turning to stone. I take a drink of my sidecar to buy a moment. The lemon is too sour this time. Even this one sip seems to give me heartburn.

I shake my head. "I'm just listening. Taking in what you have to say," I try.

He smiles a little sadly. "Of course you are, Celeste," he says with confusing familiarity. "To be honest, real listening is something I can't even recognize after all these years."

Inside, I melt, fume, refreeze in cycles. Every word he says hurts me more, and every bone in my body wants to fight that pain, to bury it in anger, self-righteousness, indignation. How many times have I asked him how things are going, asked him how I can support his art? How many times have I suggested we take a quick weekend trip to see sculpture in other places, to meet with different gallery owners, to fill his well of creativity and inspiration? It feels like thousands. The answer has always been no.

Desperate, I try one more time. "Maybe she's trying, but she still just doesn't know what you need anymore," I say, holding my hopes in my hands like a precious work of etched glass. "What would you want your wife to know, right now," I ask him, "if you could be sure she'd really and truly listen?"

He leans forward, really close to me, as if he's going to whisper in my ear, and sure enough, his voice is low and a little hoarse. "If I could tell her anything, and she'd just listen, like you are now, and not lecture me on productivity or positive work habits?" he asks.

"Yes," I say. "Tell me." I am breathless, praying the next words are something, anything, we can use to save us.

He cocks his head closer and begins to reach for my jawline. It's exactly as it was the first night we met, his hand cupping my cheek, pulling me in, a kiss just inches away. I am utterly lost in the memory of that kiss. That beautiful beginning. Until he speaks and I realize.

He's not reaching out to kiss me.

"I'd tell her that there were women out there—beautiful, alluring, feminine women—right next door, for example, who understood me better than she ever could," he says as he gazes into Celeste's eyes.

I jump off the barstool backward, hopes broken, illusions shattered. "What the hell! Are you drunk?" I ask him.

As if that somehow matters.

He grimaces, pulls his entire body back a mile away from mine. "Ahh, sorry, sorry! Not drunk." He holds up that beer, half-finished, as evidence. "Just read things wrong. I thought I'd noticed you . . . ah . . . noticing me around the neighborhood, you know?" He puts his hands up in surrender. "I thought we'd had a moment. Sorry about that, really. Misread the situation. No harm, no foul, right?"

"So much foul," I blurt out. "So incredibly much foul! You have no idea."

"Hold up, Celeste," he calls as I start to make for the exit. "Hey! I'm sorry. This doesn't have to be a thing," he tries. I pause, one foot on the sidewalk, the other still under the pergola. "We're both adults here. You were flirting with me. We know how things are."

I look at him with hateful eyes, wishing like hell he could see who I am, see what he's done. "To be honest, I didn't know how things were, though, Seth. Not until right this second."

Now I know.

And now here is one more thing I can never unknow. Like a worn knot that can take no more tugging, I feel the ties of my marriage come totally undone.

—

CELESTE

The morning after the Taco Barn, I had a mild headache, some less mild flatulence, and an early schedule. I got up humming, thinking about the conversation we had, Wendy and I, and the magic vodka that would be winging its way to my front door today. I couldn't wait to be back home, but I would not be exactly the same. I'd have a friend, a real friend, someone who I knew could understand me in a way no one else possibly could. I couldn't think of a better way to thank her than to give her some time to herself before she went back to her real life and I went back to mine.

But since she and I texted this morning, I haven't heard a word from her. Maybe in my attempt to give Wendy some overdue R&R, I've overstepped. I try to reach her, to figure out if she's mad, happy, delirious, or what, exactly. I try her on her cell, at home. But she doesn't text back, and though I borderline stalk her, I never see my minivan return to my driveway.

And there's something else that doesn't show up.

Dinnertime rolls around, then the movie, and still no magic vodka. I check every door, both houses, the mailboxes, the sides of the garages. I check the routing information four hundred times. An hour. There's no update. The message just reads, *Out for delivery.* But it's getting later and later. Soon it will be dark. Soon I will need to meet Wendy by the rosebush with the sangria ready, and neither the woman nor the sangria will be here.

I want to fall apart. I want to fall apart on the kitchen floor of Wendy's house and cry and scream and hit my fists on the ground like all three of my kids have done in turn, all at different local parks. But I can't fall apart. I have to figure out logistics for five freaking children, make sure Seth knows what to do tomorrow, and face the horrifying fact that if that vodka doesn't arrive on time, I will be presenting a sold-out speech that can either make or break Wendy's entire business. On a subject I have zero competence in. I breathe in and out a few times and then, as the *Minions* credits start to roll, I send Samuel home to Hugh and put Linus in his own bed. Then, not sure what else to do, I stall the girls with the excuse of ice cream sundaes.

The girls look at me sideways. The moment I get Zoey alone, I explain I need her to go on a recon to her house to look for her mom and check everywhere for packages. I'm 99.9 percent sure I sent the vodka to Wendy's house, not mine, but I put my own number on the shipping form, and I've had my own phone in my grip all day, just in case they called for a signature. But maybe . . . if they came earlier in the day, they'd have rung the bell at a neighbor's . . . or maybe I'm grasping at straws.

"No sign of Mom or package," says Zoey when she gets back. "Dad looks a bit worried." Zoey does, too, and I wish I could hug her and tell her that her mom is here, perfectly fine.

Instead, heart in my throat, I slip away and text Hugh. Home soon, I write optimistically. No need to worry. Just recharging my batteries. Again I refresh the tracking page. Nothing is new.

"Something weird is up with my mom," says Zoey to Bridget when I'm walking back into the kitchen. "She's been out of it this week, let-ting us do all kinds of weird stuff that's normally banned. Cartoons, packaged snacks, dressing up, computer games, and generally just letting us do normal kid stuff. And the other day I heard her say a swear word."

"Swearing isn't the end of the world," I interject, glad, at least, that parenting is something I can do even in times of extreme worry. "But it is an adult privilege. Keep that in mind."

"Well, ok, I guess, but it's really unusual for my mom," she tells me, then turns back to Bridget. "And she's been letting me watch regular TV. Like, movies other kids in my grade watch."

I keep my face neutral, but I'm wondering if maybe I haven't missed how old Zoey has gotten lately. Maybe too old for a strict diet of PBS Kids and Monopoly Junior. "How does your brain feel?" I ask her. "Totally rotted?"

"Not yet. Actually, I didn't really like the movies all that much. One was so stupid—a mom and daughter change bodies and then run around like crazy pretending to be the other person. What even is that?"

I try not to snort.

"But I did love this show about fashion designers on cable that she showed me. Bridget, have you seen that one?"

"I haven't watched anything good for, like, an entire week. I've been doing a bunch of other stuff. Mom says I can save TV for weekends now," she says, in a performative grumble in my direction. "And keep it PG."

Earlier today Bridget was found voluntarily doing her free-reading time for today *and* the entire weekend so she can goof off after her softball game—for which she's all packed and ready a full day in advance. Linus, who has no free-reading issues whatsoever, has been seen folding his laundry, including several pairs of clean undies that tell me he's kept up with the new mandate of changing his shorts every day.

The spackle on the bedroom hole is dry, the house is clean, the freezer is full, the chore wheel is spinning. I've done what I thought I came here to do. The problem is, I seem to have misplaced the woman I intended to do it for.

"Whoa. That sounds like my mom normally," says Zoey.

Both girls turn their heads to look at me. Bridget coughs. "I'm not sure they're a good influence on each other after all."

I laugh at the kids. "What is this show that's so fabulous?" I ask.

Excitedly, Zoey describes a program about designing and sewing outfits on a two-day deadline that sounds, if not meritorious, at least pretty fun. I think of the gritty fantasy drama Bridget had on earlier in the week when she thought I wasn't paying attention. It gave me the heebie-jeebies. "Here's the new content rule, Bridget, and Zoey, I bet it's the same at your house: if you can't stand the thought of your mother sitting next to you while it's on, it's a sign it's not right for our family."

She nods. "I guess that's cool. But we have to go now, Mrs. Charles. Coach says we have a curfew of nine p.m."

I look at my watch. "It's only eight thirty," I say. *Do packages still go out at eight thirty?* I wonder to myself, as the nervousness begins to morph into something more like panic. If only Wendy would get back to me. She'd know—she'd have to know—what to do.

"But all we've done the whole night is hang out with you," Zoey says, bemused. "The whole point of coming over here is to get some girl talk."

"I am a girl," I point out, and both Bridget and Zoey roll their eyes in unison. "Right," I say and realize, *It's true. Zoey is ready to grow up. She'll only trust me more if I can let her, just a little bit.* "Ok, have fun. And set your own timer so you don't blow curfew."

"Where will you be?" the girls ask me.

"I'm just going to sit out front for a minute and get some fresh air," I tell them. "On the front porch." Where I can see the mailbox. And watch for a minivan that belongs to a woman I am sorely missing.

—

WENDY

The worst thing about Seth is that when he tries to cheat on me, with me, he does it in a great bar. So I can't even get a shot of whiskey without relocating.

Is that what happened? I ask myself as I race, dazed and frantic, back up the waterfront to the parking garage where I left my car. I mean, I'm very clear on where I stand on cheating husbands, and so is Seth. But was this cheating? Attempted cheating? I mean, can you really cheat on your wife when she's not in her own body? The logistics are both mind boggling and exhausting to consider, so I decide to stop. Instead, I start ruminating about Celeste, about how Seth could want *her*, of all people. Seth has always said how much he appreciates that I have kept trim, not "let myself go," as he calls adult women walking around in bodies that have any variation from the ones they had in college—and to think I bought into that! As soon as he has half a beer, he's all over the ultimate mom. I look down at that body now, hating it, not for thighs or belly but for existing and trapping me inside it and making everything in my life seem so fruitless. Exposing it as a lie.

Before Celeste, I tell myself in anger, I had a great life. Before her, my husband wasn't a louse, just an artist. My kids weren't spoiled; I was just making up for how little time I had at home. I wasn't a workaholic; I was just in building mode. And the guy at work wasn't a crush; he was just a friend and a reliable sounding board.

God, what a pack of stupid, impossible lies.

I find the minivan in the parking garage but not the payment ticket. And then I realize that the ticket is in my card wallet, which I definitely left on the bar when I ran away from there and away from Seth. So I need to go back to the bar now if I want to ever extricate Celeste's kid limo from this concrete labyrinth. When all I really want to do is scream and drink and rage and cry and hide from this hurt inside me that has grabbed on and will not let go.

But I cannot go back to the bar because that is where I stormed away twenty minutes ago, and knowing Seth, there's a decent chance he's still there. Maybe stunned by what he did. Ashamed. I hope. But then, maybe he's waiting for the next middle-aged mom for him to hit on in the middle of a Friday afternoon. I grab my phone and call the bar. The bartender picks up with a "Yup?" and I tell him about the little yellow leather wallet that Celeste carries around inside her enormous purse. He knows the one exactly and says he can call me when the "married guy leaves" so I can come pick it up. Great. Seth is still there. Perhaps another neighbor of ours has arrived and he's trying his moves on her. Maybe the eighty-five-year-old widow from down the street, seeing as his standards seem to be anyone who has a pulse.

Sorry, Celeste, I think. In my misery I've become a terrible snob.

No, I mentally correct. I've been a terrible snob for years. Snobbery is just something I've bought into to explain my choices. Just like it's something Celeste has bought into, but her kind of snobbery is Mother-of-the-Year snobbery, and mine is Too-Busy-to-Be-Mother-of-the-Year snobbery, and the reality for both of us is that the minute you look too closely, any illusion of superiority falls right away. Honestly, what good has it done me to go to those stupid barre classes three days a week for the last five years? My husband still wants to throw me over for someone "gentler."

Just then my phone buzzes. I look down at the screen. It just says, Still no vodka. It's getting kind of late. I'm starting to worry.

For some reason, that's the final straw. The goddamned vodka is late. The stupid vodka that Celeste just had to put in her stupid sangria that has screwed up my life so badly it will never be the same. I ball my fists in rage and grit my teeth, holding back a scream, but only for a few moments. Then I can't hide under my anger anymore, and finally, though my eyes have been stinging since the moment Seth touched my face, I give in and start to cry.

There was another time, a few years ago, when I wondered if Seth might be cheating on me. He kept more normal hours with us back then, and his absences were more closely noted. I got jealous after several missed dinners and confronted him about what was going on, and then I felt like a fool when he informed me that he had gotten a public works grant and was burning the midnight oil on a sculpture that would go on to win a prestigious local prize. Boy, did that ever teach me. I had to grovel for weeks, but really, he never quite forgave me for suspecting him, and I hadn't been fool enough to do it again.

I thought I had no cause to. Seth might be a lot of things, but unfaithful? I mean, why? He rarely wanted sex anyway, and he never got enough time to himself, to hear him tell it.

I start to cry so hard I can't see where I'm going anymore, and since I'm not really going anywhere, I just sit down on a big concrete planter-cum-bench put out in front of the garage designed to keep people from parking on the sidewalk, and I give in to the tantrum that's coming over me. I wail, I screech, I carry on, and three separate people come over to ask me if I need an ambulance. Very nice of them, really. I tell them to go away because my life is falling apart and I would like a little privacy. All three of them give me a look I can't decipher until I realize that asking for privacy in a bustling business district of a major metropolitan area is perhaps a sign that I need an ambulance more than I realize.

But who cares anymore? Who cares what kind of lunatic the town thinks Celeste is? Who cares if they think *I'm* a lunatic, too, after all? It makes no difference. Where do you go from here, from this awful, horrible place I'm in? It's all downhill from here on out. I mean, what exactly is next? Divorce lawyers? Alimony? Split custody and devastated children and moving to an apartment near my sister for extra support, only to hear her and her stodgy lawyer husband say *I told you so*?

Finally, the tears start to slow as I recognize my own ridiculous drama taking shape. What an idiot I've become over the last week. Of course I'm not going to end a marriage of fourteen years over what was, in point of fact, a husband's attempt to kiss his wife. Yeah, Seth made a misstep. But that's all I can be sure of. That's all I have to believe. One misstep. He's frustrated. Maybe even depressed. In a situation like that, it could hardly even be thought of as his fault. A quiet bar, a bored housewife with a fresh hairstyle and newly discovered eyebrows, a moment where my star has begun to soar ever so slightly higher than his . . .

He was hurting. He was vulnerable. He was basically a sitting duck.

My breath comes back to me. I start to recover myself, piece by piece. As I do, I take the pictures of what just happened, the memories just formed, and fold them up into the tiniest little square of emotion that I possibly can. I fold it again and again, until the creases are bigger than the feelings themselves. I take that tiny little square of pain and hurt and betrayal and tuck it in my sternum, just under my voice box, where it is like a block of lead I only feel when I breathe. There. It can stay there forever. I can talk around it with no problem. It doesn't even hurt that much, as long as I never, ever think about it again.

And as I well know, the secret to not thinking about how awful things are is just staying very, very busy.

CHAPTER 19
SUDDENLY SATURDAY
C ELESTE

Around midnight Saturday morning, I give up on the vodka.

Before I go inside, I make my way to the front of my own house and peer inside the garage. To my great relief, my minivan is parked inside. I have no idea why Wendy isn't texting me back, but at least I know she's home safe.

I walk down the side of my own lawn and toward Wendy's. The lamp next to the living room sofa is on, and in its low light I spot my husband and Joy, snuggled up together fast asleep. My heart tugs. That giant, deep, L-shaped sofa was the best purchase we ever made. Hugh stretches out lengthwise, Joy nestles in like the small spoon and immediately passes out, and I can fit on the L when we're watching movies. Until Hugh falls asleep and his head slowly sinks from the headrest to my shoulder to the seat cushions, leaving me very little room to sit.

I miss that sofa so much right now. And if this vodka doesn't arrive—or doesn't work—will I ever get to sit on it again?

Finally, after 1:00 a.m., Seth arrives. He is visibly drunk—definitely shouldn't have been driving, but he was. *If he were my husband . . . ,* I think for the thirtieth time, with mental ellipses. When I heard the garage door open, I quickly turned out the light in the bedroom, where I'd been reading—yep, trying to distract myself with a historical novel from Wendy's Kindle—and pretend to be asleep. I listen to him stumble in, drop his keys, skip the evening grooming, and fall straight into bed. He is snoring within seconds of his head hitting the pillow.

I sit up and text Wendy for the tenth straight time. Please let me know you're ok, I beg.

To my surprise, she writes back immediately. I'm fine. Vodka?

No, I send. No point in mincing words on this catastrophe. The shipping status has been updated to tomorrow.

Another text appears after five minutes. Is everyone tucked in there?

She has never asked me that before, and I think about how recently Seth came in. I wonder if Wendy saw the lights of his car as it rounded the block, and that's the real reason she wrote me back. To check on Seth. After all this time, after all she's told me, all we've talked about.

Everyone's home and asleep but me, I write back quickly.

There's no response for a long time, and I lie flat, still clutching the phone, trying to figure out why something feels so terribly amiss. Maybe she's just insanely tired of being me. Based on her long disappearance and her strange attitude about it, I've concluded that if it's a head injury that's required to switch our bodies back, Wendy will be waiting for me with a baseball bat tomorrow morning. Hopefully the vodka works.

On that front, I decide to rip off the Band-Aid. I'll have to give the speech, I tell her.

Another long silence. I imagine the profanities that must be echoing off the walls of my real bedroom.

Fuck it, she finally writes back. What does it even matter? I'm going to bed.

With that most un-Wendy-like reply echoing in my brain, I suffer a fitful night of sleep.

—

The first thing I see in my notifications the next morning is an apologetic update from the shipping company and their "guarantee" that my package will arrive by six this evening.

Six. Too late for the speech. That means either I'm giving the speech today, or no one is.

I will not let Wendy down.

I slide out of bed, careful not to disturb Seth.

Like a character in a Hitchcock film, I spend the next hour staring out the window, watching for any appearance from Wendy, a light in the bedroom, any sign that all is well in my house right now. It's too early to text, I think. But if she's awake anyway . . . and wouldn't I normally be awake right now, if I were home? But the house seems quiet. Around and around I go. At last, at about eight, I see Hugh come into the kitchen in his ratty old bathrobe—a robe I desperately wish I could bury my face into right now—and make the coffee. Soon he is joined by Zoey, who is bouncing around nervously, and then Samuel, who will want only one thing: to eat us out of house and home, as he does every morning. Eventually I see Joy emerge with a stuffed toy I don't recognize, colored a flammable bright pink with those huge plastic eyes that are definitely a choking hazard if a kid pries them off.

Joy is almost four, I remind myself. She has never destroyed a toy in her life. She is safe. They are all safe, and all I want in this world is to walk into that kitchen as myself and have a normal, noisy morning with them. I would do anything for that. I take in a big breath, let it out slowly.

Just as I'm putting myself back together, I jump in my seat at a movement in my periphery. Wendy has let herself in the back door and sneaked up on me.

"How's the spying going?" she asks.

I'd be annoyed, but I'm just so glad she's alive and well and talking to me. "There you are!" I reply. "For a while there I thought maybe you'd taken the first flight out of town."

"I was tempted," she tells me.

"Don't tell me this swap thing hasn't made you reconsider your priorities," I tell her.

She makes a truly inscrutable face and says, "I suppose it has." Then, to my utter shock, she crosses past me to the cupboard, takes out a bottle of vodka, a can of spicy tomato juice, and a highball glass.

"Wendy! It's eight a.m.!" I exclaim.

"That's why I'm not drinking the vodka straight," she says.

"What is going on with you? You are acting really weird. You disappear all day yesterday, you sneak up on me this morning, and now you're hitting the sauce?"

She looks around furtively. "Is Seth up?" she asks.

"No," I say. "I don't think anyone is. Maybe Linus, but you know he'll just hide in his room with a book until there's some promise of food. I was just about to start eggs."

"C'mon," she says, grabbing me by the shoulder of the pretty linen sweater I put on over pajamas this morning and steering me into the pantry.

"What are you—"

"Hush," she says and closes us both into the cozy space. Organizing her pantry was one of the most satisfying parts of tidying up Wendy's life over the last week, and now I wait in happy anticipation for her to notice how clean and neat it is in here.

Instead I get, "What the hell happened in here?"

"I cleaned it!" I announce proudly. "Check out how I sorted your canned goods by expiration date!"

"You what? Honestly. What the hell is wrong with you? I don't need my canned goods organized!"

"It was a mess in here!" I say. "You had six different half-used bags of flour."

Wendy looks at me hard, a look I don't understand. Aren't we supposed to be friends now? Isn't tidying a pantry something a friend would do? For a minute she says absolutely nothing to me. Then, after an eerily long time, she says, "And?"

"What do you mean, and? I took the bags and combined the ones that hadn't expired and put them in this large canister here, and see, I made this label that says 'Flour—White, Unbleached,' so now it will be easy to find."

"This is your idea of helping, Celeste? Organizing another woman's baking supplies?"

"Well, I thought it might help us swap back," I admit, feeling just a bit silly. "I mean, I tidy up your closets and get your kids to help out, and . . ."

"And what?"

"And, you know, I learn a bit more humility about how complicated your life can be . . ."

"So let me get this straight. For the last week you've been 'fixing' all the things that are wrong with my life in the hopes that you can get your own life back but be a tiny bit less smug about how much better it is than mine. Is that right?"

I gape at her. When she says it that way—cold, mean, insulting—it does sound silly. But yes, that's exactly right, so I nod a tiny bit.

"And I suppose that part of fixing my life is setting me up with Davis, then?"

I grimace. I thought she understood where I was coming from on that.

"And tell me why, Mother Superior, you wanted to break up my marriage with Seth and send me off to live happily ever after with Davis?"

I stammer. I mean, I've let her know what I think of Seth before, in pretty certain terms. Do I say it all again? What in god's name happened to her last night to make her so angry?

"Is it maybe because that way you wouldn't have to share Seth anymore?" she asks me in a furious voice.

My jaw positively falls off my face. "What are you even talking about?" I ask her.

"Ok, sure, time to play stupid." She takes a chug from her glass. "There's no need, though, to act like a clueless idiot anymore."

"I'm not a clueless idiot!" I insist.

"Nope, you really aren't. You're a freaking evil genius. How long have you been after Seth, exactly?" she asks me. "A month? Six months? The entire time you've lived here?"

"What? No!" I say. "I don't know what you mean. I met him for real the day we body swapped. Until then I just knew he was your husband."

"Was that all you needed to know for him to be desirable, then?" she asks.

"He's not desirable!" I exclaim. Then I hear what I've said. "I mean, I'm sure he's great, if you're married to him, but I'm not into that. I'm married to Hugh. I love Hugh. You know that."

"Hugh, who moves heaven and earth to give you the perfect life," Wendy tells me. "Hugh, who takes the kids outside when I so much as give him a long look, who cleans up after dinner every single night, even if it's takeout, and does bedtime with the girls and makes enough money that you don't have to work. *That's* the guy you want to cheat on."

"I don't want to cheat on anyone! I love Hugh," I say, starting to feel panicky. I mean, I can't just fake apologize my way out of this, whatever this is. It would be like an admission, when I haven't done anything wrong and don't want to. "I have no idea what this is about, but let me say it again: this week has been like an abject lesson in how lucky I am to have a great partner. I'll admit that we haven't been in a crazy romantic place in our marriage lately, but as soon as we swap back, I'm going to grab on to him and never let go." I pause for a second. "And also, I'm sick of telling you this: I *do* work. Why do you keep insisting I don't work?" I stare at her, mystified. I thought she was starting to understand. I thought we understood each other. "What is going on with you, Wendy? Is everything ok?"

She crosses her arms and leans back angrily. "I'm just sick of being you, talking to you, having you in my life at every turn. You've made a mess of everything. When we swap again, I'm going to have to deal with an awkward situation at my office that could cause the entire partnership to go to pieces. Plus, I won't be able to find the fucking flour!" she shouts.

"Wendy!" I hiss at her. "Stop this. You're acting crazy, and you're going to wake up the kids!"

She lowers her voice, and when she does, her words drip with ice. "You're right. I'll stop shouting. Just know this: Seth thinks he ran into Celeste yesterday at the Water's Edge Bar. And he seemed to think he knew her fairly well. He seemed to think there was something started between the two of you, and it was something he was ready to take to the next level after half a glass of IPA yesterday."

I gasp. I've barely gotten my jaw off the floor, and there it goes again.

"If you've been flirting with Davis to break me and Seth up, that is a seriously shitty and maniacal thing to do. Even if you've been flirting with *Seth*, that's horrible enough. The other night, when we met up for drinks, it seemed like you were finally starting to get me, a little bit. Like you were trying to help. It seemed like you were starting to think of me as a friend and care what happened in my life." Wendy's voice cracks, and I see that under these crazy allegations and anger is a woman whose life has completely fallen to pieces. A woman with no idea how to pick them up.

"I am doing that!" I insist. "I have been trying to help, and I do care what happens in your life! Look, I'm sorry if I have been flirting with Davis just a little. He's an amazing guy, he's fun to look at, and yeah, ok, marriage with Hugh is stale at the moment—though as soon as I get my body back, I am going to change that, because like I said—he is my whole world. And yes, I've been hard on Seth, but all in the spirit of trying to help you. Genuinely help you. I thought you'd have an easier time baking if I organized your pantry. I thought Davis might give Seth the extra motivation he needs to step up, you know, the way a little competition can motivate. That's what you're always saying about softball, right?

"But I didn't know Seth would be unfaithful. I didn't know things with Davis could cause a work problem. I thought of it as kind of a fun, harmless thing." My voice is pleading.

"You brought Davis to meet my son!" she says in this weird half yell, half whisper that is actually more unnerving than just a shout. "They liked each other and talked about nerd books. That's not harmless. That's a thing."

I open my mouth to defend myself, but she's right. I've made this into a terrible mess. "I'm sorry. I see that now. I didn't think it through," I say.

Wendy shakes her head in disgust. "You and your apologies," she says. "Look me in the eyes and apologize for hitting on Seth, why don't you?"

"I can't do that, because I would never hit on someone else's husband," I insist. "And because I would never be unfaithful to mine. Think it through, Wendy. Besides, if someone did hit on Seth, it wouldn't have any effect unless your husband was already open to cheating. Your issue here . . . it's not with me."

For a second I think she's hearing me. Her shoulders sink; her anger seems to crumple up inside her. But then, as if her whole life depends on it, she turns on me again. "Really?" she says snidely. "Really? Because it sure seems to me like my life was fine before you came around and stole it from me."

And that's it. That's all I can take. I look at her, dead serious, and open the pantry door. I'm fed up. I've been an idiot, but I've apologized for it. I'm not going to apologize anymore. "Your life was not fine," I say as I step into the opening. "Your life just plain sucked. The only thing that's different now is that you finally know that."

—

WENDY

She leaves me in that pantry, so angry I can barely see. That stupid, color-coordinated, date-organized, perfectly labeled pantry, where I will never be able to find anything again. I scream in fury, swipe my hand over a row of pottery canisters I haven't seen since my bridal shower, and see them go flying across the wall, crashing, flour and sugar and . . . I don't know; I can't read the label through my tears. Porcelain going everywhere. For a few moments I can hardly breathe from the explosion of flour particles, and I cough and sputter and wipe my face. My clothes are covered in white, and I feel like such an idiot—I've made a bad situation worse. Times a million.

I brush off the legs of Celeste's sloppiest stretch pants and unzip the matching jacket I wore out in the morning's chill, then shake it out right there on the floor. After all, it will be me who has to clean it out tomorrow, if everything goes the way we think it will. Me who has to clean up this mess I made. If I possibly can.

Then I walk out of the pantry, into the bright light of day. The kitchen is empty, thank god. I close the pantry door tightly and leave the way I came, through the kitchen door, a trail of white footsteps following behind. Out in the yard, I try to push away new tears and gasp deep breaths to calm myself down, but there's no way Hugh—every bit as caring as his wife—is going to miss the state I'm in, and soon wet tracks are running through the flour dust on my face. I walk into Celeste's house with gritted teeth, slip off my dusty shoes, and pad upstairs to the shower. On the way I pass all three kids, who stare at me but don't dare speak, and Hugh, who says, "Celeste! What on earth happened to you?"

I don't answer; I can't. I just push past him to the bathroom and close the door. "I'll explain it all later," I say to him after a moment, when I hear him follow me to the door. "Don't worry. Please. Just . . . can you cover for me with the kids? I don't want them to know how upset I am. I don't want them to be scared."

Hugh's voice rings through the door clear and true. "Of course, honey. Of course. Do you want me to take the boys to the science fair on my own?"

The science fair. For which I purchased fifty green ribbons from the awards store that read *Star Participant!* Because that was the absolute least I could do for Celeste.

"That would be amazing," I say, truly meaning it. "I packed a bag by the door—be sure to give it to Dr. Randall for me, would you?" Here's a man who may not notice that I changed his wife's hair and made over her brows and put on lipstick for the first time in eleven years, but he knows that his son has a science fair today, and he was already planning to attend. Hell, he's awake, and we all know that's not the case with the man of *my* house. Goddamn Celeste. Why did she get so lucky? And why did I wreck everything between us to make her pay for it?

I've acted like such an idiot. There is no universe where I could truly, in my right mind, think she would come between Seth and me. Now that I've had my tantrum, no better than that of a three-year-old, I can see that the only thing Celeste did wrong was to be there when I was hurting.

Well, that and the pantry overkill.

"Wait, Hugh," I call. Already the thickness of my voice is fading, I am breathing again, and the fog that has surrounded me since yesterday is starting to lift.

"What's up, babe?"

"I know this is odd, but can you and the kids go straight from the fair to meet me someplace at noon? There's someone I want to support. Someone who is doing something really hard today, and she's done some very kind things for me lately."

"Sure . . . ," he says, his voice questioning.

"I know I'm acting crazy. I can explain everything, and I will. But not right now."

"Of course," he says, without so much as a pause. "Whatever you need. Celeste, I don't know what's been going on this week, but I do know I love you, no matter what. When you're ready to talk, I hope it's me you talk to. Got that?"

Those loving words, offered so freely, twist the knife. I nod silently, and then, thinking of what Celeste would need me to say, what she would do for me in my shoes, I say, "I love you too. No matter what."

"Okeydoke!" he replies, happiness forced over the top of worry. "I'll see you in a couple hours. Take your time and use the fancy face mask; we are good to go."

"You're the best," I say. God dammit, he really is the best. He's the unicorn, maybe. But I've been an absolute toad.

The shower makes me feel better. I start to get my wits again. This is my life now, postknowing, a seesaw of tantrums and acceptance, one that I would very much like to get off. I try some deep breathing and remind myself as best I can the mantra I teach my clients after a major setback: Every minute that passes, I get further from the moment Seth tried to cheat on me. Every hour that goes by, it'll hurt less. In a couple of months . . . ok, maybe a year, it will all be a fuzzy memory, something I can't really believe ever happened. Kind of like this entire switcheroo in the first place.

Until he does it again.

Of course, the next time Seth tries to cheat, it won't be with Celeste. It won't be with someone who would tell me what happened—that's for darn sure. My heart sinks back down the teeter-totter until it hits the ground. The next time may, just twenty-some hours later, have already happened.

Is Seth a serial philanderer? I finally allow myself to wonder. My first thought is that I can't imagine when he'd have the time. My second thought is that I don't actually know where he goes or what he does all day. I'm in the city working. He's in the city making art. Except there is no art to show for it, no gallery shows coming up, and not even a big materials purchase in a few months, come to think of it.

And then there's the new sofa in his studio.

It's for naps, I remind myself firmly. I'm drying Celeste's hair so vigorously right now it might fall out, so I stop, go over her curls with a wide-tooth comb, put in the new gel that makes it so amazingly shiny, and style it to perfection. Celeste looks so, so much better than when I got her. Just that tiny bit of care, a clean face at night, a nice new lip color, and some well-applied wax, but most of all a week straight of sleeping all the way through the night. Maybe that's all that Seth responded to—surprise at the instant makeover. Just a weird, complicated impulse—maybe not even so different from what I've occasionally felt toward Davis. A moment you let down your guard and something strange creeps in that's not welcome at all. It could happen to anyone. Seth just got very unlucky in the way that it happened to him.

Seth and I both.

Now the question is, How much more bad "luck" do I intend to put up with?

Celeste's words echo in my mind, and for one self-indulgent moment I imagine keeping up the argument with her. It would be so, so nice to keep pretending my beef is with her. As long as I keep duking it out with Celeste, fighting her tooth and nail on every front, turning my problems around on her, and blaming her for all the things that aren't working in my life, nothing has to change. We can drink the sangria, switch bodies back, and pretend this whole thing never, ever happened. Never talk again.

But that's just not what I want.

I pull on a loose T-shirt dress that hangs just right on Celeste, gives her a waist instead of flaring out too high and making her look like a walking triangle. The bright blue looks perfect with her hair. I just hope when she sees herself looking like this, with her family and my family together, it plants a tiny seed of forgiveness in her mind. I hope she can see through that side of me that lost it over flour canisters to that part of her—the patience, the compassion, the understanding—that has changed me for the better.

I hope she can realize that becoming Celeste is the best terrible thing that's ever happened to me.

CHAPTER 20

CELESTE

Too angry to tiptoe around the bedroom, I stomp around, determined to wake Seth, that stupid so-and-so. If I had time, I'd throw a bucket of ice water over his head. As though he can read my mind, he glares at me and puts a pillow over his head, so I turn on my phone at top volume to Broadway hits. Then, singing along as loudly as possible, I put on Wendy's stretchiest pantsuit over a feminine draped top that still had its tags and add sophisticated, if low-heeled, black shoes. I forgo the enormous resin statement jewelry in favor of a long silver necklace with two little silver charms, one etched with Bridget's name and one with Linus's. To look at me, you'd have no idea I'm absolutely terrified about this speech.

Satisfied that Wendy looks both professional and feminine—it is a women's expo, after all—I go downstairs, make the kids truly outstanding blueberry-banana pancakes without mussing so much as a hair, and get them started on their new list of Saturday-morning chores. They know the new weekend deal: those children who have done their work when I get home will get rides to the movies and the comic book shop respectively, and those who haven't will just get more chores. And now that I've been around for almost a week, they know I mean it.

Then I grab Wendy's briefcase, preloaded with her laptop and the vital slides on Productivity in Practice and Purpose, which she sent me earlier in the week in that Wendy's-prepared-for-every-eventuality kind of way, and take myself to the massive convention center set where I'm about to have someone else's big moment. Because as mad as I may be with her right now, I am even madder at Seth. And I will be great goddarned (sorry, Jesus) if I don't set this infuriating woman up for a lifetime of success so she can leave that guy the minute she gets up the nerve.

The place is crawling with other Wendys. Trim businesswomen clad in head-to-toe stretch wool or ponte, holding their free tote bags under their arms with a printed event schedule and phone in each hand respectively. It reminds me of when we had our college-internship fair, and we all dressed as fancily as we possibly could for malnourished college students and clutched for dear life three copies of our résumés on thick white paper given to us by our career counselors. So much nervous milling. So many people trying to get where they are not, all at the same time, without ever breaking away from the group.

And there are so, so many people.

Trying to hide my panic, I check and recheck the schedule myself. I am set to give the keynote over a tea service in the grand ballroom. A local newscaster will introduce Davis, and Davis will introduce me. Then I will speak for an entire hour on the subject of Purpose. I mean, if that's not ironic, I'm not sure what is.

I head to the ballroom. To my great relief, Davis is there, and he pats a spot next to him at a large banquet table on the dais.

"Wow," he says, taking in Wendy's softer look. "Have you changed your hair?"

"Do you like it?" I answer back.

He eyes me strangely, and I remember I just apologized to Wendy three hours ago for flirting with him. "You look great as usual," he deflects. "Are you ready for this?" he asks.

"As ready as I can be," I lie. He doesn't know I only had time to skim the speech—that I'll be reading it line for line out there off the PowerPoint prompter. "Are you?"

"I'm excited," he says. "Just think, when we joined our coaching practices, there were fewer than fifty women-owned businesses in the entire city—fewer still Black-owned ones. Now look around at this place. It's teeming with a diverse group of entrepreneurs and executives. The playing field is changing day by day."

The expression makes something pop into my mind, and I chase it down. Of course. The playing field. Tomorrow is the girls' first competitive game of the season. Zoey has been blowing up my phone about her nerves, while Bridget is impatient for the day and can't focus on much of anything else.

After this, it all comes down to the sangria. If it works tonight, I'll be myself again. That's what I want. I want my soft, out-of-shape body back. I want the mouth that can't eat spicy food and the stomach that can't do a sit-up and the life with no crushes and no accolades and no answer when I'm asked what I do for a living.

And without a doubt I want that body and that mouth and that life back more than anything in the world. I want to go to the game tomorrow and cheer my heart out for Zoey while Hugh and I book-end Joy and Samuel on the bleachers. I want to look behind the kids' backs, catch my husband's eye, and reach out a hand and hold his for a moment in pride for all that we've created. This feeling—this powerful longing—it's not just for my old life in general. It's for Hugh.

The audience starts to file in, and Davis gives me a killer wink, and to my surprise it just misses me entirely. Whatever appeal the man had, it falters next to the man with the ever-so-slightly hairy back who's dragging our reticent son around a school science fair right now. Thankfully, Davis doesn't notice. "Almost time. I'm going to go get my notes," he tells me. "Good luck, Wendy. Don't forget: passion wins. You've got this."

Wendy does have this. Wendy's life is hectic and stressful and kind of sad. Or it's full and accomplished and pride inducing. Whatever it is, it's hers. It's the way she wanted it. She wanted to run around like a chicken with her head cut off, and she wanted to suffer through endless boot camp workout sessions, and she wanted to work through softball practice and look at holes in the walls in her bedroom and eat truly dangerous amounts of rotisserie chicken. She wanted the roommate-style marriage and the constant mothering guilt, because that is what she knows for her life, and to her, that is what feels real. And this week has taken that reality away. Any fool can see all that anger wasn't meant for me.

But what about me? What feels real to me?

I shake my head to myself. A week ago I would have been 100 percent convinced that my life was jam-packed with purpose and meaning and that there was nothing more important than me being the secretary of the PTA and the class mom and teaching Joy American Sign Language before she gets to the ripe old age of four. But being Wendy has screwed all that up, and now 90 percent of what I was doing to fill my days feels . . . just a little empty compared to the real pleasures of my life. It's not the stuff I do that gives my life meaning. It's the people I do it for.

Why am I engaged in such competitive mom-ing, as Wendy has so cleverly dubbed it? Why have I taken the life I always dreamed of and turned it into something that has to justify its own existence?

From what seems a long, long distance away, I hear Davis thanking the newscaster, Karen Wetherby, for introducing him. He laughs as she asks him what it's like to consult with the university's athletic department—it's apparently well known around town that he's on retainer to work with the star student athletes on a regular basis—and he tells a good-natured joke about the women's basketball coach, a woman who is renowned not just for bringing home trophies but also for wearing the same underpants throughout long winning streaks.

Then, smoothly, he says that he's pleased to introduce another, far less superstitious winning woman, and the bottom drops out of my stomach. This is me. This is me pretending to be an expert on life. A coach. A winner. In front of hundreds of people in real life and who even knows how many people online.

But through the sound of my pulse racing, I still hear Davis. He is talking about all the ways Wendy has helped people, most of them entirely news to me. To hear him tell it, she's led people from all walks of life through challenging situations and helped them reorganize their lives to make room for their dreams.

It's no wonder she suspected I needed the same treatment.

I hear her name and a surge of applause from the attendees, and I know no matter how panicked I feel, I have to rise to this occasion. There are probably five hundred people in this room, all here to cultivate their own dreams and reorganize their own lives, and if I do this presentation well, they'll all line up to get Wendy to help them do just that. And through my nerves, it hits me: This audience—they're no different from me. Striving to be better, thinner, wealthier, more perfect. When in fact these people, who have Saturday mornings to spend in a convention center listening to productivity tips while they eat tea sandwiches, already have so much to be grateful for.

I should know.

I clear my throat and thank Davis for the warm introduction, and just as I'm opening the first slide, I see someone come into the nearest door of the ballroom. Someone very familiar. It's me. It's Wendy, really. And to my surprise, I find she's brought guests. Hugh, Seth, and all five of our kids are trying to skulk in quietly to hear me speak. I lock eyes with Wendy for a long time. Woman to woman. Mother to mother. Wife to wife. Finally she mouths words that are easy for me to recognize even across the giant room:

"I'm sorry."

I nod back. *"Me too,"* I mouth back. And then, *"Thank you."* I'm proud of her for getting the families here to support me—her. No, *us*. She smiles a bit, nudges the boys, and I watch them each hold up their science fair ribbons—second-place red for Linus and, to my surprise and delight, a green participation ribbon for my recalcitrant scholar Samuel.

And then, unmistakably, her eyes drift back behind me, and when I follow them, I lock eyes with Davis. He's staring at me, who he thinks is Wendy, intently, and for the first time ever, Wendy can see how he looks at her when she's not paying attention. Surprise—and something more—washes over her face. I let her feel it, and I turn back to the notes, clear my throat, and take the plunge.

"Thank you all so much for coming out today, sharing your precious Saturday with me. I think I have something precious to share with you back, something that can change your lives if you let it. But first, let me tell you about a client of mine who generously gave me permission to share with you all what she was able to achieve with the right plan."

I change slides. What follows is the story of a pro bono client I knew nothing about. She was a former addict who dreamed of returning to school to get her bachelor's in economics so she could start a for-profit investing club for women in recovery. She explained how after years of working as a bank teller before her drug arrest, she'd always been near the money, but she wasn't making much of it herself. Then, after serving six months for intent to distribute, she knew she'd never even be able to go back to working at the bank.

"She did the hard work; make no mistake," I read. "But I introduced her to a few very simple concepts, some of which we'll be discussing today." I pause and smile around the room, catch a few eyes, just as it says to do in my script. Lucky Wendy that she body swapped with someone who took a public speaking course twenty years ago, required for my minor in education.

"These are concepts that taught her to believe not just that you *can* have it all but that you *deserve* to," I read. "They can help you toss aside the limitations of your life—the things you've been told—or told yourself—that you can't do. Perfect example: Who here has said they *can't* when it comes to getting up an hour earlier every day, even though we know that getting up before everyone else is a trait seen most often in High Achievers and High Wealth Accumulators?" I wait for people to raise their hands, and they oblige. "Ok, there we go! Even in this room full of go-getters," I read, "here we are, telling ourselves we can't get out of bed for our own dreams!"

There are murmurs of recognition and nods of understanding moving through the room. I catch Wendy. She's nodding along, too, and gives me a thumbs-up. She must know this keynote like the back of her hand. She probably worked on it endlessly, sometimes at the crack of dawn when she, too, could have used an extra hour of sleep. That's how important this is to her. That's how important it is that I get this right.

I take a deep breath and tell more of the bank teller's story. How she started by getting up earlier in the morning than her young kids and recruiting help from the community center and the small business women's association. How she made investments in herself to be the person who was successful in advance of her actual success. How her posture, her attitude—even her body mass index—changed as a result of these new thoughts and steps, until she had managed to double her working productivity, get a promotion at her day job, start business school at night, and join a junior investing club that met for breakfast meetings once a month.

There is the appropriate number of oohs and aahs.

Now comes the part where I introduce her, and she stands to cheers and applause. I announce that she graduated with top honors, and her successful investment group has a waiting list. I tell how she has visited the nearby women's prisons and empowered dozens of women to start their own fiscal support groups, and she is taking meetings now with major VC firms as part of a new dream to never have a moment of downtime again for the rest of her life.

Well, I don't say the downtime bit.

Everyone claps again. Frankly, it's hard for me not to stomp and cheer at this remarkable, if exhausting, story. The business maven waves and beams with pride. What Wendy can help people do is pretty remarkable.

It's just what she's doing to herself that I take issue with.

I turn to the next slide. Here comes the part where I tell the audience what Wendy Charles Consulting can do for them, if they are just willing to believe in the idea that they really can have it all.

But when I open my mouth to deliver the big sell-in, my throat starts to gets dry. By the time I'm through to the you-really-can-have-it-all part, my tongue is a desert and my hands are sweating. I can't go on with this. It's plain as day. I clear my throat, shake my head.

"No," I hear myself say. "No. Look, no. I'm sorry. Wendy Charles Consulting is a terrific company, and there is no doubt that she—I—can do great things for you. But no, I'm not going to stand here and tell you that you can have 'it all,' whatever that means, or even that you should *want* to have it all. Not all at once. Yes, there are people out there"—I lock eyes with Wendy, see her expression of concern, but push on—"people who maybe have found themselves pushed too far to one side of things or the other. Women who haven't had time for themselves or their families, or women who haven't had—or even wanted to make—time for a career. And let me tell you—I know whereof I speak. I've been one of those kinds of women. I'll let you guys guess which kind." There's a polite, if hesitant, titter in the audience. They're not sure where I'm going with this. To be honest, neither am I.

"But you know what? I've given it a lot of thought lately, and I've realized that's totally ok. Yes, maybe my life isn't in perfect balance at this moment. Yes, there's a whole lot more many of us can accomplish, now or in the future. But do we really have to achieve every single goal and dream *right this second*? Aren't we all just kind of exhausted?" I look up, and to my happy surprise I see the audience setting down their scones, watching me carefully, a few heads even nodding. "Wouldn't some of our time be better spent figuring out how to do *less*, how to stop taking on more than our fair share of the hardships, how to free up just a little bit of extra sleep rather than pushing ourselves yet further into the land of the tired, the guilt worn, and the weary?"

I take this moment to run my gaze over the tables, locking eyes with my listeners whenever I can. The audience looks back at me, surprised but definitely engaged. Some people look genuinely stunned—maybe people who know Wendy personally. One of them may charge the stage if I don't make my point soon. So I'd better figure out what the heck my point is.

"I came here today ready to tell you the six steps to getting more done every day, and I even have a clever mnemonic for it in my box of tricks here"—I switch to the *DO MORE* slide to prove it—"but no. I'm just not going to do that to you. Not today." I click the slide to the next one, a woman on a beach looking thoughtful. It will definitely do the trick.

"Later, when the time is right, you'll all get your chance to learn how to do more. Believe me when I say I can talk for *hours* about how to do more," I say, and then I let myself smile directly at Wendy and, to my relief, see the beginning of a smile flash over her face in return. "But for today, let's be revolutionary. Today, why don't you consider visiting a productivity coach to learn to DO LESS, and do it with more joy? Wendy Charles Consulting can tell you how to take over the world, sure. One hundred percent, and you don't have to take my word for it." I hold up my note cards and rifle through them. "The testimonials in this speech are insane." The audience laughs. Then I open my hands and let the cards fall to the ground. "But this company can also tell you how to get more joy out of what you are already doing. We can help you find out what you should stop doing because it makes you unhappy or stressed out. I'm looking at you, science fair cupcakes, book club theme platters, and homemade coconut milk–collagen smoothies," I say, and the whole room laughs knowingly. "And you, filthy break-room microwave that no one else will ever clean, and office birthday parties that you are inexplicably always in charge of, and"—I reach back to when I was a teacher and somehow became the Xerox-machine repairwoman of the math department—"toner cartridges that for some reason can only be changed by people with vaginas." The audience's laughter gets louder, and someone hoots and claps in recognition.

"Look around you, ladies," I say, gaining more and more momentum from the positive responses. "Here we have a huge room full of smart, empowered women experiencing at least some small amount of privilege to be here with me today. Do you want to use that privilege to push yourself ever harder and harder until you collapse? Or do you want to hit the brakes and start saying no to this madness, not just for yourself but for every woman in a home or an office struggling with more than her fair share? At Wendy Charles Consulting, we can help you find out who needs to step up to give you the space to do what you're born to do." I try hard not to look at Seth and Wendy when I say this . . . and fail. Her eyes are locked on me, but she's not frowning. In fact, I could swear she's giving me a barely perceptible nod.

"Do you feel me?" I ask, turning back to the larger audience. "Who in your life comes to mind when you hear me talk about these things? Who did you instantly visualize when I say that you're probably doing more than other people, just because you were born with ovaries and a strong sense of responsibility? Let's hear it!" A couple of people answer me back, shouting the names of guilty parties. The boss. The coworkers. The kids. Some listeners just start clapping. A couple of cheers get loose.

"Women, we can get free from the idea that the only way to be a strong, successful feminist is to work yourself into the ground!" I cry, realizing the truth of what I say in the exact moment I'm saying it. "We don't have to compete with each other anymore." I think of the sangria, the cookie auction, the softball tryouts, and that stupid magazine-worthy pantry I thought would be the answer to everyone's problems. "We don't have to work ourselves to death! We may not have mastered every one of our life dreams yet, we may not have crossed off our bucket lists or achieved our max potential or even washed our hair in five days"—I let the laugh wave over us and see a couple of women self-consciously touch their ponytails—"but there is a season for everything, and our job today is to figure out which one we're in and EMBRACE IT! We are enough as it is, right now, exactly where we are, no matter what or who we're not!"

The audience goes wild. I mean, they clap, they cheer, they honest-to-goodness whistle. And my heart is thundering, but not with fear, not anymore. With freedom, joy. A sudden, crystal-clear understanding. I look at Wendy again, and now I know for sure: she's nodding. Her eyes are wide, and she looks shocked, but she's not mad. She's telling me, *Keep going.*

I beam back at the crowd, exhilarated. "Now, isn't this more fun than a mnemonic device?" I ask them all. There is more clapping. There is more cheering. If I don't get control of the room soon, I think there will be some light chanting.

I wait for the racket to die down a bit and realize Davis is trying to catch my eye. He is alternating between wild double thumbs-ups and meaningfully tapping his watch and mouthing the words *"wrap it up."*

"Ladies, thank you so much for coming out," I say. "Thank you for picking up what I'm putting down today. Now let me send you on your way, charged with the mission to go out and do less!"

More clapping. In a quick spark I remember why I'm there. "And if you can't figure out how to do it, navigate your phones to WendyCharlesProductivity dot com and make your introductory appointment right now, because WE CAN HELP!"

I basically mic drop. My heart is full and pounding. As I stroll from the stage, a newly minted Women's Expo Rock Star, I see Wendy staring at me, mouth open, a tiny grin forming as she slowly begins to clap. I see Seth staring at the ceiling, utterly bored. I see Davis applauding me and laughing and shaking his head in wonder. I see Anna Joy eating a bright-red Ring Pop.

And finally, I see Hugh, his arm hanging loosely around Samuel, giving me the thumbs-up and a chummy nod, the look of a man who has no idea how badly his wife is missing him. My heart almost pulls out of my chest in his direction. I wish he knew it was his own wife he was cheering on today. I want to run into his arms and say, *Thank you. Thank you for letting me do—what would Wendy call it? Oh yeah, "ef all" for the last twelve years. Thank you, Hugh, for letting me just love on our kids and take care of them in the way that felt right to me at the time. Thank you for being so. Damn. Patient with my pursuit of perfect parenthood.*

And also: *I believe, as of today, I can officially put that pursuit aside.*

I swallow all of it. As long as I am Wendy, I can't tell him any of those things. And it breaks my heart.

Up until today, until this very moment, I haven't truly understood how much I have to lose if I can't get my real self back soon. Davis is handsome and all, but Hugh is the man who taught me what I know about joy. He's the man who has let me figure out everything I finally understand about my life and do it in my own sweet time. Over the years I've told myself stories about how I'm not worth enough in the marketplace to work, how childcare costs more than I can earn, how parenting is the only thing I'm good enough at to be truly useful, to be truly of service. But that's all nonsense, and I don't need that story anymore. I *like* staying at home. I like making fruit sushi. I don't have to do it because fruit sushi is somehow necessary. I just like it.

That said, I do not want to make the gazpacho anymore.

I walk straight up to Wendy and say that to her.

"I don't want to make the gazpacho anymore."

She looks at me, stunned, and pulls me by the arm to a slightly private bit of hallway just outside the ballroom. "What the hell did you just do?" she asks.

"I blew things up," I tell her. "I'm sorry. But I had to. I couldn't take what I'd suddenly figured out about our lives and then tell a roomful of already overtaxed women to do more, more, more all the time. Think of all these people. Think of how it would have made them feel."

She stares at me a long time. I think, *Ok, this is it. This is when she snaps and kills me and hides my body in the chest freezer in my own basement.*

But instead, she wraps her arms around me and hugs tight. "I don't have to think about how it would make them feel. I know how it's made *me* feel. And I know it's time for that to stop."

Before I can respond, Davis jogs up to us and acts like I'm the only person in the room. "Did you see this?" he asks excitedly. He holds up his phone, and it's Wendy's consultation schedule for next week. It's booked solid with new business. Every opening she's offered has a name in it.

Wendy's jaw drops. Quickly, I lean in and whisper to her, "Never forget: you inspire people. Everything I said today—I figured it out from you."

She looks at me hard, her eyes glistening. "Thank you," she says. It's two words, but to me, it means the world.

Davis pats me on the back. "You killed it!" he says. And then, right in front of Seth, Jesus, and everyone, the man gives me a massive hug full of joy and celebration and just a tiny bit of something else too. Desire.

I soak it all up, just this last time. This will be it for me. This will likely be the only crush I will ever indulge for the rest of my life, because I just realized how madly in love I am with my husband. And that makes me so incredibly lucky. "Amazing, Wendy!" Davis takes me by the shoulders. "You freaking knocked it out of the park," he says to me.

And then softer, just into my ear: "You're amazing. I need you to know that, no matter what."

I pull back. Inhale the adoration. And respond just loudly enough so that only he and the real Wendy can hear me: "You know what? I am. I didn't always see it, but I am kind of amazing. Thank you for noticing, Davis, so I could notice too."

Then I turn to Wendy. "Are you thinking what I'm thinking?" I ask her.

She nods. "It's time for you and me to get very, very drunk."

—

WENDY

That night I tuck Samuel, Joy, and Zoey in bed for what I expect will be the very last time. I linger over each of them. Tomorrow I will be myself again, but I will be different, and I will miss these kids.

I will miss Hugh too. As I tell him I'm going out to have a drink with my new friend, I take in his scent—a pleasant mix of aftershave and Downy that will forever make me think of their big soft bed and lying about the state of my vaginal health. He asks me if I'd like to sleep in tomorrow, since it's Sunday. He offers to take the kids to the ballpark early and meet me there after I've gotten a few extra z's.

I mean, this guy.

That's why, before I take the sweaty glass of pink sangria that Celeste has made for me, I ask her, "You'll be good to him, right?"

"Are you talking about Hugh?" she asks. "I've always been good to him."

"I want you to be, like, crazy good to him. Unsolicited-back-rubs good to him."

Celeste nods. "When this is over, I'm going to be go-to-awkward-work-events-without-complaining good to him," she tells me. "Plus some sex stuff."

I put my hands up in horror. "Please do not elaborate."

She cracks up. Then she raises her glass to mine. "Let's drink to that."

"How do you think this switch back will work?" I ask her as we settle on the lawn just inside my yard on our big softball blankets, looking up at the pretty canopy of trees and the dark night sky.

"I have no idea why you're asking me," she says. "But maybe we just drink until we can't walk straight and then go to bed? That seems to have done it the last time."

I nod. "But what if after a glass of this we start fighting again?"

Celeste looks at me sternly. "I think you got the last of your fighting out this morning, didn't you?"

I look down. "I'm sorry," I say. "I was way out of line."

"I'm sorry about what I said back," she says. "But I do not apologize for sorting your baking supplies."

"You know what, Celeste," I tell her, shaking my head. "It doesn't matter where you put the brown sugar; I'm not baking anyway. And I'm officially completely ok with that. After all, I heard this really inspirational speech today, and it made me think maybe I could hang up some of my fantasies about what a mother is 'supposed to do.'"

"So you're not mad at all about my little, uh, rewrite?"

"Mad, no. Shocked . . . well, maybe a little."

"You're going to be making a fortune in the next six weeks, if it's any consolation. Your consult schedule is completely full through August."

"The trouble is," I reply, "those people are going to want to be told they can have more by doing less. And I've got no reason to believe that's true."

"But it is!" Celeste says. "It has to be. I mean, Wendy, look at our lives. We've seen it from both sides of the thorny shrub now, and they're both just . . . too much. I mean, I have a literal hole in my abdominals I didn't even notice! Something has to give. You must agree with that by now."

"I guess I do," I say with a heavy sigh.

"And you'll figure that out, just like you figured out how to write a business plan and fund a company and hire people and create a partnership and get A-list clients and publish planners and give keynotes," I tell her. "You'll take everything you know about productivity and—like you did with that bank teller—put it toward only the most important things in your life."

I look at her in wonder. "Do you really think I can do that?"

"Of course you can! I'm completely sold on Wendy Charles Consulting. In fact, someday I'm going to send Zoey to you to learn your mad skills."

I set down my drink for a moment. "Really?" I ask her. "You'd trust me with your daughter?"

"Don't act so surprised!" she says. "My kids have been under your care for the last week!"

"Yes, but . . . I thought I was doing a terrible job," I confess to her.

"Not really," she says. "You didn't really think that."

"Yes, really! Of the two of us, you're the good mother," I remind her. "I'm the businesswoman."

She rolls her eyes. "It's possible, just possible, that you're both."

I think on this for a few minutes. "Seth told me, long ago, that we were both too selfish for kids. And I still think about that all the time. What kind of mother would rather be at work than with her children?" I ask her. "You're not supposed to love your job more than you love your kids."

"That's idiotic," says Celeste, and I can tell the vodka is working on her. "What a silly thing to say. Perhaps you prefer the work at your office to the work of parenting, but that's not the same as putting your job before your children. That's just called being a normal grown-up who prefers doing grown-up things."

"You don't prefer doing grown-up things," I say.

"Yes, well, it takes all kinds." And then after a moment she adds, "Surely you know that just because I enjoy staying home with my kids, that doesn't mean changing diapers or playing My Little Pony for two hours is my idea of a good time."

I say nothing for a long moment, because no, I don't think I did truly get that until just now. "I tried to play My Little Pony with Joy and lasted about seven minutes," I admit.

"Better than Hugh. He falls asleep while she's still trying to teach him the rules of the game. Most of the time he ends up just being part of the terrain, and then when he wakes up, he's forced to hold still until the ponies clear off Dad Mountain."

"That's adorable," I say.

"It really is."

I look at my glass. Empty. I set it down and flop onto my back on the blanket. Celeste grabs the pitcher of sangria and tops off our glasses. In the stillness of the evening I imagine all our babies sleeping away in their rooms, and a pang surges through me. "I cannot wait to be myself again," I tell her. "If for no other reason than to have a good hug from Linus."

"He's the snuggliest," Celeste agrees.

"He's like a heat-seeking missile," I say. "I cannot believe how much I miss him."

"Why not? He's so lovable. I know I'll miss him like crazy when we switch back."

"I thought you said he was an entitled Jordan almond."

"He's a very sweet, very smart Jordan almond who is starting to get the hang of folding laundry."

"You're kidding," I say. "You have Linus helping out?"

"I have them both going on a chore chart. I have mad skills, Wendy, and soon you will learn to worship at the altar that is my parenting."

I laugh. "Consider yourself worshipped. You're freaking Mother of the Year. I have tried for years to get the kids to do stuff. No luck."

"Let me guess: it's easier to just do it yourself."

"Exactly. Easier and faster, and it gets done right."

"If you want your kids to do their laundry, prepare for a lot of pink laundry," she says.

"I can't deal. I'm way too uptight for that."

"Correction—you *were* way too uptight for that. Now you're the picture of zen."

I laugh way too long at this. "I am one with the pink laundry. Ommmmmm. Am I convincing you? I am totally not convincing myself."

Celeste just laughs.

"You know what my dream is?" I go on. "My dream is to be the kind of mom that's ok with pink laundry. To enforce the chore chart even if it's more work than doing it myself. To get Happy Meals for my kids without shame, but also to sit down and eat our McDonald's together like a family sometimes."

"That sounds utterly doable," Celeste says. "I've got your back on all of that."

"What's your dream?" I ask her.

"My dream is healthy adult offspring who can figure out what makes them happy and then make it happen. And when they're not happy, I want them to believe they can weather the storm until it passes, knowing full well that it will." She sighs. "But that dream is taking less and less from me every year, as it starts to pass out of my hands."

"It will be years before Joy is out of your hands."

She shakes her head. "Just the blink of an eye. It will happen in the blink of an eye."

"All the more reason to slow down and savor it," I hear myself say. And then, "Oh my god, I can't believe I just said that. This vodka is crazy stuff."

"More?"

"Yes, please. What's the first thing you're going to do when we switch back?" I ask her.

"Plant a huge kiss on Hugh," she says. "And tell him how much I love him."

I get quiet.

"What?"

"It's just . . . that is not the first thing I'm going to do," I say.

"I would hope not. Hugh would be very weirded out."

"I mean Seth."

She sighs. "I know you do. I was trying to be funny and distracting."

I give her a wan smile. "You're a good friend, Celeste."

She shakes her head and holds up the bottle of birch-sap vodka, saying, "What is *in* this stuff?!" with a big laugh.

"Whatever it is," I say, "it's powerful as hell."

"After this is over, I'm keeping it behind lock and key."

"After this is over. Can you believe it's been a week?" I ask her.

"It feels like it's been a year," she says, at the exact same time as I say, "It feels like it's been a minute."

We look at each other and laugh.

"Exactly," I say.

"Exactly," she agrees.

There's a long pause. Then, "What if we don't swap back?" Celeste asks.

"We're going to swap back," I tell her.

"But if we don't?"

I pause and think. This is the longest I could have ever considered lasting, these seven days away from my real life. Tonight will be a milestone, the end of an entire week, and even the slightest consideration that this could go on longer feels like an actual stone dragging on my soul. I recognize this feeling from every single December 31 I've ever had: the idea that if I don't start doing whatever resolution it is I've decided on now, maybe I never will.

"We just need to be very sure we drink enough of this stuff," I tell her, with finality, because I need my answer to be final. I cannot stand the alternatives.

"In that case, would you like another glass?" she asks me.

I grab the entire pitcher. "Don't mind if I do."

CHAPTER 21

STUNDAY SUNDAY

WENDY

I wake up the next morning, and my head is throbbing and my mouth is dry. I pinch my eyes shut as tightly as I can and hope with all my might. Then I open my eyes, slowly. Slowly.

Shit. With Celeste's crystal-clear vision I see her bedroom and her body and her pretty cream nightgown. I'm still her. She's still me. It's Sunday and a full week has passed, and if I haven't gotten my body back yet . . . will I ever? Before I can even begin to start sobbing hysterically about that, my doorbell rings.

Who could possibly be ringing Celeste's doorbell at this hour? I wonder. And then realize it's daytime and the sun is streaming in the windows and Hugh is gone, so I pound down the stairs in unison with my throbbing brain and try not to vomit on Celeste's front rug.

"Hello?" I say before the door is fully open.

"I AM STILL FREAKING YOU!" Celeste says, and just that most minor of curses is enough to get my attention. "AND WE ARE GOING TO BE LATE FOR THE GAME!"

I squeeze my eyes open and then shut and then ask her to give me a moment. She stands there in my body, tapping my toes and saying, "Are you going to put on pants or what?"

I put on pants, noting as I do a thoughtfully written note on my side of the bed from Hugh telling me to meet him and the kids at the game, and follow her to my beloved Jeep, heading right for the driver's side out of habit. "Sorry," I start to say, but she says, "No, seriously, you drive. I'm still too traumatized that I'm not me again. No offense. I really, really wanted to be me."

I nod and gladly take the wheel—I'm in the mood to drive like a NASCAR racer. "Do you think . . ."

"We're stuck like this forever?" she completes. "I don't know, Wendy. I just know I want my life back." Tears start to leak out of her eyes.

I want mine back, too, but Celeste is spinning out. "Ok," I say, because I don't know what else to do. "Try not to freak out."

"'Freaked out' doesn't even begin to explain it. I stress ate all your kids' leftover Easter candy before I drove over here," she admits, showing me a tote bag full of empty wrappers. "I don't know how to make this right. I know we're not supposed to fix things for each other, and I put all my faith in that stupid artisanal vodka . . ."

I shake my head. "That was my idea," I admit. "I didn't know what else to think." My own tears rise up again. "All I know is that I miss my kids so, so much. I miss my stupid house with the messy pantry and the hole in the wall. I miss my routine and my hustle, and I even miss my crazy sister!" The tears break out, and I frantically try to blink them away as I pull into the parking lot of the softball field.

Celeste puts her hand on my arm, comfortingly. Kindly. I've misunderstood her, underestimated her, and overruled her at every turn. And even after all that, she's been there every time the chips are down.

Only, when I put the car in park and look over at her, ready to tell her thank you for all her good intentions, even if they didn't work out quite right, I realize she's not patting my shoulder to comfort me. She's trying to get my attention. She's wheezing. Gasping like something's wrong with her windpipe. "Celeste?" I say. "Are you ok?"

Her face is red, and she shakes it no, violently. She starts to creak out a scary, airless sound. "Are you choking?" I ask her.

She shakes her head again and starts scraping at her neck, the skin over her windpipe. She's leaving bright-red marks, and her eyes are watering violently. She starts to cough, and then, when her hands move, I see them. Hives on her chest. Hundreds more popping up on her arms. Appearing right before my eyes, like she's being stung by a thousand invisible bees.

Immediately I understand.

"Celeste!" I shout. "What did you eat?"

She shakes her head but points to the door. I jump out of the driver's side of the Jeep and come around to look on the floor by her feet. There's nothing there. In fact, it's cleaner than I've ever seen it, but she keeps pointing and gasping, at the tote of food for the game, and at once I remember the candy wrappers. I dump them, and there it is—the wrapper I would know anywhere. Yellow, square, pleated sides.

Peanut M&M'S.

I'm allergic to peanuts. I drop the wrapper like a hot iron but then realize, no, I'm *not* allergic to peanuts; my body is. Celeste's body, at the moment. I must not have ever told her, and she ate some, and now she's in anaphylactic shock and needs epinephrine. I have the EpiPen in the back zipper pouch of my handbag—which is Celeste's handbag right now—which I normally take with me everywhere. It's black leather, the size of a hardcover book with a cross strap; I start combing the car for it. How is it not in this car? It's not anywhere. All I find is a huge canvas bag that I usually use for pastries and flowers when we go to the farmers' market. Large enough to fit a week's worth of produce, only now it's full of wet wipes, healthy snacks, extra socks, a kid's book, a tween book, a pack of markers, a raincoat—where exactly did this woman think she was packing for?! But there's no EpiPen. It's all spilled out on the floor of the back of my Jeep, every single item taken out and rooted through. No EpiPen. How can she be going around with a dangerous allergy and no EpiPen? Why didn't she just stick to my handbag? *Dammit, Celeste! Why did you always have to be so prepared?*

She's still making sounds, but now she's getting quieter. Her eyes are wild when I come around to look at her. I tell her it's all going to be ok. She's having an allergic reaction to something I'm allergic to. Peanuts, I explain in the softest, calmest voice I can, even though I am freaking out. I don't know if the EMTs can get here in time to administer an injection. I call 911, tell them my friend is experiencing anaphylaxis, and they ask me if there's an injection pen around, and just as I'm about to say no, I realize—*SOFIA!* Peanuts, just like me, and her mother sews an injector right into her daughter's softball uniform so she's never unprepared.

I look at Celeste—her eyes are fluttering closed. Someone needs to give her CPR while I get the pen, but I'm terrified to leave her there, and the cheering on the field makes my shouting inaudible. My brain feels hot and my pulse is racing, and I just decide, *Ok, I'm going to bring her with me.* She's in my littler body, and I've got the shoulders of a woman who still carries a forty-pound toddler everywhere she goes. The field is not even twenty feet away. I just have to run up there and get help, get someone to give her CPR while I get the pen, or vice versa. It doesn't matter, but I cannot leave her here alone in the car. I grab her by the chin and say, "Can you hear me," and she nods, and I say, "Stay calm and try to climb on my back," and then she does; she gets right on my back with her front over my shoulders like a sack of potatoes, and her legs are standing shakily in the wheel well of the car. "Ok," I say, though I am wincing under her weight. "Push!" and she gives a quick push of her legs, and we are off. I have her over both shoulders, her waist curled around the back of my neck in a fireman's carry just like I learned in some emergency-preparedness seminar at some women's expo whose details I can't even remember, and I start to stagger toward the field, shouting, "HELP! HELP! WE NEED THE EPIPEN!"

And somehow I make it to the grass, and I see Sofia, so close, right there on the pitcher's mound, and I know that pen is in her shirt, but she doesn't seem to hear me shouting, so I unload Celeste gently, as best I can, and a few dads rush up to help me, and I tell them to start CPR, because Sofia is so close I feel like I can almost reach her. I'm going to get that pen right off her, and Celeste will be breathing fine before even another single minute goes by. So I run onto the field as fast as I can, beelining for the pitcher, for the pen I know is sewn into her waistband. And I don't really notice that Sofia is letting go of a slider, and I completely don't notice that someone's bat connects with it before the ump sees me running onto the field, and then, in a startling starburst of pain under my chin, I don't really know exactly what hits me until I, and then the line drive from less than twenty feet away, hit the ground one after another. I've dropped to my knees, the world getting very white and small, only a few inches from Sofia, and somehow manage to shout to her, as loudly as I possibly can, "GIVE HER YOUR EPI SHOT!"

I swear I see someone running toward us, or many someones, but I cannot be sure, because after that the entire world gets tiny, the size of a pinpoint, of a pinpoint through closed eyelids.

And then, just absolutely nothing.

———

CELESTE

What happens next is truly beyond my understanding. I've seen EpiPens before but never had one thrust into my thigh by an eleven-year-old girl. I've never been fireman-carried by my own body occupied by someone else's brain. I've never had a peanut allergy, except it turns out that

I have for the last entire week. I wish someone would've mentioned it to me. Before I demolished three snack-size bags of peanut M&M'S.

But within seconds of getting the pen, I stop drowning on nothing and can suck in huge amounts of air. My heartbeat races a bit, and the spot on my leg where I got the injection kind of pulses. There's a teeny bit of jitteriness but nothing compared to, say, a shot of real espresso. And then, bit by bit, I start to feel better. In fact, I feel so much better and am so surprised by the whole affair that it takes me a very long time to realize that my real body is lying next to me, unconscious. Leaving me to wonder what happened to Wendy. I try to scramble to my feet to find out, but the act leaves me dizzier than I expected, and someone's strong arms—Davis's, I'm surprised to see—hold me in place.

"Stay where you are," he tells me. "The ambulance is already here."

"But what happened to Wendy?" I demand. "Did she freak out and faint?"

Davis looks around, panicked. "She's out of it," he shouts down to the EMTs. "She doesn't know who she is!"

I force myself to think. Think about the last week. "I mean Celeste. What happened to Celeste?"

An EMT runs up to me, starts taking my vitals. I'm craning my neck to see where Wendy is. Why isn't she getting up? Is that . . . is all of that blood?

"What happened? Is Hugh here? Can anyone tell me what's happening?"

Davis turns to look in the direction I'm pointing and seems surprised at what he sees. He very nearly drops me into the EMT's arms and rushes to Wendy's side, where a crowd is forming. And Hugh is already there. Hugh and the kids. Wendy's and mine, looking shocked and scared. Linus is crying.

"Bridget!" I shout. "What is going on here?"

She looks past the mask and blood pressure cuff and the EMT, confused. "Mom?" she asks quietly. Then she looks to Wendy lying on the ground and then back to me. "Something happened. Something really bad."

That is the truest thing anyone has ever said. Something is very bad. It must be the epinephrine or the shock. It must be the stress of the week that has been. In my brain is a whirlpool, and in that eddy is a muddle of events. The switch. The sangria. Baseball tryouts. Softball tryouts. Wendy in the pantry yelling and me on the dais cheering.

"Where's Joy?" I ask, but once again, air is failing me. "Where's Hugh?" I gasp. "Can you help me breathe?"

"She's going to need her second shot," one EMT calls to the other, who is crouched over Wendy, and her hands are covered with blood, and she's calling for backup, and she sounds panicked.

"It's me who is hurt," I try to tell them, but then, it's me here, and that's not me over there, and there's so much blood, and Wendy's not getting up, I'm not getting up, and suddenly not only can I not breathe, but I can't understand. Is that me over there, dying on the grass? Is this me here, holding Bridget's hands?

"Wendy's not getting up," I hear myself croak out.

"Ma'am, we're going to give you another shot and wait for the next ambulance, ok? It's going to be ok, but we need to get the other mom to the ER right away. You're going to be just fine. Is this your daughter?" she asks.

"No," I say, while she looks at me and says, "Yes."

"Bridget, go find my daughter," I ask her.

She looks at me like I'm crazy, and then I remember. She's not my daughter, but she doesn't know it. And her mother's body is in some kind of awful shock. And my body is over there, not moving. Not even seeming to breathe.

Am I going to die and take Wendy's body with me? Or—worse—is she going to die and leave me here forever?

"Ok, try to hold still now, ma'am. This is your second shot, so it's not going to be much fun."

"Baby, don't be scared, ok?" I rasp out. In my mind I'm talking to both girls, to all our kids, but I only see Bridget there.

She nods, but her eyes are huge, and I swear I can feel her heartbeat in the squeezing of her palm.

"Tell Samuel don't be scared," I think I'm saying, but after that second shot, I have no idea if any words come out. Instead I'm just thoughts.

Davis

Speech

Wendy

Hugh

I lie back down flat on the ground. Davis is back, hovering just on the edge of my blurry vision. Bridget is still holding my hand. That strange quiet drowning sensation from before is back, but without the choking that came before it. And now, sirens. I hear sirens. More and more sirens.

I'm in the parking lot, even though I feel the grass underneath me.

I'm in the back of a truck.

I'm in an ambulance.

I'm still craning my neck, hoping I can see what happened to my body, and Wendy inside it.

But Wendy isn't here, and if she's not, then how much longer can I stay here myself?

CHAPTER 22

WENDY

When I wake up, I know who I am instantly. For the last week it has been the very first thing I check every morning when I first wake up, and it is the first thing I check this time too. My breasts—they have been shorthand for my identity ever since I switched with Celeste. What I feel under my hands is small and firm and bony above and below. I am Wendy—I am in my own body!—and I can breathe. The awful splitting headache I had just seconds ago (or was it hours?) is gone. The hives Celeste had are gone. I'm just Wendy, in a normal body that works normally, and everything is going to go back to normal. The relief comes out in tears and gasping, and for a bit of time I'm too wrecked to do anything besides bask in the gratitude.

At last I try to remember what got me here. I'm in a hospital bed, and it's bustling and busy, so I know I'm still in the ER, and if I'm awake and I'm me, then I must've gotten Celeste the EpiPen after all. And someone must've gotten her to the hospital and administered another dose and started me on this IV drip and given me a walloping dose of Benadryl, which always makes me super groggy. What else can I remember? Who called 911? Where are my kids? Where is my husband, and is he still my husband, and do I want him to still be my husband? Because I am me again, but I am changed. I cannot unknow what I know.

And I don't want to try.

I sit up slowly. Nothing hurts. I have a nasal cannula—a tube that runs under my nose and pushes oxygen into it—and a blood pressure monitor on my fingertip and an IV that is only hooked up to a single bag. In other words, odds are good that I'm as fine as I feel. Actually, I'm probably better than fine. Compared to last week, my body feels great! I have abdominal muscles, and my back isn't tired from hauling Anna Joy up and down. Plus my shoulders don't hurt, because this isn't the body that fireman-carried a suffocating person onto a ball field. This is the body that was suffocating from peanuts, and this body feels fine now.

But then, that means someone is unaccounted for.

Finally I start to remember details. The pitch, the crack of the bat, the connection of ball to jaw. Dropping to my knees and face-planting into the dirt between the batter's box and the pitcher's mound. That was me, but now, if I've switched again, that means that person who blacked out is now Celeste.

So where is Celeste's body?

In the movies, people are always ripping out their IVs when they flee their hospital beds. Unable to be quite that impractical—or quite so masochistic, perhaps—I call the nurse station and tell them over the beeping that I wish to check out on a very urgent basis. Within a few minutes, a nurse comes into my room and tells me I will not be discharged anytime soon.

She slowly explains that I am in here for observation for a reason—do I remember I went into anaphylactic shock just this morning?

I don't, exactly, but she doesn't need to know that. Besides, my body remembers everything. It tells me everything I need to know about what just happened to me, and it tells me in no uncertain terms that I feel fine, if a bit groggy from the Benadryl. I shake my head, apologize to the nurse as if it's all some big misunderstanding, and rephrase: it's not that I really want to leave the hospital, per se, but that I want to go for a walk around the hallways of the unit to stretch my legs.

In that case, it seems, I'm welcome to wander as long as I stay far from Triage. She hooks my IV up to a wheelie stand I can push around, my saline bag—just saline, not even glucose, so I must be totally fine according to my *Chicago Med* medical degree—hanging from a shepherd's hook at the top. She helps me to my feet and ties a second gown around me, with the ties back to front so I end up with full coverage. And after checking another gauge, she unhooks my nose tube and tells me to come straight to the nurses' station if I feel any shortness of breath before bustling off and leaving me to it.

I totter out of the room feeling 100 percent fine, except for that dopey haze over the top of everything, and the dawning realization that Celeste is missing, and can you die from being beaned by a softball?

Of course you can. And here I am, fine. Better than fine. I can tell my body has been treated better over the last week than it has ever been treated before. Funny how I was so nice to Celeste's body—exercise, sleep—and she was so nice to mine—home cooking and a break from punishing boot camp routines—and we are both normally so awful to each other . . . and to ourselves.

When I see Celeste again, I am going to tell her just how sorry I am. I'm going to make sure she knows that I never truly suspected her—just took anger out on her unfairly, to try to keep my own stories intact. If I see Celeste again.

But I *have* to see Celeste again. The fact is, there is no way you can swap bodies without sharing so much more. No matter what we were telling ourselves over the last week, brains and bodies aren't two totally unconnected things. There's not a Wendy's brain that can float around without information from Wendy's body, and a Celeste's brain without Celeste's body. There is a third thing, which is what we have been since this started, something neither purely Celeste nor purely me.

After all, I was awash in Celeste's nursing hormones. Celeste was feeling what I feel for Davis—no matter how my brain has tried to cover it up. The person I was in Celeste's body wasn't just Wendy with a different bra size. It was someone who could take a few days off and let her business be. It was someone who opened her heart to three more kids, kids I hardly knew before and now love dearly.

It's someone who was jealous of Celeste, of how loved she was by her husband, of how she carefully, tenderly mothered everyone around her, and of how she lived outside the rush-everywhere panic bubble that I thought was just how life was supposed to go.

And what did I do? I weaned her baby, gave her kids fast food, plugged them into screens, and neglected them. I made fun of her husband instead of seeing him for the upright man that he is. I told Celeste that her life and her choices were stupid. That she didn't matter.

My face burns with shame.

I touch my own cheek and think back to that night in the Taco Barn. To the hot burn of that salsa in my mouth. I follow it to the equally painful memory of Seth leaning over to kiss me, of the weight of Celeste on my shoulders as I dragged her from the car, of the impact of that ball on my face, of the ground rushing at me as I fell forward.

I make the rounds of the ER, intrusively peering around every cubicle and curtain. Celeste is nowhere to be found. The thought is almost purely intellectual for a moment, a beat too long, and then it lands, bam, on my heart. If she's not here . . . where is she?

I cough and grasp at my chest, and my body remembers what it went through. While I was out of my mind.

The nurse is back at the nursing station. I start shuffling along the back of the wing and see an elevator come into view. I wait just a few seconds, making sure I'm unnoticed, before I push the down button, slip inside, and make a break for it.

On the reception floor I find the information desk, where someone with a name tag that specifies pronouns waits merrily. I tell them I'm here to visit Celeste Mason. They frown at me for ages. Finally, they start tapping in their computer.

The wait is interminably long.

At last, they call a number. Is it to page someone whose job it is to give bad news?

"No visitors," they tell me, at last.

"No problem," I tell the receptionist, giddy that Celeste has a hospital room. That must mean she's still alive. "I'll just go back up there and talk to her family in the waiting room."

The receptionist looks at me in my gown for a moment. Then they shrug—what do they care?—and I say, "Oh crap, I can't remember if I was on floor two or she is."

They laugh gently. "You're on two now. She's on four."

"Thank you. Otherwise I'd be riding around up and down the elevator like a lunatic," I say. Which is absolutely true. Lunacy is the perfect word for my state of mind.

And then it only gets worse. Four, it turns out, is the ICU. I feel choked up just reading the label on the elevator button panel. When I tumble out, the waiting room is crowded with truly miserable-looking strangers in a mix of dress, some in pajamas and a few with pillows and blankets, and I am hardly noteworthy even in my unique garb and accessories. I scan for Hugh or the kids. Since they aren't there, they must be with her in her treatment room. That's good news, right? Unless . . . well, what kind of treatment is she getting, exactly? Exactly how badly did I break her?

I pick up some speed in my step and bustle right past the waiting room, piggybacking on the people in scrubs coming and going without notice. Maybe the robe gives me the right look for it, because as soon as I cross the electronic double doors, I see that in all likelihood I am *not* supposed to be there in that ICU at all. There's no talking except for the buzz of a few TVs and the sound of the machines keeping digital vigils. Many of the doors are closed, and the open ones have curtains that put the patients out of view. The whiteboards outside each room have dates of birth in lieu of identifying patient names. If I'm going to find Celeste, I'm going to have to remember when her birthday is—highly unlikely—or look in every room one by one until I find her. Or until I get kicked out.

So fine. I'll look in each room. They are a picture of extremes. I peek into them only if there isn't the slightest bit of sound, no rustling even. And I quickly understand the bleaker truth of the ICU. It is not a place for healthy people. These patients are not on any road to recovery I'm familiar with. They are plugged into things from every direction, and their eyes are closed, and if a couple of them are ever going to wake up, there is truly no telling. *This is where they brought Celeste,* I think in horror. She is one of these poor people in one of these awful rooms.

I find her, eventually. Fifth room I try. The room has a bouquet of balloons from all five kids and a vase of roses just from Hugh, and it is the note, *You got this,* that makes me start to cry. Celeste has a ventilator mask and adhesive nodes on her chest, wires disappearing into her sheets and gown. She's got some sort of tensioner in place over her head to keep anything from moving. There is a bloody bandage on her head, maybe from where we hit the ground. Her face looks awful. Purple, black, and brown from the cheekbone down, and two gray circles around her eyes. She looks like she was hit with the bat, not the ball. So much for so-called softball.

Tears fill my eyes. Tonight, if I had only done every single thing differently, we'd have met by that miserable rosebush. The one that thanks to Celeste will probably actually flower again. We'd have fought about idiotic stuff—productivity and screen time and freaking Seth, of all things that don't deserve even another moment of our precious breath—and we'd have sort of ended up laughing at ourselves and the whole situation like usual, and . . .

A moment of understanding alights. Celeste, for all her pantry reorganizing, was trying to be my friend all along. No, she *was* being my friend. She was being a really freaking *good* friend, actually.

Is that why I feel as if I would trade places with her right this second if I could? A small sob wrenches loose. If there were any tiny bit of justice in this world, it would still be my brain in that dying body, and she would be alive, with the family who loves her, the beautiful life, the happiness she deserves.

But there is no justice in this world. Not now, at least. I pull the rickety guest chair by the wall closer and closer, until I can reach Celeste's hands with my own, and I begin to tell her how very, very sorry I am.

Sorry I didn't see what friendship she had to give, see it from the very start, the very first time she sat out on that lawn in that adirondack chair with her glass of wine and invited my kids to play with hers.

Sorry I missed all the wonderful things that she was in favor of the one single thing she was not.

Sorry that I got her into this, and sorriest of all that I have no idea how to get her out.

—

CELESTE

When I wake, it's from a truly bizarre dream. In it, for some reason I'm in the hospital—real me, not Wendy me—lying there with my real, freaking fantastic body—not Wendy's, but mine. Strong and pliant, voluptuous, sexy. And I'm just so freaking overjoyed about it.

But then I realize I'm hooked up to stuff, blooping, bleeping stuff that I can't make heads or tails of, and for some reason—dream logic, I guess—I'm not free to move anywhere. And then in comes a woman I could once truly call my archnemesis without too much exaggeration, and she just full-on apologizes to me for basically half an hour straight.

When I was ten, a boy stole my prized possession, a purple ten-speed my mom had found at Goodwill, from out front of Casey's General while I was inside returning cans. I had to walk all the way home with my heart flapping along on the bottom of my plastic flip-flops. Two hours later, before I'd even had the guts to report my loss to the family, that wretched kid came to our house shamefaced, wheeling my beautiful bike.

His mother made him apologize and then give me all his money and mow our front yard. Taking that Mason jar full of quarters and watching him toil in the July sun was almost as good as this dream.

In it, Wendy hits all the things I wish I could have been vindicated for. She tells me I'm a better mother than she is. She adds that I'm also probably a better wife. She talks about my beautiful, happy home, my blessed life, how she's been jealous and stupid and petty, and it goes on like that for some time. Dream me eats it up with a spoon.

She tells me Hugh is a saint and she was an idiot to put Seth on some pedestal or to think I had anything to do with his recent bad behavior. She admits she was deflecting her anger onto me to help her cope with the idea that her husband is a philanderer and that she was hoping that if it was my fault, maybe she wouldn't need to face the painful idea that her marriage is the source of many of her current problems.

Then her voice grows thick, and she tells me that she's not quite sure how she'll live without Seth, and things take a sadder turn. Crying softly, Wendy tells me she doesn't know if she can survive a divorce or put her kids through all the suffering a split would entail. Through quiet, rolling tears, she tells me that she would give anything to reset us to one week before so she could have done things differently. So she could have taken ten minutes to sit down with me one night after dinner, in the front yard, and get to know me. So she could have spent the two seconds forwarding the potluck emails to the new softball moms instead of just deciding they'd have to figure it out the way she'd had to. So she could have asked Hugh if he knew what to do with the mangy shrub between our two backyards and told Zoey how glad she was that she'd become friends with Bridget and told Samuel that Linus had a totally unused Razor scooter that he was welcome to borrow anytime.

"I wish I had brought you guys cookies."

For some reason that completely random sentence makes her cry harder.

"But then," she tells dream me, "I would have had to look up from my emails to do all of those things."

In my dream, I grab her hand and say, "No, no, Wendy! You're a wonderful mom. Your kids adore you. They're fed and clothed, happy, and they think you hung the moon!" but she doesn't hear me. She keeps right on.

"Celeste," she says, and my name is raspy through her tears, "I almost wish I didn't know husbands like Hugh existed. Ready to help when they are needed. Able to give love with no strings attached. Capable of loving children with the same fervor as a mother would."

My heart pulls at the very mention of Hugh, but because it is a dream, I can't seem to remember where he's gone to. How to get him back.

"But now I know, and I know I can't keep wasting my life with a man like Seth, no matter how much I once loved him, no matter if he's a genius or a fraud. Staying with him does my kids no favors. And it does me no favors either."

I want to nod, shout, clap, cheer. I try to. But nothing comes out. Nothing Wendy can see.

"If anything happens to you, Celeste, I will never, ever forgive myself. You've taught me so much. You've shown me the things I refused to see. You, your beautiful family . . . if something happens to you today . . ."

She chokes on a sob.

"Just know that I have your back. Today and from now on. No matter what. Know that Zoey and Samuel and Anna Joy won't be able to get rid of me. Know I will bring over a million cookies or potted plants or biryani; I will learn how to make biryani if that's what they need. If it's the worst . . ." She stammers the words. "It won't be. But no matter what, from now on, your family is my family. Your babies are my . . ." Her voice cracks, and she can't go on.

Tears spill over my hand, which she's grasping as she cries and cries, and for some reason that only makes sense in dream logic, I can do nothing to comfort her whatsoever. To tell her I'm fine, just asleep. Just dreaming.

I just lie there, as still as death in my hospital bed, and let her go on like this.

And then the dream is no longer the least bit satisfying. How can it be? Wendy isn't my archnemesis anymore, and she probably never has been. She's just my friend, who has been looking after my kids with such kindness and love, who has been doing the best she knows how, who has carved out a monumental career for herself, made her family an amazing living, and then suddenly, in the space of an instant, forgotten all she's accomplished. She's the mother of the most sensitive boy I've ever met and also of the best friend my daughter has ever had. She's had a chance, all this time, to scuttle a disappointing marriage or even cheat, and instead she has stuck to her commitments, again and again. And no, even dream me knows I'm not a better mother than her. I just took a different road.

It's like that hoary Robert Frost poem, but without the false dichotomy: Two paths diverged in our woods, and because we are women, and women's choices change dramatically with every single generation, both paths were less traveled by. And because there is no one way to have a family, no instruction book, and no trustworthy set of rules (and, trust me, I've looked), it is likely that both paths are just a little bit wrong and just a little bit right, and which one we take is simply a matter of luck and happenstance.

I fell in love with a wonderful guy who likes me, his job, and his kids. We got pregnant, mostly on purpose. Wendy fell in love with a hot artist who didn't want kids and didn't want to say no. They got pregnant, too, and yes, they were both there for that whether Seth cares to admit it or not.

Then there are those women who have no children, or more than they'd prefer. There are those who have lost their partners or intentionally misplaced them. There are those who earn more than the cost of childcare and those who make less. There are those who can feed their children and those who must take help at every turn in the road. In each house in Birchboro Hills is a woman who took one road and then another and another and now tells herself her choices are all her own and where she finds herself now, and in which body, is all her doing. Or all her fault.

I have been dreaming a long time, I finally understand. I'm coming awake now, but I must have been dreaming about the body swap and the sangria fight. I must have dreamed the Taco Barn, the softball game, the handsome coworker, and the rosebush where our backyards meet. I must have dreamed about *everything* that didn't make sense.

How long have I been asleep? I wonder, as I come to full consciousness, slowly, inch by ever-shifting inch. Have I dreamed the entire week? Have I been dreaming since that otherworldly hangover seven days ago?

Slowly, painfully, I try to come out of this confusing, unbreakable sleep. It almost feels like I have to pry my eyes open. My bedroom is too bright, there are too many flickering fluorescents, there is too much noise. My head is pounding. *This . . .* I think. This is the hangover from the sangria from that potluck all those nights ago. Everything else has been nothing but the craziest REM. Now, at last, time and reason have intersected again. And now . . . now everything is different. Now I have new eyes to see my life. My husband, my kids, my amazing, beautiful life. And I'm not so lonely anymore, because now I have a friend. Someone just like me.

What an enormous relief.

But that relief slides away faster than any dream should upon waking. I am not in my bedroom after all, and Hugh is not next to me, and my kids are not down the hall. I am in the hospital, in terrible pain that starts on my face and radiates through my body, through every inch, and Wendy's sleeping form is lying next to me in a wet puddle of tears, with her face in her arms, on the side of my bed.

And all those noises I thought I was dreaming are coming from the machines plugged into me, and as I wake and try to gasp for my own air around a ventilator, they all start beeping. Louder, louder, until the whole room turns into one startling mechanical scream.

CHAPTER 23

WENDY

I wake up being physically hauled out of the ICU. As I go, the nurse berates me. "Your friend's spine," she tells me, "has been seriously damaged. What were you doing in there? Trying to give me a heart attack?" With that, she leaves me in the waiting room, my face crusted with dried tears, my eyes threatening still more new ones.

"Wait!" I say as she turns on her heel, but before I can ask her if Celeste is going to be ok, she's gone. I turn to the room, and I see Hugh holding Joy, Bridget and Zoey watching Linus, and Samuel watching an iPad, and boom, it's waterworks again.

"Mrs. Charles!" says Zoey, jumping to her feet. And then, again more cautiously: "Are you ok, Mrs. Charles?"

I nod vigorously. "I'm fine. Just fine."

"Mom!" shouts Bridget.

She wraps her arms around me, and in a matter of seconds she is squeezed out by Linus, and I take them into my hug together. My heart fills up until the love actually hurts. I hold my kids as tightly as I can, whispering, "It's Mom. I'm here."

And then I make room for Samuel and Zoey. Even Anna Joy gets in on the action for a sweet, short moment.

When the children have peeled away, I move to sit by Hugh. "Have they told you anything?" I ask in a low voice.

"Only that there's spinal cord damage," he tells me. His face is the color of wet ash. "They say it could be hours before they know more."

I nod and swallow hard. Yes, I want to go to pieces. But now is the time for me to be a mother and a friend. I reach out my arms for little Anna Joy, and she practically leaps into them. Oof—she's much heavier now that I'm in my real body. "Other mommy!" she cries delightedly.

Hugh looks at me, shocked. I'm shocked myself, but then, just a little bit of me gets this. The little ones always know.

"Let me take care of her, and you get some rest," I tell him. "She'll need you bright eyed when she's back up and running."

He shakes his head. "They said that maybe . . ."

"Don't listen to that," I tell him with fake confidence. "She's tough as hell. And she loves you guys so much," I add. "I believe she's capable of truly anything, if it's for the sake of her family."

Hugh nods. "You're right. That's completely true. I had no idea you knew my Celeste so well."

He takes Zoey's and Samuel's hands tightly in his own. "Come on, Team Mason!" he says to them. "Everybody send up a quick prayer, and then let Mom work her magic. She's got this."

I nod. "Bridge, Linus, your dad's here, right?"

Linus looks up at me. "He's in the cafeteria," he says.

"Perfect. Go find him and tell him to give you twenty bucks for lunch—dinner—whatever meal comes next—and send him up here in your place, will you?"

"But we want to wait here with you," says Bridget. "To find out if Mrs. Mason is going to be ok."

"This is what I need you to do," I say to her, channeling Celeste. "And we know that Celeste is going to be ok, so just stay down there and wait for a text."

Hugh nods. "You go too, Zoey," he says to his daughter, peeling off a twenty from his wallet. "Samuel, you want to stay with me or go eat with them?"

Samuel looks at Linus, who shrugs. "Eat," he says.

I tell Bridget to tell Seth to buy the boys comic books from the gift shop. "For both boys," I say. "He can complain to me later if he doesn't like it."

The kids scuttle off. I make a pillow of the kids' softball blankets, and Hugh conks out instantly, and Anna Joy and I play with the busy box in the corner of the waiting room for what feels like hours. In that time I think over what I told Celeste back in that hospital room. I imagine what she would have told me.

At last, a doctor arrives in the waiting room. I sit there in my double hospital gowns with Hugh on one side and Anna Joy running circles into the floor, and together we hear the news. "She's awake, and her latest scan is looking promising. She can have visitors now," she tells us.

Hugh looks at me, and I laugh. "Go, Hugh!"

The poor man sprints away, leaving me and his toddler to fend for ourselves. Seth is nowhere to be found, but Hugh has left Celeste's handbag behind in the waiting room, and there, right where I left it, is my phone.

I call Davis. Of course I do. I call the person who has become my main confidant, with one exception: I never, ever talk about Seth with him. Now it's time to break the rule and get real. And get real with myself.

He answers on half a ring, asks me where I am, and I tell him the hospital. This he knows, somehow. "Where in the hospital, I mean? Because I'm in the ER, and you're not, and the nurses seem kind of put out about it."

I swear into the phone.

"Sorry?" asks Davis.

"That wasn't for you," I explain. "I did do a runner, because I was worried about my friend. She's in bad shape."

"Celeste?" he asks. "The woman who saved your life?"

"Yes! How do you know about all of this?" I ask him.

"Linus. When I got to the hospital, Linus gave me a full blow by blow. He was so upset. I calmed him down, explained how the epinephrine worked and that you'd be just fine."

"Oh, my poor baby," I say. "Thank you. Wait."

"Waiting . . ."

"How did you know to come to the hospital?" I ask him.

"Because I saw you get carted here from the softball game," he says.

I pause. "How did you know to come to the softball game?"

"You asked me to, remember? Late last night?"

Did we drunk text Davis last night and invite him to the girls' game? Yes, I recall, *yes, we did.* "Of course I remember," I say. "Did you see Bridge too?"

"Yes, and I don't know who else exactly I talked to. There were a lot of people there, most in softball uniforms. It was a bit of a melee. You are deeply cared for," he tells me.

"No," I tell him firmly. "I'm not. I wish I were, but those people were here for Celeste. For my friend. She's very hurt," I say, my throat catching. "Davis, she's very badly hurt, and for reasons too complicated to go into right now, it's my fault."

He makes a tsking sound into the phone. "People say stuff like that whenever they've been in a scary accident. But from what I hear, you were in anaphylactic shock when the whole thing went down, so it's pretty hard to imagine you were culpable."

"Trust me," I say. "The thing is, I haven't been in a good . . . uh . . . headspace lately. Something happened, between me and Seth. I need to talk to you."

Davis makes a low noise in his throat. "Ah . . . Wendy . . . ," he begins. "I'm trying so hard to be respectful. I'm trying to give you space . . ."

"I know we don't usually touch this subject with a ten-foot pole," I tell him. "But I think that's been a mistake. I think I should have been more honest with you about what life is like for me, even just from the perspective of a friend. Though"—I take a deep breath—"the thing is, I have feelings for you that don't stop at friendship."

The other end of the line is silent.

"Davis?"

"I'm listening," he says, without giving any indication of how he's taking this. "I can do listening."

"Ok, well, listen to this. I've spent the last week having a pretty creative nervous breakdown," I tell him. "And I've come away realizing that everything I'm doing is wrong. I'm parenting wrong, I'm working wrong, I'm friending wrong, and I'm definitely not being a great wife. A good wife would be trying to work things out with Seth—really work them out, not just hide all our problems behind overachievement and overcompensation. The truth is, if I had really wanted to save what Seth and I had, I probably wouldn't have let you come on board in the first place, because I've been attracted to you from the very first."

There's a sharp intake of air on the other end of the phone.

"But obviously I did, and at the same time, I had absolutely no intention of changing the situation, changing what Seth and I had or trying to fix it or whatever, because the way I've been running my life lately, if something's not on fire, then it doesn't get dealt with. It's strictly triage around here, and it's been making me feel *terrible*. It's convinced me that I don't deserve anything better, because I can't cope with what I already do have."

Davis is still silent on the line.

"Even after I caught him trying to cheat, I thought I could just ignore what I knew. I know how stupid that sounds now, but I really did think it was the way to play things. To keep acting like I had it all, even as I finally could say, without a shadow of a doubt, that my marriage needed to be over. And I just want you to know I'm so sorry about all that. It never occurred to me that while I was busy jerking myself around, I wasn't doing the right thing by you either. Until it did."

"During that pretty creative nervous breakdown?" he asks.

"Very creative, to be honest."

"But Wendy, why are you telling me all of this?" he asks. "I'm not the person you need to be talking to right now."

"You're right. I need to be talking to Seth."

At exactly that moment, Seth walks into the otherwise quiet waiting room. "What do you need to be talking to Seth about?" he asks, almost casually.

I ignore Seth and say into the phone. "You're exactly right, Davis. It's time for me to do that right now. Ok if I call you back later?"

"Better if you meet me in the ER when you can," he says. "That way the nurses can cross you off the AWOL list. And I can . . ." His voice drifts off. When he speaks again, the old thought is forgotten. "Good luck. Wendy. Remember our motto: passion wins."

"I will," I tell him, and end the call. Then I turn on my husband.

"I know you haven't been faithful," I start. It's partly a bluff—it's possible the move he put on me when I was Celeste was his first offense, but that doesn't seem particularly likely.

Even so, a tiny part of me wants to be hopeful when his face falls and he says, "What are you talking about? Unfaithful? When? I don't—"

I hold up a hand to stop his bullshittery. "It's too late for all that, Seth," I tell him. "Save your breath."

His shoulders collapse. "How long have you known?" he asks.

I pause and consult my heart. When was the last time he came home from the studio in a great mood about his work and in the mood to celebrate? With me? "Years," I tell him.

"Oh, Wendy," he says. He sounds sad and very tired. I am tired, too—tired of protecting my conscious from what my unconscious has surely understood for a long, long time. Why else wouldn't I push back about the city studio we can hardly afford or his long hours or the complete lack of compassion he's shown me? I am, in all other areas, a reasonably strong woman. I negotiate on the cost of printer toner and the internet bill and never, ever buy an extended warranty. But there was nothing to negotiate with Seth, was there? He was already lost to me. I had no ace up my sleeve, and I wasn't willing to walk away from the table.

Until now.

"We're breaking up," I tell him. "And doing it in a way that spares the kids from any drama as much as humanly possible. Our dissolution will be just like everything else I do: well planned, carefully orchestrated, and all for the best of our family."

Seth looks at me in shock. I don't miss a beat, though, because for some reason, every single thing is crystal clear in my mind. What to do, how it will work, when it will happen. "We'll sit down with Linus and Bridget and tell them we're going our separate ways by mutual agreement. We'll make sure they have counselors to talk to whenever they need them. They'll visit you on Wednesday nights and every other weekend, as long as you live within a drivable radius from school."

"What?" he stammers.

"Honestly, Seth, I think we'll be good coparents. And so you know how absolutely serious I am about this going smoothly, we'll split all our assets—the house and retirement savings—right down the middle. I won't put up a single fight."

Seth is still staring.

"I've made good investments," I tell him. "Play it my way, and you'll have time to sell some art before you have to worry about money."

"I . . ."

"Talk to a lawyer anytime you want. No hurry there. But I'm telling the kids tonight, and you'd better be there for that. And afterward you'd better be gone."

"Where will I go?" he asks me.

I look at him askance. "What do you mean, where will you go? You can stay in the studio rent-free, at least tonight. After all, it has a sofa."

Seth has the good sense to look ashamed. "Wendy, look. I didn't mean for things to go this way. I didn't know how bad I'd be at the two-kids, white-picket-fence life, is the thing. I didn't know how much it would kill my soul."

"You *still* don't know if you're bad or good at it, Seth," I say bitterly. "Because you never put yourself all the way into it. You never tried to be the dad you might have been. Were you even faithful to me back when we lived in the city?" I ask him. "Because now that I can see things more clearly, I think we went wrong before Birchboro Hills even factored into the picture."

He frowns. "We went wrong when you talked me into having kids before we were ready."

I look at him hard. "I don't disagree with you," I tell him, feeling not resentment for him but a distant sort of pity. "That is when you and I went wrong. But if I gained Bridget and Linus, and all I lost in the process was you, then I can only say it was totally worth it."

Seth can only nod to that. His face is red, and I'm sure there's plenty of anger in him—he hates when I give him instructions, whenever I plan things for both of us, and this breakup speech has been nothing if not unilateral. But maybe he also feels something close to what I'm feeling right now. Sheer, unadulterated relief. After all, there is no evidence that either of us has been happy together for a long, long time. And if it weren't for the week that just happened, there's no chance I would have done anything about it.

"You're off the hook, Seth Charles," I tell him. "You'll be happier in the end."

He sighs deeply. "We both will," he says, sorrow mixing with relief. "The thing is, Wendy, most of the time I feel like you and the kids are holding me back."

I take in the sting of the words, like a slap you know you kind of deserve.

"But at the same time, I sure as hell wasn't bringing out the best in you either," he adds. "So yeah. This is for the best for both of us. After all, you deserve to find someone who can do that too. Someone who will stop holding *you* back."

I nod at him, because he's absolutely right. I nod, and then I pick up Anna Joy and turn and walk away, toward the elevator, moving fast, wishing I could move faster despite the rolling IV stand dragging by my side and the kiddo on my hip. I have somewhere to be, now that I've finally done the right hard thing. Because thanks to Celeste, I know exactly the man who brings out the best in me, and I need to let him know that as soon as I possibly can.

—

CELESTE

My goodness, but my hospital room is abustle. There are so many people in here, and none of them seem interested in answering any of my questions. In fact, one of them keeps putting a mask over my face as if to shut me up. I take it off, for the third time in a row, and this time I just shout, "HELLO! WOULD SOMEONE TELL ME WHAT THE H-E DOUBLE HOCKEY STICKS IS GOING ON?"

"Did she just say 'H-E double hockey sticks'?" asks someone near my lower spine.

"Probably a good sign for neurological function," jokes someone else.

I'm about ready to sit up and walk out of there if someone doesn't answer me, but luckily someone does. A nice lady with a face shield who says, "Celeste, you're in the hospital after you were hit in the chin by a line drive to second. It snapped your neck back, and now we are trying to make sure there's no long-term spinal damage. You're supposed to be resting comfortably right now while we do our job."

"Oh. Crap," I say.

"At the very least, please leave the mask on and hold still, ok?"

I nod vigorously and let her reposition the mask.

"Hold STILL," she repeats.

I stop nodding.

"Very good. Now, the anesthesiologist is back, and he's going to start doing his thing, ok, so . . . ok, count backward from ten. Ready?"

I don't nod, but thinking it must be ok, I say, "Ten."

A few seconds later, after what seems like a very slow eyeblink, I feel groggy and achy, and somehow, Hugh is in the room with me.

"She's awake!" he says.

"Hugh!" I say.

"Wiggle your toes," he says to me. I do, and he laughs. "Nice one, babe. Nice one."

"What happened?" I ask, the fog over my eyes lifting but my words coming out very slowly. "Did I do ok?"

He gingerly leans over and kisses me softly. Our first kiss in a week. I savor every millimoment of it.

"You did perfectly."

"Oh, darling," I say through the mists of the drugs. "I've had such crazy dreams."

Hugh moves hair out of my face and smiles at me indulgently—I don't think he can understand my slurred words yet. My brain is working faster than my mouth, though. It's thinking through everything that's happened, at a surprising pace. Figuring out how I got here, what went down beforehand, and what has to happen now. Figuring out who I have to—no, who I get to—become.

And later, when Hugh can understand me again, I'll tell him all of it. Not about the body swap, maybe, not anytime soon. But about who I've been lately and who I want to be next. About how, when I said goodbye to my past and started our future, I didn't forget it all. I didn't forget the painful lessons of what it meant to grow up the way I did. The responsibility I felt to give my children something better. How beholden I felt to the man who gave me a different life and how little debt and love have to do with one another. Wendy is, as she often is, partly right. Hugh doesn't owe me anything. And I don't owe him either. We're not a balance sheet, my value doesn't come from what pennies I save us, and I'm not on my own at the end of the day. Hugh and I aren't like that. We float or sink together.

We float, I decide. We float because I am no one's anchor. What we have is buoyant. What we have is beautiful.

But there's no way I can explain all that to him right now. Instead I just find his hand with mine, hold it as tight as I can, and dream of who I will be now that I'm not "just a housewife." I'm Celeste Mills Mason, and I'm the mother of three wonderful children and the wife of a loving man, and there's absolutely no "just" about it.

CHAPTER 24

AFTER

CELESTE

Two days later, I am home from the hospital. Wendy is, too—and Seth is staying with his parents, who live an hour away. Hugh has been obsessed with building a firepit in our backyard ever since I told him everything. Not everything—he doesn't need to know he was sleeping next to his neighbor for the last week—but the home truths that have come of it. I tell him about the themed bento box lunches and the dollar-per-Dixie-cup gazpacho and the over-the-top science fair cupcakes—not that there is anything overtly wrong with them—but how instead of somehow making me worthy, they are keeping the people I want to know at a distance. They are a disguise I put on to justify my existence.

Wendy has seen right through that disguise.

Hugh's eyebrows shoot way up when I tell him I finally have a real friend and who it is, but then he catches himself quickly. "She's whip smart," he says in a quick recovery. "She can see what a gem you are."

See, this is what it is about Hugh. His Celeste-colored glasses are the best thing that ever happened to me. But instead of soaking it up when he says things like that, I've spent too much of our marriage wondering what's wrong with him to love me so much.

I wrap him up in another tight hug, something I've been doing so often lately I can't even keep count. The time has come for me to start soaking him up. To put on my own pair of Celeste-colored glasses. To tell my kids a few stories about my life when I was young. To let my story show through to anyone worthy of seeing it. Wendy was right all along: there's nothing inherently exhausting about my life—except pretending to be someone I'm not.

And I'm NOT someone who wants to go to work outside the home. Not now, and maybe not ever. I can't say for sure—after all, a week ago I was wondering about substitute teacher certifications. But that wasn't because I wanted to be a substitute teacher, necessarily. It was because I believed that once Joy was in school full time, my value to our family would be used up.

I shake my head at my stupid self. How many times has Hugh said our family has a wonderful balance? How many times have I thought that myself? How many times has a mom thanked me for picking up their kid when they were stuck in a meeting, or a teacher thanked me for coming into the classroom when they were low on time or materials?

How many times have those tiny acts filled my heart?

Why would I give all that up? There are seasons to our lives, and I'm not done with this one yet.

I finish up what I'm mixing in the kitchen and open the french doors to the screened porch. She's waiting there, my first friend in Birchboro Hills, with a bag of marshmallows and a box of graham crackers. At her feet, Anna Joy is happily making a mess with water pens while Wendy rebraids her hair.

"Don't be angry," I say when I show her what I'm carrying.

She laughs. "Pink sangria."

"*Without* vodka. It's literally the only mixed drink I know how to make." Well, aside from something my cousins used to make in a Fleet Farm bucket. "At least it's not a bag of peanut M&M'S."

"Nah. Attempted murder is really more my thing." Anna Joy squirms, and Wendy coos, "Almost done, baby."

"Manslaughter," I correct Wendy. "It's manslaughter when it's accidental, and after the week that came before it, I don't think any jury would convict."

"Thank you for being so forgiving about me almost putting you in a wheelchair," Wendy tells me as I pour her a glass.

"Thank you for being so forgiving about me almost killing off your body," I say in return and raise my own.

"There." She puts the ponytail holder at the bottom of the thick Anne of Green Gables–style braid she's made and taps Joy's head with the flat of the brush. "Shall we go see the new firepit?"

"We shall."

We step out into the yard and move past the kids. Samuel and Linus are at the picnic table drawing something, acting very sneaky, which probably means the cartoons are bathroom related.

Bridge and Zoey are hitting balls off the pitching machine on the other side of the house. I can't help but notice that the machine is facing our house, so any broken windows will be at Wendy's.

"Try to keep to grounders, ladies," I holler.

Wendy smiles. "Look at you, with the lingo."

"We tried your version of a rainy day at home," I explain. "We all piled on the sofa and watched baseball movies. Anna Joy thought *The Sandlot* was hysterical."

"That's odd," says Wendy. "All that TV, and yet . . . they don't seem like their brains are completely rotted."

I shrug. "I am forced to admit that TV may not actually be the devil. Or if it is, we're corrupted."

"Where do you come down on s'mores these da" "Processed sugar served with processed chocolate betwee of processed flour?"

"I'm very much pro s'mores," I say. "As dessert. No s'moring my kids until they eat something from a food group."

"Fair enough," Wendy says as we settle into the twin adirondack chairs, moved from the front yard to the firepit. Turns out we are a backyard family after all. "Actually, I'll go with the same policy."

I smile at her warmly. "Look at you. Respecting my rules."

"Look at you," she replies smoothly. "Having reasonable rules."

I open my mouth to say that all my rules are reasonable but stop myself just in time, asking instead, "Is the weekend going ok? Without Seth?"

Wendy exhales deeply. "The kids will need time. No question. For them it's a huge adjustment. But for me a weekend without Seth is no different than a weekend with him. Minus some snoring."

"Then you did the right thing."

"No question. I suspect issues will come up when I need help with childcare for staff meetings. But that's what babysitters are for."

I shake my head. "You don't need a babysitter, Wendy." I gesture to the kids. "You've got us."

She raises an eyebrow. "You sure? You're not just offering to try to be useful?"

"The girls entertain themselves. And the boys . . . ," I say. I don't need to finish; I can just gesture toward the picnic table.

"How weird is that? Nothing in common, and yet they're the best of pals."

I raise my eyebrows at her meaningfully. "Apples," I say, with a wave toward the boys, "and trees," gesturing at the two of us.

"And they got there without any trips to the ICU," Wendy adds.

"Kids are smarter than we are."

Wendy looks toward the girls, laughing and chattering away, but her eyes look unfocused. She sighs. "Things will have to change for me."

I nod. Wendy has a long road ahead of her.

"They'll be at their dad's at least once a week," she says. "And I know I should feel awful about it, but I just feel relieved. It's been a long time since I had extra hours to spend on whatever I want. I can use the extra time on the business without guilt and come home earlier on the other nights. On Seth's weekends I can maybe even go out."

"With Davis?" I ask.

A small smile slides over Wendy's face. "Maybe."

"You have to let me live vicariously through you," I tell her. "I've been married a long, long time." Hugh cheerfully waves over at us from the pair of sawhorses he's using to finish up a simple Leopold bench to set by the fire.

"A long, long time to a wonderful man," Wendy says, then lowers her voice. "If hairy."

"For all you know, Davis has a chest like a shearling coat."

Wendy smiles wickedly. "I'll have to get back to you on that."

"Be nice to him, Wendy," I tell her. "He's been pining a long time."

She shakes her head. "He said he wasn't a piner."

"I'm sure he wishes he weren't a piner. But he pines like anyone else."

"Like Linus?" she asks, and I follow her eyeline. To my surprise, I see him looking up from the notebook where the boys have been drawing, gazing adoringly at my older daughter.

"Oh my goodness," I say.

"Yup," she says. "This should be interesting."

"Meanwhile Samuel is too busy drawing fart cannons to even realize girls exist," I say. "My oblivious little man."

"Your day is coming," Wendy says. "Samuel is going to be . . ."

"A hellion," I finish for her. "I know. I've heard all about it from Hugh's mom."

"It's kind of a relief," Wendy admits. "Before last wee your kids were perfect. Too perfect."

"They are perfect," I tell her. "This is just what perfect looks like."

"Messy," says Wendy.

"Crazy," I tell her.

"Bookish," she replies.

"Sporty," I say back.

"At home," she says.

"At work," I reply.

"Eating sidewalk chalk . . ."

I look up. "What?"

Wendy gestures over to Joy, who is licking a stick of blue chalk like it's a lollypop. "Ugh. Joy!" I jump up to redirect her.

"Chalk is for drawing," I tell her and demonstrate its, uh, original purpose. "Would you like something to eat?"

"I'm eating blue!" she tells me, and her tongue is evidence that she's also sampled green and yellow.

"I bet you are thirsty," I tell her.

"Milk?" she asks.

"Cow's milk," I offer. "Or banana-oat milk?" There's that familiar tug in my breasts, but it is time. When it's time, you know.

Just then we hear the sound of a softball hitting something solid, and everyone in the entire yard swivels around.

"My bad!" says Zoey. Our eyes follow the sound—Zoey's line drive to third has knocked off a section of Wendy's gutter downspout and brought it clattering to the ground.

"I got it," says Hugh, with the sigh of a man who is handy and has three boisterous kids.

"You're a doll," I tell him, blowing him a kiss on the way to the kitchen to make blended banana milk, our happy compromise between breast milk and Starburst. As I go, I see Wendy go sit down by Linus and Samuel, which means she's being treated to a giggling play-by-play of their new graphic novel. Behind her, the sun is setting, bouncing golden light off the siding of Wendy's house onto the lawn, the kids, the fallen downspout, and the rosebush, which is finally starting to shoot up new wood.

Back outside, Joy curls up on my lap drinking while Hugh bends over the firepit and Wendy hovers at the picnic table with the hysterically laughing little boys. Zoey and Bridget sit as far from us as humanly possible on the finished but unpainted Leopold bench that is sure to give them splinters, whispering and giggling. Wendy calls to me through it all.

"So this is perfect, huh?" she asks me, as she waves around our backyards, kids, Hugh, rosebush, and thorns.

"This is it," I call back and raise my glass of sangria (without vodka) in her direction. "As perfect as it comes."

ACKNOWLEDGMENTS

I would like to thank my crackerjack publishing team: my agent, Holly Root; my editor, Chris Werner; Tiffany Yates Martin; Danielle Marshall; Alexandra Levenberg; Brittany Russell; Gabriella Dumpit; and the entire team at Lake Union Publishing.

Big thanks to the talented and supportive Tall Poppy Writers and all the inspiring mothers in my life who took the road less traveled by. *You* make all the difference.

Thanks and love to the Harms family; to Chris Meadow, who moved heaven and earth to get me writing time; and to Griffin, who inspires me at every turn and makes sure I am never bored.

Finally, thank you to Tui T. Sutherland, whose fantastic stories allowed my son to travel to faraway worlds while we sheltered safely at home in 2020.

ABOUT THE AUTHOR

Photo © 2020 Lea Wolf

Kelly Harms is the Amazon Charts, *Washington Post*, and *USA Today* bestselling author of five books, including *The Overdue Life of Amy Byler*, a Goodreads top ten fiction book of the year and a WFWA STAR Award finalist. Her work has been translated into a dozen languages throughout the world. She lives in Madison, Wisconsin, with her clever son, Griffin; charming Irishman Chris; and Scout, the best dog in dogtown. For more information visit www.kellyharms.com.